QUIETLY MY CAPTAIN WAITS

BY
EVELYN EATON

INTRODUCTION BY
BARRY M. MOODY

Formac Publishing Company Limited
Halifax

Formac Publishing Company Limited acknowledges the support of the cultural affairs section, Nova Scotia Department of Tourism and Culture. We
acknowledge the financial support of the Government of Canada through
the Book Publishing Industry Development Program (BPIDP) for our publishing activities. We acknowledge the support of the Canada Council for
the Arts for our publishing program.

Cover illustration: *Washing Green from the South*. E. Thresher.
Courtesy NSARM

National Library of Canada Cataloguing in Publication Data

Eaton, Evelyn, 1902-1983.
Quietly my captain waits

(Formac fiction treasures)
ISBN 0-88780-544-2

1. Damours de Freneuse, Louise, 1668?-1711?—Fiction.
2. New France—Fiction. 3. Annapolis Royal
(N.S.)—History—Fiction. I. Title. II. Series.

PS8509.A96Q8 2001   C813'.52   C2001-902581-5
PR9199.3.E24Q5 2001

First published in 1940, Harper & Brothers, New York and London
Series editor: Gwendolyn Davies

Formac Publishing Company Limited
5502 Atlantic Street
Halifax, Nova Scotia B3H 1G4
www.formac.ca

Printed and bound in Canada

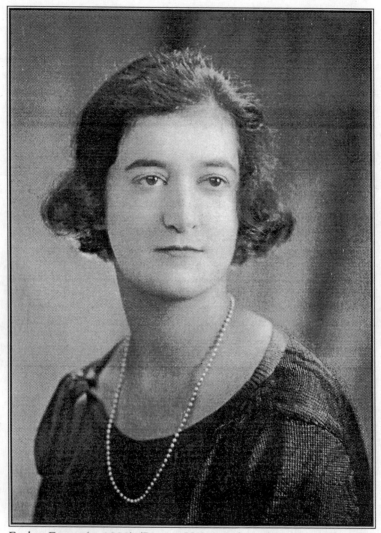

Evelyn Eaton (c. 1923) (Boston University)

Presenting Formac Fiction Treasures
Series Editor: Gwendolyn Davies

A taste for reading popular fiction expanded in the nineteenth century with the mass marketing of books and magazines. People read rousing adventure stories aloud at night around the fireside; they bought entertaining romances to read while travelling on trains and curled up with the latest serial novel in their leisure moments. Novelists were important cultural figures, with devotees who eagerly awaited their next work.

Among the many successful popular English language novelists of the late 19th and early 20th centuries were a group of Maritimers who found in their own education, travel and sense of history events and characters capable of entertaining readers on both sides of the Atlantic. They emerged from well-established communities which valued education and culture, for women as well as for men. Faced with limited publishing opportunities in the Maritimes, successful writers sought magazine and book publishers in the major cultural centres: New York, Boston, Philadelphia, London, and sometimes Montreal and Toronto. They often enjoyed much success with readers 'at home' but the best of these writers found large audiences across Canada and in the United States and Great Britain.

The Formac Fiction Treasures series is aimed at offering contemporary readers access to books that were successful, often huge bestsellers in their time, but which are now little known and often hard to find. The authors and titles selected are chosen first of all as enjoyable to read, and secondly for the light they shine on historical events and on attitudes and views of the culture from which they emerged. These complete original texts reflect values which are sometimes in conflict with those of today: for example, racism is often evident, and bluntly expressed. This collection of novels is offered as a step towards rediscovering a surprisingly diverse and not nearly well enough known popular cultural heritage of the Maritime provinces and of Canada.

Introduction

Rogues, heroes, beautiful women, love (chaste and unchaste), native attacks, heroic accomplishments — all of these and more can be found in the pages of Evelyn Eaton's novel *Quietly My Captain Waits*, which is set against the backdrop of the struggle between France and England for empire in North America. The early eighteenth-century is the time, while the action occurs in places as diverse as Quebec, the backwoods of what is now New Brunswick, the colonial capital of Acadia — Port Royal — and France's royal court. Probably the best known and most successful of her many books, this was also Eaton's initial foray into fiction.

Quietly My Captain Waits is a historical novel rooted firmly in the rich history of Maritime Canada. The middle third of the twentieth-century was the heyday of the Maritime historical novel, with such notables as Thomas H. Raddall and Will R. Bird producing most of their best work during this time. Many of these historical novels were set in the eighteenth-century rather than the nineteenth, perhaps because by the 1930s and 1940s, the previous century still seemed too close (and perhaps too dull), lacking the romance and drama of the earlier period when empires were in collision and the Native Peoples controlled much of the countryside. Historical novels are perhaps not as popular in early twenty-first-century North America, where our tastes tend to run more to courtroom dramas, high finance and international intrigue. So today's reader of *Quietly My Captain Waits* enters not only the eighteenth-century world imagined into existence by Eaton, but also the world in which a Scarlett O'Hara — not a John Grisham lawyer — would be the literary focal point.

As with the best of Maritime historical novels, the main characters of *Quietly My Captain Waits* were real people, although the usual literary licence is taken with the details of their lives. The heroine, Madame Louise [Guyon] Damours de Freneuse, was certainly real enough, as the voluminous correspondence about her attests. And she certainly did most of the extraordinary things with which she is credited by Eaton. Her notorious affair with Simon-Pierre de Bonaventure was real enough, and it is this on which the author focuses and makes the central theme of her novel. The other main characters, especially the residents of the fort and town of Port Royal and the officials in Quebec and France, were also drawn from the pages of history.

It was not Eaton's intent to write a historical account of the period, of course, but rather a novel set in the past. She was well versed in the available histories of Acadia/Nova Scotia in this important era when the French were withdrawing and the English were picking up the reins of power. But she did not rely on the few academic histories available at the time, instead, she perused the existing documents dealing with de Freneuse. And this is, I think, one of the secrets of the novel's success. There is a richness and depth to this portrait of the period and its inhabitants that could not have been gained from solely reading secondary sources.

This portrait is generally an accurate one, while also exercising the freedom needed for a work of fiction. The indifference, even hostility, of French court officials to the colonies has not been exaggerated; the hardship endured by the colonists is probably, if anything, understated; and the conflict between French, English and Native, while not accurate in every detail, is nonetheless able to convey the flavour of what living on the frontier was like. Some of the details of the main characters lives have been rearranged a bit by the author, at times to provide more dramatic deaths or convenient twists for her story. If the reader wishes to compare the fictional accounts of the lives of Eaton's characters with historically accurate versions, the first three volumes of the *Dictionary of Canadian Biography*, which was published long after Eaton researched her novel, provide wonderful thumbnail sketches of Madame de Freneuse, her second husband, her lover de Bonaventure, the various governors of Acadia and some of the townspeople of Port Royal.

Although the portraits of the people and the period are, for the most part, accurate, there is an area in which attitudes and understanding have changed considerably since Eaton wrote her novel. The novelist herself would radically alter her perceptions of the Natives Peoples, later coming to identify with this element of North American society and seeing them as noble and virtuous. However, the picture presented in *Quietly My Captain Waits* is quite different.

The Native People are referred to as "happy animals," who, "when it came to presents,... were children — greedy and curious." Eaton described the Mohawks as the "filthiest and most cruel of all the Indian tribes.... Their faces were bestial and stupid." While these were common attitudes in the first half of the twentieth-century, our perceptions have changed considerably since. Eaton also errs in her portrayal of at least part of their lifestyle. Dog sleds and buffalo hides were not typical features of native life in the Maritimes. When this novel was first published, Micmac was the common spelling of the name of the Native People of Nova Scotia and Eastern New Brunswick; it is now more acceptable to use Mi'kmaq.

If Eaton is rather harsh in her judgment of the Native People, she is equally so in her portrayal of the residents of France. When her heroine, Madame de Freneuse, journeys to Europe, Eaton puts these thoughts in her head:

> Now she was home [where everyone in New France longed to be]; she was able to enjoy the company of distinguished men and women; she went to the play at the Court and saw the King; she talked with men whose names were spoken with fervour and faith in Acadia; and she was disgusted with it all. She longed for the clean seas, the fair land, the spacious skies, the freedom, of the New France. What if there were savages, and hardship and disease, and famine? These things were in Paris; they were everywhere — worse, in the Old World, because disguised and distorted.

In contrast, North America represents freedom and the rejection of the stifling conventions and traditions of Europe. Near the beginning of the novel, an older Frenchman voices his fears about the freedoms of the New World when he speaks about "the dangerous ideas the New World brought to men: the beckoning of adventure, the ease with which all bonds were slipped, the proper obligations of a man's allegiance to his King, his country, his lands, his wife — all these could be evaded in New France." But these were the very things that so attracted Eaton, and through her, the heroine of the novel and her lover. In Paris, Madame de Freneuse "was hungry for the freer air of the New France." This contrast between the Old World and the New is a frequent theme in the western literature of the past four centuries, with North America usually viewed in much more positive terms than Europe.

Although Eaton, in a later novel, would eventually turn her attention to the Acadians, it is interesting to note that these regional inhabitants don't appear in *Quietly My Captain Waits*. In fact, they aren't even mentioned. The author does refer to the "*habitants*" of the area, but this term is borrowed from Quebec, as is the sketchy portrait she paints of them. The reader is left with no understanding of or feeling for these people. Eaton's attention is focussed on the townspeople of Port Royal rather than the farmers of the countryside. There are no echoes of Longfellow's *Evangeline* to be found here. And that is probably just as well; even by the 1940s, the Acadians were suffering from literary overexposure, having been the subject of hundreds of poems, plays and novels. Eaton wanted to look at another dimension of life in the region, without becoming entangled in the sentimentality that infused most of the literature about the Acadians.

In terms of historical accuracy, the author adheres closest to the facts in the sections dealing with Port Royal, renamed Annapolis Royal in 1710. Most of the available documentation about her heroine deals with her controversial time in that town, and Eaton was herself more familiar with that region than she was with any of the novel's other settings. Today, one can still roam the earthenworks of the French fort where de Bonaventure, Subercase and other officials lived, and stroll down the same main street where Madame de Freneuse was either greeted warmly or snubbed by the townspeople. If one wanders down to the end of St. George Street in Annapolis Royal, one can still find the site of Madame de Freneuse's home, built at government expense so long ago. While her house — and most of the other buildings of her era — are gone, the past never feels far away in this town, and one can almost imagine the figures and events that are so vividly portrayed in this novel.

Eaton's own unconventional and rebellious life probably, to

some extent, explains the obvious attraction she felt to the early eighteenth century and to the equally unconventional and rebellious Madame de Freneuse. In 1902, Eaton was born to Canadian parents in Switzerland, and raised first in Canada and then in England. In the rambling autobiography she published in 1974, *The Trees and Fields Went the Other Way*, Eaton painted an exotic picture of a rather unorthodox childhood and an even more unusual adulthood. It certainly appears to have been a passionate life, very much like the one she saw in — or imagined for — Madame de Freneuse. At one point she wrote: "I have loved men, women, children, animals, trees, the sea, stones, planes, cars, an Alaskan sea lion, a lynx, passionately, tenderly, but not necessarily, always, sexually. I have also had my share of sex. Most of it was fun and some of it was funny. I think sex should be funny, sometimes, to be right." Certainly the early eighteenth-century was, in many respects, a more congenial time for Eaton than the Edwardian era into which she was supposed to fit.

Her writing career began in 1923, with the publication of *The Interpreter*, a volume of poetry. A steady stream of books and articles flowed from Eaton's pen in the years that followed — poetry, fiction, non-fiction, children's stories — more than twenty books in all. Much of this writing was done while she laboured at other occupations, attempting to sustain herself and her daughter, having become estranged from her family. A child, marriage and divorce (in that order) did not necessarily endear one to one's family in the 1920s and 1930s.

London, Paris, Provence, Oxford and New York — during her life, Eaton lived and worked in both Europe and North America. When Eaton's need for money drove her to desperation, her literary agent in New York told her to "write an historical novel." Eaton's reply — "How can I? I never even read them" — was considered no impediment, and she was told to sit down immediately and write an outline. As she later recorded in her autobiography,

> *I sat down obediently, but I did not have much hope or confidence in the results. Still, I did remember a rainy afternoon I had spent in the fort at Annapolis Royal in Nova Scotia, when I was waiting for Terry [her daughter] to get through with the dentist before I took her to Edgehill [School].*

Uncle Tim [Col. E.K. Eaton] was curator of the muse-um there. He showed me a series of letters about a Frenchwoman named Louise de Freneuse, written between 1702 and 1711 by several French governors. Each letter praised her or damned her in words that still came crack-ling off the pages.

With a generous advance of $1000 from Harper Brothers, Eaton left New York for Victoria Beach, a small fishing village near Annapolis Royal. With help from Laura Hardy at the museum at Fort Anne in Annapolis, Eaton researched and wrote through the summer of 1939, banging out a chapter a day "on an old battered portable with keys that stuck and a ribbon that had to be rewound by hand." In the fall she returned to New York, with the manu-script and a great deal of skepticism in hand.

Quietly My Captain Waits was an immediate hit with Harper Brothers, and even before it was published it had created quite a stir. Hollywood was already interested, and was considering Vivien Leigh as the star. Leigh, of course, was still basking in the glow of her triumph as Scarlett O'Hara in *Gone with the Wind*, and there are indeed some echoes of that popular historical novel in Eaton's own work. Both novels were about very strong women who faced, and dealt with, great adversity, often by flaunting the standards and values of their times. The image of Vivien Leigh in Hollywood's version of eighteenth-century Nova Scotia is an intriguing one, but it was not to be. Warner Brothers eventually bought the movie rights for the handsome sum of $40,000, with Bette Davis in mind as Madame de Freneuse. However, even this did not come to fruition as the war slowed, and then finally halted these plans; the movie was never made.

The novel, however, proved to be popular. There were some negative reviews, and Eaton received some backlash for writing a story from a French rather than from a British perspective. Some readers thought it was disloyal at a time when Britain herself was so threatened by Hitler's Germany. However, encouraged by the general, more positive response, Eaton began writing her next novel, *Restless are the Sails*, which was published in 1942. For some time she kept her attention focussed on eighteenth-century Nova Scotia, shifting her attention to the fate of the Acadians and their expulsion from their homeland. However, she would never again be on quite the same solid ground historically as she was with *Quietly My Captain Waits*.

In 1945, she severed her ties with Nova Scotia and Nova Scotian themes as she moved on, both physically and spiritually. But the memories of the years she spent at Victoria Beach, and the impression that Nova Scotia had made on her, remained with her for the rest of her life, until her death in 1983.

Although eight more novels followed *Quietly My Captain Waits*, none proved as successful or as appealing, although most also dealt with historical themes. *Quietly My Captain Waits* remains Eaton's major contribution to the genre and to Canadian literature. Eaton would continue to write for most of the remainder of her life, but she never achieved the recognition or financial security she sought. If her life was not successful from a literary point of view, it was at least interesting. Her later years were as unconventional and as filled with action as her earlier ones had been.

Eaton's historical novels, particularly *Quietly My Captain Waits*, are strong evocations of eighteenth-century Canadian life. They are also important reflections of a significant phase in the life and interests of this complex and often unconventional author. Evelyn Eaton would eventually move away from historical novels, but in many respects she never escaped the long shadows of the past. Twentieth-century — and now twenty-first century — readers are the beneficiaries of her preoccupation with the past.

Barry M. Moody
Wolfville, Nova Scotia
2001

GEORGE
ANNAND

NORTH

W E

S

SAGUENAY

R. de Sts Marguerite

PORT NEUF plein
de ROCHERS

Fleuve de Canada ou de S.

Riviere du SAGUENAY

Port Tadoussac

Les Trois Rivieres

CANADA

P. Gaspé

Baye de Chaleurs

Le

KEBEC (Quebec)

Port Neuf

Trois Rivieres

PORTAGE des
CANOTS

Malisites

R. St. Jean

LES CHEMINS

JEMSEG

PORT NASHWAAK

FRENEUSE

Fort de la
Tour

Malisites

CHANSON

Miramichi

Les Mines

ISLES DE LA
MAGDELAINE

ISLE DE ST.
JEAN
(Prince Edward
Island)

S.

Forest

NOUVELLE ESCOSSE

BEAULIEU
R. Dauphin

PORT ROYAL
(ANNAPOLIS ROYAL)

Micmacs

NOUVELLE
ANGLETERRE

FT. PENTAGOUET

Combat

Baye Françoise
(BAY OF FUNDY)

Forest

ISLES AUX
LOUS MARINS

LA HEVE

CHIBUCTO
(HALIFAX)

Massachusetts

BOSTON C. ANNA

PROVIDENCE

PLYMOUTH

SEA FIGHT between the "SOLEIL
D'AFRIQUE" and His Majesty's
ship "THUNDER"

ACADIA
(NOVIA SCOTIA)

NEW YORK

STATEN HOECK
(CAPE COD)

SANDWICH

Isle Longue

RODE I.

NATOEKE et
NANTIKET I.

——— Voyage of Mme. de Freneuse
on the "Soleil d'Afrique" from Quebec
to St. Jean ~~ by canoe to Freneuse

•••••••• De Brouillan's march on
foot from Chibucto to Port Royal

------- Mme. de Freneuse's flight
from the British on foot to
Freneuse and across the bay
by canoe ~ ~

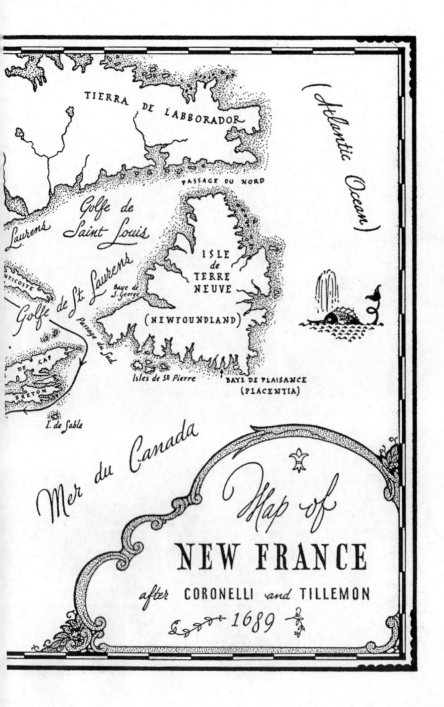

TIERRA DE LABBORADOR

(Atlantic Ocean)

PASSAGE DU NORD

Golfe de Saint Louis

...aurens

ISLE de TERRE NEUVE

...NTICOSTE

Golfe de St. Laurens

Baye de S. George

(NEWFOUNDLAND)

Passage du Sud

...DE CAP

BRETON

Isles de St Pierre

BAYE DE PLAISANCE (PLACENTIA)

I. de Sable

Mer du Canada

Map of

NEW FRANCE

after CORONELLI and TILLEMON

1689

Table of Contents

Reproduction of a contemporary map of
Port Royal showing the fort, Madame de
Freneuse's house, and where the English
camped during the last siege.

Translations of French songs in the text.

Extracts from correspondence relating to
the de Freneuse scandal in the public archives of Halifax, N. S., and originals of
the letters incorporated in the text.

Author's Note

ANNAPOLIS ROYAL, in Acadia, which comprised modern Nova Scotia, New Brunswick, and a portion of Maine, was a key position in the long struggle between France and England to establish colonies in the New World. For over a century it was hotly disputed between them, until in 1711 it passed into the English hands never to be retaken.

For the last eleven years of the French rule hardly a dispatch left New France (comprising Quebec, Ontario, and Acadia) that did not mention Madame de Freneuse, in either passionate partisanship or vehement denunciation. She charmed three successive governors; obtained a pension from the King (Louis XIV) on the grounds that she was "the only widow in Acadie"; had a child by Monsieur de Bonaventure, whose baptism is in the parish records; was banished for her misbehavior and crossed the Bay of Fundy in the coldest part of winter in an open canoe. She caused the worthy Monsieur de Goutins much disquietude, and, in fact, one of the governors, Monsieur de Subercase, left it on record that the story had been "pushed as far as hell could desire."

Out of these fragments I have woven a novel, the facts of which are accurate though the interpretation is conjectural. It is known, for example, that Madame de Freneuse's second husband, Mathieu de Freneuse, died at the siege of Nashwaak, defending the mill he had built; but whether or not there was a miller's daughter only the vanished mill could tell. Nor is there any record of Gervais Tibaut, Raoul de Perrichet, and others in the story.

No portrait has been found of Madame de Freneuse, but a contemporary map shows the site of her house, which was, in the words of the estimate, "beautified and adorned" by the French King's money.

The correspondence in Part Five between Monsieur de Goutins, Monsieur de Bonaventure, and Monsieur de Pourtchartrain, the King's Minister in France, is taken from French correspondence in the Public Archives of Halifax, Nova Scotia. The translation is mine. Copies of these letters and other letters from Monsieur de la Touche and the Bishop of Quebec are given with translations in the Appendix.

I have used the old form of the names of the towns and other places in the story, as follows:

Chibucto—Halifax
Kebec—Quebec
Port Royal—Annapolis Royal
St. Jean—St. John
Trois Rivières—Three Rivers
Baye Françoise—Bay of Fundy

My thanks are due to the Director of the Museum at Fort Anne, Annapolis Royal, for maps and material; to Miss Laura Hardy, for drawing my attention to Madame de Freneuse in the first place; and to E. C. B. in general, for her help.

EVELYN EATON

PART ONE

New France

1691

CHAPTER 1

ALTHOUGH it was after twilight, the sky was still light blue, mysteriously blue, with white stars showing.

Raoul de Perrichet, urging his black mule up the hillside toward Draguignan, in French Provence, thought suddenly of the Madonna's robe, floating over hills, above the village, along fields and vineyards, down through terraces of olive trees till blue of sky met blue of sea, a thousand feet below. The thought beguiled him. He began to rhyme:

> "My Lady wears a coat—robe—of blue,
> It spreads, flows, floats, with such an hue,
> It is the Night." . . .

The mule went slower and slower, until at last it stopped to snatch at a mouthful of thyme by the wall. Startled from the composition of his poem, Raoul kicked it angrily.

"Tsa! Get on, you ugly beast!"

He regretted having thought of the Madonna. She was his patrone, and by force of habit the thought had come; but it was unsuitable—it was even blasphemy, considering what had happened.

He kicked the mule again, and it went forward, sulkily, munching the sprig of thyme. The path twisted, continuing through orchards and a grove of orange trees. Fireflies shimmered beneath branches like a rain of falling stars in late September. The scent of crushed thyme and mountain flowers rose about him everywhere, filling his nostrils as persistently as the roar of rushing water from the mountain river filled his ears. The beauty of this night was hard to bear.

Now he could see the town, the church, the château, and

·[3]·

misery swept him at the sight, so fresh, so keen, it might have been new-met instead of his companion these interminable hours.

Vanina would be laughing, as she had laughed that night, fifteen, sixteen, no, seventeen hours ago. Vanina's laughter! He heard its low intimate amusement above the roar of the river and the clatter of the mule's feet. That throat was made for laughter, and those breasts, for now he had seen them and he knew. He choked on the remembrance.

Impossible to conceive with what fervor, in what trance, he had climbed the château wall to her window, with jasmine and white violets, to surprise her. And he had surprised her! Not with her husband, unexpectedly returned, but with the Comte de Callian, old enough to be her father and Raoul's grandfather. Bigre! Vanina laughed, deliciously, dreadfully, and there was nothing left, now, of jasmine or white violet in the world.

All those days of encouragement, of glances, of smiles, had been pet the young puppy to catch the old dog. The Comte swallowed the bait. *He* was not laughing! Out of his misery Raoul began to grin, against the aching stiffness of his face, as he remembered the old man's grotesque attitude, his purpling face, his breeches trailing . . . Ha, ha, ha!

The sequel was even funnier—scrambling somehow down the wall, stunned and breathless; gathering himself at the bottom; running in the first direction that he faced, until it brought him to the Drouins' farm. Light was streaming from their kitchen door, across the moonlit courtyard, making a red and muddy glow which darkened everything on either side of it.

Petite Marie came from watering the beasts and saw him standing there. She called to him and waved the buckets, dancing forward in delight. (He cowered in the saddle from this memory of her, laughing in the moonlight.)

He had turned fiercely, stopped her dance, and stopped the words of greeting, striding to the barn, while she, perplexed and troubled, trotted after him. There, as she drew near in her concern, he threw her down, twisting her arms, tearing at her clothes, bruising her face, listening to a torrent of filthy, wicked words which streamed from his own mouth. She screamed in pain, in terror, petite Marie, who had always loved him. It was his turn, then, to be surprised, with his breeches down, by le bon Père Drouin, his father's bailiff, and by Henri and Pierre, his boyhood friends. They chased him with pitchforks across the fields, panting savagely behind him. He reached his father's gates and slammed the heavy grille in their faces. While they roused the servants, he was saddling the mule. He got out by the back as they were let in by the front, and rode away. He seemed to have been riding ever since. Now he was coming home, for he was tired, too tired to care what sort of a reception waited.

The clattering of the mule across the courtyard roused excitement in the house. Peering faces appeared at windows, framed against the candlelight; doors opened and shut; dogs barked; there was a general scurry of rushing feet.

Raoul slid from the mule, and started toward the house. His brother, Jacquelot, ran toward him with a lantern.

"Where've you been, Ra? They've all been cross with you. Did you go to the fête?"

Raoul pushed by without answering. The full force of his fatigue had come upon him; he stood rocking in the doorway, under the stream of exclamation and question shot at him in voices sharpened by relief.

Suddenly a voice rose above the others.

"Let the lad eat and sleep. You'll get nothing out of him like this."

The speaker, a tall figure in uniform, stood with his back to the fire, keeping his wig from being scorched by holding it carefully to one side. His face stood out, dark and strong, under the wig's white symmetry, and at the first sound of his voice, though he spoke quietly enough, the confusion in the room was stilled. Monsieur de Perrichet, tut-tutting and blowing; Madame de Perrichet, lamenting and fussing; the young de Perrichets and little Jacquelot—all were dominated by authority.

Raoul raised his head. L'Oncle Pierre said to him:

"A bowl of soup, a night's sleep . . . Things will appear quite different, then—even growing up. A painful affair, but the pain will pass as one adjusts. Go, now, and sleep."

He smiled. Raoul felt the smile warm his heart. L'Oncle Pierre understood! It was the first concern that anyone had shown for him, his point of view. The others were too full of theirs. Something broke in Raoul; he began to sob—great, deep, guttural sobs that shook and tore at him.

Still exclaiming, but no longer questioning, his mother got him to bed and left him there.

CHAPTER II

TEN days after Raoul's escapade the de Perrichets were gathered at a farewell mass, which was also a mass of thanksgiving.

After a long discussion filled with ominous phrases . . . ("Certainly the Comte de Callian is important. Certainly he has the King's good ear. Certainly he cannot be expected to trust his reputation to a boy's discretion." . . . "There will be lettres de cachet." . . . "Raoul, languishing in prison." . . . "More or less interminably.") . . . they had come to a decision.

L'Oncle Pierre, standing in his favorite place, with his back to the fire, took no part in the discussion. From time to time appealed to, he shook his head or sighed, staring into a goblet of brandy which he cradled in careful hands. In the end he said:

"It would be foolish of you to keep Raoul here. Why not let him come with me?"

"You mean," asked Madame de Perrichet doubtfully, "Raoul should go into the Navy?"

Monsieur de Perrichet said nothing. He disapproved of the Navy. It was not, he considered, a profession for gentlemen, but for cutthroats and pirates. A hard life, spent among rough men, was coarsening to the fibers. Still, at this point, it was not a question of Raoul's fibers, but of his skin. Personal opinions must not stand in the way of a safe solution. And Raoul was a younger son. He continued to say nothing, while l'Oncle Pierre explained himself.

"Not just into the Navy, ma belle sœur—into the King's Fleet of New France, upon my own flagship, the *Soleil d'Afrique*. Your son will walk the deck of the fastest vessel in the world!

·[6]·

She sails, if you can imagine it, seven leagues an hour! Stupendous! And every year we think of improvements, of developments. Truly we live in an age of scientific discovery."

His face lit up with somber pride, but there was no one to share his enthusiasm. Monsieur de Perrichet disliked the modern age. He lived in, and for, the past. He disliked the conquest of the New World, the development of colonies. He grudged the money spent on them, the efforts wasted upon savages, the martyrdom of Jesuit saints, and, most of all, the dangerous ideas the New World brought to men; the beckoning of adventure, the ease with which all bonds were slipped, the proper obligations of a man's allegiance to his King, his country, his lands, his wife— all these could be evaded in New France. There were men called Coureurs de Bois, who lived in the forests on friendly terms with the savages and simply did not emerge at the King's Ministers' commands, to pay taxes, or take wives, or cultivate the land. It was dangerous and disturbing. He sank into a reverie in which he saw himself sitting beside a triangular object called a tepee, cooking a bird on a pointed stick over a fire, above his head trees and sky (olive trees and Provençal sky), around him green solitude and freedom and peace. Why, one could even walk about naked, feel the sun on one's skin, sleep when one wanted to, eat when one wanted to, do what one wanted to—though, of course, no one but a criminal would! He shot a glance at L'Oncle Pierre, kneeling beside his wife. Handsome fellow, strong fellow; gave one a dangerous sort of feeling, this Monsieur de Bonaventure, married to his wife's sister. . . . (Yes, but *he* could get away from *her*, for nine months of the year.)

"Dominus vobiscum."

"Et cum spiritu tuo."

He pulled himself back to the business on hand. Crossing himself energetically, he reflected presently that Monsieur de Bonaventure's description of the daily routine on the *Soleil d'Afrique* sounded harsh enough. It would be good for the boy to endure hardship under the protection of his uncle. It would make him a man. He rubbed his hands together in consent.

Madame de Perrichet, like her husband, was not an admirer of the modern age. Whatever men might do in the way of invention and discovery, marvelous things and beyond her comprehension, women's work remained the same. If, instead of making ships sail seven leagues an hour, men were to make water run into

·[7]·

the house, or fires light themselves, or butter churn, that would be something! But all this frantic speed, this restless haste, meant only that bad news traveled faster.

The Comte de Callian, for instance, could obtain a lettre de cachet now in half the time it would have taken him when she was young. She knew that he would do so. The Comte, though she had never told her husband this nor ever would, once had wanted her; and since nothing reveals a man so mercilessly to a woman as his desire, she knew that harming Raoul would be a pleasure to him, not only because the boy had discovered him and the Marquise de Monterroux together, but also, and perhaps more, because no one could have discovered him and the Comtesse de Perrichet in similar circumstance, and the boy was her son. She sighed. Twenty years ago the Comte de Callian had been a handsome man, as tall and as striking as Monsieur de Bonaventure kneeling beside her; yes, as Pierre, her sister's husband. (Two sisters, and one of them had all the luck!)

Ciel! What thoughts during the mass! She crossed herself and shut her eyes. Then, since in spite of herself her mind strayed sideways, she began to go over Raoul's equipment—three coverings, four shirts . . .

Raoul, kneeling beside her, was dumb with gratitude. While he was confined to his room, under his parent's displeasure, he had spent most of the time wondering how he could face the future, seeing Vanina, seeing the Comte de Callian, seeing Marie Drouin, seeing Henri and Pierre, everywhere, every day. Then he was in danger of a lettre de cachet and prison. That had frightened him, especially since his omnipotent elders were, it seemed, helpless and bewildered. In the midst of all this misery his uncle had talked of New France, of the *Soleil d'Afrique*, of the King's Service.

Now Raoul was going away. (When he returned in uniform, commanding his own ship perhaps, then Vanina would see and would be sorry!)

"Qui tollis peccata mundi . . ."

"Miserere nobis."

This would be the last time he heard mass in France, perhaps the last time he heard mass forever. He glanced past his mother to his uncle, kneeling quietly with bowed head. The possible meaning of an incident that had surprised him earlier now came to him, with thoughts of danger and of death. His uncle had

·[8]·

taken a cross from his breast pocket and given it to the curé to be blessed. It was a child's cross on a little silver chain, a strange thing for him to carry. The last time Raoul had seen one like it was on Marie Drouin's neck, at her first communion.

He did not want to think of Marie Drouin, but of this man with whom he would be sailing to a new life.

Pierre Denys de Bonaventure was born, Raoul had heard, in 1659. He must be thirty-two. He was born in the new France at a place called Trois Rivières. Raoul imagined three great silver rivers meeting in a symmetrical and impossible Y. Then he tried standing on the bank of one of the rivers, watching the water flow by. This was better; but now the river changed to the Siagne, and the Provençal country rose upon its banks. He shook his head. Monsieur de Bonaventure entered the French Navy. Last year he rose to command of a frigate at Rochefort. Now he was in command of the King's vessels on the coast of Acadia.

"Ite missa est."

(A great man . . .)

"Deo gratias."

The curé paused beside Raoul and laid his hand in blessing on the boy's head. He returned the crucifix to Monsieur de Bonaventure, who kissed it and replaced it next his heart.

They got up from their prayers. Madame de Perrichet looked stricken. Raoul moved toward her, but the horses were at the gate; the time had come.

CHAPTER III

THE *Soleil d'Afrique* sailed at noon. Raoul had been on her deck since dawn, watching cases and bales come aboard, talking with anyone who would listen, getting in the way. It was a beautiful spring morning. The harbor stretched white and gleaming, set against a hillside of olive trees with here and there a dark cypress, a pink tower, a patch of orange or of crimson, and, encircling everything, blue sky sloping down to bluer sea. The *Soleil d'Afrique* rode at anchor graciously, like a woman stopping to exchange a word or two with a loved friend. There were two other ships preparing to leave with her, the *Bonne Espérance* and the *Faulcon d'Or*; but she was the biggest, the whitest, the strongest of the three.

Raoul explored her thoroughly, from officers' quarters aft to men's hold fore. He was sharing a stowaway with lieutenants Famoisy and Nantes, as the Captain's secretary. He had a hammock and a shelf.

"You're nothing of a seaman; you're not a soldier; you'd be useless as a cabin boy; you're pretty superfluous cargo, and I'm bothered how to sign you on. . . . I have it: secretary! That will make the King laugh, and de Pourtchartrain fume. He thinks I give myself airs."

Since they stepped on board together, Raoul carrying a package of small treasures too precious to go into the wooden chest his mother had packed for him, Monsieur de Bonaventure had been preoccupied—too busy to bother about Raoul, or to speak to him even. He was free to hang about and take in all the sights.

There were plenty of these. The whole town had dropped work and taken a holiday to see them off. The quays were filled with soldiers, workmen, jugglers, nobles, priests, and women of all sorts, from the Cardinal's sister to a barefoot fishwife—all talking, shouting, laughing, pointing, throwing flowers to the sailors already on the ship, and kissing their lovers good-by. Raoul had never seen such a sight. He leaned on the railing, watching.

Three oxen were led to the ship and hoisted, pushed, pulled, aboard. They were being taken to Kebec. A barrelful of chickens followed. Cases of provisions had been coming on since dawn. At length it seemed that even the *Soleil d'Afrique* could hold no more. Monsieur de Bonaventure, conferring with the King's Ship Clerk in his cabin, signed the papers presented to him, stretched his long legs beneath the table, pushed a glass of wine to the clerk, and poured himself another.

"La santé et bon voyage!"

"And yours."

They bowed, put down the glasses, and went upon the deck. The last sailor was coming on board, his arm around two women. He stopped on the passageway and kissed them both with hearty smacks. The crowd roared comments and encouragement. He wiped the back of his hand against his lips and, grinning, waved good-by. He stumbled, coming on, and nearly jostled Monsieur de Bonaventure. Raoul, standing near, saw the change of expression come over his face, as with an effort he saved himself. It was the expression of a man who sees hell gape before him. De Bonaventure, however, looked away. The man recovered himself and went below.

A gun fired. Bells began to peal. The noise on the quay redoubled as men and women shouted their messages for friends in the New France, their good wishes for the journey, their good-bys. Girls began to throw flowers and scarves; men ran closer, pushing and jostling so that those in front pressed back, afraid of being thrown into the water.

Sixteen men in the longboat began to row, pulling the *Soleil d'Afrique* into position. Her anchor came up and was coiled into place. Slowly she began to move away.

Each one dropped what he was doing and stood to attention. De Bonaventure, miraculously in the proper place, bared his head and inclined it solemnly as the Cardinal, surrounded by his scarlet-robed acolytes, raised his hand in blessing; the sun caught his ring and sent a pin point of ruby fire into Raoul's eyes.

He blinked; and when he looked again, the space between him and the shore had widened.

Now all was motion. Men were running to barked orders from the maître d'équipage (bosun). They swarmed the decks; they climbed the masts and spread out above Raoul's head on tiny spars. He shuddered, looking up at them; but they were waving their hands gaily while they waited to unfurl the sails, when the *Soleil d'Afrique* should be far enough to sea.

A song broke out on the shore.[1]

> "Gentilz gallans de France,
> Qui en la guerre allez,
> Je vous prie qu'il vous plaise
> Mon amy saluer."

Those on the ship replied with another.

> Ils s'en vont, ces rois de ma vie,
> Ces yeux, ces beaux yeux,
> Dont l'éclat fait palir d'envie
> Ceux mêmes des cieux.
> Dieux, amis de l'innocence,

(At this a howl of laughter from the shore.)

> Qu'ai-je fait pour mériter
> Les ennuis ou cette absence
> Me va précipiter?"

Faces grew indistinct, the shouting softened, as the *Soleil d'Afrique* drew away. The men in the longboat stopped rowing and were taken aboard. The boat was fastened in its place. Now, simultaneously, at a sign from the maître d'équipage, sails were unfurled and the wind caught them in one magnificent sweep. The ship shuddered and sprang alive.

Tears came into Raoul's eyes. He was leaving all that he had known.

CHAPTER IV

HIS first day on board, Raoul ran about and looked at everything, ate and drank immoderately, and ran about again, with the result that on the second day he was seasick and lay retching in his hammock as it swung him to and fro. His uncle sent a man periodically with compôte of ginger and bowls of black coffee. On the third day he felt better. On the fourth day he got up.

They were out of sight of land, running before the wind. Raoul had never seen green-gray water before. He was accustomed to the azure sea of the South, calm, not even tidal. This strong and sullen ocean appalled him, and for comfort, since the two lieutenants hardly spoke to him, he sought his uncle's company.

Monsieur de Bonaventure sat behind a table in his cabin, doors and windows closed against the cold sea air, his slippered feet cocked upon a stool, playing a game of solitaire. He smiled as Raoul hesitated in the doorway and beckoned him inside.

"Now we can play bezique," he said. "You will be surprised how little there is to do at sea—for us. The men are occupied."

"Indeed they are!" said Raoul heartily. "I have just seen two of them running barefoot up those horrible ropes."

"The feet cling better bare."

"But in this cold! Brrr!"

"Be thankful you're a secretary and not a sailor. As for cold, imagine, then, New France in winter—snow, ice, and bitter wind!"

"But one is equipped for it, in furs, and rubbed with oil."

De Bonaventure laughed. He picked the cards up and began to shuffle, in deft movements that displayed the strength of his long hands. Raoul watched them, fascinated. He was beginning to understand why men were afraid of this man.

They played bezique until the door opened and Lieutenant Famoisy saluted.

"An English frigate à tribord (starboard), mon Capitaine."

"How far?"

"About eight lengths."

"Outsail her. This is the *Soleil d'Afrique.* Ignore all signals."

"Very good, mon Capitaine."

They went on playing.

"There's a fellow for you," de Bonaventure said presently, "who will not last a long time in New France. Can you tell me why?"

Raoul thought for a moment.

"Is it perhaps because he thinks too much of himself?"

"The opposite. He does not think enough. He is arrogant, but he has no pride. He has, instead, a lackey's soul. He hates authority, but he cringes; he resents not being trusted, but he pilfers. The savages will see through him. They respect a man; a man must be a man to deal with them. The Comte de Frontenac, tenez, though he's over seventy, has their affectionate respect, their fear. He goes among them, takes part in their ceremonies; yes, he actually dances, with feathers in his hair, and keeps his dignity.

"He speaks at their meetings, scolds them like children, sways them to his will. When he was recalled for a while, there was a massacre immediately. The new governor, like young Famoisy, was just a lackey, a king's lackey. Men, women, and children died, died horribly, because of that! Now the Comte is back, in spite of his enemies. New France demands men!"

This was the first of many flattering tête-à-têtes. Raoul was enthralled. He heard stories of the wild country he was bound for, which made him eager to see it and more eager to succeed there. He learned that there were factions and intrigues in Kebec, and men who were adventurers, just as there were men, and women too, heroic in their efforts to create New France out of a forest full of savages.

The most fascinating stories were those of de Bonaventure's childhood and youth. And one evening, when he was drinking freely and in an expansive mood, he paid Raoul the great compliment of a confidence: he told him the story of the silver cross.

It was the story of a woman. It happened in Kebec.

"I was quartered in her father's house. We fell in love. You should know something about that!"

Raoul reddened. It was strange how little he thought of Vanina now. He was still in love with her, of course, and for her sake was sailing to New France; but the pangs of unrequited love were lessening.

"He was a pretty important man, and I was nobody—nobody at all, not even a lieutenant, just a sort of ensign on the smallest ship. I asked her hand, and that was the end—convent for her, shipboard for me, heavy threats to both of us. His daughter was sixteen. He would have me imprisoned. I was ten years older than she. It would be seduction. He would break me and discipline her. But she was brave, a real daughter of New France! She had a face like a little bird, one of the brown hawks in summer rising from the forest, a small, fierce, proud, hunting face, with black eyes, high cheekbones, and thin lips."

"She sounds like a savage. Was she?"

"No, but she had the look of one. They teased her about it."

He fell into a long silence. Raoul, curious, inquired:

"What happened then?"

"What happened? We said good-by. She gave me this cross, took it from her neck and put it in my hand. I had a little leather book of poetry, by a woman called Louise Labé. Did you ever hear of her? No? She was known as Captain Loys, rode to war accoutered as a man, and they say she fought at the siege of Perpignan. She wrote good poetry. I quoted it to *my* Louise, looking out across the roofs of Kebec from her balcony. I gave the book to her in exchange for the cross. Very romantic. Her father dragged her away from me and shut her in a convent, in disgrace."

"Did you see her again?"

"Figure-toi, she climbed down the convent wall and got to my ship! When I came on board, she was waiting there, hidden in my stowaway. She had cut off all her hair; she was dressed in trousers; she had slipped on board—how, le bon Dieu knows. She was full of an idea that she could come with me as a cabin boy, poor child, that we would marry when we got to France. We could lie about her age, or find a priest who asked no questions, or do without. She poured the whole thing out to me."

"And you, mon oncle, what did you do?"

"I argued with her, and I sent her back. I persuaded her that

·[15]·

I never loved her. It was no love, I said; it was just a joke. I think she believed me in the end, for she went away. And when she had gone, I was sorry."

He poured himself another glass and drank it, smiling wryly.

"It wasn't only that her father was so powerful, you know that?"

He was looking full at Raoul, who thought he had better nod.

"It was rather . . . Oh well, does a young girl know her mind? Her heart? It may not have been love with her, but the call of life, of a man's life, of adventure; in all probability it was not love."

He stared in front of him.

"She married. Jean de Larieux told me, when he came over, that she was married and had children. So, you see . . . But I can never forget her standing in the doorway there, with the light in her eyes. I married, too. I married twice, but she was the one my heart loved, the only one. Not the heart only, the senses. You know that?"

Again Raoul nodded. His uncle was a little drunk, and he must agree with him. There must be no embarrassment when he recovered.

"That was seven years ago! Now I am going back for the first time. They say, the learned doctors of the Jesuit school, that a man changes every seven years completely. Have you heard that? Yes? It is not true. I have not changed. But she is married. I hope I do not see her in Kebec."

He reached for the bottle, which was empty.

"Va, mon vieux, I am cold and very drunk. We must go to bed."

CHAPTER V

RAOUL slept uneasily that night, dreaming in snatches of de Bonaventure and the hawk-faced girl he loved, while the wind rose, the sea grew turbulent, and angry waves struck the ship. Raoul's hammock swung in wilder curves, until the noise and the confusion woke him. He was alone, in the dark, while all around him he heard pounding and screaming, muffled through the wind.

At first he thought the ship was sinking and the two snoring men with whom he had gone to bed had left him there to die. He fell out of his coverings and dashed upon the deck. There he was buffeted by a mighty blast of wind and water and thrown against the hold, bruised and dripping. He caught a rope to save himself from being swept overboard as the ship stood on her tail and then rolled sideways until he saw the sea come up to meet him face to face.

Even in that trying moment he was conscious of a voice, above the horror, shouting orders, a calm, courageous voice, apparently quite unafraid—his uncle's voice. A sizzling fork of lightning lit up the whole wild scene. Looking upward, Raoul saw men on the rigging, men on the spars, other men climbing; and, as he gaped, the sails came down in orderly heaps upon the deck, the noise of the wind lessened, the bare masts stood up alone against the sky.

Raoul felt his way back to the stowaway. Lieutenant Nantes was there.

"It's terrific!" he said. "The ship will split!"

Raoul reassured him, out of his new-found calm. With his uncle in charge, the *Soleil d'Afrique* would ride out the storm.

·[17]·

"But I am sorry for the *Bonne Esperance* and the *Faulcon d'Or*, both smaller ships." (And without his guidance!)

"The *Faulcon d'Or* is seaworthy enough; I've sailed on her," Lieutenant Nantes said, lighting the swinging lamp with Raoul's help and tying it to safety hooks.

"We must not sleep before we put this out," he warned, "in case of fire."

"No," Raoul agreed. But it was nice to have the light. The ship was riding steadier without the sails; still, he was too aroused to sleep.

"Does it not seem strange to you," he asked impulsively, "how men can sail across all this, to that"—he waved his hand in a forward sweep—"and arrive there where they wanted to go—even when they know it is there?"

"But imagine," Lieutenant Nantes agreed, "when they didn't know, the first few times, on such small ships! That did require courage. Now we sail on these huge, trustworthy, modern vessels, taking weeks where they took months, and we know where we go. Besides, look at our science! Columbus had a compass, true, but not the perfected instrument that we have now"—and he forgot his fears for the splitting of the ship as they talked on.

Raoul heard that it was Lieutenant Nantes' first voyage to the New France, too. Together they speculated upon what they might discover. Raoul found that he liked this red-haired boy, little older than himself, with a sudden liking. They talked until it was his turn to go on duty, when Lieutenant Famoisy came back.

Then Raoul composed himself to sleep, in spite of the shudderings and heavings of the ship, the shrieks of the gale, and the mad behavior of his hammock.

It was three days before they could hoist sail again, and by that time they had drifted from their course. They continued to have dirty weather. Once they saw the *Faulcon d'Or*, beating upwind in the distance. Twice they passed English frigates.

One of the oxen died and was thrown overboard to everyone's chagrin; but its flesh was suspect, and they dared not make a roast. One of the sailors, injured during the storm, had to have his hand amputated. Raoul held the implements while de Bonaventure, his sleeves rolled up, operated. Six of the crew held down the injured man, who was made drunk on brandy; but the operation sobered him completely. Raoul heard the harsh sound of knife on bone, saw the hand fly off the block and the ship's carpenter cauterize the stump with a heated iron; he heard the yells of the patient drown even the sizzling of his flesh. That was all he saw, or knew, for several minutes. When he came to, he was being doused with salt water. De Bonaventure gave him brandy, too.

"The man will live," he said. "If I had lost my courage as you did, he might have died."

"Perhaps he would rather," Raoul choked, "than live without his hand."

But that was absurd, since before they reached New France the sailor's stump was nearly healed, and he was out of pain and perfectly merry in the thought of the King's pension he would get.

"I can marry on that," he said, "and settle down. I'll have a hook made when I get ashore. Monsieur le Capitaine is good to write me down disabled, since with a hook I could be useful still. Many a Captain keeps a sailor with a hook and expects as much from him as other men. But Monsieur le Capitaine is a gentleman and has a heart of true gold."

"A purse of the true gold, he means," de Bonaventure said, aside to Raoul, "not my own—the King's."

They continued to play cards together every evening. Raoul's affection and admiration for his uncle grew, but de Bonaventure was never quite so unbending as the night before the storm.

So the long weeks passed, until it became almost second nature to crawl out of a hammock; walk, swaying and clinging to ropes; eat salted pork and biscuits; drink out of a glass never more than quarter full; wear the beginnings of a beard; and remain unwashed, sleeping in one's clothes, with a salt-incrusted skin, under the same gray and lowering skies, the same wild gusts of wind, the same majestic bellying of the sails, the same obedient pressing forward of the weary ship.

Then, when Raoul had almost forgotten its existence, they saw land!

CHAPTER VI

RAOUL never forgot his first sight of New France. It was strange and terrifying, since he had built a different image in his mind, expecting it to be what it was called —New France.

There would be more trees, of course, since there were forests; there would be fewer towns and villages, but settlements; it would be a rougher, wilder sort of place, with savages—Raoul imagined them hairy and stupid, like the pictures of big monkeys he had seen in Draguignan.

But he was not prepared for the reality. Day after day they sailed on this enormous and unnatural river, which he could hardly concede to be a river though it flowed steadily in one direction and was, therefore, not the sea; day after day they saw rising in the distance one long, continuous, never-ending mass of dark green trees. The forest! Raoul's spine chilled when he looked at it. Savages were creeping there!

At first he was always expecting that the next turn of the river would disclose a settlement, houses, a harbor, people, lights. But nowhere was there any sign of life, only the menace of this dark hostility.

"We have days of this ahead of us," de Bonaventure said, "before we reach Kebec."

Certainly it was beautiful, especially at evening. The sunsets were superb. The air was clearer than in France; the stars shone brighter, seemed nearer. Once Raoul, watching the new moon from his favorite place on deck, saw a great yellow star low on the horizon. It twinkled and flickered energetically until he understood it was a fire, not a star. This delighted him. There were people there at last! They must be nearer than they thought to journey's end. He went to tell the others.

The news was received in a strange silence. No one made a move to go and look. The maître d'équipage and some of the men were gathered about de Bonaventure for instruction. Raoul saw the maître's face harden as he turned aside. Famoisy paled. Nantes looked as puzzled as himself. The men began to retreat, silently, with black looks. It was left to de Bonaventure to explain, after they had gone.

"If there is a fire—big enough for you to see at this point—it can only be because the savages are torturing a prisoner, no doubt one of *us*."

Raoul gasped.

After that he could not bear to look at the land as it unrolled its hostile growth on either side, nor take pleasure in the flowing silver water. When it grew dark, especially, he would not look, but shut himself in the cabin, to play at cards or talk, until one night he came on deck to go to his sleeping place and saw there were six or seven fires burning in a line, close down to the shore. He shuddered, turning sick, and shut them from his sight. But the lookout in the d'artimon cupped his hands, hailing in phrases blown away by the wind. Cries went up from the deck beneath. De Bonaventure came out, saw, and waved his arms. All the men cheered. Raoul was bewildered. These fires, it seemed, were not lit by the savages. They were signals to Kebec, by lookouts who had seen the *Soleil d'Afrique* and reported it.

"Tomorow we arrive."

The night passed in excited talk, uneasy sleep, and day broke to the sound of dull booming. Guns were being fired in salute. As the mists cleared from the river and the sun shone, Raoul could see the rock on which Kebec was built towering to the right of them. The noise grew deafening as they neared the port. Flags were flying, bells were ringing, people were shouting and jumping up and down like small black dots as the vessel put about and started for the shore.

Whistles blew, men swarmed up the rigging, and slowly, proudly, the *Soleil d'Afrique*, moving forwards, came to rest. The river deepened abruptly here, so that they were able to anchor twenty feet from shore. Raoul watched the faces grow distinct and individual, until at length he seemed to be standing just above them, looking down. The ship's sides made a barrier, so that he felt in some way free, as at a show, to stare. And stare he did, very curiously.

The first thing that struck him was the robust strength and healthiness of every face. It was the hottest part of the summer, and the sun had tanned them all a golden brown. Even the nuns (for there were six of them, standing among the children and the women of the town) had merry brown faces, sturdy arms, and probably, if one could see them, legs. The men were all robust, and as for the children, swarming barefoot all over the place, it was astonishing how good-looking and well built they were. One in particular, so poor that he had only a shirt on his back, was golden-limbed and sturdy. Raoul watched him for a moment, until his stamping and jumping on the stones made him want to feel the solid rock beneath his own feet. He went to ask his uncle if he might go ashore.

He found him in the cabin, putting on his best coat of lavender watered silk with gold embroidery, smoothing out his wig, and dabbing perfume on a handkerchief. Raoul was surprised. He was used to seeing him and all the others roughly dressed on board. He looked down at his own attire and was immediately conscious of the impression he must have given to the people on the shore. He blushed and retreated to the stowaway to change.

Half an hour later de Bonaventure, leaving the unloading of the ship for a few hours to the maître d'équipage, under Lieutenant Famoisy, was rowed ashore with Lieutenant Nantes and Raoul. They were an elegant trio. De Bonaventure, with a jeweled belt strapped round his coat that gave him a thin waist, looked as though he had just stepped out of the King's presence. Raoul wore a green suit of velour with silken cuffs and a small dress sword. Lieutenant Nantes was more modestly dressed in a dark blue coat with wine-colored reveres and a heavy sword belt, made for holstering pistols. Each carried his hat under his left arm and gloves in his right, and the whole effect would have been imposing but for the fact that their sea legs betrayed them; and do what they might, they walked with a slight lurching movement, a drunken roll.

As they stepped on shore, the crowd parted, greetings were murmured on all sides, men bowed, women curtsied, children pushed and stared. The Governor's right-hand man, Monsieur de Pesselier, greeted them officially; and soon they were climbing the hill together through the lower town to the town proper, where the Governor, the Comte de Frontenac, was waiting for them at the top.

CHAPTER VII

THE climb was steep. Raoul found himself panting as he followed de Bonaventure and the two men flanking him up narrow terraces and winding streets. Kebec was not only built on a rock; it was a rock, with houses jutting out of it. When he looked closer, he could see that some of the houses were made of wood and many more of mud, closely packed and hardened.

They reached an imposing place, where the Récollet Frères had built their monastery. Raoul paused for a moment to look back over the countryside, spread beneath his gaze like a vast counterpane. He traced the course of the broad silver ribbon up which they had sailed. Far in the distance two small acorns, with matches for masts and white specks for sails, were moving upon it.

Raoul poked Lieutenant Nantes.

"The *Faulcon d'Or* and the *Bonne Esperance!*"

They turned to tell Monsieur de Bonaventure, but he was already farther on his way, talking to the Provost, who had joined him, and to the Governor's secretary.

They hurried after, picking their path from cobble to cobble, along the steep ascent. The crowd of children and hangers-on climbing beside them dropped behind. Chatting and laughter died away. Raoul suddenly found himself passing through gates of wrought iron between stone posts. This was the Governor's residence. Sentries on guard presented arms to Monsieur de Bonaventure, who carelessly returned salute. Raoul felt his kinship at that moment, proudly. Monsieur de Bonaventure made such a gallant picture, standing in the sunlight, with his gold braid and watered silk, his tall, thin figure, and his courtly carriage. Raoul automatically straightened his own shoulders and tried to keep from slapping at midges, bigger than the midges at home, with a bothersome bite. His uncle paid no attention to them. Perhaps he was immune.

They entered a hallway. Here the group came together for a moment. Monsieur de Pesselier was saying:

"Yes, it is fortunate. We did not expect you. Such a to-do as there was when we saw your sails and could not recognize them. For, of course, the *Soleil d'Afrique* had never honored us before. Superbe bateau. Now we will know her, like the others, when she comes again. But I was saying it is fortunate that we have a greater number of people here than usual. It will be a brilliant reunion for you, Monsieur de Bonaventure. My felicitations that you command His Majesty's fleet in Acadia. So many people have come here with their families to pay their respects to Monsieur de Villebon, the new governor of Acadia, and to see him off. We heard he was to be appointed, last year, with the last boat. But you will know more than I, since you are to transport him there no doubt?"

De Bonaventure bowed.

"I am eager to hear the news. How is the King?"

"His Majesty is in health."

"Good! The Governor will rejoice to hear that. Monsieur de Villebon is with him now. He is very well liked, very well liked indeed," de Pesselier continued. "I should think the people at Port Royal will be transported with joy to have so good a man in these bad days. Have you heard about the English attack on Chibucto? . . . No? But, of course, you have hardly had time. It was shocking, inconceivably shocking. Figurez-vous, they have raised a regiment of Iroquois! Monsters! Sending those devils against us, the most ferocious of all savages; and very good soldiers, they say, except that they will stop for heavy feasting after each big fight and eat the prisoners, and that delays things for the English."

"How is the Baron de Saint Castin getting on with his Micmac troops?"

"Slowly. The Micmacs don't make fighters like the Iroquois. But he has trained them pretty well. He hopes for an encounter. Only, of course, the mere word 'Iroquois' sends them into the woods for weeks. Very disheartening. Will you come this way, to the Governor?"

De Bonaventure beckoned to Raoul and said in his ear: "Stay here. I have to go and report and give up my papers. Do something for me. Find out if there's a Madame Tibaut here, a Madame Charles Tibaut. Compris? I leave it to you."

"Compris, mon oncle."

Raoul grinned with delight. So that was the name of the hawk-faced girl! And his uncle did not regret the confidence he had made the night of the storm, as Raoul had feared. He imagined himself faced with such an encounter from the past; and he looked sympathetically after Monsieur de Bonaventure, disappearing in the wake of the secretary toward a staircase at the end of the long hall, leaving Lieutenant Nantes and Raoul by themselves.

But only for a moment. Another door opened, disclosing a company of waiting people eager to hear the latest news from France.

Raoul was presented to the company at large by a tall man who asked his name. He gave it in an undertone, blushing and furious with himself for being shy. Then he made a leg, as he had been taught in Provence, and bowed very low in the doorway. He found himself, followed by Lieutenant Nantes, being passed from one lady to another down a long line.

His first impressions were all a blur of light and color and soft speech, but presently, in the intervals of bowing and kissing the hands outstretched to him, he managed to take in some of the details. It was particularly strange to find so many well-dressed people here at the world's end. After the long voyage, the inhabitable banks of the river, and the general atmosphere of desolate hostility, it was exhilarating to find ladies dressed, if not in the very latest fashion (and Raoul was no judge of that, to him they all looked elegant; one or two wore hair à la fontange, like Vanina on state occasions), at least very sumptuously, with flowered stuffs opened upon bodice fronts of fine lace, skirts with quilled flowers and plenty of fans—the éventail brise his mother was so fond of. At times, again like Vanina, a lady was wearing her own hair. This had always seemed to him the most charming and exotic thing; it was part of Vanina's fascination, her long fair ringlets hanging shoulder length. This lady had black hair, not even ringleted. It flowed to her shoulders in natural curls. Obviously this kind of coiffure could not go unmarked in a room full of towering wigs, but the reason he noticed it so particularly was that he found himself, at the end of his embarrassing dance down the room, coming up for air beside her.

The name of the *Soleil d'Afrique* had been handed from person to person down the room, confirming the rumor they had heard from the port, but still a lady wanted to know why it was not the *Bonne Esperance*.

"The *Soleil d'Afrique* is faster, Madame. It is the fastest ship in the world. The *Bonne Esperance* could not outsail her, even though we did get out of course and drifted for three days before the storm. But for that you would not have seen the *Bonne Esperance* after us for at least a week. As it is, she's in the river now."

"Ah! Good! I expect a package by her."

"And I!"

"And I!"

"Shall we get them tonight?"

A crowd of excited ladies surrounded Raoul, teasing the officers with them by pretending to have forgotten their existence.

"I don't know Mesdames," he answered seriously. "I do not know how long it may take to unload."

"How long does it usually take? How long did it take before?"

"I don't know that. For me, Mesdames, there has not been a before."

The lady who most pestered him turned away then, with a quick movement of her large white fan, as if to say:

"Just an ignorant child!"

Raoul was mortified. He looked out of the tail of his eye to see if Lieutenant Nantes had remarked it; but the Lieutenant was deep in troubles of his own, answering the catechism of an elderly person, who seemed, apparently, from the snatches Raoul could hear, to hold him responsible for the loss of a package she had once had sent to her, years before he was born.

"If it is your first journey here," a slow deep voice beside him said, "it must have been impressive. Tell me about it, please, Monsieur."

He turned, gratefully, and began to talk to the lady with the dark hair.

She was smiling at him, and there was something very attractive about her smile. It was kind, for one thing, and her attention did not stray past him to the others, although three officers were waiting to catch her eye. They glared at Raoul, and this restored his self-respect. He told her of the journey.

"The *Soleil d'Afrique* is a wonderful ship."

"I am glad to hear it, Monsieur, because it is very likely that I shall be taking a journey on her soon."

"To France, Madame?"

"No, Monsieur, not to France, to St. Jean on the Baye Françoise, opposite Port Royal, on the other side."

"My uncle will be interested to hear that."

"Your uncle?"

"He commands her. As a matter of fact"—remembering the chattering secretary's remark—"he commands the King's whole Fleet in Acadia."

"What is your uncle's name?"

"Monsieur de Bonaventure."

"Ah."

She fell silent.

"But I call him l'Oncle Pierre."

"That—that is interesting for you. Your name is Couillard perhaps?"

"No, not at all." Raoul looked at her, surprised. "My name is de Perrichet."

("Didn't you hear it shouted out just now?" he felt like saying. It had echoed down the room with embarrassing force.)

"It's strange," she said reflectively. "I know your uncle's family quite well, his brothers and sisters and their children here. You must be his wife's nephew, aren't you? If so, I don't see what you can be but a Couillard, or half a Couillard!"

"Not even an eighth, Madame. None of us are Couillards."

"How very strange!"

"Unless"—a sudden thought struck him—"perhaps his first wife's family . . . I never did know them; but it is possible that they were Couillards, yes."

"I did not know he had married twice."

She gave a little gasp, or perhaps a snort of laughter, as though something she had said was funny.

Raoul was looking at the door. The Lieutenant Nantes was signaling; he was beginning to be restive under all this talk.

"Yes," Raoul repeated absently, "his first wife died three years ago. He married my mother's sister. That's how I come to have him for an uncle now."

"I see."

Now he thought of something else.

"Madame, could you be so kind as to give me information that I need?"

"But certainly."

"Is there here, do you know, in this room or in Kebec, a Madame Charles Tibaut?"

She looked at him oddly for a moment, as though she had not heard; so he repeated it:

"Madame Charles Tibaut?"

"No," she answered quietly, "there is no one of that name here in Kebec."

"Thank you, Madame. Allow me to take my leave."

She held out her hand. He took it, bowed, and brought it to his lips. He noticed a curious ring on the little finger, as he kissed it, and raised his eyes to her at the same time, as he was taught. She was looking down at him with a strange expression, as though she saw not him but someone else. She was certainly attractive. A little magnetic thrill ran down his arm to his spine. It would be good to have her as a passenger. It was charming that there were attractive women in New France. He had not thought of that in his flight from Vanina. Ha! Vanina would be sorry she had let him go! Just let her see this!

As he joined Nantes by the door, his place was instantly taken by a captain of the Governor's Guard.

"Monsieur de Bonaventure sends word," a page told Nantes, "he has returned to the ship and prays you both to join him."

"Entendu," Raoul said.

They left the room.

CHAPTER VIII

THE unloading of the ship went on, that day and the next. The oxen were lowered by ropes into the water between the ship and the shore. Men waded out to catch them, which was done without much difficulty, for they were weak from the hardships of the voyage. One of them began to graze as soon as he was roped. Both were led away by the Intendant's man, for the Intendant, Monsieur de Champigny, had ordered them for his grant, which he was turning into farmlands as quickly as he could. It was one of the most cultivated of the seigneuries, the herdsman said.

Raoul assisted at the unloading of oxen, hens, barrels, casks, chests, and innumerable small packages, all of which were eagerly claimed. He ran messages for his uncle and made himself generally useful, but he was impatient to leave the ship and go to the Upper Town again.

Monsieur de Bonaventure seemed in no hurry. He was relieved when Raoul told him that there was no Madame Charles Tibaut in Kebec; yet a momentary expression of disappointment crossed his face, and Raoul saw it. It dawned on him, then, that the perfume and the silken coat might not have been for the Governor's benefit.

But the unloading came to an end at last. De Bonaventure and the captains of the *Bonne Esperance* and the *Faulcon d'Or* went up the hill to the Governor's dinner, where they were to be the guests of honor, with Bishop Laval and some of his priests.

Raoul, lieutenants Nantes and Famoisy, and the other officers of the three ships dined on board, waiting until it should be time to go to the ball.

At length they set out with lanterns, walking two abreast up the narrow streets, where every now and then a passer-by stepped into a doorway to let them pass, calling out:

"Bonne nuit, Messieurs!" And sometimes a woman, with a shawl round her head, called out of an ancient, gnarled, but merry face:

"Que le bon Dieu vous benisse, les gars!" ("God bless you, lads!")

Raoul shut his eyes for a moment, trying to imagine that he was back in France; but the cold exhilaration of the night air, the size and splendor of the stars, the scent of pine, and the indescribable sensation of great space, spread out on every side, stretching, stretching ("so that a man might breathe," his uncle said when he described it on the voyage; but Raoul found it the other way—breath-taking: it took his breath before it left him, and made him gasp), proved to him at every step that he was in an alien land. But it was beautiful.

The narrow streets widened to a place, closed in again, turned and twisted in hairpin loops, until they found themselves arriving outside the Governor's house near the top.

The ball was in the big Salle d'Armes, and they could see by the lights, and hear by the sound of voices and of violins, that it was already in progress.

Raoul stood for a moment in the doorway, overcome by shyness. He had not attended many balls in Draguignan. He had been too young. Now it was different. He threw back his shoulders and went stiffly in.

People were taking their places for the first minuet, in a glittering display of laces, ribbons, Rhinegrave breeches, ruffs, cuffs, and farthingales—all the new finery that had come from France.

Perhaps it was the effect of these new fashions, or the gaiety of the occasion, that made the people wearing them smile more easily, look brighter than they had the day before, to Raoul's mind. For here were the same people that he had seen, with others added to the number, but they all looked different.

It was a lovely scene. The room was spacious; there were plenty of candles in the sockets; and a candelabra of crystal hung from the ceiling, reflecting its light in a hundred delicate glass ornaments. It seemed more suitable to Paris or Versailles.

Raoul mused that it must, like all the other things in the room, have crossed the sea from France.

He looked about him for his uncle, but there was no sign of the Governor's guests or of the Comte de Frontenac. The dinner was not yet over. These guests were dancing, en attendant, informally. Raoul bowed to the ladies whom he recognized and to some of the men. One face stood out. The lady with the dark hair was wearing an apple-green dress with low-cut lace at the shoulders and a bunch of purple ribbon, out of which her neck rose in a white curve. She was dancing opposite a gorgeous individual with one of the most elaborate headdresses that Raoul had seen.

"Who is that?" he asked a man who was standing near. "That lady wearing her own hair?"

"That is Madame de Freneuse."

"And who is her partner?"

"The Intendant. Monsieur de Champigny."

The dance came to an end. The violins stopped playing. There was a buzz of conversation; and then a new tune started, one that Raoul knew very well. He hummed the words:

"Le troisième jour, Phyllis, peu sage,[2]
Aurait donné moutons et chien
Pour un baiser, que le volage
Donnait à Lisette—pour rien!"

He plucked up his courage and plunged toward the only person whom he dared ask for a dance. Madame de Freneuse received him kindly, put her hand upon his arm, and they took their places.

Raoul was not very sure of the steps. He had paid little attention to dancing in Draguignan, leaving that to girls; and now he was sorry, for twice he blundered, making his partner lose her place in the line, though she covered it up in a clever way and did not appear to mind. She seemed distracted tonight, in spite of the brilliance of her smile and the brightness of her eyes; for she hardly spoke, although she listened, and her eyes were fixed on something in the distance, behind Raoul's head. Once or twice he turned to see what she was looking at; but there was nothing there—only the door, which he supposed she must be watching to see when the Governor arrived.

Meanwhile he was conscious of the charm of the minuet and

the envious looks he received from the officers of the three ships, who knew nobody to dance with yet except Monsieur de Blois, from the *Bonne Esperance* who had friends.

Madame de Freneuse pointed out her sister, Madame de Chauffours, to Raoul as they danced. She was a pretty, plump woman in a lavender-colored dress and a high white wig. Raoul made a note to dance with her.

Suddenly there was a noise by the door, the violins broke off in the middle of a chord, people began to range themselves in two long lines down the room, and Madame de Freneuse slipped into a corner by the window, with Raoul still beside her. Every eye was on the door. It opened. All stood up as the Governor came in. He advanced into the room and held up his hand for silence. De Bonaventure supported him. His eye passed over Raoul, standing between Madame de Chauffours and Madame de Freneuse, without any sign of having seen him there. There was a stricken, bleak look about his face. Indeed, they all looked grim.

"Friends," the Governor said, "I have bad news, sad and dreadful news. The Iroquois have attacked the settlement of Trois Rivières, set fire to houses, killed twenty-nine people, carried off six."

"The six!"

"Who are the six?"

"Names! Names!"

A group of women formed about the Governor, clamoring shrilly for news of relatives and friends in Trois Rivières. The dead were dead, but the six who were taken alive were in all probability at that moment being tortured.

"Please, doucement gently, outcry will not help us. The messenger is exhausted, ill. We will get the information from him in a moment. Messieurs, we must plan a better defense for Kebec. At Trois Rivières they were overcome by surprise. The Iroquois will be drunk with their success, and they may try to attack us here. They will certainly reattack the settlement there."

He pushed his way through the group of frantic women, followed by Monsieur de Prevost and Monsieur de Bonaventure. He disappeared from the salon, leaving a disordered gathering. Dancing was now unthinkable.

Presently Monsieur de Prevost returned, giving out the names.

"Jean Bethold, Allain Jusserand, Emile Jusserand, Felix Dourg, and two Dourg children."

A terrible cry went up from a woman near the door. "My daughter, my daughter, what about my daughter?"

"Poor thing," said Madame de Chauffours in Raoul's ear. "The Dourg children are her grandchildren, three and six years old; and the Iroquois . . . the Iroquois . . ." She controlled herself with an effort. "The father is her son-in-law."

"And the daughter?" Raoul whispered. "What about the daughter?"

"She must be dead. She is the lucky one."

Raoul stood, listening to the comments in a stupefied silence. Three and six! The Iroquois! He looked about him, shivering, while the shrieks of poor Madame Dufaix still resounded. They were taking her away, hysterically screaming.

Monsieur de Bonaventure returned and walked toward them, through the groups of men who were leaving rapidly in search of the Governor. Some of the women crossed themselves in prayer. Madame de Freneuse stood rigidly still beside Raoul. Madame de Chauffours turned her head to look at her sister, and Raoul caught her look of overpowering interest. It intrigued him. He turned his own head to see what occasioned it.

Monsieur de Bonaventure reached the group. He bowed to Madame de Chauffours and made a leg.

"Madame, your servant."

Ignoring Raoul, he bowed again, with a pas de recule to Madame de Freneuse.

"Madame!"

The word, breathed out with difficulty and force, went straight to Raoul's intuition. Mouth half open, paralyzed with interest and curiosity and another feeling that hurt him sharply, he stood, watching like Madame de Chauffours, in absorbed comprehension.

Madame de Freneuse sank in a low curtsy that was a perfect expression of cold pride in its exaggerated humility. She extended her hand without looking at Monsieur de Bonaventure. He took it in his and assisted her to rise; together they passed from the room, without a word said or a sideways glance.

Raoul came to himself, excited and miserable. Madame de Chauffours was smiling, beside him.

"They make a handsome pair!" she said. "Don't they, Monsieur?"

"Tell me," Raoul asked, "is your sister—was your sister—enfin, they have wrongly informed me! Her name is Madame Charles Tibaut, isn't it, Madame?"

"It was, some years ago. But her husband died, and she married again. She is Madame de Freneuse now. Bonsoir, Monsieur."

Madame de Chauffours moved away, still smiling.

CHAPTER IX

H OLD the glass a little higher."
Madame de Freneuse peered into the mirror she was
holding. An Indian girl knelt, holding up another.

"That's better, Dahinda. Comb out the third curl and turn it
a little . . . yes . . . tiens . . . like that. Perfect! You are better
than the best French maids."

Dahinda grunted, a sign that she was very pleased. Her dark
expressionless face leaned over her mistress' shoulder as she
fastened something inside the silken bodice, sticking it on with
pine gum.

Madame de Freneuse looked down at it.

"What's that?"

"Charm. Big medicine. Madame need it now."

Madame de Freneuse shivered and closed her eyes. Dahinda
gently passed her hand over the dark curls.

"Madame looks young, beautiful. Why do the other ladies
make themselves look old, with such white hair? My people's hair
go never white, always black, even when very old. Is prettier
so."

Madame de Freneuse opened her eyes and smiled at her.

"They wouldn't think so, Dahinda. But I agree with you. I
don't like wigs. Allons, it's time we went. My cloak, my fan,
my overshoes."

Dahinda knelt to put her mistress' feet in loose velvet slippers
with moccasin soles, made specially for her by Dahinda's brother,
large enough to go over shoes and yet quite light enough to
walk in comfortably. They were embroidered in bead patterns:
blue beads, representing heaven; red beads, representing love;

and green beads—youth, spring, growth, affection. Madame de Freneuse liked the glitter of them as she walked. Together they climbed to the château.

"Come back for me at about one hour before the dawn."

"Dahinda stay here. Night is good. She wait."

"Very well. But I do not expect you to."

"She wait. See the charm work."

Madame de Freneuse laughed. It was a thin, uncertain laugh. She stopped it abruptly and replaced it by a smile. Then she went in.

The room was already crowded. But she was safe, since *he* was still at dinner with the Governor and would not appear till later. Meanwhile she was at an advantage. She knew, and he did not, that she was here, that there would be this meeting. But to him it would be nothing—nothing at all perhaps, although he had *asked* at least . . .

The door opened. Officers from the ship. That charming, dark-haired boy who had given her the news that his uncle wanted to know if Madame Charles Tibaut were there. There was something very comic, very disarming, touching, about the boy with that obvious admiration in his eyes, too young to have learned dissimulation. Look, here he was, blundering across the room to her! Dance? Why not? It would while away the time, might calm a little this agitated blood, these leaping nerves. The boy was sweet, but not a dancer! He lost his way a little because he was looking at her. And she was looking at the door. She could not help it.

Ah, ciel! Or Quitche-manitou—she touched the charm—the moment's here!

While she looked, waiting in agony for the slowly moving door to open; while she felt the palms of her hands turning to running water inside her gloves, the smile, fixed and meaningless, hurt her lips, and her knees shake in the folds of her dress, she was suddenly transported to another moment of agony when, standing in almost the same position, her arms went round him, slipping upwards, and her fingers groped across the pattern of his coat until they touched his shoulder blades and stayed there, suddenly quiet. Adieu! There would be another, beneath the eyes of all Kebec, but this was their real adieu. He closed her fingers on a little leather book with golden clasps, smiling down

·[37]·

at her as she grasped it. She took the silver crucifix from her neck and put it in his hands.

"To keep you safe!"

He nodded, bending his wistful face framed in its elaborate wig, to kiss the hand which held the book. He fastened the cross inside his coat. For a moment they stood motionless. Then, looking up at him desperately, she had said:

"Take me with you!"

He did not answer. All the bitter things her father said crowded forward:

"If you see him again, I will have him broken, beggared like the beggar and adventurer he is, disgraced, do you hear, turned out of the Navy! Marry! Never! Preposterous, presumptuous . . . never, never." . . .

"Never."

Suddenly she had put her hands up to his face.

"Pierre . . . Denys . . . de Bonaventure . . . my . . . dear . . . love!"

The bitterness of his expression softened.

"Promise me something."

"Yes?"

She would have promised anything.

"Come here, look."

He took her to the railing of the balcony, outside this room. Together they looked down on dormer roofs, past clustering spires, over streaks of slate, across squares and terraces, along slits of cobble, to where the river, emerging from the mist, gleamed and sparkled in the moonlight.

"It's beautiful," he said. "Look at the space and the skies, and the moon over the forest. I want you to promise me that you will look at these things when I am gone, and say to yourself: 'I, Louise Guyon (she was Guyon then, mon Dieu, jeune fille!), am like them.' Never be little, or mean or ugly." (*He* had said that!) "New France is too full of grandeur for people to be little. Even the savages are big. Do you know what I mean?"

"Yes. I know."

"Then remember."

She remembered.

It was so full and clear a moon that they could see even the masts of two ships anchored at the Lower Town. The nearest was the smallest; and this was where she had looked, fixing her eyes upon it with a strange intensity. It was Pierre's boat, the *Bonne Esperance*, where he was ensign; but he would rise to second in command at least! Those two ships, so small, so far below and beyond, that holding up a finger blotted them from sight, would be going back to France over enormous waters she had never crossed, through weeks of danger and discomfort, bringing the King news of his New France, until one day, one sunny morning, they would sail into La Rochelle among the proud French fleet, drop sail, and lower anchor—home! She sighed. Since Pierre was ensign on that ship, he could not even spend the last evening with her. He was on guard—alone. Both officers and men were ashore.

Upon that ship, some hours later (now she clenched her hands and rubbed them against each other, as though she felt the torn skin from the stony convent wall, where she had grazed them climbing down)—upon that ship she had come, full of her Idea! She would be with him always, matching courage with his!

And then . . .

"No priest can marry us without your father's consent."

"Take me with you—then he'll give it!"

The answer to that was unexpected. He scooped her up and put her down outside the cabin door.

"You must not think that this is love. Petite fille, it was a joke. Go back, go quickly back. What else?"

What else!

And the climb back, through the night that was night of more than a long summer's day—night of all the innocencies, of all the dreams, of all that had been herself until that hour—night of these!

Sœur Marie de la Misericorde let her in. Like her name, she tried to be merciful. But there were the cut-off hair, the boy's clothes, the hour.

Through all the punishments and penances that followed, even the examination by the apothecary her father had insisted on, through whippings and scoldings, she walked like a small stone.

After the medical examination her father had come to see her, proposing a marriage. And like a small stone she had accepted it. She was married in a bonnet to hide the shortness of her hair!

All that was seven years ago. Now he was coming back. At any instant, in another second of this agony, his face would appear through the door. She would make him pay! Nom de nom de nom, he would pay!

The door opened. The Comte de Frontenac came in, followed by Bishop Laval and Monsieur de Bonaventure. Even as she crouched behind the mask that was her face, her eyes sought and found his. She had the pleasure of seeing him turn green, where he had only been grim before. There was a stricken, bleak look about his face. Indeed, they all looked grave.

The Governor was speaking. News about the savages. A raid, a massacre. But she paid no attention. She was looking at de Bonaventure. He crossed the room to her as if compelled by something stronger than himself, or her. The charm, perhaps, was working.

He bowed to her sister, and she found suddenly, just as she thought that she would faint, that she was strong, and glad. Strong enough to give him her hand and accept this strange, wordless challenge that he was giving, glad of it, mistress of herself enough to observe the comical expression on young Raoul de Perrichet's face—poor boy—and her sister's undisguised curiosity. Well, let them stare. She was above it—mistress of more than this—she would hear what, after seven years, he had to say.

CHAPTER X

THEY stood on the same balcony; but now she had her back to the starlit sweep, her eyes on him.

He wasted no time in coming to the point.

"Now that you are married, Madame—and have daughters?— you must have considered my predicament and have understood; perhaps you'll give me what I so much need, forgiveness!"

The last word was breathed so low she hardly heard it, but she answered:

"I have only sons. If one of them were to behave as you did to any child who loved him, he would never have my forgiveness. Nor have you."

"God knows I loved you!"

"You must not call that love," she quoted. "It was a joke!"

He flinched.

"You have grown hard!"

"I have an excellent memory, Monsieur. I quote your own words—all that you left me to reflect upon for seven years."

He straightened himself to look at her.

"Yet you have married twice! Which shows a certain forgetfulness of character, Madame, if I may say so!"

"Certainly, Monsieur, you should know, since *you* are married twice!"

She laughed joyously, sure that she had hurt him. For Monsieur de Bonaventure was a notorious wit; to lay himself open to so obvious a retort must mean that he was stung out of his caution.

Unexpectedly he laughed with her, and with his laughter some

·[41]·

of her new-found poise deserted her. She turned, so that he should not see his advantage, and looked into the night.

The stars were blurring together, through desperate moisture gathering in her eyes. Pierre's voice came from behind her shoulder, close to her left ear:

"You and I know, Louise, it would be the same if I had married fifty times!"

"I haven't a doubt of it, *Monsieur*," she replied, fighting not to let him see her emotion, "you have a—stretchable sense of humor. Any number of jokes would be the same to you!"

At that he took his hands from her arm and himself from her presence. A cold voice said from the doorway:

"I have the honor to take my leave of you, Madame."

He disappeared. The blood surged up in her in wild joy that he had not seen her emotion through her weakness. He had been hurt and had gone, not knowing his victory. She grasped the balcony rail in her hands, looking downwards. In the lantern light by the door a figure could be seen, wrapped in a blanket, crouched on the ground, looking up. Dahinda. Louise touched the charm. Leaning over, she called downwards:

"It worked!"

The answer floated up:

"Bien sure, Madame. Made by a Big Medicine Man!"

Louise leaned her head against the railing and from this position sent a gesture of acknowledgment into the night.

"My compliments, sorcerer!"

Gripping the railing with both hands, she stood, looking out but seeing nothing. She was reliving the brief, incredible conversation that had passed. They had met, and every barrier of time had fallen away, stripped aside as though it were seven hours, not seven years, since they last faced each other. He had spoken from his sincerity, and she had answered from her pride.

She needed to hurt him, to make him pay. For a fortnight, or perhaps even longer, if the winds were contrary, she would travel on his ship, with de Villebon, her sister, and the others. She would see him every day; he could not avoid her. For seven years she had been cold, dead, shriveled, beneath a calm and decorous exterior. Now, now, now she would live!

She smiled. Two whole weeks! She would not look beyond them, to her husband, the children, the settlement, position, duty, life—all these things would overtake her in due course. They would make her pay for her contempt of them, but they were in the future after those two weeks!

"The present hour is all that we have!" she murmured, remembering a favorite saw of l'Abbé Peroucet, and misapplying it gleefully. L'Abbé Peroucet had married her to Charles Tibaut—poor Charles, a querulous invalid, sick with an overdose of vanity. He had succumbed to a cold. She had nursed him, she remembered, with dutiful devotion, in an attempt to rid herself of remorse. Poor Charles, if he had really loved her, as he appeared to, he must have been unhappy till he died.

The Abbé Peroucet remarried her to Mathieu de Freneuse with phrases about not losing oneself in personal grief, thinking of others, living for the children—she had Gervais and Robert then. He and her father urged her to make this match "for the children's sake." Bah! For Mathieu de Freneuse's money, lands, and the title! Her father grew an inch in self-important girth after the wedding. "My daughter goes to her terres, to the seigneury at St. Jean!" He was like so many of the men in New France, falling over to prove himself a noble. Petite noblesse (was there anything more ridiculous, in a land of naked savages!), nobles of wooden settlements, at the mercy of a massacre. "Does he suppose his blood, or mine, will flow blue into the Iroquois cooking pots?"

Soon after remarriage her sister Marguerite had married Mathieu's brother and become the Chatelaine de Chauffours. Papa had practically beamed himself into a fit. Ce pauvre papa, so childish, so naïf! She could not see him as the ogre who had loomed so large in her childhood and youth. Perhaps, after all, he *had* been thinking about their comfort and safety? Women must have protectors.

But all these years, while living a full life (ciel, what had she not done, or been, from farmer to midwife, to Amazon?), she had been waiting, conserving herself, holding back, behind her placid smile—for what? For the inevitable return of Pierre de Bonaventure and for the meeting which must follow. Now he was here! The old mad current of sympathy existed, stronger than before. She was mature now, wise with womanhood, and they were in each other's blood.

Just as she reached this satisfactory conclusion in her meditations, a slight rustling sound behind her made her turn defensively. Madame de Chauffours stood in the doorway.

·[43]·

"Everybody is leaving or has left," she said.

Madame de Freneuse started forward without speaking.

"It is a sad affair," her sister continued. "I am so sorry for Madame Dufaix and everyone. It is dreadful for Monsieur de Bonaventure. I am glad you had a moment with him to console him. He was so fond of his brother."

"His brother?"

Madame de Freneuse was on the point of murmuring, "He said nothing to me of his brother." But she kept the words behind her lips. A rush of pity flooded her for de Bonaventure. She had been so harsh and would be harsher! What was the matter with her, this ridiculous softness? "Remember the climb in the night and the loveless marriage, the desolation and sick emptiness of betrayal, seven years of silence," she told herself sternly; but do as she would, her heart was softened. Absurd heart, still his.

CHAPTER XI

REQUIEM masses were said the next day, in the Church of the Madonna, from dawn till noon. The church was packed for the last mass, which was also one of special intention for the departing ships. The *Bonne Esperance* was bound for Trois Rivières, carrying men, ammunition, and supplies to the besieged settlement. The *Soleil d'Afrique* would take reinforcements, ammunition, supplies, and the new governor to Port Royal as quickly as possible, lest the English take advantage of the confusion and dismay following the Iroquois attack to fall upon Acadia, the settlements on the other side of the Baye Françoise, St. Jean, La Hève, Chibucto, or any of the seigneuries. The *Faulcon d'Or* would stay at Kebec in case of emergency.

All three ships took on a large supply of eels and fish, with a smaller amount of beaver. Eels formed the staple diet of New France. Raoul watched baskets filled with them, new-caught and still alive, with mingled feelings. He had not acquired the New French attitude of robust indifference to hardship where food was concerned, although he was hardened in other directions and becoming adapted to the different atmosphere.

This mass, for instance, at which he knelt was altogether different from the last mass, in France. The altar was bare of decoration and ornament, being covered with a rough spun-linen cloth and plain silk orphreys; the walls were stark and unpolished; the images of the saints were primitive and bore, it seemed to him, stern expressions. St. Joseph looked pained, the Madonna was sad, and the Child stared out upon His world with firm resignation.

Even the rendering of the mass was different. The chanting

was harsh and resonant. It had an anguished strength. The old Bishop bellowed his words, pronouncing them slowly and distinctly, so that Raoul found himself listening to the familiar phrases as though they were new. One felt that this religion was not native to this place but had to impose itself upon its surroundings, competing with a hostile atmosphere. It had to defy savage gods in the dark woods; it perched precariously here, founded upon a rock—which still might crumble.

Raoul realized, for the first time, the enormous undertaking of the Jesuit saints, the insane adventure of the colonists, the whole mad and splendid conception of New France. He realized and was afraid of it. He had not the native hardihood of these Canadians. It was his uncle's different timber that had attracted him in France. It set him apart. He moved through the precisions of the French Court and vie de Provence as though he were stifled or taking part in a child's minuet, with exaggerated care not to trample something fragile. Here he was like the others, moving freely in his full stature, standing under the sky with no one to obey but himself, the King (shrunk to a cherished miniature on the other side of the world), de Frontenac, and God, of course, who expanded here, as the King shrank, and was unapproachably impersonal.

These impressions occupied Raoul's mind during the service, while his eyes strayed from the stern, autocratic old Bishop, to the Governor, equally autocratic, the Intendant and his overdressed family, the captains, soldiers, sailors, adventurers, and nuns. Among the nuns, in a solemn row of little black heads beneath little black veils, knelt the first real savages Raoul had seen. They presented an edifying spectacle, sitting still or kneeling motionless, with blank, expressionless faces, neither fidgeting nor whispering as other children did. They joined in the singing with pious fervor, and Raoul, watching them cross themselves, found it hard to believe that they were the children of savage cannibals. But, he reflected, these were Micmacs, a gentler race than Iroquois.

Raoul partook of the host beside his uncle. He had been excluded from de Bonaventure's friendship and favor since the previous night, when de Bonaventure encountered the lady he had hoped to avoid. Raoul could find no opportunity to explain to his uncle that it was really not his fault! De Bonaventure was annoyed at having told him anything about that old affair when

·[46]·

he was drunk. Raoul sympathized—he knew from experience how it felt to have one's deepest feelings turned into a public performance for the benefit of others—but de Bonaventure had burdened him with the confidence, and should not now resent his knowing it.

Another thing was bothering Raoul. He could not feel the same toward his uncle, since he had seen Madame de Freneuse, for deserting her. There surely must have been some way . . . It was none of his affair, évidemment, but it made him restless to think of it. The existence of this intense emotion between two people near to him as these were—for he loved his uncle comme de juste, and Madame de Freneuse had been kind to him—shutting him and all the rest of the world outside of it, disturbed and distracted him.

He did not look forward to the next two weeks on board the *Soleil d'Afrique* with the two of them. Yet it could not have stopped here; he was eager and anxious that there be a continuation, a working out of the problem. . . .

He conjured Madame de Bonaventure to the forefront of his mind—la Tante Jeanne. He did not like her very much. She could not compare with Madame de Freneuse. Not even Vanina had this woman's startling charm! She knelt there by the third pillar to the right. Raoul knew that his uncle's eyes had not left her face. He, too, was watching her. But Madame de Freneuse never raised her eyes.

What was the fascination of her face, not even pretty, with its peculiar nose, odd lips, outthrust and determined chin—but beautiful, intelligent, amused dark eyes?

Raoul found himself indignantly asking why so much had happened to that face before he knew it. Why did he come late to every fete in life? Vanina laughed at him as a boy. Madame de Freneuse was climbing down her convent wall to experience all that mad, amazing, enviable emotion when he was still a child of eleven! She had married twice; she had children; she had lived; and here she was, kneeling where he could look at her, in quiet control of herself and of the situation, of the wild surge in his uncle's heart; for Raoul knew that de Bonaventure was experiencing intense emotion—he, too, was living; only Raoul was shut out of life. To Raoul life came, a succession of futile situations, of mockery at his helplessness, because he was young, outside. Inside he was a good deal older than Madame de Freneuse, if she only knew!

Mass ended. He crossed himself and rose to his feet. Madame de Freneuse looked up and smiled.

"Really, the poor boy," she was thinking, "he is rather sweet!"

De Bonaventure contrived to be beside her at the holy-water stoop. He dipped his fingers and held them out to her.

"Merci, Monsieur," she said, tranquilly accepting the drops from his finger tips and signing herself.

("What good fortune," she thought, "that the bonnet came from France in time—on his own ship—and is so becoming! I believe I am better looking than I was seven years ago. But Louise, my dear, you will never be pretty! Your conquests are rather the uniqueness of the individuality! I really think he never looked away from me the whole long hour!")

Aloud she asked:

"At what time is the *Soleil d'Afrique* sailing?"

"As soon as we can get away. In an hour's time."

"I shall be ready."

He stared, not understanding. Then, strangling the sounds that came to his throat as he understood, he made a superb recovery.

"I will send a man to help you with your things."

"Merci, Monsieur. And my sister also, may she have a man?"

Her eyes twinkled. De Bonaventure bowed and turned in some confusion to greet the Governor. But first he shot a look of black rage at Raoul.

CHAPTER XII

THE *Bonne Esperance* and the *Soleil d'Afrique* sailed together, at noon, one going up river, one down. Crowds gathered to watch the embarkation, cheering the soldiers, the Governor of Acadia, and his retinue.

Madame de Freneuse and Madame de Chauffours came on board together, preceded by Dahinda and another servant carrying last-minute luggage. Bishop Laval, with priests and acolytes, gave the Church's blessing to the two expeditions while bells pealed from monastery and convent, but the church bells tolled in commemoration of the dead at Trois Rivières.

The *Soleil d'Afrique* was crowded. De Bonaventure gave up his cabin to the Governor, the Second Officer vacated his for the two ladies, Raoul and the lieutenants Famoisy and Nantes were turned out of their stowaway to sleep on deck.

The passengers and some of the soldiers gathered astern to wave to the *Bonne Esperance* across the widening water separating them. The day was sunny and hot; but a little breeze blowing off the river, lifting awnings, fluttering flags, and undulating dresses, was pleasant upon their faces, mitigating the severity of the sun's fierce strength.

The breeze was contrary to the *Soleil d'Afrique*, but the current for her. She tacked against the wind, while the *Bonne Esperance*, with favorable wind and contrary current, made slow headway, full sails set.

"She'll make Trois Rivières before we sight Port Royal, for all that." The maître d'équipage explained to Madame de Chauffours, who stood near him. Madame de Freneuse leaned upon the bar before the tiller to the discomfort of the helmsman, staring past her.

Presently a bugle summoned them to dine. On shore the Governor and other notables dined in the evening; but this was inconvenient on the ship, and de Bonaventure followed the practice of the Navy, shifting the hours a little, to suit his men. The main meal of the day was at three o'clock, supper following in the evening.

The salon was a brave sight, with silver and napery not used on the voyage out. De Bonaventure and the other officers were in their grande tenue; the sailors who waited on them wore lackeys' coats, with buttons ornamented with a rising sun to represent the *Soleil d'Afrique* as well as le Roi Soleil, and white ruffled shirts. They were quick and nimble-fingered, so that de Bonaventure could take his mind from the progress of the meal and bend it to the conversation.

He talked first of Acadia. He knew it well, having served there in his youth. He asked the Governor if it were his intention to make Port Royal stronger or to fortify Jemseg and La Hève instead?

"A mixture of both," the Governor replied. "Last year, when Sir William Phipps seized Port Royal and carried off the Governor de Menneval and his garrison, I was on my way to Port Royal in the *Union*. We arrived twelve days after the attack, and gathered up the survivors, to give chase. We crossed the Baye Françoise to the mouth of the Rivière St. Jean and disembarked the stores and presents for the Indians into two ketches. But there was no wind, and we were forced to leave the ketches where they were, for the night, a little below Jemseg. In the morning the ketches and all the stores had disappeared, and the *Union* had also been seized by the English. I roused the Indians and told them what had happened: that our King's presents to them were stolen by our enemies, who were, therefore, also theirs, and I promised to revenge the theft if they would take me for their leader."

"Which Indians?" Raoul asked.

"Monsieur, these were the Malisites. There are three sorts of savages native to Acadia—the Canabas, the Malisites and the Micmacs—which have three different languages. The Micmacs occupy the land up to the Kebec Rivière and extend along the coast to Cape Sable. The Malisites commence at the Rivière St.

Jean and have the interior of the country as far as the Rivière du Loup and along the seacoasts, occupying Passamenquadis and all the rivers along the coast. The Canabas are those who have settled on the Kinibiquy, from which they take their name."[3]

De Bonaventure had been nodding agreement to the description, with Madame de Freneuse and Madame de Chauffours. Now he asked:

"Did they agree?"

"Yes. I am now 'Commander of the Eastern Indians' and brave of three tribes."

Raoul gasped.

"I sailed to France, and there I promised the King that I would keep the English out of Acadia, with the help of the Indians alone, if His Majesty would ratify my command of them. He did. My plan now is to strengthen all the forts and to build a new one up the river."

"Near us?" asked Madame de Chauffours.

"Nearer the de Freneuse seigneury," the Governor replied. "If we can unite Malisites and Micmacs against the Mohawks, in a string of strong inland forts, we should go far toward checking the English and establishing the fur trade for ourselves."

"Monsieur de Freneuse is friendly with the Malisites," said Madame de Freneuse. "He has been taken into the tribe quite recently."

"Madame, your husband is one of the few strong men who understand and cooperate with us in our plans for the colonization of New France. Your husband's seigneury is the best cultivated on the river. He has placed settlers on his land, with cattle and crops. Freneuse is a model of what we want the other seigneuries to be."

"I am pleased to hear you say so. I will tell my husband that his efforts are appreciated."

De Bonaventure broke into this with a brusqueness that surprised the Governor.

"When, do you consider, is the best time to attack the Indians?"

"The middle of May, or the first of June, because the Indians will all be returning from their hunting and repairing to their principal settlements in order to replant their maize, whereas in the months of August and September they are scattered in family groups along the river, living on the fish and game they kill.[4] It would be no good to attack them now, even if we wanted to.

My aim is rather to build and prepare forts, and to attack them next year, in the spring, after their hunting season, which is in its height in February and March."

"You would lead the Malisites and Micmacs against them as well as the French?"

"Certainly. When the Malisites and Micmacs see the forts go up, they will be impressed. They are ready to fight for us now; they will be readier then."

Madame de Chauffours sighed.

"I wish we could clear the country of the English and the Mohawks and the Iroquois—then life here would be worth while!"

"The country is too rich in furs for that. While the fur trade can continue, we will always have the English on our tails—the English are rapacious and traders. They would do anything for gain."

"Hmmm," said de Bonaventure, smiling, "it seems to me that the French are fond of the fur trade, too, and equally rapacious."

"That may be safe to say among ourselves," de Villebon rebuked him, "but I beg that you will remember that le Roi Soleil, our incomparable Majesty, has nothing but the welfare of the savages at heart. He wishes them to enjoy the benefits of civilization and the refining influence of the true religion. The English are damned heretics. They would take the savages with them into hell."

"While we prefer to give the savages a good taste of it here on earth, so that they will scuttle safely into heaven?"

"Monsieur de Bonaventure, even in jest . . ."

"I ask your pardon, Monsieur le Gouverneur. As you say, jesting on the subject is unseemly. Shall we take our coffee on the deck and watch the view? Soon it will be September, with perhaps an early fall of leaves. They are very beautiful here, so red, so golden; those of you who have not seen them yet will have a wonderful experience."

He bent the first smile in twenty-four hours upon Raoul and Lieutenant Nantes.

CHAPTER XIII

MOONLIGHT falling on Raoul's face, coupled with the hardness of the deck, waked him. He twisted and turned in futile attempts to find a comfortable position. The only relief to aching muscles and stiff back was to turn on his back, and then the moonlight fell directly upon his eyes. He sat up and looked about for a more sheltered place. The other side of the deck would be more protected from the moonbeams by the sails and the saloon. He got up, walking very softly in his bare feet in order not to disturb the two lieutenants sprawling beside him, and crept to the spot he had chosen. Here, after having arranged his blanket on a coil of rope for a pillow and wrapped his coat around him closely, he settled down to sleep again.

But a door opened, a stream of light from the hanging lantern flashed into his eyes, the door swung to again, and a voice spoke out of the darkness near him.

"How beautiful! Look at the moonlight on water and forest!"

It was de Bonaventure. Madame de Freneuse answered:

"You have a great appreciation of nature, Monsieur. I noticed it before—the view over Kebec, for instance."

Raoul cowered into his blankets. He did not want to listen, but to make his presence known would probably be worse.

"In each case, Madame, my remarks were prompted by the same need to cover an emotion—a very deep emotion. Shall I tell you what it is?"

"No, I am not interested in your emotions now, Monsieur, frankly—only in my own, and at the moment they are strongly in favor of sleep."

·[53]·

A rustle of receding steps. . . .

"Louise!"

No answer but the gentle shutting of the door. Raoul heard his uncle pacing the deck in jerky steps, stopping every now and then to lean upon the rail. Then he went away, and Raoul could sleep.

Just as he was about to sink back, however, the door opened again and two people came out. They walked in silence up the deck, and down again, with slow, perfectly matching steps. Raoul propped himself on one elbow and peeped out to see who it was. To his astonishment he saw Monsieur de Bonaventure and Madame de Freneuse arm in arm, smiling in the moonlight, walking up and down.

He lay back quickly, looking up at the sweep of the sail, with a strange pain in his heart.

Now and then the steps faltered and died; the walkers came to rest, looking at the sea, leaning on the shipside, but speaking no word. The strange silent tryst went on for an hour. Then there was the sound of a kiss, which startled Raoul into looking out before he could stop himself. Monsieur de Bonaventure was standing with Madame de Freneuse by the door of the cabin. He held her hand, which he had taken to his lips. ("That was the kiss!" Raoul thought, relieved and uncomfortable.) They stood there, smiling at each other, immobile, saying no word, until with a sudden, quick movement she had gone.

De Bonaventure paced the deck again, humming beneath his breath. Raoul recognized the tune. He knew the words:

"Cloris, que dans mon coeur j'ai si longtemps servie,
Et que ma passion montre à tout l'univers,
Ne veux-tu pas changer le destin de ma vie,
Et donner de beaux jours à mes derniers hivers?"[5]

He had a sudden impulse to call out, to jeer at his uncle or just to make his presence known; but he was afraid. The man standing there smiling, with such an extraordinary expression on his face, was a stranger and—dangerous. There was no saying what slept beneath the calmness of his face. Raoul lay still, and suddenly hot inexplicable tears were flowing between his hands to the deck.

Madame de Freneuse, in the cabin, was sitting on the edge of her bunk, hands clasped, staring in front of her. A lantern, shaded to allow of sleep, lit up the form of her sister, Madame de Chauffours, asleep or pretending to be.

"I shall not be able to hold out," Madame de Freneuse thought. "I shall never be able to hold out. It is worse than ever—madness —madness! I thought I hated him! I thought I was strong." . . .

She bowed her head in her hands and shivered. Madame de Chauffours sat up.

"What's the matter? You've taken cold? Quick, come into my bunk with me, where it's warm. No? Then some tisane. Dahinda left some in the jug over there. She thought you might need it. She is a devoted girl."

Madame de Freneuse allowed herself to be petted and fussed over and put to bed, where she lay sleepless, staring at the ceiling, till the dawn.

CHAPTER XIV

LIFE on the *Soleil d'Afrique* for the next few days was full of a strange undercurrent of tension, ascribed officially to the unseasonable heat. Raoul was not the only one to look a little haggard. Monsieur de Bonaventure fell into abstractions and dark studies, which the Governor, Monsieur de Villebon, observed at first with solicitude and voluble anxiety but presently with an amused silence; Madame de Freneuse was conversational in bursts and silent in turn. She looked a little pale and tired; Madame de Chauffours seemed preoccupied. Only the young lieutenants Nantes and Famoisy were unperturbed and slept in their wooden bed on deck with hearty snores. The continued heat and constant tacking of the boat got on everybody's nerves.

Then, as the wind changed and waves rose, they reached the mouth of the River and turned south through Gaspé toward Cape Breton. The ladies kept their cabin; the Governor was seasick; the soldiers herded together. Raoul found his sleeping quarters cold but much more to his mind, since he did not have to listen to the sound of walking feet and low voices every night beneath the moon.

But after the third day of heavy seas everybody found sea legs; the ladies appeared at dinner for the first time since the change of wind, and the Governor came in for coffee. Conversation was resumed with much laughter at the buffeting and rolling and the accidents which happened, as when Madame de Chauffours was spilled into the Governor's lap. Madame de Freneuse took no part in the laughter. For the most part she sat silent, as in a daze, while Monsieur de Bonaventure stared and stared. The Governor and Madame de Chauffours kept the conversation

going, by a series of efforts, without any help from anyone—
the two lieutenants were silent by nature, and Raoul was having
a fit of the sulks.

The Governor, fortunately, liked to talk, and Madame de Chauffours made a good listener. Between them they managed to get
through the meals, after which Monsieur de Bonaventure and
Madame de Freneuse disappeared together to the salon or to the
deck or to their cabins, followed at an interval by Madame de
Chauffours and the Governor with the air of people in the front
seats at a play. It was just that—a tragicomedy for sophisticated
taste. Young Raoul, for instance, could not be expected to appreciate the fine nuances of the situation—the Governor was sorry
for the boy. Madame de Chauffours attempted to make him eat.

"You must not lose weight," she said. "What will happen if
there is a battle or a famine? Eat now for future strength."

But Raoul only glowered, following Madame de Freneuse with
his eyes.

"Like a sick dog I used to have," Madame de Chauffours whispered to her sister, who started and said:

"Where?"—looking vaguely around, as though she expected to
find a poodle at her feet.

Madame de Chauffours sighed and shrugged.

They were within a day of St. Jean when the lookout hailed
from the d'Artimon:

"A sail! A sail! English ship three leagues ahead!"

Raoul rushed to the rail, peering through the mist which had
risen and was shrouding the ship. Soon everyone could see the
enemy, when the mist cleared for a moment before it fell again.

De Bonaventure became more like himself, barking out orders
for full sails set and urging the *Soleil d'Afrique* forward in pursuit
of the ship, which seemed to be making for the harbor of St. Jean
as they were.

"I don't like it," said de Villebon. "Looks uncommonly like
mischief to me. Taking advantage of the Iroquois raid to descend
on Acadia."

"There can't be many in that small boat," Lieutenant Nantes
said soothingly.

"Can't tell how many boats may have preceded this one," de
Villebon replied. "I tell you, it looks bad to me."

"Out of the way!" de Bonaventure called to Raoul at the prow.
Four men put each forward gun into position, standing by to

load and fire at command. Raoul stood aside, excited. There was a cold feeling in his stomach. In half an hour or less he would be fighting! With English devils and Indians, too, perhaps. He could not understand his uncle's calm, although he admired it as de Bonaventure, taking his eyes from the English ship, went astern to see to the ladies' comfort. He came back presently, shrugging his shoulders, and said something to the Governor which made him shake his head and spread out his hands.

"I ordered them below," Raoul heard presently, "but they insist. . . . If they were men . . . mutiny . . . women . . ." the wind blew half his words away, but Raoul could imagine them.

"Out of the way!" his uncle said again, as the decks were cleared for action.

"What can I do?" Raoul shouted at him.

"Take hold of that rope and go on holding it," his uncle said, pointing to a lashing hanging loose from the mast. Raoul obediently stretched out his hand; then the meaning of the words came to him and he flushed, dropping his hand.

"I can shoot!" he flung back angrily, "as well as any man!"

"Tra la la, tra la la," sang de Bonaventure in an incredible tenor, then, becoming serious, he beckoned. Raoul came nearer sulkily.

"See if you can persuade the ladies to go to their cabin and stay there; if you can't, get them into a sheltered spot astern. Then go and fetch one of the pistols from the armory and stand with them to protect them from an assault."

Raoul nodded. This was better; and if he could persuade the ladies to go to the cabin, he would stand guard on the deck above it. It was terrible to think of the dangers Madame de Freneuse—and, of course, Madame de Chauffours, too—might be running presently from English devils and their savages—unthinkable! He marveled at the coolness of the other men.

CHAPTER XV

IT WAS about four o'clock when the first gun thundered through the mist, which was thicker than ever. The shot fell short of the *Soleil d'Afrique*, astern, making a strange sizzling noise as it dropped in the sea. It sent up spray that splashed the two women. Raoul seized hold of Madame de Freneuse in a panic. "Go below!" he shouted. "Go below!"

She screamed back at him, but the answer was lost in the shouts of the officers and the scurrying of the crew to their places as the *Soleil d'Afrique* went about. The wind caught the sails with a wild flapping that made the ship keel over, and leap ahead.

Madame de Freneuse caught hold of the shipside and steadied herself. She was smiling as a succession of deafening crashes and sizzling noises proclaimed that the enemy had sent another salvo which had fallen short.

Monsieur de Bonaventure was endeavoring to outsail the English ship, passing across her stern to return the salvo but holding fire until then. His men were waiting by the guns, cleaning, ramming, priming, grinning automatically as they worked to the barked orders of their officers. Another salvo; and this time some of the shots went home, splinters flew up from the deck, and a cloud of flying dust blew about the hole where the shot had struck. Two of the sailors doused the debris with water and stamped on it before they ran by, answering an order.

The *Soleil d'Afrique* swung about into position, lying before the wind, bearing down upon the English ship; her guns, cleared for action, spoke together as the waist of the enemy ship came into range.

The shots went home. The gun crews cheered, and the *Soleil d'Afrique* dipped, swerved, and was by before the enemy guns could get into action. The English captain brought his starboard guns to bear on the retreating foe. A ball knocked three of the *Soleil d'Afrique* sailors into pulp and carried away a spar.

De Bonaventure shouted an order which the maître d'équipage repeated. Men swarmed up the rigging; the *Soleil d' Afrique* went about on a new tack, quivering at the brutal disregard of strain on her masts. The force of the wind nearly jerked the ship from her seams. Only a master seaman would have crammed on so much canvas, but de Bonaventure relied on his ship and the speed that she could make in outmaneuvering any other. She was the fastest in the world, and she must prove it now.

A succession of shocks and a wild shouting, followed by a spurt of flame, told of another direct hit by the English guns. Raoul ran forward to the scuttles and emptied a dipperful on the burning planks, dragging the wounded maître d'équipage aside.

"Feu!"

The French guns spoke in a sullen roar. Two of the shots shattered the mainmast on the English ship and tore away the sails; another shot landed in the middle of a gun crew, silencing the gun.

The mist had folded up now; visibility was good. Raoul, craning over, could see that the English ship was getting much the worst of it. She was smaller and heavier to handle; her guns were fewer and of an old-fashioned type. They took so long to cool that the *Soleil d'Afrique* could fire two salvos to her one, and the damage was beginning to be heavy. The decks were strewn with wreckage; and men were trying to cut away the sails from the fallen mainmast, which had put two guns out of commission. A direct hit had smashed the forecastle.

But the English sailors were disciplined; and even as he watched, the ship went about and made off on a tack that looked as though she might be trying to escape. De Bonaventure shouted another order; the *Soleil d'Afrique* prepared to go about in order to pursue; and then Raoul saw the English ship tack, go about, and bear down upon them while her forward guns spoke and her crews cheered, standing by the grappling hooks. The *Soleil d'Afrique*, caught in the middle of going about, could not tack out of her way.

"Trim!"

Then: "Helm a-weather!"

The English ship passed athwart; the ships came together for a moment; the English mizzen shrouds caught the French bowsprit and snapped it off. The English ship passed alongside, head to stern with the *Soleil d'Afrique*.

Both ships' guns fired a broadside, muzzle to muzzle.

De Villebon took a pistol out of his belt and primed it carefully. Raoul watched, gaping, while the ships came together with a wrenching, grinding crash. The men leaped forward with knives and pistols to stem off the attack; but the Englishmen came forward in a concerted rush, the grapnels were fixed in spite of all the French could do, and now it became a hand-to-hand battle. Raoul stood, stunned, while two Englishmen swung themselves aboard, on the prow, where nobody was standing to oppose them.

They ran forward, firing at the French, and de Villebon was hit as he shot the first of the boarding party by the main breach.

Madame de Freneuse snatched the gun from Raoul and brought the first man down. Monsieur Nantes tackled the second, braining him with a marling spike passed from one of the men. Madame de Freneuse reloaded and fired again, this time at a man who was getting a leg on the deck near de Bonaventure.

A sudden hoarse scream came from the Englishmen, and a party of them made a rush together. They came on in a row, heads above the deck, hurling themselves over regardless of wounds. Raoul saw the whites of their eyes and the devilish grinning lips; he heard the screams of the French sailors as they went down, knifed and bludgeoned. De Bonaventure was firing steadily into the throng, de Villebon was laying about him with a sword, and the French soldiers were firing their pistols and throwing blazing oakum.

Then the tide turned; the French dropped down onto the deck of the English ship, pursuing the retreating enemy. Lieutenant Nantes, crazy with excitement, flung a heavy iron bar down on the heads of the English sailors as they ran beneath him on their ship. The French were driven back and hard pressed. Raoul ran to the side of the ship from an overpowering need to see what was happening. Madame de Freneuse followed just in time to see de Bonaventure, pinned between the body of an Englishman and the swords of two shouting soldiers, receive an upward thrust that disabled him. Madame de Freneuse screamed and fired at the same instant.

"Pierre!"

The cry went through Raoul and startled him into action. He

hurled himself from the *Soleil d'Afrique* onto the two men assailing his uncle and went down with them in a struggling heap on the deck of the English ship. A report singed his ear; one of the men jerked and lay still. The other got a grip on Raoul's neck, putting his knee on Raoul's chest. A searing pain shot through his shoulder. The confusion above him died away as he fainted.

He came to, to find that he was being dragged onto the *Soleil d'Afrique*. His uncle was fighting beside him, and the noise and confusion were intense. He was pushed and pulled on board, and there was a sudden crack and scream as the two ships parted. The English had unhooked the grapnels in an attempt to free their ship from the French and to escape.

De Bonaventure, watching his men still fighting on board the English ship, set his teeth and signed to the gun crews.

"Feu!"

The guns spoke, and the deck of the English ship was filled with smoke and flame. Men began to leap from her—Frenchmen trying to regain their ship, Englishmen wounded or falling from the rigging.

"Feu!"

A second salvo tore the foremast down. The flames grew. De Bonaventure saw men struggling to lower a longboat, but no flag of surrender was run up. One of the English guns barked, and a ball hit the helmsman and killed the two men near.

"Feu!"

The French guns sent a deadly broadside into the hull. When the smoke cleared, they could see wild confusion, spreading flames, and more men jumping from the ship. A white flag was waved and the longboat lowered.

Raoul crawled to his feet and stood swaying by the smoking gun near the prow. He felt giddy and sick; and when he tried to raise his arm, a wet, warm trickle made him faint again in a heap at de Bonaventure's feet. His uncle stepped over him and leaned on the shipside watching the English ship, burning beyond saving while the longboat pulled away from her. There were very few men in it, and some of them were wounded. The sea was full of bobbing heads, of men swimming and men who were being swept away.

De Bonaventure gave an order.

"Stand by to pick up prisoners."

He turned away.

Madame de Freneuse was standing behind him. She had a strange expression on her face, which was black with burnt powder and streaks of blood where she had been spattered by a man shot down beside her.

"Pierre! Are you hurt?"

He put her aside with a smile.

"No. I'll come to you for dressing presently. The boy here needs attention."

He gestured to two men to pick up Raoul and follow Madame de Freneuse to the cabin.

So Raoul opened his eyes a second time to find her bending over him.

"You did very well," she said, "and your uncle's proud of you. That leap was very fine. You've got a bullet in your shoulder which will have to be probed out. Your uncle will attend to it himself in a little while. He's receiving the surrender."

"I'd like to see that," Raoul said.

"Come up with me, then, if you feel you can."

CHAPTER XVI

"CAPTAIN JOHN HUGHES, at your service, of His Majesty's vessel *Thunder*."

De Bonaventure took the proffered dress sword and bowed.

"These gentlemen?"

The tall, disappointed-looking English captain made introductions:

"Colonel Tyng, Governor of Acadia."

"Tiens, tiens!" The French officers looked amused.

"Mr. John Nelson of Boston. His son, Mr. William Nelson of Boston."

De Bonaventure bowed and made a leg. "I think I have had the —er—pleasure of encountering your uncle, Messieurs, if I am not mistaken, when I was a boy. Is he not Sir Thomas Temple?"

"He is, Monsieur."

"Ah."

De Bonaventure turned and said to de Villebon: "That is the Sir Thomas Temple who was Governor of Acadia, from Boston, about thirty years ago, when the English were in possession. He held a grant of the region now the Freneuse seigneury. Perhaps his nephew wanted to look over it? Permit me. . . ."

He led de Villebon forward.

"Monsieur the Colonel Tyng, English Governor of Acadia, allow me to present le Sieur de Villebon, actual Governor of Acadia, on his way to Port Royal. I am sure you will have much in common."

De Villebon and Colonel Tyng faced each other, smiling.

"Fortune of war, Colonel," de Villebon said. "Last year you

put me to great inconvenience and carried off my predecessor, le Gouverneur de Menneval. This year we carry you off. Thus it goes. Snuff, Monsieur?"

"With pleasure."

Colonel Tyng took a pinch and elegantly sniffed it up each nostril.

"Exchange and ransom?" he inquired.

"Yes. Ah, the ladies. Permit me—Madame de Freneuse, the lady whose husband owns the land your uncle had, Monsieur Nelson. Madame de Chauffours, whose husband owns the grant beside it. And this is my nephew, Monsieur de Perrichet."

"We have met before," said Mr. William Nelson, ruefully rubbing his chest. "I broke his fall."

"Not fall," Madame de Freneuse corrected him. "Leap!"

"Whatever it was, Madame, it was most uncomfortable for me."

"But it is I who am uncomfortable now," Raoul said, showing his bandages.

Monsieur de Bonaventure gathered the three swords carelessly under his arm and turned toward his cabin.

"If you will excuse me, I have a scratch to be dressed. Lieutenant Famoisy, you will see to the prisoners and dispose of the dead."

He disappeared with Madame de Chauffours. Madame de Freneuse started to follow, and then turned back. She went uncertainly toward the wreckage and sat down suddenly on a broken spar. Raoul went over to her.

"You are tired?"

She nodded as he took his place beside her. The English officers stood by themselves with their backs to her. The French sailors and soldiers were engaged in the work of getting the ship straightened out. She stared past them to the dark waters and the scarcely visible stretch of land behind them. Her mind was with de Bonaventure, in the cabin, but she had not dared to see for herself the extent of his wound. She would rely on her sister to tell her.

Madame de Chauffours, probing with expert fingers, for it was not the first bullet she had extracted in her life of wars and alarms, made conversation to distract Monsieur de Bonaventure from his pain. Dahinda held a basin of water and soft cloths for her to use.

"The last time I had to do this sort of thing," she said, "it was an arrow, and my nephew, my sister's second son, had been shot in the thigh."

"How many children has she?"

"Four, from two marriages."

"She is absurdly young to be the mother of children," he said, moving restlessly under the pain. "And so are you, Madame!"

"I had forgotten mine!" She made a wondering gesture with her free hand, and after a silence: "You don't suppose forgetting them could lead them into danger like the little Dourgs!"

"Nonsense!"

"They've been haunting me, and my sister also."

"Yes. And I have thought on this voyage of my brother."

She put her hand over his.

"They told me he died quickly, without too much pain, and he was spared anxiety about his wife and children. They're in France. I shall have to tell them when I go back. It's strange that they do not know. There should be a means of quicker communication."

"The Indians have drums," said Madame de Chauffours absently as she felt him wince beneath her manipulating hands. The bullet was coming out.

"That wouldn't carry across the sea."

"No."

He moved restlessly and winced again as she made another attempt to get the wound clear of dirt and splinters. The pain made him talkative.

"What sort of man is your brother-in-law? I have met your husband and the other two, but never Monsieur de Freneuse."

"Mathieu has built a mill. It's the first one here. He's fanatic about it. He gets up at all hours to see that it's still here. My husband says if something were to happen to the mill Mathieu would die. On other subjects he's reasonable, and he cares for his land."

It was not much of an answer. Monsieur de Bonaventure closed his eyes and saw a stolid, heavy-shouldered man moving about a mill.

Madame de Chauffours was asking something about his wife. To his own surprise he heard himself answer:

"My first wife wanted to marry me, and I was lonely; I needed a home, or thought I did. For a man who spends his life on the high seas or fighting savages, the need is pretty theoretical, isn't it, Madame? So I married her. My second wife is the Naval Minister's niece—I do not owe my position as Commander of the King's Acadian Fleet *entirely* to my own merits, though the merits are there. Both wives, good, loyal, devoted women—both have given me sons . . . but . . ."

"Lie still," said Madame de Chauffours hastily, warding off further disclosures. "You have fever. Do not talk. I will wash out the sword cut now, with wine, and leave you to rest."

She went to a flagon hanging by a leather strap beneath the light and moistened a strip of linen from the roll she carried, washing the second wound with the wine-soaked stuff. It was a thin sore cut from a knife, but not dangerous and bleeding very little.

When she had finished tying him up, she found him another shirt; then, motioning to Dahinda to stay and look after him as he sank back exhausted, she left him and went on deck in search of her sister.

"He's feverish," she said when she found her, "but I do not think there is any danger."

Madame de Freneuse sighed and relaxed the tension of her attitude. "It has been exciting."

Raoul stood up.

"My first fight," he said. "I wish I could tell them in France. . . . It will be so long before I do."

"Fight?" said Madame de Freneuse. "You don't call that a fight! I don't suppose Monsieur de Bonaventure will bother to put it in a dispatch. No one travels here without a few encounters. But a fight, that's something else."

CHAPTER XVII

MADAME DE FRENEUSE picked her way between groups of English prisoners playing at dice on the deck; she avoided the Governor, who was talking to the English captain, and found a place by the shipside, where she could lean over and look toward the land. She could not see it—it was too far away—and though her eyes were fixed in its direction, she was looking at things within.

Supper had been hilarious in spite of the fact that both sides had lost good men. Most of the survivors were feverish, relaxing from the tension of the battle; all of them were ready to laugh at any sally which could make them forget their wounds and the deaths of their friends. Each side had been anxious to show the other how well it could take defeat or victory.

Colonel Tyng spoke good French; he would not have been appointed Governor of Acadia otherwise, and the Nelsons had spent some years in France. They toasted the ladies and told mild stories. De Bonaventure, with burning eyes and smiling lips, was absurdly gay, amusing his guests with one mad remark after another, while the wine went round and the night grew late.

Raoul, watching, sickened of the supper, the lights, the noise, the hot throbbing of his wound, the dizziness of his head. He broke up the party, asking to be excused. Madame de Chauffours went with him to see to the dressing, and Madame de Freneuse escaped for a moment to her thoughts.

All evening de Bonaventure's eyes had questioned hers in a new, disturbing urgency. The battle and the tension afterward, his wound, his fever, had relaxed the guard he kept upon himself, and now he was giving freer rein to the four-footed, fiery, un-

·[68]·

tamed thing within. She found her own eyes meeting his and staying there, happy to be near him in the meeting of a glance. The battle, his danger, his wound, had made her own emotions more intense. Moreover, the end of the journey was in sight, and for her as well as for him a question mark was forming.

She must do her thinking now. If she waited until she was with him, it would be too late. The responsibility of the choice was still all hers; and the decision rested on a little thing—whether or not she should go to his cabin, as she had been doing with Madame de Chauffours, to talk for a while each night, and sometimes to play at cards, and once to sing. But this night Madame de Chauffours would not come, however long they might wait for her. They would be alone, not on the deck where there were hindrances and chaperones, but face to face in a small room with the door shut to the world.

She thought, first, of Mathieu. He rose before her mind, solid, silent, preoccupied, matter-of-fact, and a little coarse. What would she be taking from Mathieu? A body he no longer cared for, a heart he had never had. If she were to take from him, instead, her part in the ordering of his life, his house, his children, even the habit of her presence, that would be wrong and robbing him. But this, this secret hour of living snatched from life, an hour of the transmutation which would lift herself and Pierre to the immortal place from which one descends transformed—what was that to Mathieu? He must not know of it, of course, for, knowing, his pride might be hurt, although, if he were logical, there were his Indian women, his nights in the woods, his junketings and feasts. He would still have his Indian women; he would still have his wife, when he wanted, if he wanted. . . . What, then, did he lose that had ever been his? Honor, perhaps. "To make a man's honor depend upon what another person does *not* do is illogical," she said aloud to the waves.

Then she thought of the children. Well, the children had their lives ahead of them. Her relationship to them would not be hurt. On the contrary, it might be better for them to have a mother who once, at least, had been happy.

De Bonaventure, facing death and danger as his daily lot, and she herself, in danger, too, from Indians, raids, hardships, famine, childbirth—surely they had a right to love? Surely if two such lovers loved, the world of sunlight, shadow, stars, grass, birds, and trees would be enriched by something new, not there before, immortal, free. Or if the world were not enriched, they would be enriched. They would reach the soul's full stature through the body's ecstasy.

Then she thought of the Church. The Church had married her twice, to sons of the Church, and each time it had been deadening and horrible, a sin. "This that you would call wrong," she said aloud, "is the only right thing that has happened to me." Then: "Right or wrong, I choose it for my share of the world."

Loitering a few moments more, watching the lantern's reflection in the sea, looking upward to the stars, going through a thousand restless motions, she waited until her heart was beating so wildly that she felt it must be heard far out to sea, as an Indian drum is heard in the forest.

"Besides," she added, "this is something we will share forever. Something we cannot forget. Life has nothing better to offer than . . . a beautiful, shared dream!"

And, turning, she made her way to de Bonaventure's cabin. It was the little stowaway that Raoul had occupied on the voyage out.

"It was in a little stowaway like that that I first wanted to be his," she thought.

The door was just closing behind de Bonaventure when she pushed it open and stepped inside. It was dark in there. They stood for a moment, silent, while their clothes rustled in the dark. Before she could reach up and light the lantern, since he made no move to do so, he caught her by the hand.

"Louise!"

There was no answer. She began to tremble, leaning against the door. When he felt her trembling, he, too, began to shake. Then he gathered her close and held her against his heart.

"Light the light," she said in a whisper.

"No."

"Light the light!"

He tightened his hold for a moment, sighed, released her, and obeyed.

When the flickering light grew steady, casting an orange beam on the little room, she turned him again to face her; and as he looked at her, not daring to speak, she smiled and offered him her lips.

CHAPTER XVIII

THE sun was shining over a panorama of land and sea that ordinarily would have made de Bonaventure's heart leap with joy of living and fierce pride in his New France. Hills stood against blue sky, like the blue skies of Provence. Forests undulated to the water's edge. Green waves, ice-cold in their purity, broke on the sands in rhythmic line. The Fort de la Tour could be seen in its strategic place, untaken, evidently, by English or Iroquois, and there was great activity in the settlement. Even at such a distance men and women could be seen scurrying back and forth. Bells began to peal. Guns were fired into the woods, to serve the double purpose of greeting the ship and discouraging lurking savages.

Around de Bonaventure on the deck stood his officers, the Governor and his retinue, and the defeated Englishmen.

One of these said:

"A beautiful country!"

De Bonaventure did not answer. The scene brought nothing but heaviness to his heart and the stirrings of an inward rebellion. For one wild moment he saw himself setting the Governor and his men ashore, turning about, and going his way, with the woman he loved on board, to join the pirates. By the bones of St. Mark, if the crew were to go as well, he would not care! He could sail the *Soleil d'Afrique* single-handed, if Louise were his, and shared his fate.

It was impossible, of course. He could face the gallows if he must, alone, but not with her. And, besides, there was his duty to the King, his duty to the ship, his place in the scheme of things, Acadia, New France; there was the woman herself. Louise would not go with him on a stolen ship, facing unknown hazards until they were caught and killed. Or would she? He had half a mind to ask.

Meanwhile the circle stood, silent, waiting for his orders. He heard his own voice give them, calm and sure.

"Man the longboat. Take His Excellency and his men ashore. Colonel Tying, Messieurs Nelson, and you other gentlemen, go with him. You are on parole."

There was a chorus of assent and au revoirs. De Bonaventure did not acknowledge them. He was staring glumly at the shore. The longboat was manned and pushed off with the Governor in it, and his things, and several of the men who were with him. De Bonaventure watched it bobbing over the water.

There was a rustle by his side; he turned to find Madame de Chauffours near him.

"Bonjour, Madame," he said. "Here you are, home. Give my respects to Monsieur de Chauffours, and I hope you will tell him that we did our best to make the voyage comfortable?"

"But you will be landing yourself, Monsieur, to speak to him?"

"No. It is best for an old sea soldier to stay on his boat. We sail as soon as we can for Port Royal. The Governor is anxious to get there. He wanted to go ashore here only to inspect the condition of the settlement. He will, I believe, be coming back to you in the autumn."

"And you will, too?"

"That, Madame, is in the hands of those above."

He turned away from her and went in search of Louise. He found her, not where he expected, but on the other side of the deck with Raoul, who slid out of the way as de Bonaventure came up.

They were alone, leaning on the shipside, looking back past the waters over which they had come, in the night, out to the wide sea.

"Madame," de Bonaventure said with formal courtesy, taking her hand in his and bringing it to his lips.

"Monsieur," she replied mechanically, with a curtsy. They were both grave.

"Madame, I had a question in my mind," de Bonaventure said.

"Tell it me."

"Would you turn pirate with me? Would you trust yourself to me, to shield you from the dangers of a life—every man against us, only *us* alone?

·[72]·

"Gladly."

He breathed faster. "Then . . . will you?"

"No. But all my life I will remember that you asked me to."

"And all my life I will remember that you said you would. May God protect you, my beloved!"

He kissed her hand again with the same formality, uncertain whose eyes might be watching. Then he raised his voice:

"Raoul!"

"Mon oncle?"

"You will take Madame de Freneuse and Madame de Chauffours ashore, with their things, in the longboat when it returns. Take your own things, too. You are attached to Madame de Freneuse's service from henceforth, to serve her in any way that you can, that she may have a dependable fellow to run her errands. Does that suit you?"

"Yes, mon oncle. But you?"

"I sailed without you these fifteen years, mon vieux, and for all the use you are as a sailor, or a soldier either . . . well . . . No, don't be hurt; I jest. You have been very much a help. That is why, in a sense, if you understand, I send you ashore. You will guard"—he dropped his voice—"what is dearer to me than the *Soleil d'Afrique*, than life itself. Compris?"

"Compris, mon oncle."

Raoul threw out his chest and looked at Madame de Freneuse. But she was looking at de Bonaventure. Her soul was in her eyes.

CHAPTER XIX

MONSIEUR DE CHAUFFOURS was waiting for the longboat to arrive. He was a tall, broad-shouldered man with a weather-tanned, strong face and furrowed brows which gave him a look of discontent. He bowed to his wife as Raoul helped her out of the boat. Madame de Chauffours curtsied. Monsieur de Chauffours bowed again—to Madame de Freneuse, who curtsied, too, a little absent-mindedly. Raoul made his best leg. They stood for a moment exchanging banalities while the baggage was unshipped and set ashore. Then the longboat turned about and made for the *Soleil d'Afrique*. They followed it with their eyes.

She lay, beautiful in the sunlight, with the wind already stirring in her sails, a proud and imperious creature. Madame de Freneuse turned suddenly and took an uncertain step forward. Her eyes had filled with tears. Raoul engaged Monsieur de Chauffours' attention hastily. When he looked round again, Madame de Freneuse was leaning on her sister's arm. They all began to walk to the fort.

Monsieur de Chauffours told off several soldiers standing on guard around the port to carry the ladies' belongings.

"My brother is impatient to see you," he said to Madame de Freneuse.

"Is he well?"

"He was when I saw him last week—and the children, too. But there is trouble brewing. He wants you to go home at once."

"But, mon mari, she was to stay with us for a month!"

"I know it is a disappointment, but Mathieu is right. He has made his dispositions."

That was all he would say. Madame de Freneuse introduced

·[74]·

Raoul now more particularly to Monsieur de Chauffours' attention.

"Monsieur de Perrichet is Monsieur de Bonaventure's nephew and has been attached to Mathieu's service. He is to travel with me and control the Indians."

Raoul's jaw dropped slightly. First of all he was astonished at the calm way she shifted him to her husband, and secondly he was at a loss to understand what she meant by controlling the Indians. But Monsieur de Chauffours understood.

"A la bonheur!" he said, twisting his hands. "I was afraid that I might have to accompany you, and God knows I am needed here. Very thoughtful of Monsieur de Bonaventure, very kind. When you have occasion to communicate with him again, Monsieur, you will convey my appreciation?"

Raoul bowed.

"Now let us refresh ourselves!"

They had reached a wooden house inside the settlement, which was a little larger and more imposing than the many they had passed. Monsieur de Chauffours entered, clapping his hands. A soldier ran to take his hat and cloak, and another appeared to dust off chairs and set them for the ladies. Wine was brought and a basket of petits pains.

Monsieur de Villebon appeared with the Captain of the fort, Monsieur de Saint Etienne. He greeted de Chauffours and bowed to the ladies.

"The supplies and the troops here seem to be in good shape," he said to de Chauffours. "I have heard what Monsieur de Saint Etienne has to say. I will send what men and supplies I can from Port Royal, depending on what I find there and the activities of the English. You have heard, have you not, from the ladies that we captured an English governor of Acadia on his way to Port Royal? So much for him!"

De Villebon rubbed his hands. He accepted a glass of wine and a cake and turned his attention to Madame de Chauffours and Madame de Freneuse.

"La santé to us all, Mesdames, and my good memories of a happy voyage, graced by wit and beauty and romance!"

The last word was in a lower tone and apparently directed to Madame de Freneuse, who smiled uncertainly. Madame de Chauffours accepted the toast.

·[75]·

"We wish you a bon voyage, Monsieur le Gouverneur, and a prosperous return."

De Villebon bowed and went out, followed by his officers. Monsieur de Chauffours went to the door and then returned to sit by his wife.

"You will start for home tomorrow," he said to her, "with Armans and some of the men. He will stay up there, and Guillaume is already there with his men. You should be all right. You must take every precaution for yourself and the children. Listen to what Armans tells you, and do it."

"But if there is to be an attack," Madame de Chauffours said, "would it not be safer here?"

"It is not an attack, precisely, that I fear the most," Monsieur de Chauffours said, "and this is the most dangerous place to be."

"But what *is* it?"

She bent toward her husband. He looked over his shoulder and round the room. Madame de Freneuse was sunk in her own thoughts. Raoul had risen, for a moment, to draw her another glass of wine from the carafe standing on the side table.

"Plague!" whispered Monsieur de Chauffours. "It has broken out among the Indians. We are trying to prevent a panic here. If the English learn of it, and they have spies, they will attack. Our only hope is to hold out until supplies and men can come from Kebec or Port Royal. We've sent runners to Kebec, and—you heard the Governor. He will send us what he can."

"Does he know?"

"Yes. Perhaps that's why he toasted you la santé!"

"Plague!" said Madame de Chauffours. "The children!"

"Exactly. The sooner you leave here the better. There have been no cases near the seigneury. It is the Malisites not the Micmacs, so far. You must stay close, burning herbs, and pay attention to Armans, who has studied medicine. Look after the children, encourage the cultivation, keep a sharp watch against surprise attack; enfin, take my place, as I know you can."

"But you . . ."

"I must stay here. It is not what I planned. But if there is mutiny or panic, I may have to step in and control things. If the Indians and soldiers take to the woods in panic, the English will take the fort and the settlement. So much depends on keeping this new line of forts and the one the Governor is to build. . . . You see, I

treat you like a man, Madame, because I know your worth and
courage."

"Thank you." She took his hand and held it in hers. "I shall endeavor to live up to your confidence."

"I know that."

"There's something else you should know—you are the best,
the kindest, and the most loving husband in the world!"

"Madame, you overwhelm me!"

He bowed very low and smiled at her across the table. Madame
de Freneuse came out of her reverie. Raoul brought her the glass
of wine and sat down beside her.

A gun was fired outside; there was a noise of shouting and a
general clamor.

"The *Soleil d'Afrique* sailing," Monsieur de Chauffours said.

CHAPTER XX

THE birchbark boats shot forward. Raoul lay back in his. He was tired. There had been a long stretch of portage before they could take to the river. Eighteen Indians, carrying canoes, tents, baggage, and weapons, formed the cortege; Raoul and Madame de Freneuse walked in the middle, carrying nothing but themselves and finding it hard work at that. So much twisting and turning, so much bending and pushing aside of branches along trails not visible to a white man's eye, in the heat of the woods, bitten by the mosquitoes and tormented by the shut-in feeling of trees and undergrowth. Raoul could hardly bear it at first, imagining an Iroquois behind each bush and not being oversure of the Micmacs escorting them, in spite of all that Madame de Freneuse could say. He was acutely unhappy till they reached the river and the boats were launched.

Madame de Freneuse told him, in answer to the question why they could not use the river all the way, of the reversible falls near the mouth of it. She appealed to Nessamaquij to describe the place, which he did in broken French and with many gestures. Nessamaquij was the chief of the tribe living nearest the Freneuse seigneury. His heart and his allegiance had been won completely by the gift of an iron kettle. "Before that," Madame de Freneuse told Raoul, "and even now most usually, the Indians used a wooden kettle. Naturally they can't put it on the flames. It is made of a hollow log, and it usually is part of a tree and can't be moved. They have to go to their kettle, when they want to heat water, and this leads to the reason for many of their camping places. They heat large stones and put them into the water which they have poured into the kettle. Thus, gradually, the water gets heated; but it also gets dirty, and it is a very slow process involving a lot of work over fires and carrying of stones. When I showed Nessamaquij how to use the iron kettle, he was transported. You should have seen him! He did the dance of a great rejoicing and gave a feast to which he invited Mathieu, and he gave Mathieu a present at the end of it. Although I had shown him the kettle, I was only a squaw—so he gave Mathieu all the official thanks. And a wife!"

"A wife?"

"Yes. He gave him Dahinda, and Mathieu gave her to me."

Raoul turned his head to where Dahinda was sitting in the third canoe with Madame de Freneuse's baggage.

"Do you trust them?" he said.

"Implicitly. Because of our common enemies. They fear the Iroquois and the Mohawks. And, par conséquent, the English. We fear them also. Therefore we are friends. Moreover, we have done them nothing but kindness. Mathieu is now blood brother in the tribe. The tribe is also officially Christian. They come to mass at the seigneury church, and they admire l'Abbé Elizée. I think they look on him as a medicine man; of course, they keep their own beliefs as well."

"Wonderful," Raoul said. "And you can speak their tongue!"

"Dahinda taught me. You'd better take lessons from her, too."

They were three days and nights on the river, landing occasionally to make a fire and eat. Dahinda prepared the food for Madame de Freneuse and Raoul. Indian cooking was too dirty. Mostly dog.

"I have taught Dahinda the rudiments of decency," Madame de Freneuse said.

At night they lay in the bottom of the same long canoe, paddled by two Indians, at bow and stern. Raoul had insisted on Madame de Freneuse being in the same canoe with him, and he had his pistol loaded. In spite of appearances he was taking no chances.

But, as he lay, with Madame de Freneuse using him as a pillow, he suffered from her nearness and the magic of the night. Do what he might, by turning himself away and spreading thicknesses of cloth between them, he was acutely aware in every nerve of her body near him. He looked at the stars and inhaled the pine-laden air from the forests on either side. The bronze, impassive faces of the Indians added to the strangeness of the scene.

When they landed, he always rose and stretched himself and

walked away, trying to recover from the spell of so many hours of her intimate presence. It was a strange experience. Raoul knew nothing like it. He found it torture, but he could not endure the thought of its coming to an end. The silence of the Indians, the majesty of the night, the rapid gliding of the canoes, the glory of the dawns and sunsets, and the autumn moon were the fitting background to the rising tide of his love for Madame de Freneuse. But though she lay practically in his arms all night, she was remote from him. There was no intimacy in her nearness. She used him as a nice young pillow and friendly prop, the only white among the Indians and, therefore, her companion in a special sense; but she conveyed to him at every turn that she would have been safe without him and quite unafraid.

Raoul was nearly at the end of his tether when the canoes were beached for the last time, the Indians took them on their heads, and the last lap of portage began. It lasted an hour. Then they came out of the woods into a clearing. Raoul, accustomed to nothing but the savage undergrowth, saw a plowed field and beyond it a farmhouse. Beyond that, again, were a little church and a large wooden house inclosed in palisades.

He looked a mute question at Madame de Freneuse, on whom an odd hesitancy seemed to have fallen. She stood, for a moment, looking at the rolling hills and at the men and women working in the foreground, while the Indians waited, impassive, round her. Then she started forward, sweeping her arms in a circle.

"Tiens," she said. "Raoul, this is Freneuse."

PART TWO

Freneuse

1696-1700

CHAPTER XXI

SNOW lay deep on field and forest, stretching in drifts to the river's edge. It was piled high round church and barn, where the wind had driven it into heaps. Here and there beaten paths led from the house to the barn; but after a radius of fifty feet there were no paths, only the marks of raquettes on the snow and toboggan trails on one of the slopes. Freneuse was snowed in for the winter. All around the wooden house, as far as eye could see, there was just this dazzling, blinding whiteness, with surface snow blown up in gusts, and the sun's glare upon ice—a cold glare that gave no hint of warmth, although sometimes at noon the sun was strong.

Raoul, walking toward Freneuse with the sun at his back and the biting wind in his face, was thinking of warm food and drink and the grateful heat from the hall fire as he plodded up the hill, lifting his raquettes just the quarter inch required, expertly and quickly. The sun was setting in an orange ball behind him, swooping down to the west with surprising speed. Soon the afterglow would start, of purple light across the snow; and then the stars, enormous and silver, would appear, shining with a frosty light. But long before the sun had gone, he would be in warmth. He thought, as he often did, of the Indians in their fragile shelters; of the pioneers, Champlain, de Monts and his men, spending their first winters without houses; of the comforts and conveniences of Freneuse, with its solid wooden walls, its wide fireplace, its warmth, and the light of its candles on the walls. He could see the lights, now, on the top of the hill.

A voice hailed him from behind.

"Ohé, Raoul! Wait for me!"

·[83]·

Mathieu de Freneuse was swinging up the hill, fairly running on his long raquettes. Raoul waited for him, blowing on his gloves and clapping his arms around his waist. The sun sank lower; longer and longer shadows appeared in front of them. Mathieu de Freneuse caught up with him, and without further word—it was too cold to speak—they swung along. Raoul had hard work to keep up. Monsieur de Freneuse's legs were longer and his movements more precise. He had been born and brought up on raquettes, so to speak, whereas Raoul had only five winters' practice. Five winters! It seemed much more than that since he had come to make his home at Freneuse. He was so much a part of it, now, that it was part of him!

The last crest of the slope was conquered; they were at the top! And now the long, low wooden house spread out before them, with a welcome in its windows, and the smoke from its chimneys spiraled through the air.

Raoul stooped at the door and unstrapped his raquettes with an effort; his fingers were cold and fumbling. Monsieur de Freneuse had his off and was into the house before Raoul had dragged his against the door and shaken the snow from his feet.

A little girl held the door and danced impatiently.

"Vite! Vite! It's cold."

She shut it quickly after him, and ran before him into the hall. It was full of people. Madame de Freneuse sat at a spinning wheel near the fire, working busily. Dahinda was carding the wool, beside her, while two little boys played with shriveled chestnuts at her feet. An older boy, dressed in knee breeches and green velour coat, was practicing the flute in a corner of the room before a music stand, while another boy and two little girls were gabbling over a rosary in the corner.

The entrance of the two men broke up all the pattern. Every child was on its feet, and bows and curtsies followed each other round the room. Madame de Freneuse had risen. Her husband made her a bow; and she dipped to him in an informal curtsy, with the spindle still in her hand. Dahinda put down the wool and went to serve the master with coffee, which was keeping hot on the hob. He took the cup from her with a sigh of satisfaction.

Raoul stared at Madame de Freneuse.

"Will she forgive me for this morning?" he thought. "Boor and brute that I am!"

He took the bowl offered him and supped at it mechanically.

His large dark eyes looked over it, trying from some sign to find out how she felt. But Madame de Freneuse did not look up.

"Well, the mill's still there," said her husband heartily, "and the wood has kept the cold out very well. It was quite remarkable how warm it seemed to be inside."

"It is well built," Madame de Freneuse said, placidly taking the flute away from the boy who was playing it. "Not now, Jean-Marie, your uncle is tired. Presently we will all play. Be silent for a moment."

"Oui, ma tante." The tall child bowed, in his elegant coat. He went over to Mathieu de Freneuse and curled himself at his feet. Mathieu put out a hand and stroked his hair.

"And the studies?" he inquired. "How are they coming now?"

There was a stricken silence round the room. The children looked toward Raoul, who put down his bowl and said as gravely as he could:

"A greater attention would be desirable, Monsieur. One might imagine now that reading, the privilege of the nobility, was not a privilege but a punishment."

He said the last word with an odd inflection, looking toward Madame de Freneuse as he spoke. This time she did look up. A stab of delicious pain shot through him as he met those reproachful eyes. He endeavored to put his soul into the gaze with which he answered, but she had quickly looked away.

"Ecoutez, mes enfants," Mathieu de Freneuse was saying to the circle of abashed little faces, "and I will tell you a story. There was once a man, taken prisoner by the English. He had fought long and well, in a small boat, against superior odds, and in the end he was captured. While he was a prisoner in Boston, which is not many hundred miles from here, he had occasion to read a dispatch written by the English general to his King. He wrote down the news in this dispatch; and because he had no ink, he wrote it in his own blood, upon a piece of wood, and sent it by an Indian to His Excellency, the Governor of Canada, in Kebec. . . . Who is he?"

"The Comte de Frontenac," chorused the children.

"Bien. And because the news was important, and placed a valuable weapon into our hands, His Excellency was able to intercept a convoy of supplies and to destroy the men who were guarding it. The supplies went to the relief of one of our settlements which needed it, and turned the long winter into a period of fresh hope;

and, enfin, that man served his Governor and his King through his knowledge of reading and of writing. I want you to comprehend that. Now who do you think this brave man was, who is still a prisoner among the English?"

No one answered. Raoul, who had succeeded twice during this peroration in catching Madame de Freneuse's eyes and once in forming "Forgive me!" with his lips, brought his attention back with a start to the matter in hand. But the question was rhetorical, apparently, for Monsieur de Freneuse continued:

"I will tell you. Jean-Marie, Robert, Patapouffe, Jeanne, Denise, hold up your heads, mes enfants. That man was your father and my brother, the Sieur de Chauffours, now in Boston among the English. Your sainted mother, had she lived"—the five de Chauffours children crossed themselves—"would have been very proud of him; and she herself, as he, would tell you that it is your duty to them both to learn well your letters and your Latin and whatever else your tutor, Monsieur de Perrichet, is teaching you, and to listen well to Monsieur l'Abbé, and to your aunt, so that you may grow up true sons of a true father and of a good mother. As for you, Gervais and Robert, and you, my children, Paul-Marie and Jean-Mathieu, if you do not do a great deal better, I shall give you to the Indians! So now you know."

"Oui, Monsieur mon père, mon oncle," said all the children in the same breath. They looked toward Madame de Freneuse, stifling a yawn, and to Raoul, who was watching her. Quickly both composed their faces into becoming gravity.

When Raoul first walked out of the woods, with Madame de Freneuse, Mathieu de Freneuse invited him to stay until the plague abated, which it might do with the cold weather, and after that to remain until the snows melted with the spring. But it was Madame de Freneuse, after a stormy and passionate scene with Raoul, who found a pretext for his becoming a permanent part of the family, as tutor to the de Freneuse children, Paul-Marie and Jean-Mathieu, their older half brothers, Gervais and Robert Tibaut, and the five de Chauffours children, whom the de Freneuses had taken under their protection since Madame de Chauffours died of the plague and Monsieur de Chauffours was taken prisoner.

Raoul laughed heartily when she suggested it; the idea of himself as tutor struck him as absurd. But he would have done anything to stay at Freneuse; he was fond of the children because they were hers. It ended in his accepting the position. He taught them Latin and the rudiments of reading and writing, as well as everything else that he could remember of his own education in Provence. He had played truant a good deal, and there were more gaps in his knowledge than he cared to admit. Some of these he filled in by surreptitious study with the Abbé Elizée, who periodically visited Freneuse, and the rest he ignored or invented. He grew fond of the children for their own sakes and even developed a reluctant respect for Monsieur de Freneuse, although it irked him to be treated like a son, well paid and well looked after, by a man whom he would have preferred to hate for daring to be the husband of Madame de Freneuse. She was the star of Raoul's heaven, as remote from him as the stars. For five years he had loved her, in a restless fever that she had somehow, without allowing him the slightest hope, made easier. Unhappy herself, enduring much that he could only guess at, she knew how to soothe unhappiness in others, even when she was the cause of it.

In five years they had had almost constant news of de Bonaventure. His fame as Commander of the King's Acadian Navy grew and spread among the Indians. They called him the Untamed Bear. When supplies and dispatches came from him to Monsieur de Freneuse, Madame de Freneuse sent a letter back with the Indian carriers. Raoul knew that he was the center of her life, her share of the world, the heart that she loved, even as she moved about quiet, sensible, witty, amused, directing and ordering Mathieu de Freneuse and his existence, keeping all the threads of it together, as only she could. That knowledge did not prevent him from intruding his own heated feelings into her calm. They had been through many desperate tormented scenes together. Under the strain he had matured. He was twenty-one. He felt younger than he did at sixteen and could laugh at himself and his misery sometimes. But the desperation of his love was a driving fire, fueled every day from the intimacy of his life as a member of the family. Sometimes he feared that it would flare up as a forest fire, scattering sparks and roaring through the night, destroying all living, green, and tender things before it.

CHAPTER XXII

IT WAS Christmas eve. Madame de Freneuse, looking out across the snow, before the curtains were drawn and the lamps lit, thought, as she always thought, when she had a moment's quietude:

"I wonder how and where *he* will be spending his Noel?"

She sighed, turning back to the bustle of the day. She was making a great festivity out of the occasion, wearing her own best brocaded gown and seeing that the children and the men wore their velour. She hoped to make her nephew and nieces forget their dead mother and their imprisoned father in the innocent gaieties of the day. It was le petit Jesus whom they were honoring, and He was a child among children. They would prepare the crèche in a few moments, when the children were ready. She looked across to where Dahinda and the other servants were putting the finishing touches to the cave of green pine boughs which, in this cold land, represented the stable at Nazareth. The figures had been sent from France, all except three which the nuns had fashioned in Kebec. The cradle was made by the Indians, who would be coming tomorrow to see the completed groups.

"Maman!"

"Yes, Gervais?"

She turned and smiled at her eldest son, eleven and already at her shoulder. He looked down at her, smiling, too, with a wistful hesitancy that made him look more like his father than ever. Charles Tibaut had looked at her in just that fashion when she had been the sunlight of his short, unhappy days. How hard and cruel and young she had been to poor Charles. She stretched out her hand to his son. He took it to his lips respectfully.

"Maman, would you do something for me? Would you give me a very special present for Noel?"

"That depends."

"It's something you can do, Maman—it's something only you can do."

"Well, what is it?"

"If you would play now, just for me alone."

Madame de Freneuse looked at him for a moment. The handsome boy, dreaming away his time, always in trouble with his stepfather, had this one consuming passion, music. He could play the flute and the viol already, but his chief delight was to listen to his mother play the harpsichord; and if he could get her to sing, he was in the seventh heaven. But he took no pleasure in the little orchestra that she had trained, out of all the children; he played in it because he would not disobey her wishes, but distastefully and always as though he were holding his hands to his ears. Naturally the other children made mistakes; they were healthy young animals with more normal characters and with ambitions like Mathieu de Freneuse, whom they adored, stepchild and children and nephews and nieces alike. Only this one boy was different. He was the child she had carried in her sorrow, through that first unhappy stone-cold year of marriage when de Bonaventure had broken her heart and she had, perforce, put away childish things and a great deal besides. . . .

"Bien, Gervais," she said, smiling at him. "I will."

He ran to the instrument and lifted the cover from it carefully. Madame de Freneuse dusted the keys with a silken cloth and sat on the special chair that had come with it from France. Her skirts billowed about her as she sat, and her long dark hair (for she still refused to wear a wig, even though wigs now were less elaborate and more natural-looking) framed her face in a dark oval, accentuating the darkness of her eyes. Gervais posted himself where he could see and hear, and looked at her descending hands with quivering heed.

She played a folk song first and sang to it, nodding to Gervais to join in. She had a rich contralto with an unexpected strength to it, while he had a clear boy's soprano lacking only polished training to make him a boy soloist of any cathedral choir. Even Notre Dame itself, she sometimes told him, boasted no better voice if it were trained. They sang together happily.

Then, on an impulse, she played him something modern, something he had never heard before. The music had been copied for her by a friend in France, who sent her books and scores from time to time, since he was happily placed to do so, being choir-master of Vincennes. She propped the manuscript up in front of her and began to play.

After a few bars she began to sing. Gervais was transported.

"What is it, Maman?"

"It's a modern thing," she said, "by a great composer whose name is Buxtehude—Dietrich Buxtehude. It is the seventh thing of his I have heard, and the second I have tried to play. Do you like it?"

"Like it! It's strange and unmelodic at first, but it's—it's—it's the *truth*! It goes home, here!" He laid his hand upon his solar plexus. Madame de Freneuse laughed.

"That's where music hits me too," she said.

"Tell me more about Buxtehude."

"I know very little. I only know that he is organist at a place in Germany."

"He must be famous."

"I shouldn't say that. Perhaps among the few who know and can appreciate new art, he is known and loved; but fame comes usually after death, if at all."

"I wouldn't care, Maman, if I could write like that!"

"I don't suppose he cares, either, Gervais."

"Sing me again the amen."

"It should be sung by a big choir, I think. There are parts, indicated at the top, for many voices; but I'll do it as best I can."

"It's beautiful just like that," he said when she finished.

"You are an appreciative audience, my son. Shall I tell you the story of the thing I sang?"

He settled himself closer and looked up at her. She found herself feeling, as she often did when she looked into those eyes, guilty toward the dead man whose eyes they seemed to be, and guilty to this child who thought her what she was not. She was a sinful woman, and a woman who could not repent that sin. She was a woman who set that sin of guilty love as the only beautiful and pure thing that had ever happened to her. But a woman who had no illusions as to what her children, her present husband, and her world would say if ever they found out. She launched into the story hastily.

"In 1687, only nine years ago, a blacksmith was decapitated for

·[90]·

blasphemy against the Trinity, and this took place in Buxtehude's town. The people asked him to write an atonement to the Trinity, which would be played and sung publicly as an expression of the townspeople's contrition that such a blasphemy should have taken place. Buxtehude accepted, and this is what he made of it. It is so gentle and sweet and uplifting that I think he had understood and forgiven the blacksmith, as I am sure the Holy Trinity did, too, when they knew him better and what was the reason for his sin."

"But, Maman, that was a sin against the Holy Ghost. L'Abbé Elizée says that is never forgiven!"

"I think we cannot know, Gervais, not you nor I, nor even the Abbé Elizée what the Holy Trinity decide to do. I am quite sure that since so much good came out of the whole thing, as this music, there was probably another ending to the blacksmith's tale. Listen!"

She sang again:

" 'O Lux Beata Trinitas . . .' Isn't that beautiful? Do you like your Christmas present?"

He flung himself at her and kissed her with no regard, for once, to respect.

There was a noise behind them and a sound of voices and clattering feet. Gervais disengaged himself and darted to a corner. The other children came pouring in, with Raoul, who had been helping them to decorate the chapel with evergreen and light the stove there so that at midnight mass would not be too freezingly cold.

Raoul looked over the children's heads to Madame de Freneuse, smiling an inquiry. It was the way he often looked at her. She knew it to mean: "How are you, my beloved? Has anything happened to you since we last met?"

She gave him as maternal a look as she could manage. Raoul suffered. It was selfish of her to keep him here. But he was such a help, an ally, a friend. Mathieu liked him; the children adored him; he was indispensable. As long as he could endure it—and he did not want to go—why should she not have the comfort of his presence?

She sighed, suddenly remembering the bitter strength of emotion at his age. Just twenty-one! They had held a fete for his coming of age; the Indians had invited him to a feast; Mathieu had said pretty things. . . . The boy was, after all, better off here than alone with strangers.

"Maman! Maman! Ma tante!" The children clamored round

her as the yule log was propped into place, and Dahinda and the other servants stood back to allow Mathieu de Freneuse, who came into the room behind them, to stoop and light it.

He took his place beside her without a glance.

"Mathieu looks on me as part of the furniture," she thought resentfully for a moment. Then her sense of fairness said to her: "and what for these many years have you looked on him as— duty?" She blushed and laid her hand on his arm. He covered it with his own, unexpectedly, and led her forward. They stood looking down at the burning pine cones and crackling twigs beneath the log—that traditional bûche their fathers had gathered round on Christmas eve in France. L'Abbé Elizée came forward now from the doorway and threw grains of incense into the flames.

CHAPTER XXIII

TWENTY-SEVEN people sat down to table at two in the morning on Christmas day. More than that had come to the chapel for midnight mass. The place had been full of Nessamaquij's people, dressed in their best and taking part with fervor in the strange magic of the white medicine man. Only the French came to the meal, afterward, at the Freneuse house. The Indians would reappear later to drink a glass of wine and cement their friendship, but for the moment this was entirely French.

L'Abbé Elizée took the seat nearest Madame de Freneuse and pronounced a long and sonorous grace, while the children, hungry and sleepy at such unusual hours, fidgeted and did their best to be patient, with the smoking pork and the huge dish of boudins steaming before their noses.

Grace came to an end, and all sat down. Madame de Freneuse looked round the table. There were five women there besides herself, wives of the farmers whom Mathieu de Freneuse had settled on his land, the wife of the miller, and a woman servant. There were nine men, not counting Mathieu and Raoul, two of them soldiers in command of the Indians under Mathieu and Raoul, five of them farmers, and three youths—the miller's two boys, and one farmer's lad. L'Abbé Elizée made the ninth. The children, dispersed about between their elders, brought the number up to its full complement of cheerful, healthy faces. This *souper* was a great event to the community. It broke the monotony of the winter. Men and women alike were glad to put on better clothes, to forget the hardships of pioneer life for an hour or two, and play at being visitors. They remembered, those of them who came from France, other suppers, in their homes, among parents and friends, in the quiet country places or little towns of the motherland. Faces and memories came crowding with each toast. Those who, like Madame de Freneuse and her husband, were born and brought up in New France thought of Kebec and the old Bishop, or of Trois Rivières and other places, where at this time celebrations would be taking place, healths drunk, and they, themselves, perhaps, remembered.

Raoul thought of his father and mother and of his little brother, favorite of them all, now a big boy with five years added to his growth. He thought of Vanina, with an odd surprise to reflect that such a trivial emotion should have brought him across the seas to the middle of this forest, thousands of miles from any other inhabited place, to be with the woman he loved . . . who did not love him.

"It is destiny!" he thought, raising his glass to toast the frivolous, delightful, faithless Vanina, with an understanding smile. For now, at last, he felt he knew life, love, and the universe. He was Vanina's equal; he was a man, if an unhappy one.

Madame de Freneuse toasted de Bonaventure with her first glass, silently. The others were drinking to the King, but he would have enough toasts over his country and his colonies. Monsieur de Bonaventure would be toasted, too—publicly on his ship, and in Kebec, and even here, perhaps, if someone else suggested it— but this one toast was different.

"Oh, my love," she said to the wine, "good luck to you this year and every year. If it be God's will that we meet, then let us meet. Let me have news of you." Her mind sheered away from the thought that she might hear of his love for another woman. "He has a wife; that will keep him out of harm," she thought, and felt a certain warmth toward Madame de Bonaventure because her husband did not love her but could not marry anyone else. She smiled.

Mathieu de Freneuse saw the smile and rose to his feet.

"A toast! To the courageous woman who makes comfort to us all, the friend, supporter, and helper—to my wife!"

Startled, she raised her eyes to find the whole roomful looking at her, smiling and drinking her health. Raoul was beaming; the children were chorusing, "Maman! Ma tante!" Mathieu was looking at her gravely, with something in his eyes that she did not recognize. She heard herself responding to the toast.

"My husband!"

Too honest to qualify the word with any additions. That was what he was; and she had tried to play her part, beating down the inner fires that had never burned for him, forcing herself to be fair and to recognize his qualities, his strength and manhood, and his affection, too. But it was hard. She turned away from him.

Patapouffe was eating too much and too quickly, as usual. Greedy little boy! Denise was doing her best to make Jeanne laugh, and get a reprimand. Madame de Freneuse sent judicial frowns to the right quarters, and the meal went on. The conversation, for once, was not on the English or the Indians, or what one might expect for the crops, or the scarcity of water, or any of the other normal topics. It was, led by the Abbé Elizée, about other Christmases and olden tales. Soon Monsieur Edard, the miller, was telling a ghost story of his youth in Avignon, and Raoul added another—from Provence, too, though farther south.

Monsieur Devignes told a truly terrible story that made everybody shudder. He had been taken prisoner nine years before by the Iroquois and, while he was held for ransom, had set himself to learn their language. He had succeeded in understanding them fairly well before he was, at length, exchanged, starved and in a poor state of health from the tortures they had inflicted on him.

He said that the Iroquois had a tradition that all of them believed, and some swore to have seen at first hand. They asserted that "a nameless monster haunted the forests and that the bones of the men it had killed never lay quiet in their graves. Their skeletons were seen swimming with hideous speed and dexterity in the lake of Teungktoo." This tale of the unquiet dead brought a breath of the hostile forests with it and was easily believed by all who sat there in the room. They knew the vast desolate recesses of the forests to be full of strangeness, and they could believe almost anything of the Iroquois.

After this tale the door opened and Dahinda appeared, leading seven little children and carrying a baby. These were the younger children of the farmers and the miller, who had been relegated to the kitchen to give their mothers a rest. Children and babies were strewn on the floor, and the de Freneuse and de Chauffours boys and girls took them in hand. The older people pushed back from the table, too. Dahinda and helpers began to clear away. The door opened a second time, and a party of Indians came in.

Raoul could never get used to being on friendly terms with the Micmacs and Malisites. To him each sight of the bronze, impassive, cruel-looking faces brought a shudder and made him reach for his pistols. Although he attended when Mathieu, who commanded half a company of these Indians, drilled them every Sunday afternoon, with all the other men of the community, in the use of the guns and muskets kept in the armory, he never could feel at ease with them, and once or twice his obvious hostility had insulted Nessamaquij. It was bad to get on the wrong side of the Indians, bad for him and for the settlement. Mathieu had spoken to Nessamaquij, who said he would accept Raoul as his own blood brother for love of Mathieu, who thereupon had asked Raoul to apply for initiation into the tribe at once. Raoul refused. He was one of those people born with an instinctive horror of savages. No reasoning could get him over it.

They came in now—sixteen splendid figures in buckskin and feathers, with the peace paint on their faces, and the calumet, or pipe of peace, in Nessamaquij's hand.

Mathieu de Freneuse greeted them with a little speech in Micmac and passed them each a goblet of wine. Then together they drank to the French King, to the French and Indian alliance, to happy hunting together, and to plentiful crops.

"Good health and no more plague," Mathieu proposed, "and happy hunting in the good grounds with Quitche Manitou, for all the dead."

Jeanne de Chauffours, looking up at the stern faces and understanding her uncle's words, took them to mean for all those who had died of the plague, including her mother, and for a moment wanted to cry at the idea of her own maman, so tender and so sweet, having to go out hunting with the dead Indians. Then she remembered that l'Abbé Elizée had said her mother was in Purgatory and would be in Paradise, if she remembered to pray for her every night, and was reassured. Her uncle was talking of the Indian dead. Her mother would not have to roam the dark woods, nor swim a lake, like the skeletons. She shivered.

"Ave Marie," she murmured suddenly to her rosary, "I will pray every day for my mother, as well as every night."

The Indians drank, passed the pipe of peace around, grunted, and accepted cake. After an interval they rose to go, stepping silently into the night, gliding on their snowshoes into the woods, to their own miserable tepees where, over smoking fire, they would exist till spring. The Christmas midnight mass and the wine and cakes that followed for the men were an occasion for them, too.

After they had gone, the children of the house were dispatched to bed. The tired women began to collect husbands and babies, to depart. But another barrel of wine was broached, and all sat down for a final talk.

The farmers appreciated their seigneur's kindness to them, his friendliness. In many settlements there was not so much cooperation between the seigneur and the farmer. Mathieu de Freneuse was also Captain of the Militia, which was rare. As a rule, the Captain, appointed by the Governor, was someone chosen from the people. But it worked out very well, at Freneuse, like this.

The farmers, like everyone else in New France, went in terror of Indian attacks, but they did not have to contend with harsh laws and badly administered taxes. Their lands were rich. Winters might be long, summers brief; but maize, wheat, peas, rye, sprang up profusely, growing quicker than in France. Cattle multiplied and throve on the swamp pastures. Wild berries were plentiful; tobacco, too. Game, protected in the homeland by dreadful penalties, was free in New France to all who could kill or snare it. The farmers had stout walls, hot fires, and stout clothing. It was another Noel, and things were not so bad.

Good nights were said. With bows and curtsies, smiles and nods, everyone departed, content and satisfied.

CHAPTER XXIV

W ITH the first melting of the snows two messengers arrived. They were Indians who had run from Port Royal, keeping the tireless pace of the trail until they arrived, as they had started, seven hours apart.

When the first brown figure darted from the woods, Raoul, who happened to be standing by the window, shouted; Mathieu de Freneuse, who was in the courtyard with two of the children, caught them up under his arms and ran for the house. Gervais appeared at the door of the barn and rushed in again. Everybody in the house caught up weapons and ran to close doors and windows against the flight of arrows they expected. But as no more brown bodies followed the first one and he came near enough for them to see that he ran lightly, in the paint of a trail breaker, they put down whatever they had taken up and waited. Dahinda gave a deep grunt of satisfaction, recognizing a young man of Nessamaquij's people, whom she knew. He had followed de Villebon to Port Royal and was now his personal messenger, or, as the Indians spoke of it, "his feet."

Mathieu de Freneuse came out to meet him, making the sign of a friendly chief. The messenger shielded his eyes from the brightness of the white man's spirit and, extending his right hand, palm downward over the earth, called it to witness the truth of his brotherhood. Then he drew a package from his belt and handed it over, standing impassive while the splendid muscles of his naked body moved with the deep breaths he drew.

Mathieu called to Dahinda:

"Give our brother all he needs."

Dahinda walked before him into the kitchen, with the proud tread of the woman who was no man's squaw.

Gervais, peeping round the corner of the barn door, decided to make a dash for it and sprinted to the house, head down, legs flying madly.

"Imbecile!" he said to himself. "To hide in the barn! That was a very stupid thing to do—they would certainly get me there. Madonne, what a blessing that they aren't attacking yet! I shall have time . . . I shall still have time . . ."

The space between his shoulder blades was cold, as he ran, with the feeling of arrows sticking into it. He died a number of deaths before he reached the door and panted through it.

He found everybody standing calmly in the hall. His stepfather was reading a letter.

"De Villebon expects us to be attacked," he said. "He is coming here himself as soon as he can get away. He wants us to build new palisades. . . . Well, perhaps that is an idea, though I hate to take the men away from the work. We'll get no crops if we lose too much time." He skimmed through the letter.

"He sends his compliments to you—'Call me to the remembrance of Madame de Freneuse, of whom I retain a warm impression of charm, courage, and kindliness.' . . . Tiens, tiens, you seem to have made an impression."

"That was because I cooked his favorite pie when he was here," Madame de Freneuse said placidly. "And I suppose he expects me to do it again. How many of them will there be, do you think?"

"Forty to fifty. Fifty, say. We can put some of them into the mill and some of them with the farmers, as we did before. It's a lot of work; but if there is to be an attack, their help will be worth our trouble."

"Mine, you mean."

"Well, perhaps," he laughed good-humoredly. "You certainly have most of it, but then I have to listen to de Villebon's stories. And I think that's worse."

He became aware of the children, staring goggle-eyed at him, and continued hastily.

"Because I am not clever enough to understand them all, and the Governor is such a clever man."

·[99]·

Gervais edged closer to his mother. He was still white from the shock.

"Maman, are the Indians going to attack?"

"No, no. It's just the usual spring scare, my son. Nearly every year the Governor sends messages or somebody sees an Iroquois; but, children, from now on you will not go out of the yard in front of the house. And keep an eye on the woods. If you see anything moving, come in immediately."

"Raoul," said Mathieu de Freneuse, "come with me, and we'll put the farmers on their guard and begin to plan the palisade. It isn't a bad idea to have one made. It should include the mill, and one of the farms, and the house and barns, of course. I think we have enough men to handle that."

They disappeared together, and Madame de Freneuse, left alone with the children, called the Indian in.

He came, tall, impassive, standing in front of her with a level, faraway look in his dark eyes. She shooed the children out, summoned all her Micmac, and began to question him.

"How was the Governor? Who were the officers with him? What sort of a winter did they have at Port Royal?"

The Indian gave short, unsatisfactory answers, until she sighed and gave it up. Then he grunted, fumbled in his belt, and brought out a little package.

"The Untamed Bear sends this."

She paled, taking it.

"My thanks to the messenger," she said a little unsteadily, looking about her for a gift. Denise's doll and Jeanne's sewing basket were lying on a table near. Between them trailed a little glass necklace, intended as a present to the miller's child. She picked it up and dropped it into the Indian's hand, dismissing him. Then she opened the package.

It was a little leather book of illuminated poems. So much she saw at first glance. The pages were filled with jeweled margins and gold lettering, and there were illustrations scattered through the book. On the first page she read:

"Poems, translated from the English tongue by P. D. de B."

His own work! She sighed with delight and pressed the opened pages to her heart, then she looked at them again.

The first poem was worked in greens and gold, with pictures in the margin that at first made her blush a little and then smile with swift and secret delight. The words ran:

·[100]·

Taken from John Attye's first book of airs, 1622.

The Wakening

Once on a time the amorous Silvy,
Said to her shepherd, "Sweet, how do ye?
Kiss me this once and then God be with ye,
    My sweetest dear!
Kiss me this once and then God be with ye,
For now the morning draweth near."

With that, her fairest bosom showing,
Opening her lips, rich perfumes blowing,
She said, "Now kiss me and be going,
    My sweetest dear!
Kiss me this once and then be going,
For now the morning draweth near."

With that the shepherd waked from sleeping,
And spying where the day was peeping,
He said, "Now take my soul in keeping,
    My sweetest dear!
Kiss me and take my soul in keeping,
Since I must go, now day is near."

Medley of impressions rose within her—blue of water, white of sail, whispered words to the accompaniment of wind and wave, the motion of the ship beneath them as they lay laughing in the darkness. . . .

The illustrations on the page stood out to her eyes, and she looked more closely.

No shepherd ever wore the uniform of a captain in the French Navy; the woods or pastures where the shepherd and his shepherdess were lying bore a remarkable likeness to the corner of a deck or even a cabin. And Sylvy . . . Sylvy wore an apple-green ball dress with a bunch of purple ribbon at the neck.

"So he *did* notice it that night!" She murmured happily, turning the pages for a glimpse beyond.

"Sonnets, by Shakespeare," whoever he might be. Wyatt, Grimald, Scott, Greene, Peele—a host of poets and poems, all illuminated, illustrated, and, if one were to judge by the amorous Sylvy, all containing food for thought, fuel for love. . . .

The sound of voices and steps outside the door made her thrust the volume into her dress.

Gervais and Raoul came in, both in high spirits and laughter from a wager they had made outside. Raoul, shooting his customary look at her, found it unexpectedly answered. Something *had* happened to his beloved since he had seen her half an hour ago! Her eyes were bright, her cheeks rosy, and she looked astonishingly ten years younger, so that for an instant he thought "Who's this?" even while he glared about him for a clue to the mystery. There was nothing but a doll on a table and a child's sewing basket beside it. Madame de Freneuse brushed past him and went out.

He followed her. She wheeled about in the passage and stood facing him.

"Well, what is it? Must you speak to me now?"

The sharpness of her tone struck him like a whip. He gasped, reached forward, and took her in his arms. Oblivious to her fist striking him across the forehead and to her urgent whisper, "Let me go! Let me go!" he sought to press his lips upon hers, trembling with desire as he kissed. She ceased to struggle, compressed her lips into a rigid line, and waited for a moment till he paused for breath, moving his head back to look into her eyes. Then, deliberately, she spat at him.

The gesture brought him up short in horrified despair. Implacably she stared at him, arranging her disordered dress with trembling hands. Then she spoke.

"You are impossible. I shall tell Mathieu. If you have no respect for me, at least think of him. What would he say if he could see what you have been doing here to me, you whom he trusted?"

"What would he say if he knew what you were doing that night on the *Soleil d'Afrique*, you whom he trusted?"

This was something he had often longed to say, and never dared. Madame de Freneuse whitened; her hands clenched convulsively; she looked at him with hatred in her eyes. Then she said slowly and, considering all things, composedly:

"If you know what happened on the *Soleil d'Afrique*, you know who has my heart. Go and tell Mathieu if you like. But at least keep your hands off me."

She turned from him and started to walk away, although her knees were trembling so that she could hardly stand. At the sight of her back, so gallant, so defenseless, something broke in Raoul. He rushed after her.

"Stay! Wait, Louise! Forgive me. I am mad with misery, with jealousy." . . .

"That is very obvious. On account of this unhappy obsession I have forgiven you many things. We cannot go on like this, Raoul."

"Why not?" he demanded indignantly, forgetting that he had just asked her forgiveness. "Mathieu loves you; my uncle loves you . . ."

"Hush, for heaven's sake!"

"You do not laugh at their love. Why do you laugh at mine?"

"Raoul, you are beside yourself. You have asked my forgiveness, and I give it you. Now go, and let us have no more of this nonsense. You will force me to ask Mathieu to send you away."

"Nonsense!" He clenched his hands, almost weeping with rage and distress. "Send me away! Why can't you be kind to me? I don't ask so much. I know you cannot marry me, and I even accept that you love my uncle; but he isn't here, and I am, and I love you more than he. Why can't you be kind to me in return?"

"Have I ever been unkind?"

"You know what I mean, Louise."

"Mathieu and I have both been kind to you. We have treated you as we would treat a son. I am fond of you, Raoul; and if you could only control yourself, I might in time become even fonder."

"Fond!"

"Yes, fond. It is all I can promise you, and more than many have. Is friendship nothing? You and I have that."

She looked at him, smiling, and his heart turned over.

"But I don't think you can stay here, Raoul. I will ask Mathieu, without telling him why, to find some way of sending you home, perhaps to France. Would you like that?"

He saw by the calm sweetness of her face that she meant what she said, and broke out into pleas.

"I promise you . . ."

"You have promised before. You never keep your word."

"But I will this time. Is there nothing I can do to show you that I mean it, that I love you enough? Don't send me away!"

A sudden thought struck him.

"Will you let me stay if I do what Mathieu wants, if I let the Indians take me into the tribe? I'd be more useful then. I could command a troop, like Mathieu, or take over his. It would be a good thing for the settlement."

·[103]·

Madame de Freneuse bit her lip to prevent herself from smiling. Just as earnestly as he was urging now, so he had urged against it, pouring out a flow of words to explain why he, Raoul de Perrichet, would never go native and become blood brother to a breed. "Dirty beasts," he had said; "we should make them take to our customs and not pander to theirs."

Now he was offering what to him, and she knew it, was the supreme sacrifice—that, in spite of his fear, horror and contempt of the savages, he would submit to being initiated painfully into the tribe; and this not for any promised reward, not for a night of love, nor for a kiss, but just that he might be allowed to stay near her, constantly tormented, constantly in stress.

She smiled. As he had found her back pathetic and touching, so now she found his young flushed face.

"You may stay," she said, "and I am glad you will be initiated. It will help the settlement, as you say, and Mathieu will be delighted. You will have power among the Indians now. Who knows how that may serve us? Perhaps you will have to use it one day in the woods on my behalf."

His face lightened at that, and he looked at her with adoration.

"Will you forgive me for just now, and for what I said?"

She beckoned in answer. The kiss he had tried to take and been denied was given him, now, full upon his lips. He sighed and closed his eyes.

She left him there, rustling away, as he stood still in his dream. She had hardly turned the corner before she took out de Bonaventure's letter again; and then Mathieu, the children, Raoul, the world itself, faded from her mind.

CHAPTER XXV

THE morning after Raoul's great resolve, Mathieu de Freneuse waked early. He turned his great frame over to lie upon his back, and the grim procession of things he hoped to evade, thoughts he dared not think, began to march across his brain. He raised himself to look at his wife. She was lying beside him, heavily asleep. He looked at her avidly, smiling at the child-like bundle that she slept in, all hunched up, with little curls escaping from her nightcap. She might have been a child of twelve, asleep before Noël, with the firm expectation that in the morning her shoe would be filled with magic that would change the world.

Actually she was thirty-two, mother of five children. And she was his wife. He knew what would happen if he waked her with his longing. She would look up at him with faint distaste and mild alarm. Then, if he persisted, she would resign herself and, like a good wife, give him what he wanted, in such a way that she gave him nothing and left him shamed. Then she would pat his hand reassuringly, turn over, and pretend to be asleep; but from the slight ripples and shudders that went through her he would know she was not asleep, but fighting to control her nausea.

Why, why, why? A man should be able to make love to his wife without being made to feel a boor and a criminal! It was absurd! No, it was he, Mathieu, who was absurd, to expect so much from her. His marriage had been arranged, like other marriages. His wife had borne him children and kept his house, like other wives. Was it her fault that he had wanted love within his marriage, too? Love matches were frowned upon in New France as elsewhere. With reason, if they led to fevers such as this. And he had given her no indication that it was a marriage unlike any other at the start. He had married a widow with two children and a good estate; he had taken her to his own estate; and there suddenly, out of the blue Canadian skies, he had fallen in love. He remembered the day.

"Louise, Louise, you were enchanting and bewitching that young spring. You filled the house with gaiety and with delight. I came upon you one night in the cherry orchard that we planted together, walking beneath the moon. I kissed you then on the neck, do you remember? It was more of a bite than a kiss, and you turned to face me with such a look, such a look! Oh, my one love, why could you not respond to this in me? But there, it is not a thing to command, or I could have commanded it away. I tried to when I knew how it was to you. A man in love with his wife! Jealous not of his honor, but of her thoughts! My father would have called it an unmanly weakness. Certainly it has ruined my life.

"If I could think that she were cold—a cold, virtuous woman who could not be set on fire and would not if she could . . . But no, Louise is passion itself; it is in her walk, in her eyes, in the turn of her head, and in all her tormenting body—it is there. It is there, but not for me. For whom then? It began long before the boy was here, or it might be for him. Easy to see with half an eye that he is seas deep beneath his love for her. A boy's first love! There is nothing like it in height, in range, in intensity, unless it be a mature man's one love after many. Raoul, mon vieux, I think you are in for eating misery. I do not think you are the man who is responsible for mine. Misery.

"Yes, it is misery. Here she is, not an inch away; we are touching each other; she is mine to take, and if I take her she will not deny me. I shall find myself clasping only a cold shadow, something that gives but does not yield, or yields but does not give; I shall find myself only farther away than ever from her and uncomfortable as though I had raped a nun. Ciel, why should I be made to feel so, why? By God, there are other women, passionate and warm, women who like to feel my body against theirs, who laugh and sigh and press me closer. . . . Yes, there are plenty of those, and I serve them as she serves me. Thus it goes, and where's the sense to it? A man needs a companion in this life. Not that she doesn't do what she can to share Freneuse. She does. Our heads can get together. I should be content. Oh, Dieu, she's going to wake and find me here, propped on an elbow looking at her so. She'll sigh and resign herself. Unbearable!"

He sank down on his side of the bed and pulled the cover up, biting nervously at the fringe of it. Madame de Freneuse woke, gave an experimental pat, and turned her back on him. Then he sat up.

"I think I'll go out," he said.

No answer. He slid the cover off and stood up, naked in the morning sun. In summer there was no need for clothes beyond the sheet. It was in winter that he accepted nightshirts and nightcap. Madame de Freneuse wore hers the year round.

Naked, he ran down through the courtyard and to the stream. He would begin the day with a swim. That might make him feel better. But when he reached the stream, he was first startled and then amused to find Raoul already there, shaking the water out of his ears.

"Ha!" he said, to tease him, "if you had been initiated, I should say you were back from a night in the woods. I can't imagine why a young blade like you doesn't want to be blood brother and chief to the Malisites, when it means that you can have your pick of the squaws. If you went after them now, you'd be tomahawked, of course, and serve you right. They don't ask much—only that the man who takes their squaws shall be a brave man, like themselves."

"I don't want squaws," said Raoul sulkily, stamping on one foot to free his ear from the last imprisoned drop.

"Are you by any chance considering turning monk?"

There was no reply. Mathieu took off with a laugh and felt the icy stream tingle against his heated flesh. Then he turned round on his back and let himself be carried down the current to a little fall, stopping himself on the brink by clutching at a rock.

Raoul had been following on the bank, evidently speaking, though he'd missed half of it. He was saying now:

". . . so don't you think it is. But I've come to see that I could help you better so and command the Indians in your place or under you. I can't be much use in an attack without it, I see that. So will you tell Nessamaquij?"

"Tell him what?"

"That I am ready to be initiated now."

"What? Good man! Bravo! That's the best stuff!"

Mathieu climbed out of the water to thump Raoul on the back

and kiss him on both cheeks with enthusiasm. They walked back to the house together, naked and brown, talking about the Indians as they went. Now that he had accepted the idea, Raoul was suddenly eager to know all about it, to look on the glamorous side of the Indians, and to forget the dirt.

Denise ran out and pulled a face at her uncle, seeing him naked. She was neither surprised nor abashed. Life in New France taught women and children not to be squeamish, and there was nothing Denise did not know. She had assisted her aunt with the care of women brought to bed and washed new-born babies. A naked man or two about the place was nothing to her; and these were relations, if one might place a tutor in that class.

She contented herself with saying:

"Coffee is on the table. My aunt is up."

"Next time you see Raoul," Mathieu de Freneuse said, pulling her hair, "you'll have to address him in Malisite! He's going to be an Indian and learn to protect us all. He'll be whooping round the place seven times a day now, dressed in feathers and beads."

"Nonsense, mon oncle," said Denise, winking at Raoul to show that she understood. "You mean he'll be like you, a chief among the Indians, not that he'll whoop at all."

Mathieu did not answer. He was thinking:

"And then he'll take a squaw and leave my wife alone. He's tired, poor boy, of hanging on like this. That shows at least that she hasn't encouraged him, hasn't given him anything."

At the thought of what she might have given he scowled so blackly at Raoul that Denise was astonished and cried out:

"Mon oncle!"

He paid no attention to her, brushing by.

"If it is," he was thinking, "if he is the one, and I am wrong, I'll have him killed. It would be easy enough, in the woods, by the Indians at the initiation. Well, we shall see. I'll keep a better eye open, yet I think the boy is as unhappy as I am myself. A likable enough boy if he could fall in love, and not with Louise! Perhaps the Indian women are the answer."

They went in.

CHAPTER XXVI

A WIND blew through the forest, high among pines and silver birch. It shook the branches so urgently that wafts of heavy scent descended in waves below. It roamed between tree trunks, over bushes, by boulders, through clearings, across glades, until it filtered into a sheltered hollow where men were sleeping in the sun.

There were ten of them, Indians, lying in a circle with their feet to the ashes of a noonday fire. They inhaled the rich air, relaxing more completely in their sleep.

Suddenly a dead twig snapped, and Raoul sat up with a start. He looked about him. The others were still there, motionless. He could not tell if they had heard or were still sleeping; but if they kept so still, there was no need for him to strain, to listen. . . . There could be no danger that these would not hear. He sank back, reassured.

The forest symphony above them gathered in strength. Its muttering lullaby, fierce whispers, and strange groans, drugged him into heaviness. He sank through the floor of the world into bottomless slumber.

When he awoke, he was alone. The others had vanished, Hamogom, Neloo, Wosedek—all gone, stolen away. It was the third time it had happened. Raoul was annoyed and a little afraid. They did it to tease him, like children, having fun, enjoying his bewilderment. But they could not be far . . . or could they? How long had he slept? Now that the sun had moved, even the direction would be hard to find. He scrambled to his feet and stood peering between trees. They might be gone moments or hours; they might, smiling silently, be watching him a length away. It was all part of his initiation, which, please heaven, would soon be over, giving him authority over the Malisites not acquired in any other way.

Well, he must trail them and not blunder this time as he had before. He stooped to the ground where Hamogom, nearest to him, had slept, and looked for the marks of his rising. The fire had been carefully removed, the ashes covered. He circled on his hands and knees a moment. If he could find an indication . . .

He looked above the trees. The sun was changing color. The earth was dipping away from it perceptibly. He stood with his feet pointing toward the east and took his bearings. Then he began to walk through the underbrush, bending and twisting, straightening up from time to time, to make sure the sun was behind him in the same angle to his direction.

It was hot and tiring, this constant scrambling over rocks, between resisting bushes, along fallen tree trunks, and sometimes over little bogs. These were the worst. With all his strength Raoul loathed the slime around his feet, the horrid sucking noises of the swamp.

He went steadily onward. He did not want night to fall and find him closed in among the hostile things of the forest. He was very wakeful now and full of energy, some of which he wasted slapping at mosquitoes. They rose in whining droves now that the wind had dropped, and beyond them was a waiting silence.

Raoul crashed on. He was making a great deal of noise, but he did not care. Now and then he stopped to listen in case some body, animal or human, might be following. He heard a great many sounds that sent his heart pounding and his brain hurriedly explaining them away.

The underbrush grew scantier, the trees more huge and thinly spaced. Other sounds broke in upon the silence, in front of him, the gurgling and rushing of water over stones. The sun was down behind the trees; behind him the forest grew dark and full of menace.

Four men stood in the clearing ahead of him. They grew taller and taller as Raoul went forward to them. Each of them wore a different dress. Raoul's eyes traveled from one blaze of rich color to another, coming to rest at last on the man in the center, who was wearing the warrior headdress. This, Raoul thought, watching the wind make every feather come alive, was surely the proudest of all the fantastic head coverings man has devised.

When he grew near enough to see their faces clearly, he drew in his breath; his hands closed nervously; he forced himself to walk a little slower. These were four Indians he had never seen. Their impassive faces, with wise dark eyes above outthrust chins and thin-lipped mouths, disconcerted him.

As he approached within about six feet, the first chief took an abrupt step forward, touched his shoulder with the right hand, and swept the back of it against the ground in front of him. He said no word, looking fixedly at Raoul, who was overcome with discomfort. That sign, he knew, was one of those made only to a chief, a big chief who had accomplished great things for the tribe.

The whole world waited round him while he thought. Then into his mind's mirror flashed a tiny Raoul, bent low, holding his hands between him and the sun. He copied the gesture before he had time to stop himself. A grunt of satisfaction rose around him, composed of many relaxing sighs, released at the same moment, sounding as though they came from one big throat.

The second chief stepped forward, hand extended beneath Raoul's face. Again there was a dreadful silence. This time no helpful picture came to him. Mathieu had said: "Humor them, mon vieux, treat them with respect, as though they were superiors. The English treat them like the savages they are, and that is why they do not like the English and why they like us. What difference does it make, a little politeness? Of course, you must not go too far, and you must comport yourself as a chief *after* your initiation; but before that, humility and politeness."

Desperately he took the hand, put the back of it to his forehead, and waited. There was a deep, unbroken, ominous silence. "I've gone too far," thought Raoul.

The chief freed his hand. All four chiefs turned their backs and marched away. Raoul stood up, dazed. Others, behind him, were moving forward, too. He began to walk rapidly, looking neither right nor left.

It seemed to Raoul that he walked for several hours, following the man in front of him. His eyes ached from peering for a safe footing. The back of his neck was scorched, and he was bitten in great welts by the mosquitoes.

Actually it was a very short time before they came to a stretch of water. This was an inland lake that Raoul did not recognize.

Rock formations stood out in it; water lilies grew in great patches. In the middle was an island.

There were canoes at the water's edge, and Indians waiting in them. Now Raoul recognized Hamogom, Neloo, and others, grinning there. He was pushed into a canoe with two others; a paddle was put in his hand.

The sun was setting in crimson and mauve. Peach-colored clouds floated above Raoul's head. He dipped his paddle into burnished gold. When he lifted it, the drops ran off in purple and silver loops.

He was watching them, and he did not see how close they were to land until the canoe slid into the beach with a rasping noise. The men behind jumped out, dragged the canoe out of the way of the others gliding up. Raoul stooped to help them.

A soft hood made of skin was thrown over his head. His arms were grasped, and he was led away. He tried to walk steadily forward, showing no emotion before the unseen eyes that were, he knew, scrutinizing his arrival. But the shock of being blindfolded so suddenly was shaking him. A great horror of the dark descended on his shrinking spirit. If they would let him see, he would go anywhere, do anything; but this—this was impossible. He drew in his breath as his foot struck against something soft and horrible. In another moment he must scream and lie down on the ground and give it up, give everything up! He was at the end! But before he could take another breath, the grasp on his arm slackened and left him, the hood was taken from his eyes, he was pushed forward, something fell into place behind him with a soft thud. He was alone.

As soon as he could see, he looked about. He was in a small square room, made or lined with skins and heavy quill decorations in brilliant colors. There were no windows to this room, no fireplace—only a small brazier in the center of the room, which was not lit. There was no furniture, either, except for a couch made of pine wood with a raised head and foot, covered with buffalo and bearskin.

Raoul made for it at once and sat down. His glance traveled about him for signs of the opening or door. He could not find one. The light, now that he was used to it, was dim enough. It came from the roof. There was a space between the walls and ceiling which allowed light and air to enter.

The ceiling was painted like the sky, with stars and moon.

Only, when he peered more closely, he saw that it was not paint, but quill work; and he marveled. He had never seen such beautiful examples, such rich coloring. He was too tired to look further. Taking off his outer clothes, he laid them on the biggest buffalo skin, carefully. Hidden eyes were probably watching him. He remembered Mathieu's advice and stood in the center of the room before lying down, raising his arms above his head, palm turned inwards. He commended himself to Quitche Manitou in a clear voice. Then he lay down; and after a few moments of uneasily turning his head to look for the invisible opening, he sank into sleep.

CHAPTER XXVII

HAMOGOM came in the morning to prepare Raoul for initiation. He put a hood about his eyes and took him to the sweat house. As soon as he was allowed to look, Raoul saw that this was a low tent, covered with skins and heavy cloths which cut off all air from entering it.

Hamogom stripped him in the doorway and pushed him in, alone, with instructions. Raoul sat down by a huge stone jar filled with water. Presently others, whom he could hear outside busy with firewood and rocks, began to roll in heavy heated boulders, one by one, beneath the opening flap.

Raoul poured the cold water from the jar onto these as they appeared. A hot, stifling steam rose as water met stone. It filled the air in a damp cloud. Raoul stayed there, almost unable to breathe, faithfully dowsing each stone as it rolled in, drinking fistfuls from the jar to stimulate the sweat which was pouring down his body.

At length, when he felt that he must die unless he could get air into his lungs, the stones stopped coming. This was his signal. He dashed out and raced to the river bank. It was quite close to him. He reached it and plunged in.

The delicious coolness of the stream set his nerves tingling, soothed his pores, and made him feel stronger than he had ever felt.

But Hamogom was shouting from the shore. Reluctantly Raoul came out of the water. Hamogom seized him, blindfolded him again, and flung him down. He felt himself lifted and carried away. Presently he was put down again, on a bed or table. Three pairs of hands began to rub him expertly with bear grease and oil. Raoul gave himself up to the rubbing and tried to relax. So far, so good. The rest of the initiation might not be so pleasant.

When he was very nearly asleep, the rubbing stopped. Footsteps came toward the place where he was lying. They came slowly, heavily, and there was perfect silence round them. Raoul felt the hair on his scalp tingle and the back of his neck go cold.

A deep voice began to speak to him. The words were spoken impressively. It reminded Raoul, fleetingly, of the voice of the old Bishop chanting his mass. Though it spoke in Micmac, he seemed to have no difficulty in understanding. All that was said to him was said behind the language it was spoken in, behind words, even, so that his brain received it in a series of pictures or flashes of "this is true; this is the meaning." He knew Micmac and Malisite as well as Dahinda had been able to teach him, but not well enough to understand long flowing passages like these. Yet now he knew. The voice was asking him if he were wavering, if he would be blood brother to Nessamaquij and lead the Malisites. If he would go forward through the rites, if he would carry the sakamoundel steadily. . . . If not, he might retire now.

He saw himself, a small, deserted, disgraced figure—the white man whose courage failed. He saw Madame de Freneuse measuring him against her husband, and he remembered something else. . . .

There was a silence. Raoul said slowly:

"It is my wish to be a chief."

Immediately he was turned upon his face. A sharp, unbearable pain seared through his back, between his shoulders. He gasped but did not cry out. The pain was terrible. A gush of warm blood ran down his back. He imagined a great gaping hole; from the pain it seemed immense. Another searing agony went through him, a little to the left of the first, and more warm streams flowed. Now he knew what it was. He forced himself to lie there without moving. Above all, he must not move nor make a sound while they were fastening the wedge. L'Abbě Elizée had once described to him a ceremony among the Malisites—it must be that. He felt like fainting from the pain and the uncertainty. A terrible sick loneliness came upon him. Why was he here among these unseen torturers? Who were they? What would they do to him? Had something unforeseen gone wrong? Was Mathieu there? Had Mathieu, perhaps, betrayed him? A subtle way to take revenge. . . . But no, Mathieu was good; one knew that when one once got down to it.

An intolerable longing swamped him, to roll over, to snatch the bandage from his eyes, at least to see; but before he could move a muscle, someone drove a sharp stake through the two holes, a great yell went up which drowned his shriek, and left him still quivering, but silent, waiting.

A rawhide rope was being fastened to the wedge and to the ceiling.

Somebody stepped forward with a medicine bag. He placed it in Raoul's hand.

"Sing to the Great Spirit."

They hoisted him to the top of the room till he dangled four feet from the ground. Then they spun him round and round, faster and faster, with all his weight hanging from the hole in his back.

"Sing! Sing!"

Raoul could think of nothing, nothing but a vast gray space with pain in it. He was fast losing consciousness. The more he twirled, the further he was sinking into dim emptiness.

They called again:

"Sing to the Great Spirit."

He opened his mouth. It seemed to him that he had sung before, somewhere, some other where, and differently. A moan came out, a long ascending moan. Faster and faster he swung, and the pain rose up in a red slashing wall and fell on him. It towered and sank; it was alive. It was the biggest thing alive; biggest of everything, and red and gray.

It held him like a catapult, and like a catapult it shot him from his body into space. His body was still singing down below, but he was free and could look down on it.

He saw a circle of grave medicine men in full regalia, with deerskins and bearskins down their backs, standing round a small, black, swinging body that was his. They carried, each man in his hands, a wooden mallet, painted like an ax and having feathers hanging from it. They were dancing.

Raoul saw them grow smaller as he rose into high space.

He went to a place where there were many animals. The door of their tepee was guarded by a buffalo. He turned Raoul round, pressed the animal's hairy head in the middle of his back, with just the round tips of the little horns touching the two holes. Then he let him in.

The animals were sitting in a circle, smoking the pipe. They looked at Raoul in silence. Then a crow got up.

"Oh, the crow, our Father,
He is all in all,
Oh, our Father Crow!
A e-yo he-ye he-ye yo!"

The crow stood in the middle. He was the messenger of the Great Spirit, black as black paint and meaning good. Around him rose the Arapo and Pawnee warriors, dancing the spirit dance together although they were not of the same tribe. Because they knew the wisdom of the crow, they were together here; and other savages danced with them.

(6) "Ah, now my spirit stirreth
With the coming of the nightfall.
Caw-caw, like the crow I cry,
Caw-caw, like the crow I cry.
All the night we shall wait for the star,
Till the star riseth here."

"What is my name?" said the crow. Raoul could not think of his name.
"What do I do?"
"You fly with us to the star," Raoul said.
It was true talk, and so he passed the crow.
Then the dog got up. He was painted for the feast, with a stripe of red down the back and red on the jaw. He growled and yelped at Raoul.
"What, then, am I?"
Raoul did not know.
Dakota Indians got up and danced. They wished good eating to the dog. They danced the Young-Dog-Dance song.
"What do I do?"
"You bay at the moon and the stars. Man's friend are you."
It was true talk, and so he passed the dog.
The bear rose up. He had wonderful power, obtained from the sun. He was wearing Mother Corn and Father Hawk. Pawnees and other tribes, and the very great Bear Society rose with him, dancing. They danced the Song-of-the-Spirit dance, "Kehare Katzaru."
"What, then, am I?"
Raoul did not know.
"What do I do?"
"You give the power of the rising sun to warriors. You make

·[117]·

them conquer. There is honey on your tongue and on your paws, honey of the truth."

It was true talk, and so he passed the bear.

The otter rose, with the morning and the evening star beside him. From before his feet went the pathway of departed spirits, parting the heavens into east and west. Otter carried the sacred bundle.

"What, then, am I?"

Raoul did not know.

"What do I do?"

"You bring the messages of wisdom. You teach medicine and the properties of herbs, roots, and all that is above and below the ground."

It was true talk, and so he passed the otter.

Tirara's bird, the eagle, rose. He held two eggs, one on each claw. His feathers were pure white and black. Behind him rose a multitude of dancers, young and old.

"What, then, am I?"

Raoul did not know.

"What do I do?"

"You show the twofold path. You have two eggs, one woman and one man. Your feathers are in two colors, half and half. You are the two; the day and the night, the left hand that beckons and the right hand that strikes, the good and the evil are you."

It was true talk, and so he passed the eagle.

The frog rose up and croaked:

"What, then, am I?"

Behind him rose the whole Algonquin race. They danced the dance of the changing form.

Raoul thought he knew the answer, but he was not very sure. He decided that he would not risk half knowledge, so he said:

"I do not know."

"What do I do?"

"You live in three elements and have three forms."

It was true talk, and so he passed the frog.

Then there was a silence. Dancers disappeared. Raoul watched the animals grow large and small in the smoke from the pipe.

Out of the mist came Father Hawk and spread his wooden wings.

"What, then, am I?"

"You are he who sees and who can heal. You are power and knowledge. Facing you, I face the east. You are my wings."

Then Raoul and the hawk together rose above the clouds. They went to the spirit land and found the spirit camping grounds. They knocked on the tepee door; they went through the hole in the door of the lodge, and Raoul saw splendor. Raoul heard a voice. It said to him before he fainted and fell downward through the stars: "Ruwerera."

And this, though it was not a word of his language, he took to be his word. Star of Evening, Star of Morning, or Father Sun—any or all of these this word might mean.

CHAPTER XXVIII

WHEN Raoul came back to his body, it was lying between two men who were pouring oil upon the pain between his shoulders. He moved, and they helped him to sit up.

The first thing he saw, when he was able to see, was Mathieu de Freneuse grinning at him. The medicine man was speaking:

"You have passed the tests to be made a chief. For a white man, you did well. But you could not name the very olden animals. You did no more than enter the tepee in the spirit encampment. You could not smoke the pipe with those within. You are chief, but you are not so far along the road to Kuluskape as are the Malisites."

He paused for a long time. Raoul sat still. He was weary and exhausted, but the pain had left him and he felt at peace. He felt also proud of himself, in a queer way, as though he had come to a second maturity. At any rate, he knew now that he could endure great pain.

The medicine man continued:

"You have taken Father Hawk to be your master. You must follow him. He will bring you by the road of ruwerera when your wings leave earth. Father Hawk has guided many of us."

Raoul stirred, prompted by Mathieu's expression. He held out his hand above the earth and thanked the medicine man in a weak voice. He greeted all the Malisites as brethren and foretold that victory would be to the white men and the red men fighting together against their common foe, the cruel and ferocious Iroquois, the treacherous Englishmen. The Indians shouted when he had finished speaking, and the dancing began.

Everyone took part in this, squaws and children, too, leaping in circles. Mathieu de Freneuse helped Raoul to his feet, putting an arm about him and guiding him in the shuffling steps of the fire dance.

"Soon," he whispered, "they stop all this, and we can take a woman. Look around you. Which one would you like?"

Raoul considered the question. He had known, of course, that it would be presented and had accepted the answer, but now that the moment was upon him he hesitated.

The whole subject of sex was in a tangle. When he was sixteen, it was simple enough; he slept with the village girls and was physically in love with Vanina. But since the voyage to New France and his life at Freneuse, the hardships, the danger, the constant toil and backbreaking exercise—perhaps, too, something in his hopeless passion for Madame de Freneuse—had damped down the fires and kept his urges low. True, there were moments, particularly in the long winter days and nights when he was restless, nervous, and ready to boil over with unexpected temper. It was chiefly to correct this and to make his relationship with Madame de Freneuse easier for them both that he had at last turned his mind to the Indian women or, more accurately, his body to them. Mathieu had always urged him to. Mathieu had scores of women and several children scattered through the woods. That was a different proposition. Mathieu ought not to turn to squaws—he had a wife.

"But I am glad he does! I could not have stayed at Freneuse if Mathieu and Louise . . ."

There were times, he knew; but Mathieu usually . . . "Enfin!" he dismissed the thought, impatiently.

Nessamaquij's daughter detached herself from the dance and came to Mathieu's side. He sighed as he slipped his arm beneath her. Raoul had a sudden flash of insight into Mathieu's mind.

"He is not happy," he thought. "Of course not, the poor devil! It is the same for him as for me, only worse. He is her husband, and everybody blames him for the marriage being a failure. They talk about his Indian women and shake their heads and say he isn't worthy. They pity her. Perhaps he's made his infidelities so public on purpose, to protect her from any blame? I wonder if he knows who the other is? And if he does, why he is so nice to me?"

Mathieu pushed the girl a little aside and said to Raoul:

"Woboek says Nessamaquij's niece is the one for you. She's just coming, this side of the fire—see?"

Raoul looked and shrugged.

Mathieu laughed.

"You know, mon vieux," he said, tossing his head over a broad shoulder, "I've never seen a young man so remarkable for sobriety! Is it genuine, or posed?"

He laid his hand on Raoul's shoulder with a sudden friendly squeeze.

"I want things to be right for you. I'm fond of you; you are part of Freneuse. Louise has been much happier since you came; and I, too. It is a great thing to have someone who can talk of books and music with her, and look after the children, and be gay and young—but not too young. There are few men, I suppose, who could trust a young man about the place, as I do you; but then Louise is not an ordinary woman. Other men have to be careful with their wives."

He broke off for a moment, and Raoul stared at the dancers, desperately hoping that Mathieu would not take him too far into his confidence.

"One hopes, of course, that you will marry," Mathieu continued, a little shyly, "but not yet. Not on the pay of a militia lieutenant and the pocket money for a tutor! That would not keep a beaver in his dam. And you are much too young, to my way of thinking, to be caught by matrimony. One of the great things about New France, mon vieux, is that no one can enforce the marriage laws against us. There"—he swept his arm about him and brought it to rest again on the girl's shoulder—"is our way of escape!"

Raoul nodded.

"So what remains?" Mathieu pursued, determined to do his duty to the boy and get it over. "Hands off the farmers' women, and there are no peasants here. We are all too interdependent to fool with one another's wives and daughters; and even if it weren't disastrous, in a small and struggling colony, to risk one's neighbor's friendship, you, being, as I was, virtuously brought up, would not want to. . . . No, don't answer that one, let it rest! But one is not a monk, n'est-ce-pas? So nature has provided a perfectly delightful solution for us colonists, in the Indian women. We do them an honor, they do us a service, and nobody expects anything beyond the moment's pleasure. It *is* a pleasure—they are happy animals. Look on it that way, Raoul, when you have scruples."

"Oh, I haven't scruples," said Raoul a little ruefully.

Before his mind rose a sudden startling vision of Madame de Freneuse lying naked on a couch. He caught his breath desperately, but not before the pitiless imagination finished the portrait in a shimmering rose, gave to the familiar neck and shoulders and to the laughing, enigmatical face, the glory of the unknown rest. As Raoul watched, fascinated, bending over that glowing delight, a shadow stepped between, and a man wearing a naval uniform, with straight back and gallant shoulders, insolently shouldered Raoul's watching self aside and flung himself full length upon the vision, which was blotted out; the two intertwined figures revolved intolerably for a second, and dissolved into a spot behind Raoul's eyelids.

He rose and made for the dancing figures, dragging one of them a little roughly aside, snatching at the jug of spirits which another held. In two moments he had taken a long draught and pulled Nessamaquij's niece from the crowd. Then the dancing began again, wilder than ever. The men leaped and shouted and flung themselves about in frenzied ecstasy; couple after couple dropped off, and made for the woods, laughing together as they ran.

Raoul took the young, dancing savage and slipped aside with her into the darkness.

He found himself thinking as he threw her down:

"She has to have all the discomfort, twigs and stubble in her back. . . . What a good thing to be a man!"

There were other reasons why it was good, too; and now that he tasted his first experience with a savage, he wondered vaguely why he had delayed so long.

The girl beneath him smelt of pine cones, and fire water. It was exciting, the darkness, the place, his initiation, the laughter all about him from others frankly enjoying themselves in this perfectly natural ending to the feast.

"Ha!" said Raoul, gathering the eager young creature beneath him into a firmer hold.

CHAPTER XXIX

RAOUL was carried home in the morning by grinning Malisites. Madame de Freneuse, who remembered her husband's initiation, had a bed ready for him and a soothing tisane for him to drink. She had also prepared some poultices for his back and was waiting with them when he arrived.

Raoul, somnolent and exhausted, had strength enough to smile at her concern. He felt very proud of himself and opened one eye now and then to see if she were taking in the extent of his wounds.

"Poor boy," she said as she bandaged his back. "What barbarians they are! Did he do well?"

Mathieu, helping her on the other side, said: "Well enough. They were pleased with him. Nessamaquij gave him permission to recruit another platoon. This should help us quite a bit in the settlement. They gave him Nessamaquij's sister, too."

Raoul stirred and tried to turn over. He wanted to bury his face at this cold mention of the night.

"Lie still," said Madame de Freneuse. "You will chafe your back."

There was a little smile at the corner of her mouth that showed she understood the emotions passing through him.

"That was good," she said demurely. "Will she be coming to live with us, as Dahinda did?"

Raoul squirmed. He looked reproachfully at Madame de Freneuse, who gave him a maternal pat and asked wickedly:

"Nessamaquij's sister? Which is she? I don't remember a virgin in that family. I must remember to look for her next time I go in the woods."

Raoul groaned and shut his eyes. Mathieu de Freneuse said:

"Seems to be a bit exhausted. Perhaps he had better sleep."

Madame de Freneuse nodded, and they both stole out. Raoul, who had been hoping desperately to get a word with her, groaned again and presently called out her name. Dahinda, passing from the kitchen, heard and hurried in. She offered him tisane and patted his pillow; she smiled and hung over him, while Raoul impatiently tossed on his side. The sight of her bronze face and black eyes reminded him of the other laughing, lithe savage he had crushed against him, and filled him with a mixed emotion of remorse and pride. He had been unfaithful to Madame de Freneuse, which disturbed and distressed him even though she had urged him to be initiated and he had done it for her sake.

Up to that moment he had believed she did not know about the savage woman whom he must take, and he had hoped to keep it from her. He would languish, deriving the utmost attention from her for his wounds. Now the picture changed. She knew about Nessamaquij's sister; it stirred no feeling in her breast, other than mild interest. "I must look out for her when I go into the woods." That was unbearable! Now if he tried to arouse her love or her compassion, she would say: "You have an Indian woman. You do not need me." Worse, she would never believe that it was possible for him to love one woman so desperately, so hungrily, and to sleep with another. Women did not understand such things, especially goddesses like Madame de Freneuse.

Dahinda still hung over him.

"Mister Raoul now a man!" she said, and laughed her low laugh.

"Get out," Raoul said, closing his eyes. "Get out of here."

He would make her believe somehow. He would say that the reason he refused so long to be initiated was not from any fear of the savages . . . fear? Why look at what he had undergone without a moan, without a tremor even! Certainly not fear! But his desire to keep himself for her. "I knew," he would say, "that one must take an Indian woman. That is why I did not wish to be initiated, Louise. There is no woman for me but you. Now I have made the supreme sacrifice. I have given up even my own fidelity to an ideal." Yes, that would be the thing to say. But an uneasy, feverish notion of his mind made him hear Madame de Freneuse answer: "Supreme sacrifice? For one who has just made the supreme sacrifice, you look remarkably well and full of life. You have never looked better, Raoul. You look superb."

He frowned and shook his head. That would not do. Confound

Mathieu and his wife. Between them they had made him look ridiculous. It was true he had never felt better, but for this pain in his back. It was true that it had been a wonderful night! He smiled, threw up his arm, and went to sleep.

Madame de Freneuse, spinning in the salon by the open lattice, with the breeze from the forest wandering through her hair, was thinking:

"Now, perhaps, I shall have a little peace. My love will be glad we have not had to send away his nephew, as I thought we would have to do. He will lose himself in the forest, with his Indian, and I will have the best of him. He can be sweet at times."

Mathieu de Freneuse, watching her from the doorway, thought:

"How cool she looks! She is like some drink from the depths of the earth. A drink with a star in it. I love her so. My little dark head. A crow's wing, or a blue-black shadow on the hills. The hills lie there like a naked woman, like Louise. Oh, I mustn't start this, so early in the morning. Mustn't start this at any time. Louise. In that bright dress she reminds me of a tulip. There used to be some in the Bishop's garden. I wonder if they would do well at Freneuse? I might send to France, when I am writing, for the roses. It will be good to have roses, as well as useful plants, and for a change. The fruit trees have come on this year. No fruit for me."

"Well," he said aloud, "the boy's got one thing over. It's an advantage to be blood brother to such a well-known chief as Nessamaquij. He will be more use to me. It was never much of a man's job, tutoring the children. Not my idea of things at his age."

"You were a cadet in the garrison at Kebec."

"Yes," he said, pleased that she remembered what he had told her once. "And you, I suppose, were a little slip of a thing in a convent. I think I remember you."

"No, you don't, Mathieu; you had gone away by then. You only came back afterward."

Her voice faltered on the last word, and he looked at her sharply. "Afterward?"

"After I had married and was a widow."

"Yes."

A strained silence fell between them. Madame de Freneuse got up as though she needed something. He watched her for a moment. Then he said:

"I am going over to the mill. I'll have my meal there."

He bowed. She dipped to him in a curtsy, though they were alone, but she did not look up from her work to see him go.

CHAPTER XXX

RAOUL woke up early, on a day in June, and went to the window. His room was a partition in the attic just under the roof. He could see the sun on apple blossoms and the wind laughing through clover, across a field and down the hillside, till it ran between the trees of the forest and rippled on the river in the early-morning light.

The wind's mood decided him. Snatching up a cloak, he let himself cautiously out of the window and with the help of a rosebush climbed toward the ground. He passed Madame de Freneuse's window, underneath his own, a little to one side. By craning to the left he could look in. She was lying with her dark hair toward him, the pillow on the floor and one hand clutching at a ribbon on her shoulder, which in her sleep she thought was the sheet. He smiled idiotically at her attitude, thinking how annoyed she would be if she knew that the sheet was at the bottom of her bed and she was all uncovered to his view. "Darling!" he muttered, and his heart began to pump.

A rustle behind him startled him so that he nearly lost his balance and fell. A hummingbird darted into the creepers, fluttering by his ear. Madame de Freneuse stirred, and Raoul hastily went on, dropping to the ground and running off, trailing the cloak behind him, glad of the clean air.

He walked across the grass lightly, past the courtyard, wells, sleeping barns, orchards, to where the stream ran through the woods, falling in rapids half a mile away. Here it was deep and even-flowing. Raoul plunged in.

The water was virgin-cold. It sprang against his naked body in a wall of icy strength. He tingled all over, gasped, and swam against the current, upstream.

There was a brook to his left, tumbling over shallow rocks in a great hurry to join the main stream. Raoul swam to its opening, waded up its miniature falls, found a submerged boulder covered with moss, lay down against it, clasped it with his hands, and let the water pound and beat upon his shoulders, over his hips, against his legs, and so to the stream.

The force of the water was surprising and soothing. It massaged him from head to foot with joyful thumps and bumps and steady pressure. While it worked on him, it sang; and Raoul, lying with his face to the foam, began to sing, too.

It was a tuneless little song about Madame de Freneuse, sleeping, and the goodness of being alive, and the general well-being he felt in every nerve, the excellent thing it was to have an Indian woman so that he could be free to love Madame de Freneuse without morbidity. He laughed at that, because it struck him as funny. The water laughed back, spouting merrily over him, sounding a deeper note. Raoul turned on his back and looked up at the sky.

Now he was cold and wanted to go out. He waded back to the main stream and swam to the other side. As he clambered up the bank, naked and tingling, with the morning light burnishing his brown skin, he saw Mathieu de Freneuse walking toward the woods and hailed him with a shout.

Mathieu shouted back and pointed in front of him. Following his outstretched hand, Raoul saw a brown figure dart from the forest, followed by another and another and another. They were all carrying packages and bundles, and some of them had guns. Raoul drew his cloak about him and waited while the procession filed past Mathieu de Freneuse, saluting him with nods and smiles and grunts of admiration and affection. Mathieu de Freneuse was well liked by the Malisites. At the tail of the procession came de Villebon, carried in a hammock, lolling and smoking a calumet.

He sat up when he saw Mathieu de Freneuse, and waved to him. There was no love lost between the two men, but they did their best to conceal it. De Villebon thought the four brothers insufferably conceited and suspected them of finding himself tedious (as they did) and of laughing at him behind his back. Worse than this, he knew that they had made a good deal of their money in trade with the Indians and that even now, when the law was stricter than it had ever been, they still did a good deal of trade. That, in itself, might not have been so bad; it was no use blinding oneself to the fact that all the new French traded with the Indians whenever they could. But Mathieu de Freneuse and his brothers gave the Malisites such bad prices and drove such hard bargains that the Indians, in revenge, traded with the English, instead, and were disaffected and disloyal to the Governor, de Villebon, himself.

Moreover, he had never liked the de Freneuses as much as he had liked the de Chauffours; it was a real sorrow to him when Madame de Chauffours died, and one of his most tiresome tales was the story of the saving of the Chauffours seigneury by the wit of Madame de Chauffours when a large English force marched against Fort Nashwaak. Monsieur de Chauffours, as usual, was on his boat, and Madame de Chauffours wrote such a disarming and witty appeal to the English commanding officer, and pinned it to the door, that he was touched and left the place standing, while the de Chauffours children hid with their mother in the woods near by. Moreover, Madame de Chauffours had paid attentions to him on de Bonaventure's boat, the first time that he met her; she was an estimable person, a woman one could sentimentally respect—not as alluring, perhaps, as her sister, but . . . but . . . ah, well . . .

He stepped out of the hammock and embraced Mathieu de Freneuse ceremoniously, while Raoul cut through the woods to warn them at the house.

CHAPTER XXXI

D E VILLEBON'S arrival turned Freneuse into a camp. The Governor, though a bit of a bore, was no fool and probably knew more about the workings of the savage mind than any other commander in New France. He was fresh from two successful campaigns, every detail of which he described to the wearied hearers.

"Why is it," Raoul asked Mathieu de Freneuse, in a moment when they were alone, "that the Governor makes even the most blood-curdling excitement sound like an ordinance read out by the Procureur?"

"It's probably due to his worthiness," Mathieu said, "He's far gone in worth. You know, I don't think when he was initiated—and he has been, several times, into several tribes—the evening was culminated. I am sure he didn't get as far as that. And I rather think café au lait was drunk, instead of the fire water you lapped up. Still, we mustn't hold it against him, tedious though it is; he's an able man, and if he says—and he does say, seventy times a day—that he thinks we're in for trouble, then we probably are in for trouble. I've taken the men off the fields and put them to digging a trench around the palisades, and another well. Thirsty things, sieges; though, of course, water's a tame sort of drink and, when once it gets going, we can't be sure of it. . . . I mean, if it runs from a stream or anything, the Iroquois would be likely to poison it. Dear me, I am catching Villy's longwindedness." And he shook his head.

Raoul looked at him affectionately.

"You're an unaccountable person," he said shyly. "You've been gloomy and reserved all winter."

"Reserved for what?"

"Oh, just reserved."

"And don't you think that may be just the reason I have been gloomy?" said Mathieu wickedly. "Hanging around reserved for nothing?"

Raoul blushed and rushed on:

"And now when the one man you always say depresses you to tears turns up for a long stay with us, and turns your place into his headquarters and a military camp, you brighten up and become the wine of the party."

"Perhaps I've found a new and dusky maiden."

"You haven't been to the woods in an age. I've noticed that."

"It seems to me, Raoul, my friend, that you are altogether too observant; but there are phenomena, such as my moods, that no one, not even myself, can begin to fathom. So I would take it all off the mind, in case of strain or anything, and devote yourself to digging. Villy wants a trench around the cows."

"That was dug yesterday," said Raoul, sighing.

Mathieu caught him by the neck and ran him a few steps across the room, where they collided with the children gathered round Dahinda, who was carrying wine and cake to the Governor's room.

Mathieu stopped her and took a glass and a cake, broke the cake in half as an afterthought, and gave a piece to Raoul.

"Here's your tutor, cabbages," he said. "Take him away and do your worst."

He strode on, in the direction of the mill, and Raoul found himself being pulled and pushed in various ways at once. Denise was clamoring at one ear and Jean-Marie at the other.

Over their heads he saw Madame de Freneuse coming slowly to the door, carrying a bowl of eggs thoughtfully before her. He stared at her for a moment, stared past her, caught her by the arm.

Her husband was running back through the courtyard, shouting and waving. Two of Nessamaquij's Malisites ran beside him, in their war paint. Raoul's heart sank. Everyone turned and stood waiting. Gervais shrank against Madame de Freneuse, and the other children stopped their clamoring.

"Tiens, tiens," said de Villebon, appearing at the door of his room as though summoned by the situation. "A week earlier than I expected. One of you boys cut along and ring the chapel bell."

"It may not be that," faltered Madame de Freneuse.

"War paint? and scalps?" said the Governor. "At least it can't

·[131]·

have been a surprise attack. Those two men have thirty scalps or more. Look at them!"

Gervais hid his face.

The runners reached them, and Mathieu said:

"The attack! They'll be here in an hour. Nessamaquij is dead."

"An hour?" De Villebon said. "Are you sure? Why not before?"

"They have stopped to make the fires. They are angry that we fought. They will amuse themselves with the prisoners," said Nessamaquij's son.

Gervais put his hands to his ears. Before his brain went pictures, sharp and terrible and endless. He felt sick. Madame de Freneuse stroked his head with one hand, while with the other she mechanically made the gesture of welcome to the Indians. The chapel bell began to ring in a most extraordinary jangle, now tolling, now pealing, now hiccuping wildly. Robert and Jean-Mathieu had taken the Governor at his word and were merrily pulling the ropes, which in normal times they were never allowed to touch. Up and down they went, leaping half up the rope and swinging from it, kicking and sprawling, while the noise clanged out above them across the field to the forest. The bell had come from France, and was true of note and highly prized by Abbé Elizée.

"I wish," panted Robert, swinging round, "we could do this every day. I think a siege is fun."

Jean-Mathieu, hauling in the slack, looked up at him.

"What's siege?" he inquired.

The door below them opened. Mathieu de Freneuse's head appeared in the trap.

"That's right. Go on ringing. Some of the men are fishing. See if you can bring them back. And here"—he reached in his pockets and threw them a bit of chocolate, in a long thin twist—"chew this."

They let go of the ropes and the bell protested madly.

"I suppose," said Mathieu de Freneuse to himself as he went down again, "I should have kept that for later, in case . . . But when one is that age, chocolate is more than—more than a woman or a night of love. And there may be no nights for me, no chocolate for them. . . . The Iroquois . . . Ciel, what a barbarous country this is for a man to raise his children in! Ohé!" he shouted to some Indians who were taking their places on the palisade. "Wait a minute for me."

CHAPTER XXXII

AFTER the third day even Robert and Jean-Mathieu thought a siege poor fun. The children were kept in the house; forbidden to go near door or window, although they were heavily shuttered; forbidden to light a candle to play by, in case the siege should be long and the candles run out; forbidden to eat all they wanted; forbidden to drink water without having it given them by their mother from the water jugs which had been filled before the Iroquois came; forbidden to bother with questions. . . . There was nothing they could do.

Men were shouting and fighting outside; arrows whirled through the air, falling plop against the walls and on the stones of the courtyard. The savages howled, and the wounded screamed. The Governor's soldiers kept up intermittent firing. Now and then the door would burst open and a man stagger in to get more shot, to get some water, to have a wound attended to.

Inside, the children sat in darkness while Gervais told stories or played to them. He was quite patient, now, when they made mistakes in the music and didn't remember the notes. He laughed and said:

"Let's try again."

The first day of the siege Jean-Marie de Chauffours had started up.

"Let's see if we can't fight, do something, help the men. I'm sick of being mewed up here among the babies. . . . Come on, Gervais —and Robert, too."

The three had rushed to find Madame de Freneuse, who was rolling a bandage with Dahinda's help.

She looked up when they came in.

"Yes," she said, "I think you all can help. Jean-Marie, you can load the shot and powder into the horns and clean the pistols. Robert, you can help me with the wounded; you can hold the water and the scissors and help Dahinda keep the man steady if he's French. The Indians stay steady, even when one is drawing out an arrow head. Aren't they wonderful? And you, Gervais," she continued as the others darted off, "you can help me most of all."

She put her hand beneath his chin and raised his downcast face to hers.

"Helping isn't all blood and noises, dear. I need someone patient and understanding to be with the children. Someone responsible, whom I can trust. Will you do that for me, Gervais? Will you stay with the children and look after them?"

"Mother . . ."

"Yes?"

"Don't be . . . Don't be ashamed of me!"

"Dearest, there isn't any reason to be ashamed of you."

"Oh yes, there is! I'm not brave like your husband"—Gervais never called him Father—"not even as brave as the children. Robert and Jean-Mathieu ran to ring the bell; I didn't go. I keep on seeing things, over and over in my head. They stop me from running; they stop me from doing anything."

"I know, dear, but there's a courage besides the courage that Robert and Jean-Mathieu and the others have. After all, Gervais, perhaps they run so quickly and do so well, outwardly, just because they can't see things, as you can, in your head. Dear, the greatest artists, the greatest musicians, everyone, or at least some of the ones, who have left the world better for being in it haven't all been what's known as brave men of action; but they have been brave in a far better way—even if they stuffed their ears and ran from noises. There is a courage of the soul, Gervais. I'd rather you had that than anything; and it's because I think you have it, more perhaps than any of us have, that I'm asking you to look after the children. So run, dear, while I get on with this. And remember, the siege will be over, and the Iroquois beaten, and even a time will come when all the Iroquois are beaten out of New France, and perhaps a time when there is no more danger here; but there will never come a time when there is no more danger in the world of real things, the world of the spirit, and never a time when courage of soul is not the highest, the most lovable, thing to have!"

Gervais took her hand and kissed it. She busied herself with the bandages. Then suddenly she looked at him and said:

"I know what it is to be a coward, too."

"Mother! You're the bravest person I ever knew! Your husband says so; we all say so; everyone knows that!"

"But I wasn't always, Gervais. I was frightened of life, when I bore you. Courage of soul is a thing one has to acquire by degrees. You have a great deal of it now, gotten since you were a child. You're not a child, Gervais; you're a boy, and a very fine musician. Now go back; and if I don't come, put them all to bed and don't imagine too much. Keep that great gift for the time that you'll write music."

So Gervais had come back and had taken charge ever since, inventing ways to keep them all amused and patient, preventing squabbles, and distracting their attention when the arrows flew thicker or the shrieks grew worse. Now and then he saw in his head what would happen if the doors burst open and the Iroquois came in. After one such vision, he went out again to the room where Robert and Jean-Marie were loading guns. He took a heavy pistol from the table and a little heap of bullets.

"I know how to shoot," he said to himself, with grim mouth. "If the Iroquois come, I will shoot us all. I will begin with the youngest; I'll line them up against the wall, pretend it's a game, shoot true—through the heart." . . .

He put the pistol down beside him when he came back, and said:

"Do you remember when Abbé Elizée used to drill us as they drilled when he was young in the seminary?"

"Yes."

"And do you remember how Father—your uncle, Jean-Mathieu and Paul-Marie—used to exercise us?"

"Yes."

"Well, let's play a game then, mixing up the two. When I say 'One,' you run against the wall, in a long line—you, Denise, and you, Jeanne, at each end; the others in the middle. When I say 'Two,' you shut your eyes and keep them shut no matter what noises may go on. The one who opens his eyes loses. Now, then!"

Finally he had them so that he could poke them, make them scream, bang a stick loudly, and they didn't move.

"That will do," he said to himself, and went to find his mother.

"Mother," he said, "have you a moment?"

"Well, just one. What is it? Has something happened?"

·[135]·

"No, but I wanted you to know," he gulped. "Mother, if the Iroquois do get in ——"

"They won't, Gervais; they're being beaten."

"I know, but if they do . . . I want you to listen. . . . You needn't worry about the children. I have it all arranged. I'll kill them. I've practiced it so they won't be frightened, and it won't hurt—too much."

"Darling . . ."

"You trusted them to me. I just want you to know the Iroquois won't get them, ever!"

"That's why I trusted you, Gervais; but I think it's very brave . . ."

"It didn't seem to be as bad as other things—as bad as seeing in my head what would happen if I didn't kill them."

"Don't start too soon," said Madame de Freneuse a little shakily. "I'll come to you if . . . if anything should happen, and we'll look after things together. . . . Look!"

She showed him a little pistol hidden beneath her dress, and a knife beside it.

"Also, if there's time, I have a poison here. Your father, your real father, Gervais, gave it to me years ago. But we are talking non-sense; for the Governor will beat the Iroquois with his soldiers, and we will not need any of the things we have. . . . Go back now, dear."

Gervais smiled and walked back slowly, thinking: "She is proud of me!"

CHAPTER XXXIII

ON THE eighth day of the siege twenty of de Villebon's men were dead and seventy wounded, the Malisites, under Raoul, had lost almost as many, and the militia was cut in half. The Iroquois showed no signs of letting up; on the contrary, they pressed their attacks one after another, keeping the weary men continually alert. Food was short; the water supply was getting very low. The wounded groaned and tossed from the fever of their wounds. Everyone was haggard; everyone was dirty—water could not be used for washing, only for cooking and drinking. The children were pale and listless from continual confinement in one room, and the howling of the savages was getting on raw nerves. Madame de Freneuse, looking in on them, remembered suddenly that she had set some cheese in the dairy, the day before the siege, and that there were sacks of corn in the loft above it.

To get them meant to venture across the courtyard twice, under a flight of arrows. But one might choose one's moment, dodge, and run.

"Children," she said, "do you like baked maize?"

There was still enough fuel, praise St. Anthony! Faces brightened a little; poor cabbages, they were really hungry. She smiled at them and went out. As she peered between the shutters in the hall, Mathieu came from the salon turned into a hospital.

"That man with the poisoned leg will do now, I think," he said. "Perhaps he may not lose it, after all."

"Oh, Mathieu! That is good!"

"Why all this sudden interest in the great outdoors? Not thinking of going out, were you?"

"There is some maize over the dairy, and I think some cheese."

"Cheese! Some savage in Raoul's troop will have stolen it; still, it's worth investigation. Stay here, while I report."

"No. Let me come, too."

He hesitated.

"Please, I must have air or I shall stifle. . . . Oh, listen to them! Aren't they horrible? Why did the bon Dieu make such brutes?"

"Think of them as animals, not men; that helps. But even so, it's pretty foul. Wait! . . . Now!"

They threw open the shutters, slammed them shut, raced across the yard, and were in the doorway of a little outhouse before the flight of arrows rained against the door.

"They must keep their faces close to the palisade," Mathieu said wearily, sitting down on an upturned pail.

"It's nice to see you alone for a bit," he went on more cheerfully. "I had almost forgotten you weren't a nun, or a surgeon, or a soldier; you've been such a mixture of all three. But, then, you always were brave."

"Pretty speeches, Mathieu."

She raised one grimy hand and looked at it with interest.

"If my face looks like the rest of me . . ."

"I praise your soul, your essence; and you think of your face! Dearest, you *are* a woman!"

She shied away and bent down over the cheese.

"It seems to be all right," she said. "Now let's get the corn."

They climbed in silence to the loft and dragged out two big sacks.

"More than I thought there was," she grunted. "Mathieu, how long do you think it will go on?"

"I don't know. There are hundreds of them out there. We may have to run for it."

"Run for it?"

"Half of us create a diversion while the other half escapes. Better half than none. They may set fire to the place any moment now. We can hardly beat them back, wave after wave, all fresh; and we're so tired."

"Why?" she cried. "Why? We only ask to live in peace, to cultivate the fields and clear the woods. We don't interfere with them. Why don't they leave us alone?"

"The English have stirred them up against us, just as we stir the Malisites against them. All for greed. Trade, trade, trade—we think of nothing else. One must be rich nowadays."

"Do we need so much?"

"We don't; but the King does, for his wars and his women."

"Mathieu!"

"High treason. Will you tell de Villebon? It's true, you know."

"I suppose it is. Oh, Mathieu, *must* they shriek so horribly! All the time, all the time!"

"Poor heart! Forget about them; let them howl. Do you know what day this is?"

"Day? Thursday, isn't it?"

"Our wedding anniversary."

There was silence.

"Mathieu, I . . ." she looked at him.

"I understand; I have begun to understand—much better than you think."

He took her fingers to his lips.

"I envy the man who has your heart, and with all mine I regret that our marriage should have . . . I regret the wrong I did you when I married you, in fact."

She looked at him, startled.

"Did you think my idea of marriage with you was to run in the woods?"

"You didn't always run in the woods," she said.

"Oh, my dear! I was young, and greedy, and impulsive, and the high seas deep in love! But I should have seen; I should have known. . . . How could I see, how could I know, Louise?"

"You couldn't. And, Mathieu, the wrong, as you call it, was already done before I married Charles— At least, of course, it wasn't in that way. I mean . . ."

"Thank God for whatever it is you do mean! I've often wondered what I would have done if I had seen and known, right from the beginning. I'm afraid I would have married you just the same, and hung on just as desperately afterward, until even I couldn't pretend to be blind any more. Of course, if I hadn't cared ——"

He squeezed her hand between his arm and his heart.

"And even so, you know," he continued, "I've had great luck. Companionship with you, of any kind, is more than most men ever get—gay, diverting, loyal, brave, and always understanding."

"I don't think I've been that, Mathieu, from all you say!"

"Well, perhaps a little preoccupied."

"I want to tell you who it is. May I?"

"I have hoped you would."

"Pierre de Bonaventure."

"Pauvre choux! You can't have seen him very often."

"Only once, since the beginning."

"And?"

"It was heaven, Mathieu, the reason for all life."

"Thank you for telling me. I am glad you at least had that.

"But he's married," he continued presently; "so that even if I get killed at this siege, as I've rather hoped . . ."

"Mathieu!"

"It won't be as much use as it should be to you."

He tried to speak in a falsely fretful tone, and turned away to hide his emotion; but she put her two hands strongly on his shoulders and pulled him round to her.

"Mathieu, I never gave you any false assurances, did I?"

"Never. The most honest friend a man might have!"

"Then you must believe what I say now."

"Out of generous pity?"

"Out of the naked truth!"

"Naked! My dear," he twinkled, "between us?"

She shook him, laughing.

"Listen. I do want you to hear. You've just said you grew in growth and understanding. Ever since that growth, I've grown, too, in . . . in . . ."

"Be careful," he said, still attempting to joke, while his eyes grew hungry.

"In affection, in warmth toward you, in warm friendship, Mathieu. Tenez, I love you and Gervais next to—next to Pierre."

"Thank you, beloved. You mean Gervais and me, don't you?"

"Do I? Well, perhaps a trifle, because—because *he's* so inadequate in front of life!"

"I know. Well, after this rather exhausting conversation, for which"—he made an exaggerated pas de recule and kissed her hand —"I thank you with all my heart, Madame. Shall we go, rather fast, across the courtyard and see whether Dahinda has succeeded in cooking some of our overlooked moccasins? Passionate avowals always make me hungry."

They grinned at each other, perfectly at ease. Mathieu tucked her stained hand beneath his ragged elbow, and they started to the door.

CHAPTER XXXIV

I'M GLAD we built this so substantially," croaked Madame de Freneuse, "with three rooms downstairs instead of one, and two partitions in the attic. Everybody said it was tempting le bon Dieu, and ostentatious; but I could not have endured this in one room."

It was the seventeenth day of the siege. The Iroquois were attacking with more science, wasting no arrows on stray shots but moving methodically round the palisade; shooting at those who went across the courtyard, especially to the well; building big fires close to the palisade; and several times a night attacking with torches of pine and resin.

"They're waiting for something—English troops, I think," de Villebon croaked back. He was wounded, and rested in the room where the children were. It was the only habitable place in the seigneury. The long hall was filled with wounded, in a groaning restless line; and the dead were heaped in a corner under linen sheets, which came from the big store chest by the bed. They could not bury the dead, except at night; and then it was difficult, not only on account of the risk, but because at all hazards the Iroquois must not know the number of the dying.

Three farmers' wives, Dahinda, and the miller's family moved about the long hall and the kitchen restlessly. The stench and smother were beyond bearing, and always outside the howling and shrieking of the savages mingled with the sound of arrows falling on the roof or against the shuttered windows. The children lay in a corner, too listless to raise their heads.

De Villebon was worried. Most of the food was gone; ammunition would give out, at the rate it was being used; and the reinforcements he expected from Port Royal and Kebec might not arrive before the English enemy. It was better, of course, to fall into English hands than Iroquois'—if they could hold out. He had the satisfaction of knowing that without him and his soldiers Freneuse would have fallen long before, burning to black pulp. That might happen yet, but at least he had done his duty toward the settlers. De Villebon came from a long line of soldiers, governors, ambassadors, and men of state. Somewhere, ingrained in him, was the idea that the King must keep faith with his people, especially his people of New France. He did not like Mathieu de Freneuse or his brothers; but he did like the spirit with which they had interpreted the King's wishes, settled tenants on their lands, built bigger houses than any others in that part of the world, except the Governor's in Kebec; cultivated crops; raised cattle; and (two of them together) built a mill. Mathieu de Freneuse was defending the mill now, with a detachment of his Malisites.

De Villebon thought of the effort required to start a settlement in this hostile wilderness, and sighed that it should come to nothing once again. He did not think they could save the place and was beginning, with a sick familiarity, to wonder whether they could escape a massacre—slow-drawn-out torture, death.

Madame de Freneuse stirred, to put a log on the fire. Even in siege it must not go out. Flint and steel were luxuries that the de Freneuses did not possess. The fireplace was nine feet across and burned logs which had to be hauled into the house by oxen. They had eaten the oxen now, but fortunately several logs had been laid up before the attack.

Her eyes ranged over pans, posnets, skillets, trivet, kettles, spits, and several other implements of brass before she picked up a wooden ladle. A pot au feu was hanging from a hook; it would have to serve for all of them that day, doled out in spoonfuls. She took off the lid and stirred the mixture, thinking rather dully how wonderful it would seem to take off her clothes, stand in a tub of heated water, drink some hot soup, eat a roast of pork, and then lie down and sleep—when suddenly the shrieks outside rose in volume; there was a new booming, crashing noise above the other sounds, and a horrid silence, while the Iroquois howls changed to grunts of satisfaction and endeavor.

De Villebon sprang up and went to the shutters.

"The mill!" he said, peering out. "It's burning!"

"Oh! Poor Mathieu . . . the mill!"

"They're running from it. They're . . . trying to make the house!"

Madame de Freneuse was on her feet, rushing to the shutters of the long hall window nearest to the mill. A group of women moving about among the wounded straightened themselves as she passed, and followed, crying:

"What is it?"

"What has happened?"

"Are they getting in?"

"The devils! The brutes! Sales bêtes!"

Through the shutters, where they crowded together, they could see the whole disaster, the thick cloud of black smoke and flames enveloping the mill and part of the palisade. They could see Raoul de Perrichet running and shouting, followed by the miller and a handful of Malisites, blinded by smoke. Mathieu de Freneuse, last to come out of the mill, was fighting with a tomahawk in one hand and a smoking pistol, useless, in the other. Raoul snatched a bow from the nearest dead Indian and picked up a quiver. He dropped on one knee, wildly shooting at the Iroquois.

Suddenly Mathieu stumbled and dropped, transfixed by a flight of arrows. Three Indians scooped him up and ran for the house. Two of them went down as they struggled to get him through the window.

Madame de Freneuse received him in her arms and laid him on the floor of the hall, while the other women crowded round them, crossing themselves. She called for wine and held it to his lips.

Blood was running from his forehead and his breast; two arrows were imbedded above his heart, another in his stomach. He coughed, and a stream of blood ran down his chin.

Suddenly, as she stared down at him in angry pity and bewilderment, she was roughly pushed aside. The miller's daughter, a big, sulky, dark, good-looking girl whom she had never liked, shouldered her out of the way, knelt, and took Mathieu de Freneuse upon her breast. Cradling his head, she murmured over and over:

"My love, my love, my love, my love . . ."

Madame de Freneuse stared, wide-mouthed. Mathieu's eyes slowly opened. He looked up at her. Suddenly he smiled and made an effort to shrug a shoulder as their eyes met above the girl's bowed head. Then his face whitened and his eyes closed.

The miller's daughter gathered him closer and kissed his lips.

Oblivious to the staring women around her, to de Villebon in the doorway, and to his men getting ready for an attack upon the house—hearing nothing of the screams and shrieks outside, which were growing in triumph; seeing nothing, not even the face of the wife she hated—she held him till he died.

Madame de Freneuse found Raoul beside her, his face twisted with feeling and his hand upon her arm. She shook it off and sank upon her knees. The other women followed her example, fumbling for their rosaries, staring past the two locked figures and over the head of the kneeling wife, to where the Indians were battering at the shutters and the men grunting and sweating as they held them closed.

"We must make a sortie or be smoked out like hornets!" de Villebon shouted. "And the women and children must run for it, soon."

"It is an hour to evening," Nessamaquij's nephew answered him. "They will stop at sundown, to feast and torture and drink. They have taken prisoners today; they will build the fires close, and let us see and hear. They know, now, we cannot escape. They will grow careless for a little while, when the sun sets and they are tired. Then will be the time."

CHAPTER XXXV

THE sun set, and the Iroquois drew off. They had come upon the miller's store of wine and several pigs in the second farm they burned, and they had prisoners. The rest could wait.

De Villebon gave orders.

The women and children were to creep out at the back, with the Malisites, while he and his militia feigned a counterattack. They were to run and keep on running till they got away.

"You will all go ahead as soon as I give the signal. Follow Woboek. Run as hard as you can, when you're past the sentries; run and don't look back."

The miller's wife had her arm about her daughter, who was staring at the corner where Mathieu de Freneuse lay.

"I will not go with her," the girl said. "I will stay with him!"

"Hush," hissed the women about her, "the children are here."

Madame de Freneuse went up to her.

"I'm glad," she said quietly, "that you made him happy. You must come with us and be brave for his sake. We cannot leave you here."

Gervais looked at his mother curiously. The girl shrank back, but she said no more.

Presently, so quickly that Gervais did not know how it happened, they were out of the house and crawling to the woods. At a signal, given a little too soon, they rose to their feet and began to run.

Behind them the burning palisade cast a red glow over the ground they stumbled on; shouts and shrieks rose in the air; shots, the sharp whistling of arrows, and the wild pounding of their hearts mixed with the pursuit of panting brutes behind.

Gervais, running, head down, breath sobbing, saw Denise's face over the shoulder of the Indian carrying her, watched an arrow pierce his chest from back to front, heard him grunt and stumble, and saw him go down. A moment more, and the Iroquois running behind them would pick her from the ground.

"Get up, Denise!" he screamed. "And run! Run, quick! You'll be all right! Quick! Quick!"

He watched her wriggle from under the dying Malisite and scamper on her short legs after the others, flying for the dark forest. Then he turned and raised his pistol. He fired at the first savage, bounding toward him, reaching for his tomahawk; then he rushed on, overtaking Denise, and dragged her with him. They ran through brambles which tore the skin off their hands and legs and stubbed their toes on stumps.

Suddenly she shouted, pommeling him:

"Look!"

He turned his head. Three of the Iroquois were almost upon them, silent, grinning savagely.

"Run, Denise!"

He pushed her ahead of him. One of the savages was shot from behind, as he watched; the others still came on. The pistol had cooled; he loaded it and fired again, wounding the nearest, who fell, rolling over and over, kicking his legs out jerkily. The other stopped to snatch at his arrows.

One of the Malisites turned and came back for Denise, swung her on his shoulders, and leaped forward, entering the forest. Now they had the protection of the tree trunks between them and the flying arrows. Gervais took his pistol by the muzzle, liking the feel of it in his hand, as a slight defense, and ran as hard as he could down a little path between the bushes, panting, sobbing, not daring to turn round. He had almost reached the shelter of the forest when he heard a whistle, followed by a plop, and felt the sting of an arrow through his back. He ran on grimly, expecting any moment to be caught and swung about.

Woboek came back through the trees to see if those entrusted to his care had all escaped. It had been an easy thing. Only the sentries followed. The body of the Iroquois were drunk, quarreling over prisoners. They would not start on the warpath till the dawn.

Just as he emerged, he saw Gervais running, head up, shoulders back; saw him wave and shout, before he fell. Woboek loosed his tomahawk at the head of the brute bent over the child and caught him on the skull. He went down, and Woboek ran forward.

Madame de Freneuse turned from the running women and followed him. They rolled the Iroquois aside, pulling Gervais up. He had two arrows through his lungs, and another through his leg.

"Mother," he gasped as she took him in her arms, "I wasn't frightened. I wasn't frightened, Mother; I'm not afraid!"

"Of course not," she murmured, lifting him, "I'm proud of you." She had hardly got him up when his head fell sideways; he choked once, and died.

She carried him half a mile before they dared to stop to scratch a shallow grave.

All the time that she carried him, she thought:

"This is my son. It's too dark to see his face. Dead. Killed. Gervais. He wasn't afraid. It can't have hurt. Safe now. No torture, even if they catch us, not for him. Safe. I must think of that. But Gervais! I have his hands. They're warm. He's heavy. Woboek has his feet, but I have his hands, his heart, his head. My son. Gervais. Swift and beautiful. The beginnings of things. And the end. I have the other children. I should be thinking of them, of getting away, escape. Mathieu's dead, too. Oh, moonlight falling on his face—so small, so sensitive, a face. He seems to be smiling. My darling, my darling, my son. My son. Dead. Killed. Stupid, brutal animals. Not men. Grinning devils in the dark. They're torturing the others now. The poor brave others. Soldiers. Gervais wasn't old enough to die. Why should he die? Oh, God, be good to him. Madonna, his patron, mine, holy angels and all the saints, Jesus, Marie, Joseph, and all the angels of Paradise! I . . . Perhaps you won't hear me; but he is a child, a little child, with music in his heart and on his hands. . . . Oh, Gervais, the music is over now, lost, broken. . . . Be good to him; take him to the Paradise, where there is light and song. Holy Mother, pray for him and for me, and help me to be a better mother to the others, now that my son, my son . . . Let me look at him. . . . Good-by, my dear. I shall always be proud of you, Gervais. . . . Gervais, do you hear?"

Someone touched her gently on the arm. It was Raoul. He looked haggard in the moonlight.

"We must go on," he said, "at once. We must travel all night. Woboek says we must hurry. Come, my dear."

She stooped, signed the cross on the grave, and then stood up. Raoul took her arm, and they walked on. But when she had taken a few steps, she stopped and looked round again, as though she were waiting.

Raoul put his arm about her; Woboek beckoned. The others were beyond them, scrambling through the undergrowth—away from the shouts of the Iroquois and the screaming of the prisoners, which they could hear faintly, borne on the wind.

Behind them Freneuse was burning. The dark woods stretched ahead.

CHAPTER XXXVI

RAIN swept over hills and forest, driving down toward the bay. It fell so heavily that either shore was swathed in mist; the narrow waters of the inlet leading to Port Royal disappeared before the prow of a small ketch, trying to make the settlement before the turn of tide.

Its damp sails went sluggishly about; a group of wet and weary passengers, huddled by the hatch, bowed their heads. After every tack they looked inquiringly at the helmsman (who was owner of the ketch) pitting his skill against the swift currents.

To miss the tide would mean six hours' wait in drenching rain and bitter chill. He frowned, and shook with fatigue.

On shore the mist hid everything. From the fort itself nothing could be seen but gray shapes, portions of the palisade, stretching to the water's edge. The steady battering of rain on wood drowned all sound but the sentries' mournful challenge.

Everything was dank and disagreeable, thought Monsieur de Villieu, sipping his coffee in front of the fire before beginning the work of the day. A grim and peppery little man, he sat nursing his crippled knee, swearing at the weather, and turning over papers from the Ministry in France.

There was a memorandum on the fur trade, another demanding a detailed report of the mineral resources of the colony. . . .

"Mineral resources!" snarled de Villieu. "When we cannot even cut a log, but must import wood from France or be massacred by savages. And look at this!"

He flung a third paper down upon the table. The young officer respectfully attending on him picked it up.

It was a memorandum decreeing the earlier marriage of the

colonists and advocating a bounty on babies to encourage larger families.

He put it back a little hastily. De Villieu grinned at his grimace.

"Better get started soon, jeûne homme; bachelors will be penalized."

The door opened.

"Well?"

One of the watch came in.

"A boat has arrived, mon capitaine."

"From France?"

"No, from St. Jean. With fugitives. One of them wants to speak to you."

"Another beggar, I suppose. Did he say what his business was?"

"It is a woman, mon capitaine."

"A woman? Show her in."

The watch disappeared. There was a moment's pause, during which de Villieu dipped bread in his coffee with one hand and with the other smoothed his beard. The young officer, watching his expression, smiled and hid his smile.

But the woman who came out of the mist was not the kind he associated with his captain's mood. She stood in the doorway, tall and gaunt, lifting a haggard face toward them proudly.

Monsieur de Villieu put aside his coffee cup and rose to his feet, even before she addressed them with the beautiful tones of the noblesse.

"Monsieur, I am come to beg the King's protection, from your person. My husband is dead, our lands devastated—in the hands of the Iroquois. I have with me, besides my own children, the five helpless children of my sister, whose husband is a prisoner in Boston."

"Madame, I beg of you to be seated. Monsieur Desbardes, order refreshment. I am Monsieur de Villieu, Madame, at your service."

"My name is Madame de Freneuse."

Monsieur de Villieu made a leg, and the young officer bowed on his way to order wine.

"I fear I have bad news for you. Monsieur de Villebon and his men are in hard case. When we fled, they were alive; but that is all that can be said. They had no food, ammunition was failing, and the Iroquois had burnt the palisade. There may be more news when the others come. The ketch that brought me here has returned to fetch them now."

·[150]·

"The others?"

"Monsieur de Perrichet and some faithful Malisites."

She slumped a little in her chair and gripped the arms of it nervously. Her face was gray; her eyes were sunk in her head; there were scratches and mud on her cheeks; her mouth was set in a desperate line; her face was so thin that her skull seemed to be thrusting through it. Monsieur de Villieu, looking at her with respect, thought:

"This is the most vital woman I have ever seen," and was disturbed.

"In Monsieur de Villebon's absence, I am in command," he said. "I have heard of your husband and, of course, I know his worth. I have the warmest memories of his younger brother, Monsieur de Plessis, with whom I did my service. I shall be glad to do whatever is in my power to make you comfortable. I . . . I . . . permit me to offer my most respectful condolence. Monsieur de Freneuse is a great loss."

Her expression did not change. She did not speak. Monsieur Desbardes came back with a servant bearing wine and food. She lifted the bowl to her lips mechanically.

"Are the children fed?" inquired Monsieur de Villieu, watching her.

"The sergeant of the watch took them to his quarters. His wife will feed them there."

Still no change on the woman's face. "What is she looking at? What has she seen?" thought Monsieur de Villieu, fascinated. "Torture might make her look like that, or imbecility, or great fatigue; but it is not a silence even of these—it is something else . . . a waiting stillness, a . . . a . . ."

"Madame," he said, "more wine."

The boy filled her cup; she cradled it between her hands. Suddenly an extraordinary change swept over her. She half rose from her seat. Her face altered as though a swimmer struggled up from the depths and at last broke through, into life again, from the drowned. De Villieu turned.

The door behind him had opened. Monsieur de Bonaventure stood there. The *Soleil d'Afrique* was in port for repairs.

"They told me outside that you were here," he said, ignoring the others completely. She stood up, and he took her in his arms.

·[151]·

PART THREE

Port Royal

CHAPTER XXXVII

THE settlement of Port Royal consisted of the fort—commanding all approach by sea from the Baye Françoise, through the Gap, up the Basin—a convent, forty-three houses, two mills, and a church, sheltered from land attack by the forest—which made the transport of men and supplies difficult for the English and a tribe of friendly Micmacs scattered through the woods, always on the lookout for the Iroquois.

A main path ran through the settlement, following the curve of the shore; smaller paths divided from it, to the sea and to the forest, so that from above it looked like a deformed caterpillar, looped and hairy. Raoul saw it so as he emerged with nine Malisites and a Micmac guide from the southern end of the Mochelle trail.

They had not been able to find a ketch to take them to the Port; but a man who had business with the Indians in the mission on the north shore offered to take them in his boat, over the Baye. From there they made their way across the Dauphin River, at low tide, along its southern bank.

They were very tired. They walked with the nerveless tread of men pushed beyond endurance, silent, in single file, in the wake of their guide. Raoul, walking in the center, tried to divert his mind from its main preoccupation—Madame de Freneuse. Over and over he thought:

"I should not have let her go alone. The ketch may never have reached Port Royal. The English may have captured it. The owner of the ketch may have been in league with them. She was exhausted. She leaned on me. That last night in the forest she slept like a tired child in my arms. I dragged her along. Perhaps she knows now what my love means. She saw Gervais die. I shall always be glad that I was with her when he died. What would have happened to her if I had not been there, in command of the retreat? The Indians might have treated her as they would treat a squaw whose man had been killed. They might have saved themselves. She would have stayed there with Gervais if I had not dragged her away. A moment like that must bring me nearer. She must think of that sometimes. She must remember. She must begin to love me—she must, she must!"

"Look," said Nessamaquij's nephew, "my uncle!"

Raoul, startled, turned his head, half expecting to see the dismembered Nessamaquij behind him. There was no one there. He realized, with a sense of the grotesque, that he was Nessamaquij's blood brother and would from now on take his place, even to being addressed as "Uncle" by this brave considerably older than himself.

"What is it?"

"I can see the soldiers in the fort. They are frightened. We come in war paint."

It was true. Raoul had forgotten to give the order for the Indians to wash away their paint. He looked at them with a critical eye. A more grim and forbidding group of blood-stained savages would be hard to find. Hamogom had scalps in his belt, in a blood-caked mess of hair. The others had tied theirs to tomahawks and one to his moccasins. The red and white war paint covered their faces, accentuating the grim thin-lipped mouths and outthrust chins.

He looked toward the fort. He could see two sentries on the nearest palisade halt in their march, raise their rifles in the air, and, while he watched, fire an alarm.

Immediately doors in the nearest houses slammed, heads appeared at windows, guns were thrust out of loopholes. The convent bells began to ring. Raoul halted the group.

"I will go forward and speak to them."

He adjusted his torn clothing; passed a hand over his beard, which was ragged and full of brambles; drew himself up to his six feet three inches, striding forward. When he was within shouting distance, he sang out:

"Vive la France!"

The sentry raised his arm and signaled to another man to take his place, while he went to make his report.

"Tell me," said Raoul to this second man, "is Madame de Freneuse here?"

The youth—for he was only a boy—looked over and grinned. Raoul tried again.

"Did a woman reach the fort with her children, a refugee?"

The sentry held one hand up to his ear.

"Say that again," he ordered.

Raoul repeated his question, adding that he had helped the lady and her children to escape, that he was very anxious, and (as an afterthought) that his uncle was Monsieur de Bonaventure. The name had no magic effect. The sentry seemed to be listening to something else. He leaned down unprofessionally to say:

"By your accent you're from the Midi, you have the Provençal speech. Are you from Marseilles? It's not so long since I played on the Cannebière. And you?"

Raoul smiled back.

"I'm from Draguignan."

"Té! I was there on a Sunday off and on. My uncle's the notary."

Raoul cast his mind back so successfully that he could almost smell the notary's office, with its shelves of dusty leather-covered books, and see the withered little man with spectacles who sat in front of them.

"Not Maître Félicien?" he said.

"The same. Then you know him? A stuffy old woman if ever there was one. He's the why I'm here. Not that I grudge it now; I like the life. If you've come to enlist, you'll like it, too."

Before Raoul could embark again on his reasons for being there, the first sentry returned and signed to him to follow. He stepped forward, all his nerves trembling. Now he would hear what had happened to Louise.

The sentry halted at the door of a room to the right and presented arms. Raoul found himself entering the room at a run. He brought up short in front of a table where set a choleric-looking man whose whole attitude seemed to be saying an impatient "Well?"

"Monsieur," Raoul stammered, "I am Raoul de Perrichet, at your service, in command of a Malisite company cut to bits at the siege of Freneuse seigneury at Nashwaak. Only nine of us remain. Monsieur de Freneuse is dead. I helped Madame de Freneuse and

·[157]·

her children to escape. They embarked on a ketch which should have brought them here. Have you news of them?"

Monsieur de Villieu inclined his head.

"Madame de Freneuse is here," he said, "safe and well. So are the children. They have been taken to the convent." He clapped his hands. The sentry who had escorted Raoul stepped smartly in.

"Sound the Cease-from-alarm," said Monsieur de Villieu.

CHAPTER XXXVIII

THE Convent of the Sacred Heart of Mary stood between the fort and the Petite Rivière, looking out upon the forested slopes of the southern shore. Its grounds were cultivated with careful precision, even to a row of cranberry bushes in the swamp by the river. Corn, beans, peas, potatoes, and cabbages grew in the first two fields. Beyond them the convent rose out of an attempt at a flower garden. It was two stories high, strongly built of mud and logs, with an earthen floor. The bottom story had a row of windows dear to the ecclesiastical authorities, letting in neither light nor heat of the sun, suggesting to the passer-by both a church and a prison, which, in fact, it was—a church for worship, a prison for the little savages mewed up in it.

Raoul halted his detachment of Malisites, for the second time, at the convent gates and went forward alone up the path. The bell had ceased pealing for the alarm, but the rope was still swinging in the wooden framework that served for a bell tower; the nun who had rung it could be seen feeding a goat, tethered to the wooden bars.

Raoul advanced toward her anxiously. She raised her mild face with its shrewd eyes, folded her hands beneath her wide black sleeves, and waited for him to announce his errand. Just as he was stammering out, "Madame de Freneuse . . ." a piercing shriek deafened him. He turned, startled. Two small heads bobbed up behind the corn and disappeared, to emerge a moment later. Denise and Jeanne de Chauffours sprinted toward him as though the savages were after them.

"Raoul!"

Denise reached him first, flung her arms round his neck, and

danced on tiptoes as he struggled to get rid of her and stand upright. Jeanne seized hold of his arms. Both children danced and
shouted:

"Raoul! You've come to take us home!"

"But no!" he stammered, disengaging himself, while the nun
frowned and shook her head at the little girls. "I've come to see
you and your mother, but not to take you home. At least . . .
Home is destroyed now—burned, you know. You remember?"

"Did it *all* burn down?"

"I imagine so. We didn't stay to see, did we?"

"Have you been there since?"

"No."

He turned, while they clasped him each by a hand, and said to
the nun:

"I really came to see Madame de Freneuse. Will you take me to
her?"

An ominous cloud passed over the nun's face and was reflected
on the upturned faces of the children.

"Jeanne and Denise," she said.

The children dropped Raoul's hands and stood awkwardly before her, dropping their eyes.

"Monsieur, only close relatives of the children are allowed to
visit them," the nun continued to Raoul, "and then only with
written permission and at stated times. It is not," she added, "a
measure against the French parents of our children so much as
against the savages, who come out of the woods at all times and
hours to see their daughters, bringing the whole tribe sometimes.
They disrupt everything, so that Reverend Mother has made new
rules. I am sure you will understand."

Raoul recovered speech.

"It is true, ma sœur, that I am not a close relative of these children, in one sense; but, in another, I am privileged, since for the
last five years I have been their tutor at Freneuse."

The nun stiffened. Her glance traveled over him with an inde-
finable expression of hostility and distaste. She made no reply, but
motioned Denise and Jeanne to retire. They cast piteous glances
at Raoul. He smiled at their anxious faces.

"I am sure that their mother will allow them to receive my
visit," he said, "if you will just take us to her now, ma sœur."

Again the children looked a little frightened beneath their distress. The nun replied in a toneless voice:

"Madame de Freneuse is not here."

"Not here?"

"No, Monsieur, not here."

Her tone implied that the last place in which to find Madame de Freneuse would be the convent.

"But I thought . . ." Raoul stammered, remembering the last words of the Governor:

"Madame de Freneuse is here, safe and well. So are the children. They have been taken to the convent."

"I distinctly heard from the officer in command of the fort that she was here."

"She is not here," said the nun icily, sweeping the children before her. "Good day, Monsieur."

There was a scuffling sound behind her. Denise broke away and came back to him.

"They're horrid here," she panted. "They hate us. Raoul, come back and take us away. Take us to ma tante. She's living with Monsieur de Bonaventure. That makes them cross. That's why they won't let us speak to you. . . . Raoul . . ."

The nun strode back with long angry steps and took her by the arm. Denise became silent; she let herself be led away, not even looking back. But Jeanne, waiting for her, called out:

"Good-by, Raoul. Tell ma tante how we are. Good-by. Come back to us. Don't forget us!"

Her voice died away as the nun caught up to her, still holding Denise by the arm. Raoul watched the trio disappear, stupefied. He was still standing, rooted to the spot, when he heard a sudden cry, and then low sobbing, more screams and cries, then silence. Denise and Jeanne were being punished. Raoul started forward to the rescue; but as he took the second step toward the convent door, he realized the hopelessness of the situation. He could do nothing to help the children until he had found Madame de Freneuse. Then she would have them taken away—home, as they said, poor mites.

A sudden wave of anger swept him—anger at the nun; anger at the Governor, who had misled him; anger, white-hot and wild, against his uncle.

"Living with Monsieur de Bonaventure!" he muttered furiously. "I'll find him! I'll—I'll kill him! I'll show them! Uncle or no uncle!"

"But she always was in love with him," he muttered desolately a moment later, turning toward the road.

·[161]·

CHAPTER XXXIX

BACK along the road toward the fort, accompanied by his weary, silent troop; a word to the sentry from Marseilles, sniggering directions, across the fort grounds toward the chapel, behind the chapel to the Governor's residence, attached to the Governor's residence a little annex. Raoul halted and knocked on the door.

"Monsieur de Bonaventure?" he called.

The door opened. Dahinda, smiling, beckoned him inside. He found himself in a bare log room with a table of cedar wood, roughly nailed together by wooden spikes, and five birchwood chairs; a fire burned in an open chimney, lined with mud to prevent the shelter catching fire. Over the flames, suspended from an iron hook, a pot of stew simmered giving forth good smells. But the fire made the room very hot. Raoul passed his hand across his brow.

A curtain at the far end of the room moved, twitched aside; Monsieur de Bonaventure and Madame de Freneuse came in. Raoul looked from one to the other silently, a mist blurring his eyes. Monsieur de Bonaventure thrust out his hand.

"Eh bien, Raoul," he said. "So you got here at last!"

"Yes, mon oncle," Raoul replied mechanically, his eyes never leaving Madame de Freneuse's face.

It had changed—no longer drawn, tortured, haggard, wild; no longer the face that had lifted to him in the moonlight as they carried Gervais through the forest. This was the face of a woman satisfied. She greeted him, smiling.

"What took you so long to get here? I was worried."

"I went to the convent," he said slowly, "expecting to find you there, where you should be. Instead of that, I find you here with him. Your own nieces suffer on account of you. The settlement has set you down for a whore."

He had hardly got the word out before he felt a stinging blow across the cheek; his uncle thrust Madame de Freneuse aside and pushed Raoul back, with one hand at his throat.

"Swallow that word!" he said. "Vermin! Swallow it! Down on your knees. Apologize!"

But Raoul held his ground.

"You have placed her in that position, mon oncle," he said quietly, into the formidable face close to his. "You may challenge me; but that will not make things any better for her, or for you."

"Challenge you!" De Bonaventure sputtered. "Whippersnapper, I wouldn't think of challenging you except with a birch rod across your bare behind. That's what one does to a troublesome little boy like you, who meddles with his betters!"

Raoul drew back his fist, which had been clenched at his side, and struck his uncle full on the nose.

Madame de Freneuse called out: "Raoul!" and then: "Pierre!" Neither heard her. They were too busy fumbling for their swords. Raoul drew his first. He stepped backward, toward the door. De Bonaventure followed, a little sheepish in his rage. He had just remembered that the boy not only was his nephew but had saved Madame de Freneuse's life and brought her safely through the woods. This, however, only irritated him. He felt, illogically, that no one but himself should have been there. Then he tried to be just. Naturally, after living at Freneuse so many years, the boy might feel concern for Madame de Freneuse, and some sort of responsibility for her. Indeed, if he had not, de Bonaventure would have been furious. It was true enough that the settlement was shocked. A fig for that!

Another thought struck him, as he looked at Raoul's purple face. All these years Madame de Freneuse had lived with this young cockerel dancing attendance on her. She was unhappy with her husband. Might she not have trifled a little with the boy, to divert herself? No more than that, he was sure, but enough to upset the boy's composure. Then he remembered the episode that had led to Raoul's hasty departure from France, and wondered. The boy had had one affair with a married woman. What was to prevent him from pursuing Madame de Freneuse with his attentions? Mon Dieu, perhaps she had taken him—after all, her husband was notoriously unfaithful; she was passionate; and he, de Bonaventure, far away and, he must confess, faithless, too, if one went into that. Who could expect a man not to be, except a woman? She might have taken exception to that. A series of terrible pictures formed in his mind, so that a black mist descended upon him. He could think of nothing, stifled in the rising fumes of hatred, rage, and misery.

Meanwhile Raoul was speaking.

". . . if it is because you have nowhere else to go, that is not true. There are nine of us, and we are loyal to you. I became Nessamaquij's blood brother for your sake, and now that I am in a position to make use of it, to serve you, to take you away . . . Louise, come with me, before it is too late, before you are fatally compromised. Already at the convent . . . I know you have given this no thought. . . . I know you love my uncle; but if you live with him, you will be ruined. He is married. At least keep your intrigue a secret. You can still see him. Yes, I would be willing—yes, even that. Louise, I offer you marriage, a devotion as great as his, and the protection of my name."

De Bonaventure laughed.

"Protection! A boy young enough to be your son! What sort of a marriage is that! On what would you live? On milk and kisses? Stop babbling and get out of here. This lady has all the protection she needs under this roof. Get out, I say."

Raoul paid no attention to him. He was looking at Louise. She had paled to a sick gray.

"Raoul," she said, and she tried to smile, "it was good of you to come, and to—to offer me marriage. I feel honored. I know how you have loved me."

De Bonaventure stirred angrily, and she held up her hand.

"I have leaned upon it many times. I may again. But you should marry a young wife of your own, a girl who would love you. As Monsieur de Bonaventure says, I am old enough to be your mother. Let us speak no more of this. We are lucky to be alive."

"And you will stay here as this man's mistress—you who were so proud, who have had the love and respect of everyone!"

De Bonaventure sprang forward again, but Madame de Freneuse stepped between.

"Yes," she said quietly. "I belong here. I always have. Monsieur de Bonaventure is not able to offer me marriage, as you are. We will leave it at that. I am grateful to you for your help in the past and for your friendship; but I think you had better go now, Raoul."

"Once more, and for the last time, Louise, will you come with me?"

"No."

Raoul stood for a moment, braced to meet the refusal he had provoked, then he sputtered:

"If you will not think of yourself, think of your children, Gervais . . ."

He had no sooner pronounced the name than Madame de Freneuse gave a low moaning cry that went through de Bonaventure like a knife.

"Get out," he said, between his teeth. "Never show your face here, you ungrateful whelp."

Raoul turned on him with all the force of his anguish; speechless, trembling, exhausted with his rage, he spat in his uncle's face.

CHAPTER XL

MONSIEUR DE VILLIEU, on his way to pay his respects to Madame de Freneuse, paused in the doorway at the sound of clashing swords and barked an order to the men behind him. They ran into the room and threw themselves upon the duelists. Monsieur de Bonaventure offered no resistance; but the other, a furious young man, struggled madly and threshed his sword about, wounding one of the men who held him.

"Messieurs, what is this?" said the Governor sternly. "Dueling is forbidden in New France. Madame"—he bowed to Madame de Freneuse, standing white and silent in her corner—"may I appeal to you to know the truth of this encounter? Who challenged? Which is the aggressor?"

Madame de Freneuse looked quickly at the two angry faces, de Bonaventure's dark and mottled with rage, Raoul's hot and puckered.

"Neither is to blame," she faltered. "They drew swords in fun, and . . . and Monsieur de Bonaventure pressing too hard upon his nephew, the fun turned to earnest as your Excellency came in. I cannot think it would have continued so."

"Hmmm," said de Villieu, "men have strange notions of fun. Young man, you have wounded one of my soldiers. For that there is a penalty. You shall pay a fine of forty louis. Monsieur de Bonaventure, you will see that he appears before me in the morning for the case to be recorded. Madame, I came to beg your company this evening over a steak of bear."

Madame de Freneuse sank in a curtsy. Before she could open her lips, Raoul cried out:

"Monsieur le Gouverneur, I appeal to your justice. I drew my sword because this gentleman"—his lips curled over the word contemptuously—"struck me after I had spat in his face, as any honorable man would have done. He has injured Madame de Freneuse by compromising her good name. I wonder that your Excellency has allowed such a thing to happen here, under your jurisdiction, so that all the settlement are calling her a whore!"

It was the Governor's turn to be angry, but he did not raise his voice.

"Take him away," he said to the men holding Raoul. "Throw him into the cachot for a damned disagreeable dog. That will teach him manners. Monsieur de Bonaventure, your servant; Madame, accept my apologies that such a young ruffian should have reached you here. Allez! Take him away, and sharp!"

Then something happened which was unexpected. Raoul shouted, over the shoulder of the man who was propelling him toward the door:

"If there is no honor, no decency, no justice, here, I spit upon you all, whoremongers, lecherers." He raised his voice, in the long, echoing Malisite war whoop.

Before his hearers had time to recover from their surprise, nine Indians in war paint were among them, striking right and left with their deadly tomahawks. Hamogom scalped the man holding Raoul's shoulder; the other dropped his hold and drew his dirk, crumpling an instant later at the Governor's feet.

Raoul shouted at his uncle: "The Indians have more decency than you, than the whole filthy pack of you. If this is the King's representative, this two-faced Governor here, down with the King! Down with New France! Vive les sauvages! Let us get out of here, into the clean woods!"

His last words soared above the confusion. A moment later there was an explosion and a sharp pain in his head. As he sank to the ground in a dark whirl of red spots, he felt a drag upon his arms and saw a row of faces, grotesque in their surprise, in front of him. They lengthened conically and fell away in strips. They grew green instead of red and swayed in long shadows above him. They merged into one kindly face bent over him. He opened his eyes.

He was beneath the forest trees, carried between two Indians. Hamogom was looking down on him.

"Better," he grunted. "Ruwerera better. Ugh!"

Raoul groaned and threw his arm up. Now the scene came back to him.

·[167]·

"What happened?"

Hamogom told him, pointing to the scalps in his own belt and those in the belts of the six Indians with him. Three of them were dead; but seven of the white men had been killed, four scalped.

"The Untamed Bear shot you," he said. "So then we fought the soldiers till we got to you. The white squaw ran between, so we killed her."

"What!" said Raoul, cold with horror.

"There's the scalp."

He tossed a shrunken object into Raoul's hand. Raoul turned it over, sick with fear. But it was blond, not black.

"What white squaw?" he asked, still apprehensively. "Madame de Freneuse?"

"No. She held the Untamed Bear in her arms, drawing him away. She his squaw now."

Raoul groaned. The picture of her clasping his uncle was too vivid. But there had been no other woman there.

"It was a squaw who ran in from outside, from the big house," Hamogom said indifferently. "She carried guns and bullets to the white chief in the hut."

Raoul wondered whether she could be the Governor's wife and, if so, why the soldiers had not followed them. Hamogom supplied the answer.

"We fought and ran, and hid in the woods. Night covered us. Now we are here and wait your orders. It will not be healthy to go back. Ruwerera must stay Indian now."

He smiled. The other Indians crouching round him smiled, too. Raoul stretched out his hand.

"My brothers," he said, "we will hunt together. We will be enemies to the white man, English and French alike. We will restore the red man to his rights!"

Between his teeth he muttered:

"I will show her where her true protection lay. She will be sorry when the French are driven out. She will have to turn to me then."

A strong breeze lifted the hair from his forehead. It was pleasant to feel; but it reminded him of the colder winds to come and that he must face them in the forest, cowering beneath a smoke-filled tepee like the Malisites. He shivered suddenly.

"White man feels the snowbird walking on his grave," one of the Indians told him gravely.

CHAPTER XLI

A SOFT wind blowing from the Baye Françoise skimmed the dark hills between it and the mainland, passing over the wide waters of the basin and tugging at the masts of the *Soleil d'Afrique*, anchored off Isle au Chèvre; left the water reluctantly, racing with the tide toward shore. It shook the palisades and wandered on the banks of the fort, lifted a sentry's heavy woolen coat, flapped a flag of fleur de lis, hesitated for a moment to lose itself among the coils of long, dark, and perfumed hair.

Madame de Freneuse raised her head, standing at the window, with the comb in her hand.

"Spring!" she said over her shoulder. "I can feel it today. It's coming, Pierre. The snow will melt."

De Bonaventure came to the window behind her.

"My spring came with the fall of leaves," he said, "last year."

She turned her head. They stood for a moment, smiling at each other. A long procession of pictures went through both their minds. Winter and the howling winds without, with their icy, malevolent breath; within, the comfort of a warm fire, themselves sitting hand in hand in front of it. Supper, a bowl of hot strong soup with a roll of new baked bread, eaten together in the little rough log room; afterward, by the light of a candle, low-voiced talk, long silences; then a warm bed made of pine wood, smelling of the forest. It rocked and creaked with the storms without, and the whole shelter shook like a ship at sea. It was close to the palisades, and sometimes as they lay there in the darkness, listening to the noises of the night, they could imagine savages a foot or two away. Then they reached for each other's hands and, finding them, felt safe. Madame de Freneuse thought, a little sadly, of Raoul, crouching in

·[169]·

the woods beside his braves. He had become an implacable enemy of the settlement. There was now a price upon his head. Often she woke in the night with a sick sort of wonder, reliving the last scene, seeing him struggle with the guards, hurling insults over his shoulder, breaking away, a savage, now, among the savages. Raoul! The bitterness of a dead friendship lay heavily upon her.

In contrast there were evenings of official invitation with de Villieu in the Grande Salle of the fort; officers in uniform conversing with de Bonaventure, resplendent in gold braid; ladies in crinolines with high wigs and acid faces, looking askance at Madame de Freneuse in a long dress that showed her figure, clinging closely when she danced. There was quite a lot of dancing. Sometimes Madame de Freneuse played while one of the officers sang. Sometimes she sang herself, heartily applauded by the men, coldly by their wives.

Monsieur de Villieu as Acting Governor could and did force the society of the settlement to an outward civility, making Madame de Freneuse preside at all his parties; but the women resented the open intrigue all the more. Their own love affairs were conducted with more secrecy, not to say hypocrisy; some of them, having made attempts to capture Monsieur de Bonaventure's interest, were loud in indignation at the loose-living ways of de Villieu and the inmates of the fort. But they could do nothing about it, having to defer to him, and their virtuous indignation only stimulated Madame de Freneuse to provoke it in ways that might amuse him. He was good to them. He enjoyed their company together at his table and would often come to theirs.

"This," de Bonaventure gravely told him after the duel with Raoul, "is a work of charity. I am taking Madame de Freneuse under my protection as a mark of respect to her and to her children."

"Tiens!" said de Villieu, smiling quizzically. And again, a little later: "Charity should always be encouraged. So good a servant to the King, with talents we cannot duplicate, is free to be charitable, however eccentric this may appear to the vulgar world. You can count on my support."

He was better than his word. They came to love him as he stumped about, nervously snapping his fingers, swearing at the savages, the King, the cold, the world.

"What," said Madame de Freneuse at the window, "will the new Governor be like?"

It was a question that perturbed them both. Each had secretly hoped, when de Villebon's death was confirmed officially, that de Villieu would succeed him. De Villieu himself warned them otherwise.

"I am the logical man for the place and, therefore, will not get it."

"But why?" Madame de Freneuse asked, watching him shrug and shake.

"De Pourtchartrain never could stomach me. We were cadets together," was all that he would say. And once: "They will keep me on as second in command. Somebody must know the place. Somebody must do the work. I'll wager a chestnut that somebody is me."

So it was not unforeseen, but disconcerting, when Monsieur Jacques François de Brouillan was appointed Governor of Acadia. The news reached them in March. It would be some months, however, before he could arrive. He was at Plaisance, governing Newfoundland.

"I don't know much about him," de Bonaventure mused. "He was with d'Iberville and me in the attack on Pemquid. He was difficult and domineering then. He did not want to share the enterprise with d'Iberville. He left and attacked St. Jean."

"Those are only some of the things he did. What is the man himself?"

"Well, a Gascon, to start with."

"Oh. Proud and vain. Bad-tempered. I can see why he didn't get on with Monsieur d'Iberville. Tell me more."

"He has the reputation of being rather a tartar in his command, quite severe."

"Oh. Pierre, I suppose . . . I suppose it is certain that he will send me away?"

"I don't see why he should, beloved. You have only to charm him. Look at de Villieu!"

"Dear de Villieu, I wish he were Governor."

"So do I. Don't worry. Where you go, I go. Things will be all right."

Madame de Freneuse smiled thoughtfully.

"Perhaps I had better get the children back from the good nuns, who hate me so, and appear before him the first time draped in maternity."

De Bonaventure laughed.

"Let's wait and see if he likes children first," he said, putting his arms around her suddenly and knocking the comb from her hands as he gathered them beneath his own, crossed upon her breasts.

"At any rate, the winter has been heaven, hasn't it?"

She sighed.

"Answer me!"

They kissed in full view of a group crossing the Governor's yard.

"Ciel!" said Madame de Freneuse, deliberately finishing her kiss, "that was Madame de St. Vincent. Hates me worse than hell."

"Because she would have liked to be in your place," de Bonaventure said complacently.

"In that case"—Madame de Freneuse craned—"give me another. She can still see us if we lean this way."

CHAPTER XLII

SPRING came, followed by early summer. Word reached de Villieu that the new governor had sailed from La Plaisance, and the settlement was all astir. New uniforms arrived on a packet from France, ordered by Monsieur de Villebon in a moment of enthusiasm. They were three years late and completely forgotten, but de Villieu found them very opportune and blessed his predecessor. He reviewed the garrison, selected the best-looking men to form a guard of honor, doled out the new equipment to them crossly, and gave orders for the palisades to be strengthened, paths cut and cleared, the Governor's house repaired, the silver cleaned. Then he shut himself up in his quarters with a bottle of old brandy and his new Rhinegrave breeches spread out on a chair.

Madame de Freneuse found herself much alone. De Bonaventure spent much of his time on the *Soleil d'Afrique*, waiting in the Basin for the first sign of the Governor's ship. The ladies of the settlement, even if they would be civil, were engaged in a frenzy of refurbishing their clothes.

The days were fine and mild. Madame de Freneuse wandered in the fort grounds, which were green and pleasant, loitering to watch the bustle, stepping out of the way of running orderlies, raising her head to watch the sweep of cloud on the long curved line of distant hills, across the basin, calm and still.

Her own clothes, she reflected, were past praying for, completely out of fashion, some that were found in the fort and could not be rearranged. De Bonaventure had written to France for more, but they would not arrive before the Governor. She did not care. The chances were, clothes or no clothes, she would be sent away.

No clothes—that was the trouble; she had been too naked and un-ashamed, too happy. Madame de St. Vincent, and others, too, were only waiting for this de Brouillan to arrive, to complain of her. Monsieur de Bonaventure would defend her with his sword; he talked wildly of fitting out the *Soleil d'Afrique* and joining the pirates. He said he could not live without her. He would turn traitor first. She pursed her lips in a sideways movement that was a trick of hers.

Raoul, too, had turned traitor for love of her. The poor boy, how had he survived the long cruel winter in the woods! But he had, for they had news of him raiding an outpost with his men. Ruwerera was becoming a legend, so stoutly had he organized his braves, recruiting Micmacs to the Malisites until he now had a big company. The new Governor would likely proceed against him. He was become a menace.

The new Governor would certainly proceed against her. She tried not to think of that—no use meeting adversity before it got you by the throat—and certainly she contrived to be gay enough for Pierre when he was there. But it was with a sinking feeling that she heard the guns firing and the convent bell ringing, be-cause a sail had been sighted in the bay. . . .

The guard of honor marched out, trim and perspiring. They would embark on the *Soleil d'Afrique* and sail to the gap to meet the Governor's ship and escort her in. Then they would march him up from the quay with all the honor possible. Other years it might not have been wise for so many men to leave the fort at once, but scouts reported the savages quietly engaged in their pursuits and not expecting any attack from Iroquois or Mohawk. Ruwerera was reported on a beaver-trapping trip; he openly en-gaged in the contraband trade, a further thorn in the side of the settlement authorities. The English were keeping quiet, too. It seemed a propitious time for the Governor to arrive. Enough sen-tries were left to man the palisades. De Villieu himself joined the guard of honor, the fort was left to silence and expectancy.

Madame de Freneuse wandered through the grounds. She thought she might go down to the convent, brave the nuns, and see her nieces. It was very near, so that in case of attack the nuns and their charges might reach the safety of the fort. She mounted the first low bank that led to the palisades and stood looking down at the water. She could see the longboat rowing out to the *Soleil d'Afrique*. She watched it arrive, saw little black figures climbing out of it, a running to and fro on the deck, and then the great sails unfurl, the wind catch them, and the ship move forward. Tears blurred her eyes. The sight of a sailing vessel always moved her, even when it was not the *Soleil d'Afrique.* Now she was thinking of de Bonaventure and the refuge she had found in his love.

"Sweet, sweet Pierre, my love, my lover, and my precious, wistful, yearning, cross little boy, seeking comfort, but sometimes defiant—I love you more than ever, through rough times and smooth, up to the glorious passion which only you and I know, and will always know together until life holds no more passion for us and there comes a final peace. I shall miss you every second of this coming hideous, lonely time. I am sick of loneliness. Through the years I have groped, lonely, until I found you and your love at last, your understanding love. Give it to me always. Come to me when things are pressing in upon us and, please le bon Dieu, never find me wanting. Forgive my ugliness and stupidity and know they are because of the very great love I have for you, my darling. Oh, my perfect darling, love me as I love you, and earth can hold no greater happiness; happiness we will take with us somewhere else, wherever that may be."

She propped her chin upon her hands, gazed over the water, sending her thoughts to him as though they were written on the clouds or borne by the swift sea gulls swooping round the ship. She sat for a while, lost in thought, before, saddened by the menace hanging over them, she became restless and moved away.

She disliked uncertainty, change, and hardship. She had had enough. It did not matter that she was a pauper—house burned, lands laid waste—nor that she was still, after months of rest, slowly recovering from the shock of the siege and the journey through the woods, so terrible that it had shattered her. None of that mattered; she could take it all—all but that other sorrow, never to be spoken of, unbearable, Gervais' death. Beneath the frivolity of her manner, beneath her very real happiness and love and the lighthearted days she had spent at Port Royal, there was a quivering creature, raw in every nerve. The one great healing thing that had come to her was Pierre and his love, and that because he did not know that she was sad. How could he guess? He had seen her with the other children. A child was just a child to him—to her, too; but not . . . ah, not Gervais!

Pierre was happy, seemingly, in her love. He was still in love.

He was a much deeper, dearer person than the figure of glamour she had made of him before they lived together in this small log room. It was strange to think that he had never seen her in her vanished role—Freneuse, the biggest house, the most successful settlement, of all the seigneuries. He thought of her here, or sometimes as a child in Kebec. She was the refugee who had come to him out of the mist, frivolous and gay, charming de Villieu, flouting all the old hags of the colony. But of the anguished and bewildered mother, bereaved of her son, of more than her son—a patch of the eternal sunlight dimmed forever, youth fled from her and from the world—he could not know.

She turned to the right, making for the portière. The sentry mounting guard smiled and made way for her. It was Jean La-touche, droll young devil from the gutters of Marseilles, with something wrong in his chest. They had exchanged quips before now. She stopped to talk to him.

Just as they were settled to their duel of wits, Madame de Freneuse running beside him so that he would not be out in his count, a commotion caught her eye on the edge of the forest.

"Look!" she said, turning pale.

He shielded his eyes; and both of them were silent, picturing the disaster if the savages attacked.

"Ruwerera!" said the sentry.

"Raoul!" breathed Madame de Freneuse.

But the men coming out from the trees were soldiers.

"Is it the English?"

"No. They're in our uniform. Not ours here, but French."

"Mercy, Jean, could it be, do you suppose, the Governor?"

Jean's jaw dropped. Sixteen weedy men in badly fitting uniforms and the Governor!

"I do believe it is," said Madame de Freneuse, jumping to get a better view.

"Perhaps our people are with him."

"Not a soul. How could there be? They've gone up the bay. Sound the alarm, Jean, they're getting near."

CHAPTER XLIII

A SOFT breeze from the southeast filled the sails of the *Soleil d'Afrique*, carrying her past Isle au Chèvre, down the basin to the bay. The water, smooth and gray, reflected in black shadow a long line of the hills. Sea gulls circled round the sails, squawking, diving after herring, rising again from the water with silver-colored wings. Monsieur de Bonaventure, watching them skim and swoop, thought incoherently of Madame de Freneuse. The freedom of their wings reminded him of her, flying to meet the storm.

"And yet," he murmured to himself, "they slide into the waves and rest there, secure. Perhaps she, too, will float. Please God."

"A tribord!"

The slacking sails swelled with the veering breeze.

"A bâbord!"

"Trim!"

"Ah!"

The exclamation rose from many throats as the opening of the inlet came in sight and they could see the sails of a two-master tacking toward the gap.

"The *Bonne Espérance*!"

This was not the Governor's ship, but the schooner from France, bringing news, provisions . . .

"And," de Bonaventure thought, twisting his mouth in a sudden smile, "new clothes for my love. At least she will have the satisfaction of sailing about in hoops, if hoops are in the fashion nowadays."

De Villieu beckoned.

·[177]·

"Drive her close," he said. "They may have news. Perhaps they have sighted the Governor's ship."

There was an explosion and a puff of white smoke from the *Bonne Espérance*. The *Soleil d'Afrique* saluted in return. The wind was with her, the racing current against. She wore round and came up at the mouth of the gap. The men in the rigging, silhouetted against the blue sky, cheered as the sails came down and the anchor splashed overboard. The *Bonne Espérance* held on through the gap until she has passed the dangerous, rocky channel. Then she, too, lowered sail and anchored.

The longboat from the *Soleil d'Afrique* set out.

"Heavy weather," said de Villieu, nodding toward the *Bonne Espérance* as they came up with her. "Look how the shipside's battered and the sails are patched."

De Bonaventure said nothing. He and any sailor aboard his ship had seen and gauged exactly what had befallen the *Bonne Espérance* when she had first been sighted, beating in from the bay. But one could not expect a soldier to have sailor-sight.

They slid alongside. The ladder was over; de Bonaventure, followed by de Villieu and two officers, went up. The mate and the crew waited in the longboat, cautiously hailing heads that popped out of portholes, exchanging news and quips in an undertone.

The Captain of the *Bonne Espérance* had little to tell. He had not seen the other vessel. He had run into a gale. Three of his men were swept overboard. The King was in good health. The Minister for the Colonies had offended Madame de Maintenon's niece. He would be retired. It was rumored that Madame de Maintenon wore a hair shirt. Her influence over the King was growing daily. All the ladies wore black veils like penitents, to please her. In confidence, of course, it was an odd world.

"Can we make port with this tide?" the Captain asked, when the gossip was exhausted and toasts drunk in wine that had suffered somewhat from the trip. "I have sick aboard, and we need fresh water."

"Yes," said de Bonaventure. "Follow the *Soleil d'Afrique*."

Up went sails on both boats; the sea gulls squawked and screamed; the *Soleil d'Afrique* went about, tacking toward the north; the *Bonne Espérance* proceeded slowly, using contrary breezes with less skill than the bigger ship.

Presently they could be seen, like two gigantic swans, angry and ruffled, muddy from a storm, going along the smooth waters between the forested hills.

The guard of honor, bored and hot in the new uniforms, marched up from the quay, followed by a procession of men with bales and casks. De Villieu, de Bonaventure, and the Captain of the *Bonne Espérance* walked up together, leisurely, relaxed. It was only when they reached the gates of the fort itself, behind the joking, jostling carriers, that they saw a new large flag flying from the Governor's house and realized the Governor must be among them, unannounced.

De Villieu turned quite pale.

A group of men resting in the shade of the bastion stood up and saluted. De Villieu stopped and spoke to one of them.

"Overland?" de Bonaventure heard him say. "Impossible!"

The man repeated his story. The Governor, driven ashore at Chibucto and the winds continuing unfavorable, decided not to wait and set out overland by way of La Hève and Minas, over a trail no white man had ever traveled, to walk out of the forest tireless and calm.

"Ciel!" said de Villieu.

They went to pay their respects. A sentry at the door of the Grande Salle presented arms. De Villieu noticed the shabbiness of his uniform, compared with the guard of honor, and bit his lip. He opened the door and entered, baring his head.

A dark man with broad shoulders and a ruddy face looked up as they came in. He was laughing, throwing his head back, showing very white teeth. Madame de Freneuse was laughing, too. They sat together before the harpsichord, their hands poised above the keys. As though the opening of the door were a signal, the music started, filling the room with unexpected force.

It was, thought de Bonaventure, fascinated, like a forest of great trees, swaying in the wind, with patterned light darting through branches. He stared. The players' heads, visible above the instrument, stared back at him, attention riveted on their hands. They looked alike, suddenly, with the same expression of controlled strength and passion, the same dreamy glazed look in the eyes.

"Like a couple of pollack," de Bonaventure thought in rage. He stood there, helpless, till the music finished; de Villieu stood with him, petrified. Tone-deaf, liking to wag one finger at "au clair de la lune," de Villieu found all music incomprehensible, and now the Governor, whom he sufficiently dreaded anyhow, was musical! Quel fléau! Wouldn't that be his luck!

The chords came to an end, the players stood, and de Villieu began to stammer excuses.

Monsieur de Brouillan held up his hand.

"Reception? Nonsense! Uniforms? Guard of honor? Tut! I have had the best reception of my life, mon vieux. I have found here not only an intelligent, and a beautiful, lady; I have found an artist!"

He thumped de Bonaventure between the shoulders. Madame de Freneuse smiled demurely at him as he choked and coughed beneath the Governor's buffet.

"Do not spoil everything by saying such a reception was not meant! 'Here,' I said to myself, 'they have set forth their best; they have given the garrison over to a goddess and have retired themselves discreetly to a distance. What could be more delightful, more refreshing to a heart? These people,' I said, 'have genius. And besides genius they possess among them an artist!' Ah, I can see that my séjour here will be very different from the barbaric life at La Plaisance! Conceive that I have found here a twin soul, an admirer of Buxtehude, a skilled performer, and a harpsichord! Madame, I entreat you, tonight again, is it not? Monsieur de Villieu, do not stand on ceremony, and Monsieur . . . Monsieur . . ."

"De Bonaventure."

"Why, of course! Did we not sail with Monsieur d'Iberville when he made a fool of himself at Pemquid? Certainly. I place you now at once. I have followed your career since then with interest. I will see you again, Monsieur."

Dismissed, de Bonaventure turned to the door. White rage was shaking him, and jealousy.

"Tonight again!" he swore between his teeth. "Ventre Saint Gris! Not if I know anything! Fop! Fool! Fiddler! Fichtre!"

He strode after Madame de Freneuse, disappearing in the distance at a pace that suggested a disinclination for conversation with him till he had time to recover. He followed her, striding so purposefully that he almost collided with an orderly bearing a tray and a bottle of wine.

"Here!" he called.

The man halted and came to the salute. De Bonaventure reached out for the flacon. He took a long swill and handed it back. Then he jerked his head.

"Get on with it."

The man grinned and proceeded on his way. Monsieur de Bonaventure, wiping his mouth with a hand still shaking, went toward his door.

CHAPTER XLIV

ON JUNE 22, 1702, Monsieur de Brouillan summoned the inhabitants to witness his installation as their future ruler and to receive his first commands. The day was hot and cloudless, after a misty dawn. Soldiers, drawn up in the fort inclosure, stood in the sun presenting arms, while the inhabitants of the settlement, grouped in the center, listened to the Governor's speech.

It was harsh and to the point. The group of notables, standing a little to one side, winced and whitened at the terms he used. In two days he had, apparently, perceived every defect due to carelessness or dishonesty in the settlement and its affairs.

Monsieur de Villieu heard that the representative of the King had a duty toward His Majesty even greater than the duty he must carry out toward the settlers, and that was to see that everyone in the community was contributing his, or her, utmost to the general good. The nuns, drawn up with their scholars to the right, heard that the new Governor did not propose to countenance inefficient methods in education or able-bodied women shirking behind closed walls. The notary and justice, Monsieur de Goutins, heard that the Governor considered ill-kept archives a crime against the King; that differences between settlers which came up to the courts should be disposed of quickly, with clarity and justice, while the mere suspicion of a bribe would mean a countercharge of treason, a military inquiry, and short shrift. The peasants and farmers heard that the community depended on their labor, that the yield of fruit and vegetables was not what it ought to be—

more cattle must be bred, better crops harvested, and this in spite of their help being required to build new palisades.

Three new ordinances were read out solemnly. A list of promotions followed, then a call for cadets.

"Monsieur Robert Tibaut, Monsieur Paul-Marie de Freneuse, Monsieur Jean-Marie de Chauffours are herewith enrolled."

There was a murmur among the ladies, rising like a wind, a few hissing whispers, then all was still again.

Monsieur de Bonaventure, standing at the Governor's right hand, turned his head sharply, taken by surprise. Madame de Freneuse on the outskirts of the group caught his eye and smiled. She was wearing his present, the biggest hoop of all, and round her head the new black veil, the only de Maintenon headdress in the settlement. The other ladies stared at it, dismayed. Nobody had thought of ordering black material. Madame de St. Vincent thought of the new black dress she had sent for, in mourning for her brother, wondering whether she could bear to cut it up and sell the stuff for veils.

The Governor barked a final warning, beckoned to the priest, bared his head for the blessing, turned on his heel, and left. The farmers and the peasants closed their gaping mouths, shook their heads, took themselves off, and shambled home. The group of notables turned in upon itself, smiling and bobbing, uttering platitudes. Madame de Freneuse moved slowly, in the new mystic walk she had practiced that morning to go with the veil, with de Bonaventure laughing as she gravely glided before him.

He caught her up and took her hand.

"Madame."

"Monsieur."

They delighted in the formal kiss-the-hand and curtsy.

"So now three of the children are well upon their way. Cadets! I hadn't thought of that. Why hadn't I?"

"Chut! Madame de St. Vincent is on your tail."

"Hein? An impossibility! I have never let her near it."

He turned, grinning, bowed, and made a formal leg.

"Madame."

"Monsieur."

Madame de St. Vincent bobbed her portly buttocks, recovering them from the curtsy with a stately snatch. Madame de Freneuse stared with an expression of interested concern, until she had righted herself, and turned away. But Madame de St. Vincent padded after her.

"Our sons," she panted, "quite of an age . . ."

"Indeed?"

"In the convent, you know, among the good sisters. Comrades at play, comrades at work . . ."

"It sounds like a song," said Madame de Freneuse. "I have often meant to ask you, do you sing? I have *seen* you, of course, at Monsieur de Villieu's gatherings; and by your expression I have sometimes wondered whether you did not want to sing, rather than listen to the performer. So tiresome, performers."

"No, yes, I have not been blessed with a voice like yours, my dear Madame." . . .

("Merciful heavens! What's come over her?")

"But about our sons, as I was saying . . ." She broke into a trot and began to splutter: "Comrades in work and play, comrades in arms, cadets, a noble training, so excellent for the character, so loyal to the King." . . .

"So perfect for the purse," said Madame de Freneuse, rolling her eyes up demurely beneath the new black veil.

"One word from you, dear Madame, to the Governor . . ."

"Ah, yes, what do you think of the Governor? Will you be with us tonight?" . . .

"I thought that last touch would kill her," de Bonaventure said, as they watched Madame de St. Vincent retreating purple-faced. "She thinks she'll be there as a matter of course."

"It's the effect of the hood. Do you know, I can see now why Madame de Maintenon wears it. She has to cope with the King, and I with the prudes. It gives one the oddest feeling, indescribable."

"That is as well. For I will not give you a chance to describe it. I am not Madame de St. Vincent, and I want to talk to you now."

"I regret, Pierre. I promised I would practice the toccata with the Governor. There he is now, looking this way. With such a fierce, determined man and all those penalties—did you like the one about the ducking stool?—ringing in our ears, I could not . . ."

"Oh, very well then, go!"

"Pierre! Your face is all red, and you sound very cross."

"Go on, go! There he is waiting for you! Go!"

"Could it be that Monsieur forgets some certain things?"

"No, but it might very well be that Madame does," said de Bonaventure, laughing again between his teeth. "Take—oh, take—that veil away."

"Surely that would be a little unsafe?"

"Mon Dieu! Was ever man so baffled? Listen, my heart's life, do not drive me beyond bounds in this. We should both regret it. A bientôt. Be good!"

CHAPTER XLV

THE Governor's first banquet was an event. It took place a week after his installation. The long room in the fort was lit with candles that had come from France, instead of clumsy tallow dips the settlers made and used. Two refectory tables were laid for the guests of the evening, officers of the garrison, civil authorities, their women, and their sons.

Monsieur de Brouillan presided at the first table, with Madame de Freneuse on his right, and Madame de Goutins, the notary's wife, on his left. Nobody watching his endeavors to make himself pleasant to the company would have recognized the martinet of the previous week, nor, reflected Madame de Freneuse, in these gracious ladies talking to her with such animation, the same who had slighted and cold-shouldered her before he came.

A lot had happened since then. Monsieur de Brouillan had granted her a pension from the King, on the grounds that she was the "only widow in Acadie," a distinction which, he observed, would touch the King's heart. Two of her sons were provided for as cadets, and one nephew. Her place in the community was well assured. With the Governor's favor, and she had the Governor's favor, what more could be desired? She looked at him.

He was showing his white teeth in a characteristic grin. "Never," thought Madame de Freneuse, "have I seen a man so all of a piece in his contradictions. A brilliant musician, a harsh disciplinarian, a dull dependable general, a hot-tempered irascible enemy, and each of these, I should think, to the exclusion of all else while it lasts. It's a good thing," she mused, letting her eyes stray from him to de Bonaventure, looking glumly at his plate, "that first impressions apparently stay with him."

She gave a little, low, reminiscent laugh and found de Bonaventure scowling at her. Poor Pierre! He looked quite bilious. She must get Dahinda to make him a tisane. He might get jaundice if he persisted in making himself miserable. Jealousy! What a potent dose, turning the most likable people into caricatures—veins swelling, eyes popping, chins shaking, hands clawing, and that other last degradation: the wheedling, nauseating "Do you love me?" stuff, that makes the questioned person laugh unpleasantly. Mathieu, when he was jealous, had walked around, perfectly polite and reasonable when he had to be, leaving a trail of Indian women for her to be commiserated upon. And there was that poor girl, the miller's daughter—what a picture, sitting on the ground in that murky room, cradling her dying lover on her knees! Yes, Mathieu had technique. If all jealous lovers acted so, at least respect and fondness might remain. But all this cloying! And as for scenes! Disgusting burlesque. She could not love that way. What would be Pierre's method of being jealous? So far he just scowled, like a sulky little boy.

He had walked around a little cockily before the Governor came. Men, even when they loved you—and Pierre had, he did!—must not be allowed to feel too charitable. Compassion, yes, if they knew how; but condescension, never. Perhaps it was as well for their love that the Governor was here. Music! The Governor could play. He had the right hands, but it was curious that a man of his profession should have remained a performer and such a brilliant one. He must have carted an instrument with him wherever he went. He had explained that one was on its way from France, because he had not expected to find a harpsichord here—or her.

She raised her eyes. Monsieur de Goutins had been talking to her for some time. She wondered whether her "Yes" or "No" had been à propos. Madame de St. Vincent was glaring, and Madame de Goutins looked as though *she* might have an attack of jaundice, so they must have been pretty pat. Monsieur de Goutins looked like a greedy nun in the convent at Kebec, who used to work her jowl in the same surprised, self-satisfied jerk when there was an extra piece of bacon on her plate or the soup was thick. He seemed very excited. She turned from him and caught Pierre's eye again. The sick misery in them stirred her heart. It was so silly, with all that he must know.

"But how shall I break it to him?" she wondered, framing phrases

·[187]·

in her mind, for the Governor had told her something that morning which might hurt Pierre very much. Looking round at her, after the last note of the adagio died away, he had taken her hand and stroked it reflectively.

"I think we must build you a house. The King is making an extra grant for building operations in the settlement. I know of no work so pressing as that you should have a home. The King owes your husband's memory that."

She was surprised. It had not occurred to her that Monsieur de Brouillan had given her position in the settlement a moment's thought, other than to be glad that she was there, but he had. He had even spoken to de Bonaventure about it, in a man-to-man, frank way with just that tinge of authority that made it hard to reply.

De Bonaventure realized for the first time, fully, what with the Governor's coming he had thought of dimly—that Madame de Freneuse was not his, in the world's eyes, at all. Through the long winter, under de Villieu's protection and his friendship, he had come to find her presence in his quarters not only desirable, heartwarming, natural, but settled. He would have said, if questioned: "I suppose it must come to an end, sometime; the new Governor may object," or when his wife wrote of coming to New France to join him: "I suppose that would mean Louise and I must separate," but he had never felt those things. They were vague and far away.

Now, sitting at this banquet, where another man presided, with her playing hostess, he remembered scores of scenes. . . . Louise, in the morning, reaching for her comb, eyes screwed up, still half asleep; Louise in the green cloth dress, old-fashioned and becoming, walking across to the fort; Louise, laughing at him, mimicking his accent; Louise stretched out, waiting for him, head turned half away; Louise . . .

He smiled suddenly.

Louise!

He saw a girl, dressed as a boy, stand in the doorway of a cabin, wide-eyed, trembling; another cabin, and a woman, offering her lips. "Once on a time, the amorous Sylvy . . . " She had been nearer since; and the hunger he had carried in his heart, fed. But now, suddenly, inexplicably, his heart ached again, with the old bitterness.

He looked up and found her watching, with a new expression in her eyes.

CHAPTER XLVI

DANCING followed the banquet. Monsieur de Brouillan's men, besides being soldiers, trappers, and guides capable of traversing the forest, were also chosen because of their musical ability. There were three very fine performers: a boy who could flute, a fiddler, and a French horn. The long room took on the air of a salon belonging to any bigwig in a provincial town in France, whose inhabitants kept up with the times, one eye on Paris fashion; but beyond the lighted room there was only the forest—interminable, hostile, unexplored—and these glittering figures moving in quadrilles, wearing high-towered wigs, ribbons, furbelows, were men and women roughened by the hardships of a pioneer life. Most of them had seen relations or friends scalped, tortured; many of them would face the same horrible death. In the meantime they were bowing, posturing, flirting, gossiping, intriguing for the Governor's favor for all the world as though they were at Court.

The lighted windows threw patterned shadows on the palisades, where, listening to the music and remembering his Paris, a sentry paced, alone beneath the stars, stopping now and then to peer into the night.

Presently the dancing ceased. The door of the Salle d'Armes opened; lanterns were lit and could be seen bobbing toward the settlement. Voices exchanged good-bys in courtly tones, as though they were not going to meet tomorrow, sweating at necessary tasks. Madame de Freneuse came out and stood looking up. The stars were brilliantly silver. She did not remember ever having seen a more beautiful night. There was the archer, shooting his eternal arrow at an enemy. She shrank suddenly, remembering an arrow drawn from a little boy, and put her fingers to her mouth.

·[189]·

Feet sounded behind her. A man's tall body loomed through the starlight, and a voice said close to her ear:

"Shall we go home?"

It was Pierre. She turned and slipped her hand into his. They set off, slowly, toward his quarters, saying nothing to each other. He walked stiffly, as though he were tired. She could feel the discouragement seep out of him and knew what was the matter.

They reached the rough log door and passed inside. Dahinda had lit the lantern hanging in the ceiling from a hook. The room looked rather like a ship's cabin, with its built-in bed of cedar wood, log table, and log chairs. De Bonaventure dropped his cape on the table and unbuckled his sword belt. It rattled onto the floor. He stooped to pick it up, and then he spoke.

"It will not be long now before I am alone here, I suppose."

She came to him and took him by the coat.

"Need we speak of it tonight? There is such a lot to say, and I am tired. I would rather rest in your arms."

But he was not to be diverted.

"I know it is not much of a place," he began, "not like Freneuse; but I, at least, have been happy here."

"And so have I." She said it quietly, in a deeper voice than usual. "I could stay here always with you and be very happy."

"Then why is the Governor building you a house?"

"Because he thinks it best." She spoke as though to a child, soothingly. "He has granted me a pension. Be reasonable, Pierre. I cannot continue to be supported entirely by you."

"Why not?"

"Because"—again the reasonable tone with the unreasonable child —"you have a wife and children of your own, and very little money."

"That is not the point," said de Bonaventure huskily. "I think it is right that you should have a pension, certainly; I am glad of it. I am glad about the children being made cadets; but I don't see why you should leave me, and go and live in his house."

"It isn't his house; it will be mine."

"At least I do see why, of course," and he laughed.

"Oh, nonsense, Pierre. The Governor is carrying out his duties; he is thinking of my husband."

"Always, always everyone thinks of him. No one considers me. If you can live in the Governor's house, why can't you live in mine?"

"I've told you, it isn't the Governor's house; it will be mine. The Governor isn't doing anything about it, except to use the King's money."

"We are all living on the King's money. My money is the King's, too. Why won't you live on it?"

"I have. I do."

"You know there's only one answer."

"Do I?"

"Yes."

But he could not bring himself to put into words: "You are in love with him." He fidgeted unhappily.

"I know one thing," she said, laying her cheek against his. "I've been heavenly happy here."

He tightened his grasp about her, the lump in his throat a little eased.

"Heavenly happy. Our first home."

"Do you remember how you came out of the mist?"

"Yes."

She did not add: "I have never been able to forget for an hour, for a moment, not even in your arms, from what I came—Gervais . . . Gervais . . . Gervais . . ." Instead, she drew him to her.

"Pierre, I have lived in your house. Why do you mind living in mine?"

"Living in yours?"

"Yes. You don't suppose, do you, that I should have a house, and you not there?"

"But how can I? I thought that was the whole point. I thought the Governor disapproved of my compromising you. He said so this morning."

"I think the St. Vincent woman has complained. The Governor just doesn't want any grounds for complaint. What I do in my own house is different."

"Even if the King pays for it?"

"Even then. Can't you see it's different? You're on the garrison staff."

"I chose to be," de Bonaventure growled. "I could have gone back to the sea, instead of laying the *Soleil d'Afrique* up here in the Basin."

"Of course, you could have. But you didn't. And if you had I couldn't have lived with you at all. It would be impossible for us to be together on a ship. And don't you see this is just the same?

·[191]·

A week or so ago you were gloomy because you thought the Governor might turn me out, and now that he is giving me a pension and a house you are gloomier than ever! Why can't we be happy, having what we have? Lovers, separated for years—living on memory, on hope—together in this little room for months, alone, nights and nights and nights, Pierre, and we're unhappy. Why?"

"Because I'm jealous," he said thickly, taking her in his arms.

"Ah!"

She gave an exultant laugh and slipped from his grasp. He sprang after; but Dahinda, entering silently to help her mistress undress, got in his way. With trembling fingers he began to take his own things off in the adjoining room, trembling and glowing with desire. It was as though he had never known the body waiting for him in the darkness, as though there were a strange mysterious woman there—and yet Louise.

He stood waiting while the familiar sounds went on, until Dahinda departed. Then he was kneeling by the bed, his face buried in her bosom; then he was in the bed, gathering her cool firm body to him; then he was embarked on the voyage to a far country, beyond the stars, returning always to find himself against her lips.

CHAPTER XLVII

THE longboat from the *Soleil d'Afrique* pulled toward the rip tide at the gap. Four men were rowing. In the stern Madame de Freneuse was trolling with an absorbed expression, letting the line slip through her bare hands after an inspection of the bit of lard she used for bait. De Bonaventure, steering with one hand while with the other he gave an occasional jerk to a line fastened to a stone in the bottom of the boat, smiled gaily at her enthusiasm. She had caught a good-sized cod and two pollack already, and was hoping for a third.

They had stolen away at dawn for a day to themselves, without waiting for the Governor's approval, knowing what he would think of a woman deep-sea fishing in so dangerous a place.

"It's our duty," Madame de Freneuse whispered, "to think of the settlement. The Governor said so in his speech."

"Fichtre with the Governor!" de Bonaventure answered, kissing her into silence. "What a night, mon amour!"

"And one of the settlement's needs is food for the winter. Indubitably. Let us get some fish, Pierre, to be salted down. I've always wanted to go fishing with you in the bay."

At first he had laughed, then he had succumbed to the temptation of a whole day on the water by themselves. He did not count the four men; they were sailors under his command—so much furniture; useful to bait the hooks for Madame de Freneuse, to help her land her fishes, and to row.

The day was fine; the fish were biting well; his love had obtained her wish, and he was reassured. But it was a hazardous proceeding, for the tide was racing strong, the woods were full of savages if anything should happen and they had to make for shore. De Bonaventure bent his mind to seamanship, while on the surface lazily content.

"There!" said Madame de Freneuse. "Look at the gulls all swooping down! If there's a school of herring there, the pollack and the cod will be there, too. Let's make for it, Pierre, quick. If I don't catch another soon, I shall die."

"Pull on the starboard, there!"

The men smiled.

"I've got one! I've got one! It's a big one this time!"

Madame de Freneuse stood up in the boat, excited, triumphant. She began to haul the line in, hand over hand, panting hard as the weight against her pulled the wet line out of her grasp.

"Help Madame."

"No, no. I want to pull it in myself."

"Stand by to help Madame if she wants you."

Hand over hand, blistering her palms, the long line wound in. At the end of it, showing as a silver splash—now on the surface, resisting; now, as the line slipped a little beneath the water, trying to escape—a huge silver pollack was dragged toward the boat.

"He's enormous! He's superb!"

But when the fish was landed, nearly knocking her over, it was smaller than it looked.

"About twenty-five pounds, twenty-six perhaps," de Bonaventure said. "Hooked in his stomach. That means that they're hungry. We had better anchor and try the hand lines for a while."

While he spoke so calmly, so judiciously, he was thinking:

"I don't believe it happened. I don't believe they did. It must have been the music after all. Perhaps some men have a passion for music as others for women. Perhaps he would give her a pension and a house just because she played to him that afternoon, and nothing else. Perhaps. I was out here then, and she was there; and when we got back, they were"—he crossed his fingers—"just like that! Close friends. Friends? I will believe it was so. I must believe. I cannot bear it to be otherwise. 'If my love swears that she is made of truth, I will believe her though I know she lies.' That English poet. I translated some of it in the book I sent her. Not that poem though. Fichtre! I must never ask. But all the same, an understanding like theirs, when he looks at her and she smiles . . . And now she will have her house. She says it will be the same for me, that I will come and be there all the time. So, no doubt, will he. Music! Well, I suppose I must take it. What else can I do? My love, my life's one love."

He looked at Madame de Freneuse's flushed face, smiling, with her hair pushed back by fishy hands, a blob of bacon bait on her cheek, and smiled, opening his mouth to speak. Before he could say a word, the sailor nearest said:

"Sail bearing down upon us, sir."

De Bonaventure looked behind him toward the entrance of the gap. A ketch appeared, sailing skillfully before the wind. It was the same little boat that had brought Madame de Freneuse and the children, months before. She recognized it and remained staring, though a fish was on her line.

"More fugitives?"

They watched with curiosity. The ketch came very near.

"Why, it's a priest," she said, screwing her face up and squinting.

They hailed the ketch, and it went about to come closer. Presently they were able to get a good view of its passenger. He was tall, spare, and forbidding. His expression when he saw Madame de Freneuse finally haul in her fish was rich in emotion. Monsieur de Bonaventure began to laugh.

"Mercy! What disapproval!" Madame de Freneuse said. "Hush, Pierre. What do they want?"

The ketch came alongside now, and the sail was furled.

"I am Father Francis," said the priest as he stepped calmly into the longboat. "My mission has been burned. I am on my way to Port Royal. Will you take me there? This good man must go back for the others if they are there. There was no sign of them when we left. Benedicite."

He settled himself in the stern, opposite Madame de Freneuse, and closed his eyes. De Bonaventure made a face.

"We are not going there at once," he began. "We have come to fish."

"I doubt whether we will get a bite with such a Jonah," Madame de Freneuse said. "We might as well go back, I think."

Father Francis opened his eyes to take a bundle from the sailor, thanked him, and said a prayer for his safe return. The occupants of the longboat said an uncertain amen and looked at one another.

"Pray, continue fishing," Father Francis said.

Madame de Freneuse, embarrassed, felt another bite.

"I've got a big one," she said in a very small voice.

Father Francis took out his breviary. In an awkward silence the fish was landed, flopping over his feet, which he moved aside.

Then de Bonaventure's line had a bite, and soon the other men were putting out their lines, and the fish began to come in—flip, flop, haul. Father Francis turned his pages; everyone forgot that he was there.

CHAPTER XLVIII

FATHER FRANCIS found himself attached to an annex of the Convent of the Sacred Heart, where seven young boys were being educated for the priesthood. The oldest of these, Paul-Marie de Freneuse, showed exceptional feeling and aptitude. Father Francis made him acolyte.

They were strolling one day past the first four houses of the settlement, by the water's edge, at the opposite end from the fort and the convent, reading their breviaries together—the one a little shadow of the other, pacing solemnly beside him—when their attention was caught by an unusual bustle. Soldiers and peasants were putting up a house. The earthen foundations were already there, stamped and hardened into place. On one side part of the wall was standing, a rough row of logs laid horizontally. More logs lay heaped in the sunshine, and there was a teamster with an ox to haul them into place.

Priest and boy paused to watch the scene.

"Here," said Father Francis a trifle sententiously, "is a house going up; a roof to shelter human joys and sorrows; a little defiant castle, threatened by savages, by fire, by everything. If man showed the same confidence in his God in the building of spiritual shelters as this man, whoever he is, shows in the building of a home, all would be well in Mother Church. I suppose some young couple is married and starting life together." He mused and—not for the first time—thought of his own wrecked plans for marriage, made in France twelve years before and come to naught, so that he entered the Church embittered, a hater of women.

A man standing, like them, to watch, turned round and smiled.

·[197]·

Father Francis blessed him, asking whose house it was. The man looked cautiously about and beckoned them near.

"The Governor's doxy," he whispered. "Madame de Freneuse."

Paul-Marie was stupefied.

"The Governor?" he repeated stupidly; then as a thought came to him, formed from half hints and whispered among the other boys: "You mean Monsieur de Bonaventure?"

"No, he's the old one. He had her all winter. Now the Governor's come and wants her for himself. Can't say I blame him; she's a tasty piece. And doesn't she know how to work him, too! Got all her kids in the garrison—cadets, drawing a salary. Got a fat pension out of him for being a widow"—here he spat. "Guess if she hadn't been, she'd have gotten a thrashing from her husband instead of a pension. And now she's getting a house. All the garrison out working on it; and the laborers, too. And us needing a granary—not to mention repairs to our houses, none of *them* paid for by the King. But that's the way it goes, pardi."

"Monsieur," said Paul-Marie stiffly, while his chin trembled and his knees shook, "you must be mistaken, altogether mistaken. I know the lady you speak of, she is my ——"

"Do you now? Well, well. What did you give her? Your virginity?"

Paul-Marie, beside himself with fury, raised his arm and struck the man with his fist across the face. Instantly he found himself on his back in the mud, with a cut to the jaw and a ringing in his ears. He struggled to sit up. Blood oozed from his lip where a tooth had cut it.

"Don't raise your hands to me," said the man contemptuously, "nor you either"—to Father Francis who bent over Paul-Marie to help him up. "I'm the butcher; and the blacksmith, too. My name's Etienne. No one crosses me."

His expression changed.

"Here's the Governor now. Come on; get up out of that. And if you open your mouth to complain of me to the Governor or any of 'em, I'll cut your liver out. Merde to the lot of you!"

He moved away. Paul-Marie crawled to his feet and stood nursing his jaw, looking about him. Father Francis murmured something, laying a restraining hand upon the boy's arm.

A little group of people had arrived. The tall, red-faced man with the frowning, beetling brows must be the Governor. The boy had never seen him. With him was another man, hat in hand, obsequious, the builder in charge or the carpenter. He was dressed in working clothes. On the Governor's right, with her head turned away from him, toward the house, was a lady. Paul-Marie could not see her face, and the fashionable clothes, wide hoops, black hood, were new to him; but by the sudden fierce commotion in his blood he knew, even before she turned her head, that it was Madame de Freneuse, his mother.

She looked straight at him, and then she cried out and rushed toward him, hands outstretched.

"Paul-Marie! What are you doing here?"

She crossed herself to the priest, and then turned to the child again.

"I did not know they would let you out. What is the matter with your face? Your lip is bleeding, did you know? Have you been fighting, my little priest? The good father here will tell you that is not the right thing to do!"

She faltered before the hostile gaze of Father Francis, looking at her sternly, with contempt, and turned to the Governor with an uncertain smile.

"Monsieur de Brouillan, you have not met my last son, Paul-Marie de Freneuse. He is studying for the priesthood here. They seldom let him out."

Paul-Marie made a leg, sulkily. The Governor bowed, affability in his face. Then he looked inquiringly at Father Francis, who raised his fingers and blessed him, still without a smile.

Paul-Marie looked from one to the other. Suddenly he darted forward and pulled his mother's hand. Standing on tiptoe, he whispered something into her ear. She paled. Her eyes sought the priest's. He stared at her, a world of condemnation in his gaze. Her eyes lowered. Paul-Marie extricated himself from her grasp and went to the priest's side. Father Francis took him by the hand and led him away.

Madame de Freneuse watched them disappear, hardly listening to the Governor's words at her side. She smiled nervously, gripping the ends of her black hood, while the Governor and the builder discussed the proportions of the building and the disposition of the doors; then, when they began to measure the height for the window, she stepped back. A sudden, overpowering loneliness came over her.

"So that is what they are saying!" she thought. "So that is what it is!"

·[199]·

CHAPTER XLIX

ENISE DE CHAUFFOURS woke in the convent with a sense of pleasurable excitement. It was Thursday, not only a half holiday, but also a saint's day, September the eighth, the Nativity of Our Lady. The whole convent was astir already in the anticipation of a fete; but it was not the fact that after mass there would be recreation and a special kind of sugared cake, and after that again games and even dancing, that was making Denise sit up in bed and hug her knees with such an ecstatic smile. She balanced backwards and forwards, taking a firmer grip, thrusting her small pointed chin fiercely downwards, muttering:

"We shall see ma tante! We shall see ma tante!"

A small form on the bed next her grunted and turned over. Denise detached one arm and gave it a sharp poke.

"Wake up! It's arrived! It's the day, Jeanne; we shall see the tante."

The figure beside her rolled over and sat up rubbing its eyes. Jeanne was younger than Denise, dark-haired, dark-eyed in contrast to her sister's russet-colored hair and gray eyes. She yawned and stretched and was about to slide back into sleep when Denise, clutching her, said:

"There's Mère Marghérite! Quick, Jeanne, don't do anything to be put in disgrace! Think, if you couldn't come today to dine at the tante's! Oh, quick!"

She made an effort to haul her sister out of bed, at the same time dropping to her knees at her own bedside and pulling out her rosary. Mère Marghérite, stumping through the room, was edified to find all the children kneeling meekly, beads in hand—even Jeanne, usually en réprimande for her morning torpor.

The de Chauffours sisters were not very popular with the nuns, first on account of their early training, which had made them independent and able to think for themselves, and then because of their aunt, Madame de Freneuse, of whom the nuns disapproved. Was she not leading a shameful existence, a life of sin with Monsieur de Bonaventure, and now, it was rumored, with the Governor as well? Depending, as they did, upon the Governor's approval for many of the factors in their temporal life, they were careful not to show their feelings publicly by any discrimination against the two little girls; but there were occasions when a rebuke might be administered or a commendation withheld which would not reach the ears of the world outside or, if it did, could be excused on grounds of general discipline. More, however, than specific acts, the de Chauffours sisters felt the unspoken weight of disapproval, tinged with a certain malice and contempt, hang over them. They did not understand, but they knew better than to probe or to complain. They accepted things and clung more closely together than they might have otherwise.

On this particular day they came into their own. Promptly at noon they were sent for and departed, dressed in their uniforms of black stuff dress, blue apron, and white coiffe, to spend the day with their notorious aunt.

As the convent gates shut behind them, Denise threw her head back and Jeanne smiled. They walked down the center of the path, kicking at stones and scuffling through the fallen leaves. The time had not yet come for the maple trees to stain the hills with crimson and with gold, but the elms and poplars and the apple trees in the settlement had turned and dropped their leaves.

Presently the far end of the settlement came in sight. There, close to the water, stood their aunt's new house, built for her by Monsieur de Brouillan out of the King's money. It was quite small compared to Freneuse but large according to the standards of the settlement, where nearly every house had just two rooms with an attic above them. This house boasted three. A garden ran down behind it to the water. Madame de Freneuse had sent for flowers from France. This was the second year that they had bloomed; already the garden looked quite civilized.

As they drew near, sounds of music could be heard through the living-room window. Somebody was playing the harpsichord.

Jeanne nudged Denise.

"Do you think it's the Governor?"

"Probably," Denise nodded, with a frightened feeling in her stomach.

The Governor was such an awe-inspiring man, so powerful, so dreaded in the community, so harsh. There was the story of the soldier stripped in the coldest part of winter and thrown out to die. People said the Governor had soused him with water first, so that he would freeze more quickly into solid ice. Everyone knew, too, that the Governor had stolen an island, known as Hog's Island, from a poor habitant to whom it belonged and had threatened him with torture if he so much as complained; it was very dangerous to have anything to do with such a man. It made la Tante Louise all the more of a paragon that she could sit so calmly with him, playing a duet. They laughed together often and were as gay as though he were not the Governor, but just a man. Denise could not get over it. She loved her aunt with the wholehearted passion of a lonely child. She could still remember the days at Freneuse when she and the other children ran wild and played, when it had been her home. She did not see the boys now more than once a year.

Everything seemed to have changed sadly for the worse since the dreadful siege, l'Oncle Mathieu's death, and the escape. All through the long first winter, before la Tante Louise had the new house—when she lived with Monsieur de Bonaventure at the fort and only came to see them now and then—they had been unhappy at the convent, so alone. Now they were getting used to it; and things were better, too. Madame de Freneuse sent presents of chocolates and books and of flowers for the altar, which the nuns threw away. They never told her that; it would be too mortifying for la tante to bear—but it was so. Never once had the beautiful flowers been placed where they belonged, upon the altar, except for one mass—when the Governor came. Then la Mère Supérieure made haste to tell him:

"These were sent to us by Madame de Freneuse."

The tinkling chords came to an end as they approached; they heard laughter and a man's voice.

"It is he!"

Denise took hold of her sister's hand, convulsively. Together they entered the room, took a deep breath, and curtsied without looking up.

"Hello, cabbages," said a voice above their heads. Their aunt took them by the hands. "Ciel, what young ladies! Grown out of recognition! Let me see you both."

·[202]·

They looked up, blushing, and sank in another curtsy to the Governor. He was standing by the harpsichord, turning over some music, but he dropped what he was doing to make them a grave bow. Jeanne's heart turned over. If Mère Marghérite could see her now!

"Well, children," said their aunt caressingly, "now that you are here, the party is complete. Monsieur de Bonaventure, will you propose a toast? Children, take glasses; let us toast the day."

A tall man in the corner, whom they had not seen, rose, glass in hand:

"The King, and His Majesty's representative in New France, Monsieur de Brouillan, Governor of Acadia."

Everybody drank, the children excitedly rolling the rich flavor round their little tongues.

"His Majesty's Navy, and Monsieur de Bonaventure."

It was the Governor responding. They all drank again.

"That is enough," said Madame de Freneuse, forestalling a toast to her and the awkwardness of who would propose it; "we will drink again at dinner. Here is Dahinda now."

The Indian servant, smartly attired in maroon with a lace apron and a long streamered coiffe, stood in the doorway demurely smirking.

"Madame est servie."

The company collected and passed out of the room, Denise still grasping Jeanne's hand in her own and Jeanne making a face at her. The fete, so far as she was concerned, had only now begun.

CHAPTER L

THE meal Madame de Freneuse offered her guests was
typical of New France. Eels, bear steak, pumpkins, maize,
and a sweet syrup, popular among the Indians, over new-
made bread. She sat at the end of the table facing Monsieur de
Bonaventure, with the Governor at her right, Denise next to him,
and little Jeanne opposite. Denise watched her aunt's vivid face
beneath its de Maintenon dark hood, intrigued by the faint resem-
blance it bore to the headdress at the convent, worn by the nuns.
She tried to compare her aunt's animated, laughing eyes with the
grave eyes, dulled by lack of imagination, of Mère Marguérite
and with the sly eyes of Sister Augustine. Only the sparkling eyes
of la Mère Supérieure resembled them, and that because la Mère
had been, as everyone knew, a great lady in the outer world.

So was Madame de Freneuse a great lady. Everything she did
betrayed it. Her very sins were great—open and undisguised like
herself. She did not hide them beneath a veneer of respectability.
Denise admired her for the courage that could allow her to go her
way so serenely through the insults and hatred of the settlement.
Father Francis had refused her the sacrament. He chose a very
crowded mass to do so. She merely lifted her head beneath its
veil, stared at him until his eyes were lowered, turned her back, and
left the church. But her presents of flowers, of money, and of food
and clothing to the convent continued. So did her permission for
her youngest son to become a priest.

She continued upon her way uninfluenced by any authority.
Here were the two men reputed to be her lovers dining at her
table, as polite to her and to each other as though they were dining
at Court. Each a great man in his way, wielding much power.

Monsieur de Bonaventure—still Commander in Chief of the King's Acadian Navy, seldom at sea these days, occupying an anomalous position ashore, treated with great deference by the military authorities in the person of Monsieur de Villieu and with apparent friendship by the Governor—was a figure of peculiar glamour to the children. He was handsomer than ever, with a sparkle in his dark eyes that had not been noticeable the first time that they saw him, after the flight.

The Governor was the Governor! It was hard to connect that legendary figure with the mild-mannered, jovial person who sat at the table sipping his coffee from a bowl like any other thirsty man. He told them stories of his childhood in Gascony and even stooped to tease them. Denise wanted to pinch herself, to make sure that she was awake.

But it was hearing news of Raoul that made the day for her, even though the news was not reassuring and he was mentioned in anger. Denise had always nourished a secret passion for her tutor. She had been saddened for two weeks when she first heard that he had gone native, disappearing with the Indians. She had laughed up her sleeve when he had sent insulting messages to Monsieur de Villieu, and presents to Madame de Freneuse of beaver skins and other contraband. Once he had sent her copper, saying that he owned a copper mine. Denise, hearing talk of him by snatches on her rare visits to her aunt, conceived a very romantic idea of his occupation. It was exciting to think of him, bronze as Dahinda, shaking his dark head at the French, twinkling behind their backs to Denise, with whom he would share his secret.

"It's the Coureurs de Bois," Monsieur de Brouillan was saying, "that are the enemies of civilization."

"On the contrary, its vanguard, Monsieur le Gouverneur. Who else keeps an eye on the Mohawks? Who hears the movements of the English? Who, when you come down to it, bears the brunt of an attack? Such captains of Indian tribes, such Coureurs de Bois as Saint Aubin, de Bellefontaine, de Saillian, Denys de la Ronde, de Saint Castin, de la Tour . . ."

("Bravo la Tante!")

"But not de Perrichet," said the Governor dryly. "I am sorry he should be your nephew and a friend of Madame's"—he bowed slightly in Monsieur de Bonaventure's direction and then again to Madame de Freneuse.

"Not as sorry as I am," said de Bonaventure grimly.

"But he is beginning to be a real thorn in our sides. He would be invaluable if he were, as you say, a Coureur de Bois like Monsieur de Saint Castin or Monsieur de la Ronde, both very rough figures in their way but loyal to the crown. De Perrichet, on the contrary, is hostile to his own country and his own country's rule. He has amassed the biggest troop ever commanded by one white man. They say his forces amount to over a thousand men, scattered throughout the forests. He calls himself by an Indian name and lives like an Indian. He has deluded his poor savages by speeches promising the red man his lands and his freedom. He is an enemy and a traitor with a price upon his head. With all that, if I could make a treaty with him to stay neutral in the next attack or, better still, if I could win his favor, I would give a year's pay. And that," he grimaced, "is saying a good deal in these days of hard times!"

Monsieur de Bonaventure stirred uneasily at this speech. Madame de Freneuse looked into the fire, thoughtfully. Denise smiled. The Governor continued.

"The English are preparing a descent upon us. They left us alone last year on account of the plague. It hit them even more than it hit us. But they'll certainly be sending a landing party this year. If we have to contend with a thousand savages as well, not to mention the Iroquois and Mohawk that the English let loose on us, I do not like to contemplate the picture. It will be worse than anything that has happened so far in New France."

"Why do you not attempt to get in touch with Ra——, with Monsieur de Perrichet?" Madame de Freneuse asked. "You could offer him an indemnity for himself, for his followers. You could perhaps enlist his services in the war against the English."

"Why," said the Governor bluntly, "when he hates us bitterly?"

"That is just a young man's temper. He will yield to the right approach."

"Will he? He hasn't so far. I've tried and tried. I've sent emissaries and messages without the slightest result."

"Have you?" Monsieur de Bonaventure looked startled. "I did not know that."

The Governor shrugged.

"Why should you?"

There was no answer to that. Madame de Freneuse clapped her hands for Dahinda. They rose and made their way back to the other room.

·[206]·

"He sends the same message back to me each time," the Governor continued, when they were seated by the window looking onto the garden. " 'I will not treat with you.' My scouts tell me his men adore him. It is strange, is it not, for a man so young to hold a place of such importance, and a white man at that! I shall never understand the savages."

"It is because he is blood brother to a chief," Madame de Freneuse said suddenly. "That is why he has influence and power. The chief was called Nessamaquij, a really remarkable Indian. This boy is supposed to have inherited all Nessamaquij's force with his blood pact. Nessamaquij was killed at the siege of Nashwaak when the—when my husband's seigneury burned. It was on account of my husband and myself that Raoul went through his initiation."

De Bonaventure glared. Jeanne leaned forward.

"His back was all bloody," she volunteered, and was frowned into silence by Denise.

"Well, it was."

The Governor grinned.

"Nothing to the state a lot of people's backs, and heads, will be," he said, "if he decides to join the English."

There was a silence.

"He's nothing but a half-grown puppy," said de Bonaventure crossly.

"He bares the teeth of a grown dog," the Governor retorted. "You should have whipped him more when you had him with you, Monsieur de Bonaventure."

Madame de Freneuse said, as though to herself:

"I should like to speak to him. I don't think he can have changed. Tenez!" She clapped her hands together and raised candid eyes to the Governor. "Authorize me to go to the forest"—and before de Bonaventure could protest, she swept his words aside and went on rapidly: "Give me an escort, if you like, and let me try."

The Governor sat, twisting his hands together, without looking up. There was a frown of such concentration on his face that even de Bonaventure did not dare to interrupt.

"But would he keep his word with us if he did make a treaty?" he asked.

"I am sure of it."

The Governor looked from her to de Bonaventure. His gaze fell once more.

"You understand," he said, "the situation is graver than anyone knows but myself. I had dispatches this morning. The English have already sailed from Boston. They will be here before we can expect any help from Kebec. We are in a position to stand a siege, even a long siege, if we can maintain relations with the Indians and get supplies and food from them. Also, I had hoped to use the Micmacs against the Mohawks that the English will let loose on us. I am loath to waste good French soldiers on savages, if there are other savages to bear the brunt. But my scouts report only thirty Micmacs that have not joined Monsieur de Perrichet."

"I had no idea," de Bonaventure stammered.

"Oh, but you will be invaluable, Monsieur de Bonaventure, in command of your ships. We shall look to you to keep the English out of the Basin. Then they will have to land on the north shore and make their way overland to a position facing us. They will probably go to the foot of the Maillet. If we could let loose some Micmacs on them, between us and the north shore . . . That is why, unbidden, I have dined with you today, Madame—the possibility of sending you as an emissary *had* occurred to me. Now that you have offered spontaneously what was in the back of my mind to ask, I am as usual, indebted to you, as all New France will be should you succeed."

"Impossible!" De Bonaventure, furious, was on his feet.

"What is impossible?" the Governor asked him with assumed mildness. "That New France should feel gratitude?"

"That Madame de Freneuse should trust herself to that young rakehelly scoundrel! That she should set a foot in the forests among savages! Surely, Monsieur, you must have some grain of imagination! Madame de Freneuse escaped from the savages only a few years ago. She has seen the ruin of all her fortunes and her property. Her experiences during that dreadful journey should forever put her out of the possibility of encountering them again, no matter what is at stake!"

The Governor stood up also, to his full burly height.

"Madame de Freneuse escaped from the savages with the help of this same Ruwerera, who is Monsieur de Perrichet. I understand from Monsieur de Villieu, here at the time, that the young man put her on the first ketch and traveled overland. When he arrived here, after hardships that we can only guess at, his reception, Monsieur de Bonaventure, was such as to turn him into the bitter enemy of the settlement and the settlement's rulers that he has become. I understand that, instead of according to him the honor his exploits demanded, you drew your sword on him. Your sword, Monsieur de Bonaventure, has been used to better purpose."

Denise and Jeanne, looking at the angry faces, huddled together, forgotten, by the window. Monsieur de Bonaventure spoke:

"If I drew my sword on Monsieur de Perrichet, it was because he insulted Madame de Freneuse; you would have done as much, had you been there. Monsieur de Villieu, indeed, took my part. He ordered Monsieur de Perrichet to the dungeon."

"Monsieur de Villieu has recounted to me all I need to know of that deplorable affair. Madame de Freneuse has had, I think"—his eye swept the room significantly—"no cause to complain of the treatment the settlement of Port Royal has accorded her. The King's money has been spent to beautify and adorn her house; she receives a pension. I cannot feel that she would refuse an occasion like this in which to earn it."

Madame de Freneuse paled. The Governor had never spoken so brutally or with such an insulting meaning to her before.

Monsieur de Bonaventure fumbled with his sword but, catching her imploring glance, dropped his fingers. The Governor smiled contemptuously. Turning to her, he said more gently:

"I am glad that you so bravely offered to go on this mission, for the last message I had from Ruwerera, which arrived this morning, said: 'Send me Madame de Freneuse, or I will come and fetch her; and if I have to come and fetch her, I will burn the place about your ears before the English have to put themselves to that trouble.' That is his message."

"I will go," said Madame de Freneuse.

"I will speak to you in private," said the Governor.

For the first time he seemed to realize the presence of the two frightened little girls.

"Come here!" he said.

They advanced, trembling. This was the Governor they had always heard about. He crooked out his finger.

"Not a word of any of this to your comrades or to the nuns."

They nodded.

"No one is to know that the English are expected, yet."

"No." Denise spoke, looking at her aunt.

"Your aunt has intrepidity enough to tackle anything," he said, with a ghost of a smile, "and she will be protected. Moreover, she

·[209]·

has power over Ruwerera. You will understand that better when you are older."

He patted their heads kindly, turned his back, and marched out of the room.

Madame de Freneuse, hesitating a moment, looked toward de Bonaventure, fuming by the window. Then she followed the Governor. An uncomfortable silence fell.

CHAPTER LI

THE sun set across the hills of the north shore in purple and red, casting gold and copper shadows on the water of the Basin; a breeze moved along the tinted ripples; leaves fell, swirled and splashed. Madame de Freneuse's garden took on a quietude; the little house behind it, mystery.

Monsieur de Bonaventure, standing at the window, his arm about her, spoke.

"It is not only that I have to stand by while another man disposes of you on a fool's errand, that I cannot draw my sword and run him through the guts . . ."

Madame de Freneuse laughed. He turned suddenly and drew her close to him, groaning a muffled word into her hair. She put up a hand and disarranged his wig, pushing it a little to one side so that she could run a finger through his own dark locks.

"What does it matter?" she said soothingly. "It may even be a good thing for me to do. People are increasingly rude. The Governor may get tired of protecting me. Oh, I know they come to my parties and are polite to my face, with one eye on the Governor. If he abandoned me, they all would turn."

"Then I would take you away on the *Soleil d'Afrique*."

She patted his ear.

"I know you would. But that would ruin you. Don't you think that, if I do this, and the Governor is pleased, and the colony owes me something, everyone will be nice to me? I don't say like me, but be grateful. Don't you?"

De Bonaventure was silent. He could not bear to say:

"No. They will only say 'Couldn't she be content with the

·[211]·

Governor and the sailor without running off into the woods to sleep with the savages?'"

It seemed an unkind thing to say, but it tortured him. He wondered what methods she would use to make Raoul see sense. There was one method—no . . . no . . . no! He clasped her closer.

"Wouldn't they?"

"I don't know," he said huskily. "I'm not worrying about that."

"What is the matter then?"

"It's the journey and the danger. And I don't trust Raoul. He's insane with jealousy. He thinks himself in love with you."

"Thinks himself?"

"Well, is then—is! All the worse. I don't trust him. I tell you it is a cruel thing to expect a man to do—stand aside and let you go into God knows what!"

"You trust me, don't you, Pierre?"

"Yes; oh, yes!"

But all the same, he said to himself: "The Governor is not acting like a casual friend. I wonder what there is between them? Music? Hmmm."

Fragmentary pictures flashed behind his eyes. The Governor passing his quarters with the strut of a cock, making toward the little house by the water; and while he, de Bonaventure, paced distractedly, waiting for the Governor to return . . .

"Louise," he said suddenly, "mon amour, look in my eyes!"

She turned her head and looked at him. They were silent for a long moment. She was thinking:

"There never was anybody like him. I am his completely. He should know it. There is something grand about him, like his element, the sea. He has simplicity and strength, passion. He is the captain of my ship. His hand is on my tiller lines. I could not sail without him there. And yet this jealousy is good for him, good for our love. I am no longer the child he spurned from the *Bonne Espérance*. If I were, what hope for either of us now? He would not be easy to hold unless he felt an element of risk. I love him; I love the way his eyebrows grow, and the little line of hair from ear to beard. I love his graying beard and his natural hair. I love him naked. Enfin, I love him, the ridiculous little boy!"

Much of this her eyes were saying, while his, anxious and searching, looked into their smiling shadow, flecked with dancing lights like the waters of a shady stream at noontide. He spoke:

"Do not go!"

His soul was in the three words, dragged out of him. She laughed.

"I must. You heard what the Governor said."

"To hell with the Governor!"

"Treason, Monsieur de Bonaventure. You might be hanged for that."

"Louise, our life here is uncertain, unsatisfactory, sacrificed to my career. A fig for my career! I care no longer how it goes. There, in the Basin, is the *Soleil d'Afrique*. A word from me and she will sail with both us on board her. We will turn pirate like de Morpain and his crony Pierre Maisonat. There is a good living to be made as a corsair—without scruples, you understand. And with you! You would be really mine then; mine alone, not at the beck and call of any governor. You offered, once, do you remember, to sail with me?"

"You refused."

"I beg you now!"

"You were right."

"I am right now."

"I was a child." She sighed.

"I have saved my pay this winter, and I had also bought some beaver skin when Monsieur de Brouillan turned his interfering back on me! I have a good many louis laid up, a hundred livres."

"Rich man."

"I am tired of living in a garrison like a footling foot soldier; tired of all the carping tongues that wag at us, here in this silly settlement; tired, above all, of being made jealous! Dieu, how you have made me pay for making a mistake when we were young! Louise, be kind. Come with me now, and let us live on the *Soleil d'Afrique* in peace and the clean air."

"Pierre"—she put out her hand tenderly and crooked it through his arm, "do you think the King's ministers would sit idle and let you steal the fastest ship in their Navy, the fastest ship on the seas? They'd send a fleet against you, to get it back, and hang us both."

"That's my business. Not the hanging, but the ship. I've given it much thought. We would be safe. There's an island off the coast, unmapped, unknown—even, I imagine, to the savages. I've a notion we could anchor there and build up a settlement of our own. Eh bien?"

"Eh bien, no!"

She swept her hand in a vague circle. "I love this little house."

·[213]·

"De Brouillan's!"

"Our home. We have lived many happy hours here. I do not want to venture on the seas. Time was I would have; now I need this background and this peace. I know that, and besides"—she looked him firmly in the eyes—"I do not trust you as I did."

"Louise!"

"If I were alone with you on the *Soleil d'Afrique* day after day, year after year, always supposing we were not caught and punished, your love would die; you would get tired of me, and want a change. You would discard me on the island that you talk about. No, no. Here, I keep you a little guessing, is it not? That is good for you."

She smiled and tweaked him by the left ear. He bent his lips to hers. A long time they stood there, velour coat pressed to satin dress, white wig ruffled against black hair, eyes closed, minds dreaming. Then, still locked together, they stirred and moved toward the couch.

CHAPTER LII

THREE canoes rasped to the shores of the Dauphin River, forty miles above the fort. Two carried women, seated in the center, with men paddling bow and stern; the third held two men, a keg, some canvas bags, and a bale of bright-colored cloth.

The man who paddled bow in the first canoe sprang ashore and offered his hand to the woman. She took it with a smile and, gathering up her skirts, prepared to leap; but the man behind her caught her up in his arms and stepped into the water between them and the shore. He landed her, stood back again, and grinned.

"There!"

Madame de Freneuse grinned back. In the early light of the day her face had the startled look of a sleepy child, astonished yet eager. Her hair was tangled from a night in the canoe. She opened a reticule and took out an ivory comb. Turning her back on the others, busy beaching the boats, going about their preparations for a meal, she shook out her long black hair and began to comb it. Dahinda came up behind her and took the comb away.

"Madame tired," she said. "Madame leave to me."

Madame de Freneuse surrendered the comb and submitted to these ministrations with a faraway look. She was tired. She would have given anything to be back in bed in the little room with wooden walls and mud floor and bottle-glass windowpanes. She would like to stretch and say to herself, "Pierre will be coming soon"; or, better still, turn over to find his head beside her. The Governor refused to let Pierre come with her. He had been peremptory and harsh. She knew why and twinkled in the sunlight. The Indians found her smiling as they stepped out of the wood.

There were twenty of them, dressed in peace paint, with beaver skin coats and leggings of deerhide. They were all tall and young, with handsome proud faces. They emerged so silently that she was startled, accustomed though she was to the savage stealthiness. One moment there was nothing but the trees against the sky, along a deserted shore line; the next, color and movement filled the scene. Now there was a silence. Dahinda went on calmly combing out her hair. A French soldier brought her the first cup of coffee. She drank it while the Indians waited.

Then the spokesman said:

"We have come to take the white squaw to Ruwerera. But she must come alone. Ruwerera does not wish the site of his camp to be discovered nor the copper mine. Ruwerera does not trust the white man's words!"

Sergeant Labiche said:

"Here! That's no way to be talking. Our orders were to go with Madame, and go we will. When we have finished eating, you shall show the way."

But the Indian spokesman said they were not to come. He grew insistent about it, and very angry. At one moment it looked as though he might make sure of Ruwerera's wishes being carried out by having the white men killed. The sergeant scratched his head.

"Go back, Labiche," said Madame de Freneuse. "I'll send word to the settlement. You must leave me here. Unload the stuff, and tell the Indians to take it if they will not have you."

"But, Madame," the sergeant stammered, remembering what Monsieur de Bonaventure had said to him before leaving, and what would await him if he should go back without her, "I cannot do that. To leave you alone among savages . . ."

"Take hostages," said Madame de Freneuse, "if they will give you some, and get going, Labiche. Nothing annoys a Micmac so much as an argument. They have their orders, and I trust Ruwerera."

She spoke confidently, but she was far from feeling so. She had no desire to be left with twenty savage warriors forty miles from the settlement to undertake a journey through the woods. They had a litter of pine branches covered with a bearskin, on which she apparently would travel. The thought of what would await her if she returned without carrying out the Governor's wish made her throw her head back with a determined smile. She did not desire to lose his protection, to be sent into exile to her husband's devastated seigneury; still less did she desire to have de Bonaventure disgraced, turned out of his command, sent back to his ships. All this was in the Governor's power. If she turned back now, without even seeing Ruwerera—Raoul—the Governor would let things take their course. He was unpopular enough with the settlers without persisting in protecting a woman whom they hated as much as they hated her—notary, notary's wife, butcher, baker, candlestick maker, and the Church, of course. Father Francis would bring her down with his teeth in her throat. She shuddered; that was absurd . . . but all the same, she must please the Governor.

"Dahinda," she said, "is there danger for me if I do what the Micmacs say?"

Dahinda shook her head.

"I will go with you," she said to the spokesman. "I am ready. Dahinda comes with me."

The Micmac nodded. Silently the others moved about her, closing in. Before the sergeant could make up his mind, they had vanished, carrying Madame de Freneuse and Dahinda with them into the woods.

They left the provisions and presents where the men had unpacked them by the shore, the first time in the sergeant's experience that such a thing had happened; when it came to presents, the savages were children—greedy and curious. He shook his head.

"We'll camp here," he announced, "until the supplies are gone."

Delay might bring her back, or news of her. Delay might save him from the unpleasant fate de Bonaventure held in store for him. They sat down on the sand to play at cinq et un.

CHAPTER LIII

CRIMSON deepened on bush and tree as Madame de Freneuse was carried farther into the forest. After the first sharp strangeness wore off, the days took on an unreal quality that fascinated her. She had nothing to do but think as she was carried along, not too uncomfortably, on the litter of pine boughs, in and out of a portage trail. After a while even thought deserted her; and she was content to be wafted along at unusual angles, jerked and tossed, in impersonal silence. None of the Indians spoke, except low-voiced among themselves at the evening halt. She got used to their silence.

The first night was cold. They stretched two strips of deerhide between stakes, covered them with branches and, in the center, a bearskin. Then with Madame de Freneuse and Dahinda on the bearskin, they all lay down, and were covered with a longer hide by the last to climb up at either end. Dahinda clasped Madame de Freneuse in her arms, and when, on a given signal from the end man, they all turned over, the Indian next her did the same. Thus, all night long, she was warmed and held in place by clutching arms. Once, she dozed beyond the borders of consciousness, but not so far as sleep, and, fancying the arms were Pierre's, gave them answering pressure. It happened to be the man who was holding her. He gently took her hand and put it back into place, neither tightening nor relaxing his grip upon her waist. She woke with a start and was kept from moving, sandwiched between her human coverings. Then she was amused, imagining Pierre's face.

Every night they slept in this way. She got quite used to it, accustomed, too, to meals cooked for her by Dahinda out of the stores the Indians carried specially for her. That Raoul thought of her food on the journey reassured her. However he might have changed, there was still solicitude. One can do much with that, she reflected, dreaming for the hundredth time of bearing back the treaty through these same flaming woods, lying in triumph on a bed of pine, making an entry into the settlement to receive the Governor's congratulations. All his petulance would melt; they would readjust their relationship till even Pierre would be happy and the St. Vincent harpies brought to heel.

Meanwhile the journey grew more tiresome. She ached from lying in the same position. The nights were cold and gave her cramp. There was no one to talk to. Every day's march took her farther from the little house and Pierre. It was with extreme relief that on the fourth day, toward evening, she first sighted Ruwerera's camp.

The Indians carrying her grunted and set her down unceremoniously, so that she nearly fell, while they raised their hands toward the sunset, exclaiming in chorus: "Nagoóset dèpkèk, Ruwerera!"

Madame de Freneuse, who had been half asleep, thinking of the evening halt and wondering when she would sleep on a feather bed with a woolen cover over her instead of like a turnip on a string, was taken by surprise and jolted to her feet, looking about her curiously.

She saw a clearing in the forest, like other clearings they had crossed, with this difference—that in the center there was a lodge constructed of mud and logs, with no windows and a small hole for the only door. Around it were grouped tepees and shelters, out of which Indians were emerging silently in surprising number. A small, better-built log cabin completed the picture. It had a chimney, and what looked like a window space, closed over with hide. Madame de Freneuse started toward it mechanically. She was pulled back by one of the Indians who had escorted her. He said something too quickly for her to follow. Well as she knew Micmac, this was not the Malisite form of it familiar to her from the seigneury. Dahinda interpreted.

"He says stand still. He says do not go near the Chief."

Madame de Freneuse stopped and waited. Nobody came forward to welcome her. None of the Indians took any notice of her. They gathered round the braves who had carried her in. They brushed past her; they pushed Dahinda aside; but they said no word and gave her no direct glance. She was tired, hungry, and a little cross. She plucked at one of the Indians.

"Where is Ruwerera? Take me to him!" she said. The Indian looked past her with an indifferent glance, turned his back, and glided away. Madame de Freneuse stamped her foot. One of the older men said something over his shoulder. Two of the Indians laughed.

"He says," Dahinda whispered, "Ruwerera will not get much comfort out of that string bean. Better have taken another Indian wife. He says Ruwerera has three wives, and any of them is better than this caterpillar spit. He is saying something rude now; I not tell."

Madame de Freneuse could not help grinning as she wondered what could be ruder than caterpillar spit, but she was impatient.

"Ask them to show me my sleeping place," she said to Dahinda.

"If Ruwerera will have you, your sleeping place is with him"—the answer came through Dahinda's lips—"if not, you can crouch in there." She nodded her head toward one of the tepees. Madame de Freneuse walked to it without a word. The Indians watched her go, indifferently. She had sense enough to subdue herself, to wait for Raoul's appearance before she let go. She sat down on the tree trunk in the tepee, trembling with rage.

Presently the flap was thrust aside, a bowl of crushed maize appeared, the hand that held it vanished as Dahinda took it in.

"Madame eat this," she said. "Dahinda go presently and find the true talk."

She smiled up out of her honest face, and Madame de Freneuse felt comforted. Raoul, she tried to tell herself, was away or sick. As soon as he returned, she would see him and laugh at this. . . . String bean, indeed! She would tease him about his wives. They would have good fun. Then he would sign the treaty and she would return.

She looked about her for a place to sit; but there were only the tree trunk and a pile of pine boughs, nothing else. Dahinda took the bowl and set it down, while Madame de Freneuse wiped her fingers on her fichu. There had been no spoon. That most of all depressed her. She began to cry tears of fatigue and weariness, tears of disappointment. She realized that she had looked forward to seeing a friend, and now she felt a chill foreboding. Whatever the reason (she was already not allowing herself to think too closely of that), the friend was not to be seen. Unaccountably that made her cry. She was still sniffing a little when the flap was thrust aside a second time and a tall Indian entered, grunting. He spoke to her in Malisite, which she understood. He was one of the nine Indians Raoul had taken with him from the settlement, one of the survivors of the siege. She remembered him.

"Hamogom," she said, "good hunting here!"

Hamogom disregarded this.

"Ruwerera," he said curtly, "sends you this message: 'Tell the white woman she is my prisoner. Someday—it may be soon; it may be late—I shall have the curiosity to look at her. Till that day I have other matters of more importance to attend to. Bid her be quiet, submissive, and resigned. Give her this.'" He held out a piece of quillwork, crudely started. "Through the long weeks ahead, and in the winter months, she may finish it."

He turned on his heel and was leaving the tepee when she caught at him.

"Tell Ruwerera to come to me at once," she said, "if he values his security. Tell him . . ."

Hamogom disengaged himself and went his way. Madame de Freneuse threw herself down on the pine boughs and was very sick. Dahinda held her head and scratched a place in the earth to bury the vomit. There was, she explained, a brave outside the tepee who would not let her pass.

CHAPTER LIV

WHEN Madame de Freneuse woke next morning, Dahinda was cooking breakfast on the fire she had made in the center of the tepee between two stones. The smoke spiraled out the top; but some of it went wandering round the inclosure, waking Madame de Freneuse, getting in her nostrils, making her throat burn. She sat up dizzily, with a feeling of nausea and bewilderment. Then she remembered where she was and lay back again, discouraged. She did not move till Dahinda brought her coffee sweetened with maple sirup, instead of sugar, and no cream or milk. She watched her mistress solicitously as she drank.

"Madame is tired," she said.

Madame de Freneuse nodded. Her eyes filled with tears.

"I do not know what is the matter," she said. "I never cry like this. I feel discouraged and sick."

Dahinda patted her hand.

"Let Madame rest," she said. "I will go out and find Monsieur Raoul."

Dahinda never called him Ruwerera. A thought struck her.

"Make marks on paper," she said, "and I will take them to him."

Writing a letter awed and fascinated Dahinda. She could not understand how information could be deciphered from scratches; and in common with most Indians, even the medicine men, she looked upon writing and reading as very potent magic, pleasing to the White Man's God. Having once seen a missal with printed pages, she was confirmed in this idea.

She watched while Madame de Freneuse searched her reticule for the little gold quill pen that de Bonaventure had given her. Then she looked for the bundle in which her clothes were packed.

They were there, and also a chest of supplies the Governor sent. Dahinda opened the lid; got out bottles of wine, a heavy scarf, two leather boots with fur, a second cloak, and several packages of coffee. There was a writing set at the bottom, made of carved wood, with a lid that opened, forming a tablet on which to write; two bones for ink and sand; a stoppered bottle containing dry ink, another containing water.

She mixed the two, cut off the end of her quill, trimmed it, and began to write.

"Raoul, I am sick and unhappy. Come to me. For the sake of old friendship, let us meet. I have communications for you from the Governor; and besides that, you are my friend, as I am yours, Louise de Freneuse, this day of October, 1702."

She took a long time composing this, writing with the legible script the nuns in Kebec had taught her. Then she laid it down and stared, musing, at the embers of the fire in the center of the tent.

"I cannot think why I feel so ill," she said.

Dahinda took up the paper reverently. It was torn from the book of poems Monsieur de Bonaventure had given her mistress. She remembered it. She knew that it was precious to Madame de Freneuse, like her rosary and book of prayers. Such potent magic as that should surely prevail. She lifted a corner of the tepee, away from the flap, and rolled herself out.

Madame de Freneuse listened but could hear no sound. She lay down again to wait for Dahinda's return.

Raoul was in consultation with the medicine man when Dahinda reached the door of his log shelter, unchallenged, and crept in. She found herself in a big, rough room decorated with quill work, and furnished with buffalo and bearskin stretched between tree trunks, for beds and couches, a table roughly carved of birchwood, and a stone fireplace of French design.

Raoul was lying on one of the bearskin couches, dressed in a blanket. Dahinda saw at once that he wore it draped upon his shoulders in the State of Hesitation, and that his face was painted with the Ladder, from left corner of mouth to right eyebrow, so that the Spirits might rise in him and give him of their wisdom. The medicine man wore his buffalo horns. His blanket was draped in the Attitude of Discussion, with one corner over his left shoulder, right hand extended, left foot advanced. His face was painted with the half loop of the vault of heaven, from whence comes lightning—meaning rapidity. Dahinda bowed to him, creeping to a corner silently.

The discussion continued. The medicine man threw his hand out in front of him, raising the forefinger.

"Man," said Dahinda to herself.

Then he took his forehead between his thumb and forefinger and pinched it.

"White man," said Dahinda, "or man who wears a hat."

Then he thrust his two first fingers forward in a fork.

"Snake's tongue," said Dahinda; "that means lies."

Then he beat his two closed fists against each other.

"War," said Dahinda.

Raoul took his blanket and pulled it over his face; then he let it fall backwards, exposing it.

"I am in love. Do not bother me," Dahinda read.

The medicine man took his blanket in both fists and pulled it violently over his head in the gesture of State of Anger, Pierced to the Bone, and covered himself from all regard.

Raoul turned his back. The medicine man uncovered his face, looked at the Chief, and flung his hand up in the gesture of My Heart Is with You and with God. Then he went out. Dahinda crept forward.

"Monsieur Raoul," she said, profferring the note. He took it, read it, and remained silent.

Then he said: "I am torn between two fires." And again: "What is the matter with her?"

Dahinda shrugged.

"She is ill. She is tired."

"Let her rest."

"She is sick at heart at this greeting. You have scalped her heart. I cannot go back without medicine. Come with me, Monsieur Raoul."

"Monsieur Raoul is dead. There is Ruwerera now."

"Let Ruwerera come and see for himself, and tell Madame what he requires of her."

"Ruwerera does not go to a squaw. There are other things afoot. War is in the air. War that may make the red man lord of Acadia."

"Even so, Monsieur Raoul has time to spare for his friend."

"I tell you no!" His voice was harsh with pain. "I sent for her because I wanted to see her. Now that she is here, I do not want to see her. That is all."

"Then send us back."

"No. It may be that later I shall change my mind. Let her wait. You have seen me wait, Dahinda, in the days when Ruwerera was Raoul, haven't you?"

"The Untamed Bear will not wait," said Dahinda firmly. "He will not wait. He will strike."

"The Untamed Bear!" Raoul snapped his fingers. "He has let her come to me alone, without protection, who knows where? That for the Untamed Bear!"

"Nevertheless . . ."

"Woman, squaw, be quiet! Get out of here! Tell your mistress she may stay where she is. . . . Is she really sick, Dahinda?"

Dahinda nodded.

"I will send the medicine man."

"Madame will never suffer the touch of . . ."

"Then she may suffer sickness. Get out of here! I am busy."

"I heard Ruwerera tell the medicine man he was sick with love?"

"Yes, for my new, third wife! The Dance of the Autumn Leaves will be danced tomorrow night. Madame de Freneuse will see it. Tell her I said so; tell her she is like an autumn leaf to me!"

Then suddenly he burst into sobs and beat upon the couch. Dahinda rose from crouching and went to comfort him. Before she could get there, the door of the shelter was flung aside and a squaw came in. Dahinda, looking at her face, painted red for marriage newly accomplished, decided to retire. She had learned a good deal and surmised more. She went back to her mistress and found her sick again.

CHAPTER LV

RUWERERA spent a restless night. Even the devotion of his third wife failed to calm him. He thrust her from him angrily. The others came with a steak of bear and, when that failed to soothe him, poured him a bowl of his own brandy, taken from de Morpain in exchange for pelts. They left him alone, finally, with his mood. It was a black one.

For nearly two years he had lived among his Micmacs and Malisites without seeing any white face except an occasional Coureur de Bois, an English emissary, a missionary priest who had told him tales of the debauchery of the colony at Port Royal—in particular, the Governor's affair with Madame de Freneuse. Raoul had the man thrown out in the snow for his foul-tongued impertinence. Then he fell to brooding.

Madame de Freneuse so obsessed him that he could think of nothing else. All the while that he was building up his chieftainship, taking over more and more Malisites, planning larger and larger campaigns, he was thinking of her, dreaming of her, and wanting her. The image of her shifted from the woman he had known, became distorted until he thought of her, most of the time, as a whore—someone he desired and should have. Then the Governor sent messengers to sound him on his attitude in the forthcoming struggle with the English. He perceived the strength of his position and saw that he could overthrow the settlement, wipe out the French, revenge himself upon the men and the woman who had slighted him. He had had no quarrel with the Governor, who succeeded de Villieu's temporary administration, until the missionary father told him of his liaison with Louise. Then—ah, then —he hated de Brouillan, too.

For months he had worked with the Indians, patiently building up his reputation as their leader, taking part in endless festivities and ceremonial dances, marrying two chieftains' daughters, contracting for a third, winning the alliance of neighboring Malisite and Micmac tribes, forming a war council of braves. Now he had them solidly behind him, crazy to attack first the French and afterwards the English. He could, when he lifted a finger, loose them on the settlement. At this point, before he decided, he wanted to see Madame de Freneuse again. He sent for her. Now he was afraid to see her, in case all his new-found strength and leadership should melt away and leave him the awkward, troubled, country boy who had tutored her children and pillowed her escape without demanding more than the right to love. . . .

Well, yes, he had demanded more, but he had never expected . . . And now she was giving herself right and left to everyone. De Bonaventure she professed to love, more than anything or anyone—more than poor Mathieu de Freneuse. De Brouillan? What was that affair? Women like that should be punished. They take the heart and the guts and the dreams and the soul of a young man and twist them till there is nothing left. What was he doing, crouching in this rough log hut, more majestic than any of the tepees he had shared in the beginning of his exile among the savages, less comfortable than the meanest house in the settlement; warming himself by smoking fires; eating dog's meat, bear, otter, beaver, raw sometimes, badly cooked always (until he could train the squaws); constantly summoned to dance and leap and hurl himself about; even being wounded with knives and burning torches in order to impress the braves and the medicine men? . . .

He, Raoul, an educated Frenchman, softly brought up in Provence—he remembered Vanina's boudoir, for instance, comparing it to this!—painting his face in streaks and brilliant colors according to the times and seasons or the message he should express —all because of this woman! For her, he had been initiated in the first place. For her, he was here. Without her, he was unhappy. Why should he not have her, as others did? If she could give herself to the Governor for a house, as the priest had said, and for a pension, she could give herself to Raoul for other reasons—to save the settlement or her skin. It did not matter which or what, so that he had her! Always at this point black sadness swept him. The vision of her as she had been intruded itself· he cursed his thoughts, his lusts, and his foul-mindedness.

The Governor sent him further emissaries. They arrived at a time when he was lonely, crazy with desire to see a European face. He sent back his message: "Send me Madame de Freneuse." Then he waited, half hoping they would refuse indignantly. But they sent her alone, unprotected, trusting her to him as though she were nothing to be guarded. She was here. He had only to cross a few steps to look at her, but he could not bring himself to it. He did not want to see her changed. If she were not changed, then he was more miserably hers than before. It could not be. Moreover, there were the medicine men. Such a display of unmanly weakness would ruin him with the tribes.

He looked at her note and crumpled it in his hand. A need of impressing her rose to the fore, as it had many times in the last two years. He would show himself strong, a man, a great chief, holding the greatest position among the Indians of any white man since the colonies began; he would show himself indifferent, hardened to pain, uncaught by any wiles; he would show himself a married man, with the pick of the squaws for his wives; and he would dance the Dance of the Autumn Leaves until its savage beauty made her swoon. Then he would take her.

At this point he stopped pacing and buried his face in his hands. Unless she were his as she gave herself to those others—freely, wanting to be, with passionate cries, with all herself behind her embraces—it would be nothing, no conquest worth the having; it would never set him free from this obsession.

Dawn came up behind the spruces. He went to the cabin door and stood there, looking out. The moon disappearing on the left reminded him, in its pale inaccessibility, of Louise. He sighed, breathed deeply, looked toward her tepee. Then with an effort he went inside and shut the door.

CHAPTER LVI

MADAME DE FRENEUSE did not come out for the autumn dances. She lay in her tepee and was sick. So she did not see the splendor of Raoul's dancing, the beauty of his wives, or the fervor with which he was greeted. An Indian came to the door of the tepee to bring her out, but Dahinda pushed him outside. She was anxious about her mistress and angry with Raoul.

The dancing wore on; the night grew late; the braves paired off with squaws and went into the forest. The flap of the tepee was thrust aside. Raoul entered, dressed in his regalia. He was still carrying the wooden club of authority, carved into a tomahawk, with feathers and beads dangling from it. His face was painted with the snowbird, combated by Father Hawk.

Dahinda started up as he came in. He brushed her aside, bent over the pine boughs where Madame de Freneuse lay, and looked at her in the light of the torch he held. She was asleep, pale beneath her disordered hair, one cheek on her elbow. He stooped nearer, shading the light from her eyes, and looked his fill.

"What is the matter with her?" he said at last. Dahinda shook her head.

"Madame sick," she said. "Madame very sick since she came here."

Raoul was silent. Then he beckoned behind him. The medicine man entered in his regalia of the sacred feast.

Madame de Freneuse stirred and opened her eyes. Her glance fell upon Raoul without recognition. He looked like any other painted savage to her. The medicine man she recognized from his horns, and it was to him she spoke.

·[229]·

"Tell Ruwerera I must see him," she said. "Tell him it is necessary for him and his people. Tell him I have a treaty here that he must sign."

The medicine man did not answer. Raoul stared at her. Now that she was awake, he could see that she had not changed. There was the same childlike light in her eyes, the same candid gaze. Impossible to think this woman could be guilty of the sordid tales he had heard. Impossible!

He said to the medicine man in Micmac:

"Bring her to my wigwam. If she has something to say to me about the Indian people, I will hear it. Bring her now!"

He swung on his heel and went out. The medicine man laid hold of Madame de Freneuse and dragged her to her feet. Then he pulled her roughly outside of the tepee toward the log hut door. Dahinda followed them, throwing a coat round her mistress' shoulders, smiling because she had known Raoul and read the trouble in his face beneath his paint.

Madame de Freneuse staggered, weak from sickness and want of sleep. She was furious, but relieved to think that soon she would be with Raoul. She could tackle him alone. She had not wanted to meet him for the first time at the Autumn Festival, even if she had felt well enough to stand the noise, the shouting, and the smell of Indians sweating through the fire. She could meet him now.

They reached the door of the log hut; she stepped inside and looked about. Her face fell when she saw three Indian women, crouching over quill work, and the savage who had been in the tepee with her and the medicine man. The savage stood up and advanced toward her. Something in his walk told her who it was. She looked closer. Beneath the savage expression of a chief, painted for the Autumn Festival, she recognized Raoul. This was the greatest shock of all. She was still trembling when he said to her:

"Sit down."

One of the squaws slid forward the tree stump she was working on, and Madame de Freneuse was glad of its support. The medicine man took his leave. She rallied herself and held out her hands.

"Raoul!"

He made no move to take them, but stared hungrily as though he could not have enough of looking at her face.

"It is nice to see you again," she said in conversational tones. Then rapidly: "The children are well and send their respect. They have not forgotten you."

He cleared his throat.

"I hear that Jean-Marie is to be a priest?"

She nodded uncomfortably.

"Here," he said in Micmac to the women behind him. With one sweep he tossed off his headgear and ran his hands through the long locks falling on either side his face.

"No wigs," he said with a smile, "among the Indians. Will you have some soup? I think you have not been eating well since you arrived."

"Quite well," she assured him gravely, the conversation seeming more and more unreal to her, "but they would not let me see you. I have a message from the Governor."

"I know," he said. "At least I can form a guess at what he says." He dismissed it with a gesture, propped his chin in his hands, and stared at her again.

"What sort of a winter did you have?" she asked. "We had a hard one at the settlement." Then suddenly: "Raoul, speak to me as you used to speak; I look about me for the old Raoul, the friend. It frightens me not to find him!"

He shook his head.

"Friendship and other things can die when a man is too much alone," he said. "I've lived like a savage so long I even think like one of them now."

"And you used to hate them so!"

"Yes. I think I even had a premonition about them, as though someday I would have more to do with them than I liked."

"You needn't have. You could have stayed in the settlement."

"And seen you living with my uncle?"

She lifted her shoulders in perplexity.

"Why not? Would it not be better than—this?"

"This, as you call it, means power, means leadership, means being needed. Sometimes when I go out, and say a casual word, and know that word is law to thousands of men, I feel exalted. For instance, now I hold the fate of the settlement in my hands, the fate of New France perhaps."

"Raoul, you couldn't fight against your own people!"

"Why not? What is a man's people?"

"Everything, Raoul! If we don't hang together, here at the edge of the world . . . Oh, don't you see? It is a splendid, a magnificent, thing for the colonists to create a civilization here."

"Civilization!"

"Yes. We are showing the savages how to live, how to be clean."

"Every morning every Indian goes to the running stream. The man walks ahead and the woman follows—or the woman walks ahead and the man follows—because they believe a man or a woman must be alone with the great clean Spirit at the moment of Ablution. Then they plunge in."

"I wasn't talking of physical cleanliness. I daresay—in fact, I know—that the Indian washes. I meant cleanliness of life."

"Huh!" he snorted. "Tell me one vice, one weakness, that the red man has—he caught it either from the French or from the English, or he shares it with them."

"All that may be quite true; but, Raoul, it's beside the point! You belong to the French. You're a part of France and of New France."

"A man belongs where he is needed. I can serve these"—he swept his arms in a circle.

"You could have served us; you still can."

"Us?"

"New France, then."

"New France has discovered that since I became a power in the forest and chieftain of a large host. New France had nothing for me but a dungeon before that."

"Raoul, don't be absurd. Of course, Monsieur de Villieu had to prevent dueling."

"Why didn't he offer to lock my uncle up? According to what you told him, he was to blame for the encounter, not I."

"It was difficult for the Governor. Monsieur de Bonaventure was an important man, of equal rank."

"There! That is what I tell you! Now I am the important man, and Monsieur de Villieu sings another tune!"

"Raoul, you make us in the settlement sound very small. If you but knew the admiration with which men speak of you, the legend you have become. Denise, in the convent, follows all your exploits carefully. She is proud to have known you. So are we all. We think you have done a great work in uniting the Indians. I have heard Monsieur de Brouillan say many times that if he had been Governor when you first came he would have received you more politely, more in keeping with the services you had rendered on the retreat and at the siege, but then there might have been no Ruwerera. When you sent for me—Why did you send for me?"

Raoul waved his hand.

"When you sent for me, he asked me to give you this message —that he begged you, in the name of the King and on behalf of France and the New French, if you could not join with us against the English, at least to remain neutral. He has sent a treaty for you to sign."

"What inducement has he to offer me?"

"Anything within reason that you want. There is, of course, from the moment that you sign, an indemnity for the past raids and exploits you have engineered, the price removed from your head, and free access to you and your men."

"Any Indian who catches de Brouillan gets a string of beads. I suppose he would wish the price upon his head taken off."

"Of course," she assented gravely. What a baby he was!

" 'Anything within reason.' There is only one thing that I want, only one thing that will make me sign the treaty."

"What is that?"

He did not answer for a moment. He came near to her and threw himself down beside her in an old gesture he had often used. He took one of her hands and put it on his hair. She started to run her fingers through it, as she had often done, but the hair was greasy with bear oil and smelt. She removed her fingers and he took the other hand, looking up at her.

If she had seen the old Raoul, with his clear, fresh complexion, his boyish face, she might have been prepared for what was to come; but this painted savage, smeared and streaked with crimson and blue, where only the eyes were Raoul's, seemed a stranger to her. She had forgotten the urgency with which he used to plead and was startled when he said:

"Louise, will you marry me?"

"No, dear," she said, recapturing the words and the tone she had always used. He stayed silent, still beside her, for a moment; then he looked up.

"You see," he said, "it is all words. They will not give me what I want!"

"But," she stammered, between laughter and rage, "that is not within reason, Raoul."

"Why not? You're free and I want you."

"I am older than you."

"If I don't care, that doesn't make any difference. So is Wosedek, there, and she's my wife!"

·[233]·

"Wosedek and the others are a good reason why I cannot marry you. Do you expect me to be fourth squaw to a chief?"

"Never mind what I expect! The Governor sends me a message. Whatever you want, in reason, he says, but spare the settlement."

"Well, not quite like that."

"I answer, I want to marry Louise de Freneuse. That's in reason. I might have said I wanted a thousand livres in gold or the resignation of the Governor. I only want a woman."

"Raoul"—she leaned forward, feeling mistress of herself and sure of him—"you do not want me, a reluctant and cold victim, a woman who hates you and despises you? You would like me to marry you, if such a thing were possible, to save the settlement and then to live here with you, hating you as I would? There would not be much satisfaction in that bargain! Look at me, you know that I am capable of hatred!"

He did not answer.

"You would not want to marry me, knowing I loved another man and always would?"

Another vague gesture of the hand. Then, vehemently:

"Why not? For years I tried to make you love me. You wouldn't . . ."

"Love isn't a thing one can command."

"If I cannot have you, loving me as you should . . ."

"Why should I?"

". . . then I will have you anyhow. I have married wives enough to know that what the woman thinks doesn't matter!"

"Then why bother about wanting one woman more than another? Take a young and beautiful Indian, leave this 'autumn leaf' alone!"

"Listen," he said hoarsely, sweeping her out of the tree stump, where she sat, into his arms, "if I do all you want, sign the treaty, let you go, help the settlement against the English, will you forget for a little while that you don't love me? Will you pretend, just pretend, that you do? Will you let me love you while you are here, just a few days, just a few hours, only tonight?"

He did not wait for an answer, fearing what it might be; he shut his eyes and pressed his lips upon hers, holding her close.

Rapidly, her blood beating unnaturally, she thought. Then, putting his face between her hands, she smiled into his eyes.

"Raoul," she said, "I can't do that. I can't. Raoul, listen to me.

·[234]·

Oh, listen, I am so alone; I have only you. . . . I'm going to have a baby. I can't sleep with you!"

He looked at her. Then suddenly he sprang apart from her arms.

"Whose is it?" he sneered. "The Governor's or my uncle's? Whose?"

"Your uncle's," she said quietly. "I have never given myself to the Governor. I would not be here if I had. This is his idea of a revenge, as it was yours. Men when they love can be cruel. Go ahead and raze the settlement. Why should I sacrifice myself? I might have, perhaps, but I am in love with Pierre de Bonaventure; I bear his child."

"Why did he let you come?"

"He does not know."

There was a silence. Then Raoul said wearily:

"They told me you were sick. When my wives bear their children, they are well, and no complaint. They bear warriors without a cry."

"They are younger than I, Raoul. I am too old to bear a child with safety or with comfort."

She raised one hand in a gesture that was automatic with her when afraid or moved. He had seen it, last, by Gervais' grave.

"Louise," he said huskily, moved beyond bearing, "I love you even more than I thought I did. I will sign the treaty. I will send you back. I have had my chance, the thing I have dreamed of through countless nights for years. I am fool enough to hand it back to you, fool enough to let you go, fool enough to be hungry for you all the rest of my life. . . . Sewea," he said behind him.

One of the motionless women rose. The other two looked up as she escorted the white squaw out of the hut. Raoul looked after her.

CHAPTER LVII

FROM dawn to dusk the Indians gathered, Malisite chief and Micmac brave, until there were a hundred unfamiliar faces round the fire in the clearing in front of the lodge.

Raoul perused the treaty with Madame de Freneuse, in the shelter of his hut, while his squaws served endless berry juice and cakes of maize, in the French manner. Raoul was master of himself and gay. Now that he had made the grand gesture of renunciation, he found himself impressive and wished Madame de Freneuse to think so, too. He explained the importance of his position among the Indians in a deprecating fashion, as different from his boasting of the night before as his friendly deference was from his passion. Madame de Freneuse looked thoughtfully up. She was wondering how long she could remain there in the heat of the hut without being sick, and also how long it would be before she could get home. She was disappointed, when finally Raoul had come to his senses, to realize that the signing of the treaty was not his affair alone but must be brought before the council, and that pipes of peace would be smoked and the whole long tiresome rigmarole gone through before the thing could be settled. She sighed and shifted her feet.

"Hmm," Raoul said, "I see that the Governor wishes me to undertake the patrolling of the north shore, between the Baye Françoise and Point Maillet."

"He thinks the attack would fall there," Madame de Freneuse said.

"He does not offer us much in return."

She gathered herself together to expound to him, as one would to a judge, all the time thinking:

·[236]·

"I really don't see how I can go through with it. A child! I wonder what Pierre will say?"

She lost herself in anticipation, while Raoul frowned and argued, nodding his head at length to the flood of reasoning she poured at him.

The noise outside grew louder. Shouts and chanting announced the beginning of the dances of deliberation. All night they would keep it up and all next day and the night after that, and so on for a week. It would be a week at least before she could extricate herself and the treaty and go home, if Raoul didn't change his mind. He was all right now, but let him once begin again . . . It could not be good for a man to live alone among the savages. Raoul was an undisciplined, uncontrolled boy. But rather sweet in his intensity, she thought, smiling at him over the treaty. He caught the smile and caught his breath. He took a step toward her. The door of the hut opened, and the medicine man came in.

"We are ready in the lodge," he said, "and are waiting for you to open it."

Madame de Freneuse motioned Raoul to go on. He sighed, shook his head at her, and left. Then she sank down on the couch where he had been sitting, too preoccupied to give her a place to sit, and beckoned to his wives. They came forward impassively, the latest rather sulkily, and stood before her.

She studied them curiously. What a strange assortment for Raoul to be living with! She asked for a drink and told them to fetch Dahinda. Then she lay back and made herself quite comfortable. She did not intend to go out to the dances. Savages affected her strangely, ever since the siege. These were not Iroquois, but one savage resembled another. She did not care for them.

She could hear Raoul's voice lifted in a long harangue. He was telling them the wisdom of giving in to the Frenchmen's wishes, of the riches and the glory they would gain from an alliance. He invited them to enter the lodge and smoke the pipe of peace, which he would carry to the French general to be smoked.

"Let the Frenchman come here!"

"Here! Here!"

"Let him smoke before us all!"

"He cannot do that; he is at war with the Englishmen, who are also our enemies. He has sent his emissary."

"A woman! What talk is that to chiefs?"

"Nevertheless, she is the Governor's emissary. She shall smoke

·[237]·

the pipe for him, and afterward I and any of you who care to follow will go to the Governor and watch him smoke it again."

"Ruwerera told us, not many moons ago, the Frenchmen were our enemies."

"Ruwerera said the red man would drive the white men out!"

"Ruwerera still says that. But set the wildcat on the wolf, and less work for the hunter. Let the French wipe out the English, with our help."

Discussion followed. One by one the chiefs and braves rose from the fire, draped their blankets to show their thought, and entered the lodge, stooping their proud headdresses to pass through the little door. Inside they took their places, and the ceremony began. It lasted several hours. Madame de Freneuse was asleep on the couch when they sent for her.

She stumbled across the clearing, bowed her head to enter the lodge but drew back dismayed. A heavy, fetid stench of many perspiring bodies rose up in a cloud to greet her. The air was thick with smoke. Raoul, indistinguishable from the rest, swaying and thumping with his hands on a skin drum, shouted and pointed at her to sit in an empty space between two villainous-looking chiefs. She looked about her, rather wildly, then crouched on her knees and sank to a sitting position. Her head was beginning to ache, even before she had settled herself.

Silence fell. The medicine man leaned forward and kindled a flame from embers in the center of the lodge. With it he solemnly lighted a long calumet of polished wood with feathers and beads hanging from it. He puffed three times and handed it to Raoul, who puffed three times. Then it went the round. Madame de Freneuse, gazing fascinated as each cruel-looking mouth closed about it and thin lip after thin lip rested on its stem, began to wonder whether she could go through with it. She was more squeamish than usual because of the child she was bearing; the thought of putting her own lips to the filthy thing, after so many others, made her dizzy and sick, but it must be done if she wanted to return with the treaty. She did want that. It meant that the Governor would forget his grudge against her and would let her stay quietly in her little house with the man she loved. It meant that the Governor would leave him in peace and unmolested, in all the thousand ways a Governor could molest de Bonaventure—it meant a great many things, for a little while. So, as the last brown face puffed thrice and the last bronze hand held out the pipe to her, she took it and put it between her teeth without a tremor, shut her eyes, drew in her breath, and puffed it out again three times like the others. She cast a piteous glance at Raoul to see if she might go, after this, but he was staring at her body.

Suddenly a wild thumping and drumming began. One by one the bodies swayed and shook. Suddenly a man stood up, another and another. The lodge was filled with dancing, singing men; the smoke grew denser. Firelight from the center fell upon wild faces. Madame de Freneuse groped for the doorway. Unless she got out of there, she would swoon. She found herself in the starlight, with Raoul by her side.

"Send me home," she said. "Raoul, please, tomorrow!"

"I can't," he said, "not for a while. The first snows are falling. By the time the men started, traveling would be bad for you. You must wait now for the second snow, then you can use the dogs. I will come with you then. Now I cannot go. You have not thanked me for the treaty."

With an effort she smiled at him. Then she clawed the flap of her tepee aside, and staggered in. Dahinda was waiting for her, with a heated stone.

"Put this under your feet," she said.

Somewhere she had acquired a bearskin and a caribou hide. She draped these on the bed to make it warmer.

CHAPTER LVIII

ON A cold day near the end of November three sleds of dog teams made their way over the Mochelle trail, down the banks of the Dauphin River, toward the settlement. The foremost sled bore Madame de Freneuse, wrapped in a bearskin, covered up to her eyes, with another as a robe across her feet. Raoul stood behind her, on the running board, cracking his whip. The wind whipped color into both their faces. Madame de Freneuse was smiling. She was happy. At last she was going home, having succeeded in her mission. She would be seeing Pierre. She was hungry for news of him.

Raoul was happy, too, in a melancholy sort of way. He had shown the woman he loved what a power he was and what she had missed by not loving him. He had been magnanimous, always a warming feeling. He had earned the right to return to the settlement. He would be condescending to his uncle and treat him, not only as equal, but as a man having command over a thousand Indians. Incidentally, the campaign against the English would be good for his men. They were beginning to miss the continual scraps with this or that tribe, now united under his command. A little warfare would establish him more firmly as their leader.

"Hya, haw!"

The dogs bounded forward, straining at their harness. Madame de Freneuse leaned back and looked at him. Their eyes met. Raoul smiled. The passion he had felt was waning from him. The existence of his uncle's child came between them far more sharply than Mathieu de Freneuse or any of the other obstacles had. He did not mind de Bonaventure so much as de Bonaventure's child, which was strange reasoning. But the nerves and the blood do not reason. It was so; he wished that he had come to the settlement instead of brooding over her. He would have been less lonely. But less chief, he reminded himself. He had worked in order to forget. Now he was in a good position for a young man of his years. He had a copper mine, a corner in the fur trade. He would be able soon to retire with a moderate fortune, perhaps to return to France, perhaps to settle in Acadia, though, remembering Mathieu de Freneuse, the destroyed mill, the seigneury, he wondered whether he would have the heart or the faith to stake his all on the land.

The sun shone in his eyes; he blinked; they turned a corner. There, before them, lay the outposts of the settlement. The dogs slowed to a walk. He halted them. The other teams came up in silence. One bore supplies, and the treaty in a case; the other carried the second chief in rank. The medicine man had been left in charge.

They climbed out silently, and stood watching the tufts of smoke curl up from the houses and the glint of the water flowing past the shore. Then, as it was bitterly cold, they shivered, rearranged themselves, and the cavalcade swept on.

A few inhabitants looked up as the dog teams jerked and lurched along the snowiest part of the street. One man made a motion toward his gun; but the foremost team had a white flag tied to its harness, which waved and fluttered as the dog ran. The streets were deserted. They reached the fort without incident.

"If I had known how easy it was to attack this place!" Raoul muttered.

At the fort it was different. They were brusquely challenged. Madame de Freneuse got out and staggered toward the gate.

"The Governor is expecting me," she said, "and I bring a friendly chief—Ruwerera, or Monsieur de Perrichet. Tell Monsieur de Brouillan we are here, and also Monsieur de Bonaventure."

She said the last word in a different tone. Raoul looked sharply up at her.

Then, as the wind was bitter, she returned to the dog sled, pulling the robes about her, endeavoring to be patient, all the time thinking:

"Pierre! Pierre!"

The sentry returned.

"Will you come this way?"

He led them into the Salle d'Armes and left them waiting there.

Looking about her, Madame de Freneuse saw signs of trouble and want. There were rents in the hangings, as though parts of them had been ripped away. A sack of ammunition stood half opened in a corner. Dust was thick along the walls. The whole place had an air of haste and disarray. She had no time to ponder more before the door opened and the Governor appeared.

"Madame! Your servant!" He kissed her hands. "The sentry reports that you bring a friend and, therefore, I infer success?"

She nodded at him.

"The treaty is signed."

"Mes compliments! Alas, Monsieur de Perrichet ——"

"Ruwerera, Governor." Raoul bowed. "It is in my official capacity that I am here."

"A thousand pardons, Chief. If you could have come to our aid in time, you would have helped us much. I suppose you are well informed of the distresses we have suffered recently?"

Raoul looked blank.

"Perhaps you were otherwise occupied." He looked from Raoul to Madame de Freneuse reflectively. "One does not always keep one's ears and eyes alert when matters of more personal immediacy arise. Monsieur de Bonaventure was setting out for the forest with the purpose of bringing you back, Madame, treaty or no treaty, when he was set upon by a band of English soldiers who had landed above the river and were planning an attack on the settlement. He was wounded ——"

"Wounded!" Madame de Freneuse cried out.

"Yes, Madame, so badly wounded that he was almost taken prisoner. He crawled here somehow, with a remnant of his men, too late to take part in the attack on the settlement; but, nevertheless, we beat them off. We lost some of the inhabitants and a great deal of ammunition, food, supplies. We were looted, in fact. The worst is, they may return. They are encamped at Point Maillet, the other side of the river, where they have dug themselves in for the winter. I cannot credit that you did not know of this? Monsieur de Bonaventure has been quite inconsolable. He figured when you heard of it, a month ago at the least, you would return."

Madame de Freneuse was silent. A thought struck her. She looked reproachfully at Raoul, but his expression of astonishment was so sincere that she could not believe in his duplicity.

"At any rate, we are here to support you now," he said. "I will

·[242]·

send a runner to my braves at once. How many warriors would you like?"

The Governor drummed his hands together.

"Do you think you could spare three hundred?" he said. "Then we could make an effort to smoke them out before they can travel in the warmer weather. They will not expect an attack, knowing our forces and relying upon the difficulties of campaigning in the cold. Besides, they will, I imagine, be relying upon you and your Indians to keep us occupied till spring!"

Raoul was silent.

Madame de Freneuse started forward, laying a hand upon the Governor's arm.

"How is Pierre?" she said. "May I go to him? The treaty is signed. Monsieur de Perrichet will show it to you. I have done what you wanted." She looked him full in the eyes.

"In this particular, Madame," he bowed, "I think you have made it plain you would rather face the horrors of a journey through the forests of Acadia alone and unprotected, toward a hostile chief, than accord me what I wished!"

Madame de Freneuse blushed, a slow rising red that was not lost on either of the men.

"I concede that you have charmed the Chief"—he nodded toward Raoul—"and that does not make me feel that I am to be envied. But the bargain was of my making. You have kept your part of it; I will keep mine."

He was silent for a moment while some struggle occupied his mind. Then he said suddenly:

"I like gallantry. Both you and Monsieur de Bonaventure possess this quality in a large measure. It is the reason for which I choose my—friends."

The last word was spoken low, with his eyes upon her. She looked searchingly at him.

"Friends?" she asked.

He bowed.

"I would have you think me so."

"*Both* of us?"

He bowed his head, smiling at her.

She curtsied.

"Monsieur, these sudden friendships are not reliable."

"Love can turn to hatred, hatred to friendship," he said quietly. "But if you want deeds—to show you that I regret the recent danger you have undergone on account of my enmity—I have named Monsieur de Bonaventure my representative and deputy Governor here during my absence."

"Absence, Monsieur?"

"Yes. As soon as this little matter of the English is satisfactorily settled—and with Monsieur Ruwerera's help it should be easily disposed of soon, when the weather breaks—I am to go to France. In my absence Monsieur de Bonaventure, with you by his side, will be supreme, sole authority in the settlement. It is little, but it may please you and console him for the discomfort of his wound."

"Wound!" said Madame de Freneuse again.

"He is in your house," said the Governor.

CHAPTER LIX

MADAME DE FRENEUSE walked down the road to the far end of the settlement. Her heart beat unsteadily as she passed the mill, the bakery, the de Flang house, and came upon her own. It lay in the pale November sunlight, small and welcoming. She walked down the path toward it eagerly, feeling rather faint.

The curtains were drawn against the bottle-glass bow window that had been her pride. The door was shut. Dahinda's brown face was not to be seen peering round the corner. Dahinda would be coming back from the Indians on the next trip, bringing presents with her. She had stayed behind to get married. Poor Dahinda! The man who had married her would not be able to keep her as a squaw. She was too white in her ways. She had done it only as a gesture; she wanted to show the world that she could marry, too.

The latch was down; the house was very silent. Madame de Freneuse knocked upon the door. There was no answer. She lifted the latch and walked inside. This was home. The living room was cold, no fire lighted. The earthen floor had not been swept. There was a litter about of bandages and food. The bandages frightened her. She ran forward, swiftly, into the other room.

"Pierre!"

He was there, lying upon a couch with his leg in the air, supported by a strap from the ceiling. His face was very white, his gray eyes enormous in his head. He wore no wig, and his own hair, black and tousled, served to emphasize the pallor of his face. He sat up, startled. Then, with a clumsy gesture, he opened his arms. She ran across the room and put them round her, burying

·[245]·

her face on his breast. With trembling hands she began stroking and feeling him, to see where he was wounded.

"I thought you might be dead," he said in a husky voice. "I suppose you were a prisoner. I never wanted to let you go. I started after you . . ."

"I know; the Governor told me."

"The Governor is a devil. When you were gone, he insulted me. He told me things. . . . I knew he loved you. He said he sent you from revenge. Then the English came."

"I know; I know."

"Why didn't you come back? I suppose that devil wouldn't let you come? How have you escaped him?"

"I didn't know till today about anything. I hurried here. The Governor and Raoul are at the fort, discussing the campaign against the English."

"Raoul's here?"

"Oh, yes. The treaty's signed. He brought me here."

De Bonaventure was silent for a moment, turning his head from side to side. Then he said in a toneless voice:

"I suppose it's true what the Governor said, that you're in love with Raoul."

"Pierre!"

"He said so. He said: 'Let her go and she'll get round him.' He was right. You got the treaty signed. It's obvious how."

"Pierre, you're ill and feverish; you've been unhappy. You don't know what you're saying. Tell me, tell me, how are you wounded? Is it only your leg? Why have you got it tied like that to the ceiling?"

"That's the only way it lets me rest. A poisoned arrow got it. The English have taken to Indian ways. It's swollen still. I thought I'd lose it."

"Who's been looking after you?"

"The leech. And Father Francis."

"Father Francis!"

"And the good sister. She is out, getting me some food."

"I see. Well, I will take care of you now, and Dahinda when she returns. She's married."

She described the wedding, and how Dahinda would not stay with her husband but was following them after she had obtained all that she could of maize, sugar, sap from the maple trees, and furs for herself.

·[246]·

Then she sighed.

"I'm very tired. It's glorious to be home, Pierre, home! With you."

He said nothing to this. Suddenly he turned his face to the wall and began to weep. She gathered him close.

"Dearest, dearest, what is the matter?"

"It has been so long," he muttered.

"But I am here now. We are together, mon amour."

"Why didn't you come sooner?" he whispered fiercely, pressing his head against her heart.

"I couldn't at first. Raoul wouldn't see me, wouldn't sign the treaty. Then I was ill. I am having a child."

She said it quite simply, feeling that he would understand and comfort her. Instead, he sat up so suddenly that she was pushed from the couch. Black with rage, he struck her, across the face, across the breast, on the hands, and all the while he was shouting:

"Whore, beast, whore! Go and have your bastard in the woods, with its father! Go, get out of here!"

Aghast, Madame de Freneuse crouched by the couch, bewildered, trying to explain; but he shouted louder:

"I'll have no child of Raoul's in this settlement! Get out of here!"

He towered above her, slipping his leg from its strap, groaning with pain as he struck her. She kneeled upright and caught at him.

"Pierre, Pierre, it's yours! It's ours, Pierre! By the Holy Virgin, it is true!"

Then the room darkened about her and she swooned. A tearing, rending pain brought her back to consciousness for a moment. All that she could feel was dim, confused. She thought that she lay in a pool of her own blood and that her entrails were being torn from her. The child was leaving her. That much she knew before she fainted in good earnest. She did not see de Bonaventure kneeling beside her, wringing his hands, endeavoring to raise her to the couch. She did not hear him cry:

"Forgive me, come back to me!"

Nor did she hear his cries for help. The nun arrived. Madame de Freneuse was bathed in warm bear oil, bandaged roughly, and somehow heaved onto the bed before she was able to open her eyes; then, seeing de Bonaventure bending over her, she flinched and flung up an arm as though to ward off further blows. He groaned at this. But all his attempts to reassure her failed. She was

·[247]·

delirious, and soon she began to mutter. Her mutterings were full of her love for Pierre, her pride at bearing his child, her wish to return to him, her hurt that he had not accompanied her but had let her go alone, her fear of the woods and of Raoul, her dislike of the savages, her delight as she got back home. "And now," over and over she repeated, "Pierre is dead. I shall be dying soon. I shall be dying soon. Don't strike me! Don't strike me! It hurts. I had a lover once and loved him all my life. He struck me. He struck me. Sister, will you pray for his soul? He's dead."

De Bonaventure held her close—his own wound forgotten, though the leg was swelling fast—until the nun took him away perforce and put him to bed again. Thus they lay, reunited, sundered by her fever, through the long first night.

When morning came, she was quieter. The nun thought she might leave to fetch the leech.

PART FOUR

1703-1706

CHAPTER LX

THE spring of 1703 was an eventful one in Port Royal. Never in the memory of its inhabitants had there been so gay a season. It was as though with the shifting of the winds dullness shifted, too. Even the weather contributed its sparkle. Never were June nights more brilliantly starlit; never were soft spring breezes more refreshing. There was a feeling of well-being in the air.

The English, driven off, were keeping quiet; houses burned, rebuilt. There was unaccustomed plenty in the settlement, and the *Profond* with the *Soleil d'Afrique* had arrived with extra provisions from France.

Some of the older people found it disconcerting to have so many Indians in the town. They had delivered the settlement, but they were loath to take to their woods. Monsieur de Perrichet did nothing to disperse them. The younger people admired him and thought that fluttering feathers and beaded leggings lent their touch of color to the spring festivities. Denise de Chauffours, meeting an Indian round a sudden corner, all decked out in peace paint and beads, felt a stirring of the pulse and strange excitement. She was enjoying herself. The nuns were polite to her now; she knew why and laughed at them, secretly, up her modest sleeve. This was her time, if ever, to make hay! The new administration might not last. Everywhere she heard muttered pros and cons.

Monsieur de Brouillan had been driven out of the settlement, accused of harsh administration, sailing on the *Profond* to justify himself before the authorities in France. This was the work of a clique headed by the St. Vincents and the de Goutins, with Monsieur de Flang and Monsieur Pilou, to get the Governor out of the

·[251]·

way. He interfered with their little games and mortified their pride, for he would never permit anyone to forget that he was the King's person. It was as good as a puppet show to see him take his seat in the chapel, frowning at any man who presumed to follow him too close or rise from his prayers too soon. But, chiefly, his friendship with Madame de Freneuse offended certain ladies. They had not rested till complaints poured forth to the Minister in France took their effect. The Governor was recalled. What happened? Denise chuckled. He had appointed Monsieur de Bonaventure in his place, which he had a right to do—passing over Monsieur de Villieu, Monsieur de Labat, or the notary—so that now the settlement was governed by her aunt! Madame de Freneuse was everything. The ladies had to stomach it until the Governor's return.

This evening, for instance, there was a musicale, and everyone would go to it. Denise would be there, too. She would see Monsieur de Perrichet—Raoul—and perhaps, if she were lucky, dance with him. Her color deepened at the thought. The nuns could not prevent her now from speaking to Raoul, not even Father Francis. Denise sighed. Father Francis felt the new administration deeply. Each time that he was called, perforce, to celebrate mass for de Bonaventure and Madame de Freneuse chose to attend, he was distracted to the point of rage. He called it disgust, privately, to the nuns. Thrice he refused her the sacrament. After the third time Monsieur de Bonaventure called at the convent and gave him to understand that "one more indiscretion" would remove him from his post.

"My jurisdiction does not extend very far," Monsieur de Bonaventure said, sweetly smiling, "but it does include a dungeon."

That was the story. It thrilled Denise. It must be wonderful, she thought, to be championed by a man. What would Raoul do in similar case? She lost herself in daydreams as she thought of it.

Father Francis continued to avert his face from her aunt when they met in the street, and to avoid encountering her. But Denise noticed he devoured her with burning eyes from the pulpit, and she knew he revenged himself privately by poisoning the mind of her son. The poor boy already said long penances for his mother's sins, and looked upon himself as sacrifice and scapegoat. He was a pale, dreamy, sensitive lad who suffered much, losing himself in study only to be recalled, wincing, to the harshness of the world.

Denise had never liked him much, but she hated Father Francis for hurting him through his mother.

Madame de Freneuse sailed on. Denise thought of her sometimes as a beautiful boat with sails set. She seemed to take a naughty delight in flouting the ladies of the settlement. She jested and mocked and laughed at them before their faces and behind their backs, alike. She said they spent their entire time in gossip, ruminating over their morning fires what they would invent when they next went abroad. Most of them did their own housework and cooking, with coarse stout petticoats tucked up around their legs and with hair in tails. They were never fit to be seen unless they expected a visit. Madame de Freneuse, always neat and soignée from the time she waked, used to imitate the flustered de Goutins woman caught in her own house. After the afternoon coffee the women would dress and sally forth in their high, ridiculous headdresses, to shake them together over the latest scandal.

One or two houses were frequented almost daily—those of such leaders as Madame de Bellisle, for example, and, since de Bonaventure's appointment, Madame de Freneuse. Denise knew that her aunt served the best food and the best talk in the settlement; but she was hated, whereas Madame de Bellisle was dull and stingy but a pillar of the church. Father Francis haunted her house. It was just rebuilt, having been looted and burned by the English. Madame de Bellisle had tried to call on the King's money—as Madame de Freneuse had done, only that autumn—to have her house "beautified and adorned" as the estimate said; but Monsieur de Brouillan, knowing what everyone else knew—that Monsieur de Bellisle had left his widow a fortune, made out of his dabbling in the illicit fur trade years before—refused her request. It was an evil day for him, and had stirred up all this enmity. Nevertheless, he was right, on the face of things. Monsieur de Bellisle had done so well, before the laws restricting the trade to the King's representatives were enacted, that many people wondered why his widow did not return to France and live there. She preferred, however, to be a large toad in a very small puddle. At Port Royal she was a force to be reckoned with; in France she would not have counted. She and Father Francis wanted to rule the settlement between them. Checkmated temporarily by Monsieur de Brouillan's retort to the complaints they had poured out against him, they were biding their time to see how he fared before they bared their fangs too openly against his temporary successor and, of course, Madame de Freneuse.

They were inseparable. Since her aunt's mysterious illness and Monsieur de Bonaventure's wound, they clung together more closely than ever—he tender and attentive, she wistfully smiling. She went with him to review the troops and, later, with Raoul to speak to the Indians, thanking them prettily for their share in driving off the English.

Denise had heard that this incensed Madame de Bellisle.

"Is there no one to thank the Indians, in the name of the settlement but *her*?"

Monsieur de Goutins, whom Denise disliked, had answered:

"Don't forget she stayed with them. Doubtless she knows them more intimately than you or I."

He was a man of fifty-odd, round-bellied and bald, with stooping shoulders and a little frizzly pointed beard. His skin was yellow as though he suffered from jaundice; it was well known he suffered from his wife. It was also well known and discussed among the pupils in the convent that when Madame de Freneuse first came to the settlement Monsieur de Goutins pursued her with his attentions, haunting the places where he might find her. It was rumored that he had begged her to run away with him. Gossip had it that Madame de Freneuse laughed—unguarded laughter. Now he denounced her more violently than did Father Francis.

Denise shook her head. She loved her willful, laughing aunt and hated the carping spirit of the settlement, but she feared its power. Someday, she thought, one of them would bring her down. It would be like the deer in the forest, running full of arrows, game to the last. Yes, it would be like that. Meanwhile Denise made much of the brilliant parties, the pleasant hours. Everywhere she met Raoul; and so for her the spring was magic, and she looked no further than the gathering that night.

CHAPTER LXI

MADAME DE ST. VINCENT, cramming her portly person into the new gris-de-lin dress that had come for her from France on the *Profond*, was thinking of the evening's musicale. It would be prudent not to miss it, and, besides, there was one's natural curiosity and a desire to see how far shamelessness would go.

Nowadays Madame de Freneuse not only took the place of Governor's lady (one wondered, by the way, what that poor woman Madame de Bonaventure might think of it, stuck in France; one almost considered sending her a missive) but also appeared everywhere with the young de Perrichet, who, after incurring a price upon his head (very properly, too, no doubt) and turning completely savage (the nasty, low-down creature), was now the second most important man in the colony—deferred to, perforce, at every turn—just because he had fought one battle (one small engagement, mark you) with the English and driven them back to where they came from, by pure luck; whereas men like Monsieur de St. Vincent, who gave their very lives in the King's service, daily and hourly, went unrewarded. It was a queer world.

Madame de St. Vincent was beginning to think it might have been better not to have forced the Governor home to France. He might have been arbitrary—indeed, he had been—but in his time Madame de Freneuse had not lorded it over the settlement. Ah, no! He built a house for her, shameless enough, but she stayed in it; and when he went to practice music (or to practice anything else, if it came to that) with her, at least he did so in private; and she was not continually under one's nose.

Madame de St. Vincent draped her de Maintenon hood about

·[255]·

her head with a jerk and called to her husband, who was in the next room struggling with his best uniform jacket, grown a little tight for him.

"Félicien, do you think this will go on?"

"What, my dear?"

"The de Freneuse baggage!"

"Until the Governor returns, no doubt. After all, Monsieur de Bonaventure has no one to do the honors. He is bound to have a woman there. Madame de Freneuse is the widow of a great gentleman."

"And the whore of another. Do not speak absurdities. It is unsuitable to expect us to meet such a woman."

"You could stay at home, my dear."

"And have you thrown into prison on the slighest pretext? Remember how he threatened Father Francis. A wife's duty is to her husband, despite unpleasantness."

Monsieur de St. Vincent smiled. He did not think his wife's absence from the evening's entertainment would mean prison for himself. As to Madame de Freneuse's morals, or her relationship to Monsieur de Bonaventure, he remembered the time when his wife had run far enough and fast enough after the handsome sailor to make her husband more than anxious, and with encouragement she would have run to the end.

It was lucky for him, since he did not relish cuckoldom, that Monsieur de Bonaventure preferred Madame de Freneuse—lucky and natural. He sighed, thinking of the wistful pallor of the woman in the fort, whom he would see that night, and of his wife's superfluous bulk crammed into a dress too tight for her. Hussy Madame de Freneuse might be, one thought the better of her for it; she was a charming hostess and an alluring woman. He sighed again. Some men had all the luck.

"Félicien!" said his wife. He shrugged and went in to her.

Together, a little later, they walked toward the fort. They fell in with the de Goutins, also dressed in their best, and all four pressed forward. The two women eyed each other's headdresses, half hidden under the obligatory black hood, and ran a cursory glance over the embroidered dresses, crooked up on their arms so that the dust of the spring path should not spoil them as they walked. The two sedan chairs of the colony were bespoken so far into the night that in order to get to the party at all it was necessary for ladies of secondary rank to walk, a circumstance that did nothing to put them in good humor.

When they reached the fort, they could see lights and hear music. A perfunctory challenge from the sentry halted them for a moment, while their escorts called the countersign, "Louis," and the sentry answered: "Pass."

They walked across the grass behind the palisades in silence, each meditating with what countenance he, or she, would greet Madame de Freneuse. Beneath the blissful eye of Monsieur de Bonaventure, it must needs be gracious greeting. The difficulty of feigning cheerfulness and courtesy was increased by the fact that Madame de Freneuse was not deceived, and like as not would tell them so by some malicious quip too low-pitched for him to overhear.

When they had left their outer garments, and the ladies had put a last-minute touch to the set of the dark hoods, they were announced at the door of the Salles d'Armes. A brilliant spectacle met their eyes. Hundreds of candles blazed from sockets on the walls and from two chandeliers in the ceiling. The floor was polished with beeswax and bear grease until it shone like the two long mirrors at either end, imported from Versailles.

In the center of the room, receiving the curtsies of her guests, Madame de Freneuse was standing, near de Bonaventure. The two ladies, entering, shot a sharp glance at her. Audacity! She alone of all of them wore no hood. Her long dark hair cascaded freely down her back in three long curls, from which the hair escaped, here and there, at will. She wore a flame-colored dress, unfashionable in shape because too billowing. It flowed around her, rippling as she moved, concealing all of her but bust and shoulders, which were naked, the bust barely covered by the thinnest tulle lace. She was looking radiant, and well she might! She turned her little pointed face toward them, and a twinkle filled her eyes.

"Madame," she said with becoming gravity, as Madame de Goutins curtsied. "Monsieur de Goutins, have you come to judge our little assembly? I declare I fear your sentence."

Before the embarrassed man could turn this off with a professional quip about the courts, stripping her at the same time with his eyes, she had welcomed the de St. Vincents.

"Ah, Madame, how good of you to remember us! And the son? A cadet, is he not?"

Madame de St. Vincent controlled herself with some difficulty.

"Not yet, Madame," she said with some meaning, as she sank in a curtsy with a wobble and shake, "but one hopes for happier times."

"Monsieur, how happy you must be to reflect upon your son."

Since everyone in the colony attributed the boy to de Bonaventure, this was a shaft that might have wounded her as well; but she did not believe the story and brought it up to annoy the St. Vincents. She was rewarded by the flush that lit the husband's face. They escaped from the necessity of talking to her and wandered down the room.

Musicians at the farthest end struck up. A quadrille was formed. Madame de Freneuse tucked her hand through Monsieur de Bonaventure's arm. Happy, flushed, for all her maturity almost the youngest-looking woman in the room, Madame de Freneuse moved through the dance demurely, raising her eyes now and then in a mischievous twinkle. Raoul, dancing with Denise de Chauffours, smiled as he caught her eye. The rest of the time he was counting and calculating. Dancing was still a hazardous thing to him. He remembered himself as he had been that evening in Kebec when she had piloted him through and he had blundered, asking her for information about a Madame Charles Tibaut! She did not seem a moment older, nor changed in any way, except that she looked fragile now and paler than her wont. A rush of tenderness went out from him. She must have felt it, for she looked up and smiled with a new expression. Denise, following his gaze, gave him a slight understanding pressure of the hand. He looked down at her, astonished. She indicated that he was to look behind him. He turned his head. Monsieur de Goutins, standing by the great stone fireplace, was staring hungrily at Madame de Freneuse.

Monsieur de Goutins was thinking of the letter he had written to the Minister in France, asking that the "affairs of one Madame de Freneuse" might be looked into, hinting that interesting disclosures amounting to treason would be found. No smoke without fire. If he created sufficient smoke around her, the authorities might be trusted to find fire. Fire! With her careless, laughing insolence she had kindled one in him that never would go out! If he could have her tortured, burned, he would sweat to bring it about and assist at the execution eagerly. Then, perhaps, as he watched her body burning, naked in the sunshine, and took his fill of seeing it, his own fires would be quenched and he would be at peace.

Madame de Freneuse had her own problems as she danced.

·[258]·

Well she knew this was a breathing space, a lull before the storm! She kept her own counsel, went her own way, enjoying the power Monsieur de Brouillan had flung her through Pierre. Pierre was at the height of his strength. He worked for the good of the settlement and its affairs in a way that made her smile sometimes. She saw more clearly than he where it was leading to, but she encouraged him. Pierre was too clean, too simple, too much of the sea to be a courtier or a statesman. Poor Pierre, he dreamed of succeeding Monsieur de Brouillan in earnest, not realizing that if the Governor fell he and all his friends would fall. Only such time servers as the de Goutins, the de St. Vincents, and the rest would creep further into the rotten apple core that brought success.

Meanwhile life was sweet; her little house was full of happiness; Pierre was more thoughtful, more tender, more devoted as a lover than he had ever been—more passionate, too! Ciel, what memorable nights and days they spent together, everything forgotten! Each time they loved, it was new; yet each time known, familiar—traveled lands explored afresh.

Pierre, remorseful for her illness, for his anger, and for all the things that had happened, nearly a sevenmonth ago now, made amends very prettily for the lost baby by giving her another, just as soon as he was well. Before that, they had recuperated together, under the care of the disapproving nun. Her vows forbade her to gossip!

Madame de Freneuse smiled. If things could continue as they were, if only time would stand still now while Pierre still loved her, now while she was safe!

CHAPTER LXII

MONSIEUR DE BROUILLAN returned in the last week of August. He confided to Monsieur de Bonaventure, when they were alone after the dutiful welcome of the enraged colonists, that he had spent a fortune and even then had only succeeded in getting his case deferred.

"Those yapping curs may bring me down in the end," he said; "in the meantime, let them look out! I shall have to redouble my efforts, and scrape and scrounge, and meddle with new taxes, to get back what they have made me lose, let alone amass enough for my old age, when I'm disgraced. They shall find out now what harsh administration means, I tell you that! I'm in no mood to be trifled with."

De Bonaventure bowed. Monsieur de Brouillan looked at him quizzically.

"We have not been good friends," he said. "I am sorry for my part in that. I have tried to show you, by my appointment, that I wished the past forgotten. Although you were the best man for the administration of the colony, there were others I could have named."

De Bonaventure bowed again. The Governor held out his hand.

"Frankly, mon vieux, we cannot afford to fight. We are both honest men. We must stick together among the rogues!"

He held out his hand. De Bonaventure took it in his and tapped his sword hilt.

"There is nothing I wish more than to be your friend, Monsieur," he said quietly, looking de Brouillan in the eyes. "I cannot conceive of any circumstances arising to render that impossible."

The Governor cleared his throat.

"How is Madame de Freneuse?" he asked.

Monsieur de Bonaventure hesitated. Then he decided to take the risk—here would be the first test of the Governor's new friendship. In brief words he confided his own trouble.

"Tiens!" said the Governor. "That will bring the place about our ears!"

De Bonaventure could have hugged him for saying "our."

"When do you expect it?" he went on, and then, not waiting for an answer: "Well, we must do the best we can. I like you both. If ever I saw a woman with courage, it is Madame de Freneuse; but, of course, you know, mon cher, this will give the de St. Vincents and the rest something tangible to yelp about. Up to now the authorities have ignored the charges made against you—yes, I happen to know there have been charges, chiefly by the notary. What have you done to Monsieur de Goutins that he should hate you so?"

"Nothing. I'll kill him," de Bonaventure said.

"And hang for that tapeworm? You'll do nothing of the sort. They asked me about you, of course. They've got a whole dossier there. Wouldn't you think they'd have other fish to fry than what we do out here, so long as they get their revenue punctually! But no! Envy of our freedom, I suppose. Anyhow, I told them the truth. I said that you were one of the best men the King ever had, impeccable in your public life while privately you lived very quietly with a widow of one of our colonists. I pointed out how much better this was than carrying on with the Indians. They agreed, but asked if you hadn't a wife. I said you had, and she lived in France with her children. I added artlessly that, of course, you would need a decided increase in your salary to be able to support her decently out here, and that the colony was better off without too many ladies unfitted for the roughness of our life. They appeared to be satisfied. But now . . . this!"

De Bonaventure sighed and puckered his brow.

"Mon pauvre vieux!" said the Governor. "It isn't as though she could help it; after all, the best of them breed. That's what they're made for, drôle de chose, when you come to think of it, isn't it? But we must plan ahead and see what we can do for the best for all of us. I can't afford to condone too much of a scandal here. And babies—God knows why—are a scandal, unless they're like the puling St. Vincent brood, where there's a husband to take the blame. Anyhow, voilà. I would find some pleasant habitant family up the river; and when the baby is born, I'd have it taken there. Has anyone noticed her condition? Does it show?

"She's been clever," said de Bonaventure. "She wears full-flowing clothes, and has from the start of the season. The women think it's because she wants to look different. She has always flouted the fashions. Then she looks well, and she has danced a lot. She is quite thin. I don't think anyone suspects, as yet."

"That's good. I'd hate to see them all get their teeth in her."

He shuffled some papers wearily. "And now to work."

De Bonaventure pointed out what he had done in the matter of the building of the new fortifications. The third bastion was almost complete.

"The Indians helped," he said. "There have been incidents, of course, against them. Mon Dieu, Governor, one would think these people imagined themselves to be divinities. Not even the King himself expects such regard. Time and again Monsieur de Perrichet has had to calm some wounded chief who has, perhaps, three hundred braves at his beck and call and finds himself spat upon or shouldered aside by a whippersnapper of a white, with nothing to his name but a tarnished coat. I refer particularly to the younger Flang. I have a good mind to give him to the savages to take away. He's no good to us, and they might find some fat on him somewhere for their dogs."

"Ciel!" said the Governor. "It is high time I came back. What would the Minister think if he heard such talk! Indulging in trade with the savages and not setting aside seven-eighths of it for the King, of which a good five-eighths will go into pockets that are pretty well lined as it is! And cannibalism, to boot. All the same, I agree with you."

De Bonaventure drummed on the table for a moment with his long fingers; then he said abruptly, looking the Governor straight in the eye:

"Monsieur de Perrichet knows of another copper mine," he said, "and the Indians say there is gold in one of the north-shore hills. We could take a boat and look there, for ourselves."

"Hmm," said the Governor.

"We would not, of course," said de Bonaventure carefully, "report our findings to the Ministry—too soon. We could, for instance, say we were charting the entrance to the bay. It has not been done for some years, and never very thoroughly."

"That," said the Governor, "is a good idea. We shall need as

·[262]·

much money as we can get—you to defend your woman, I to defend my head. I suppose we could count on Indian labor? And can Monsieur de Perrichet guarantee no talk?"

"He would—for her!"

"Ah!" said the Governor.

CHAPTER LXIII

IT WAS a fine autumn day, with leaves yellow and gold and red against green spruce and purple hill, that Monsieur de Goutins chose for his great enterprise. He closed his door against the world and dragged a heavy chair up to the table. Then he fetched the tools of his trade, pen and inkhorn, sand and parchment, and began:

"Sir,[7]

"There is here an affair which causes grave disorder and has afflicted all parents by reason of the bad example it has given to their children. I speak of the accouchement of the widow de Freneuse, by the Sieur de Bonaventure, which happened on September 7th last between six and seven in the evening without the help of any woman, without preparations or plans to receive the child, Madame de Freneuse being all alone with Monsieur de Bonaventure, the servant being in a room next to that in which the birth took place.

"I will pass over the details which are publicly discussed here, in regard to the mother's evil plans, to speak of Monsieur de Bonaventure, who left at that moment for the fort, where he was seen, all excited, having difficulty in buckling on his sword and from where he returned to the said lady, where he gave some water to the child. They also sent immediately for Mademoiselle Burat and her servant; and the same evening at about ten o'clock a soldier on duty at the port, together with the wife of Nantais, a habitant, took the child about four leagues from here, to another habitant's house, to be put out to nurse.

"If this had happened to others, I would have acted in order; but not being able to, as things were here, I went next day to Monsieur de Brouillan. I told him that the danger the child was in of not being baptized was being publicly discussed; and after having mocked at this, he told me that he had sprinkled it himself and nobody should put himself out on that account.

"This affair being made public, Monsieur de Bonaventure, knowing that people spoke of it, gave us to understand that if he learned that anyone was rash enough to mention it he would have that person put to death beneath the bastinade.

"Doctor Poutz, our surgeon, being in company where it was being talked of, and this being reported to de Bonaventure, was sent for after sundown. Monsieur de Bonaventure said to him: 'It's you, then, bloody rascal, who have been talking about Madame de Freneuse?' When he wished to justify himself, Monsieur de Bonaventure struck him several times with a cane and had him thrown into the dungeon. Monsieur de Poutz was warned; but not understanding what was required of him, he fell into disgrace and was made to endure all the mortifications possible, they even going so far as to take over, without compensation, the house he had built himself, to serve as a hospital."

He had reached this point in his missive when he was interrupted by a scratch on the door.

"Come in," he said, rather irritably. The *Profond* was sailing in three hours, and this dispatch was to go on her. It would be annoying not to finish it.

The door opened; Father Francis appeared. Monsieur de Goutins crossed himself politely. Father Francis blessed him, looked about for a stool, and sat himself down.

"Well, what does she say?"

Father Francis shook his head, raising his eyes to heaven.

"I was not allowed to see her. I fear she is impenitent."

A strange sound—half satisfied grunt, half horrified groan—escaped de Goutins' lips.

"I applied to the Governor, for permission to force myself in. Monsieur de Bonaventure was opposing me with violence, and I thought the Governor would not lend his countenance to such a scandal. I asked him for soldiers to protect me if I made the attempt.

"What did he say?"

"He said: 'This is no business of the secular arm. Use your own muscles, Father, or stay out!'"

"He did!"

·[265]·

"I am writing to Monseigneur in Kebec, and to the other churches, warning them that there is a state of irreligion here. I shall ask for masses with a special intent. Tomorrow I shall preach on the text, 'Cursed be the fruit of thy body. Deuteronomy 28.' We shall exterminate the viperous brood!"

De Goutins said nothing. A faraway look spread over his face. In imagination he was walking down the pathway to the house, scratching on the door, opening it, and walking in—past the living room, into the bedroom at the back, up to the bed—and there . . . there . . . there lay Madame de Freneuse, exhausted but radiant, delivered of his child. There he stood, ready to protect her with his sword as Monsieur de Bonaventure would protect her now. Grr! Just let him try! They would bring him down, the impertinent overbearing oaf, and his doxy with him! They would hunt and harry and yelp and tear until they had torn her pride and her laughing insolence into little pieces, the whole respectable religious yelping pack of them! And he, de Goutins, would unleash the pack! It was no more than she deserved for torturing him.

Father Francis coughed and recalled him to himself. The gleam in the pale eyes faded.

"I see that you are busy? Dispatches for the *Profond*?"

"Yes, Father."

"I will not keep you, but I thought you might need—this."

He held out the great leather-covered folio he carried under his arm. It was the Parish Register. In it, inscribed in Father Francis' neat script, appeared the words:

"Antoine, illegitimate son of Pierre Simon Denys de Bonaventure and Louise Guyon de Freneuse, baptized on the seventh day of September, 1703, within the bounds of this parish."

CHAPTER LXIV

SNOW lay thick among the trees, piled up in drifts around the fort, and covered the rivers to their mouths. The basin never froze. Its blue water sparkled against the whiteness of its banks. Denise, looking out of the window of her aunt's house, thought how pretty it was, how bright and clean, what a fitting background for her hopes. And when the skies were gray, clouded, full of the menace of falling snow; when the wind whistled and moaned about the walls or a blizzard blew, what fitting background to her fear! She was in love with Raoul de Perrichet, and he did not notice the space she occupied. Whenever she spoke to him, he started as if surprised that she had a tongue or could make sounds that were intelligible. At least she saw him often. He came to the house every day. Since the bad time when Madame de Freneuse was set upon and thrown down in the mud by a bunch of ruffians, half drunk, in front of the church, Raoul set his Indians on guard around the house. Madame de Freneuse seldom went out; but if she desired to, there was the escort, grim and competent, to take her where she would go. For the most part she lay on a day bed that had come from France and watched the landscape of the basin and the north-shore hills. She was very often silent, all the day, until de Bonaventure came in from the fort. He lived in the house, going forth to his work in the morning, returning home at eventide. Then she would rouse herself and be very merry, and he would be tender and considerate. Or they would sit silent, hand in hand, looking out together at the falling snow or the frosty stars, or, sometimes, at the strange northern lights that spread their curtain across the sky.

Sometimes Raoul came with him, then they would all talk and

laugh together while Dahinda served hot drinks. Ciel, the countless cups of coffee they were drinking in that house! Sometimes the Governor called. Then Madame de Freneuse would rouse with an effort, and they would play a duet together.

"Lacking spirit!" he would say, sadly shaking his head. "I might as well play solo nowadays."

Or she would sing. Her voice was richer, deeper, with an undertone not heard in it before. It seemed to make the men uncomfortable. They shuffled with their feet and looked away. It sent the cold shivers up Denise's spine. Sometimes her aunt would say:

"Poor Denise! It's lonely for you here, with no one of your age."

Then she would protest that she was happy. But, in truth, she missed the gay parties at the fort where she could wear her brocaded frock and dance, sometimes with Raoul, sometimes with her cousins, the cadets, and with her brother, too. They never came here any more. No one came but Monsieur de Bonaventure, the Governor, and Monsieur de Perrichet. Not even her aunt's own children came; nor Jeanne, still at the convent with the nuns. When Denise suggested Jeanne should come and live with them, too, her aunt had said:

"Let her be. She's young. They can do more for her than I can do. I should not have let you come."

"I wanted to."

Denise would embrace her aunt and smile at her. It made her heart ache to think of the beasts outside. Just because of the poor little baby—her cousin! That was strange. Red-letter days were when the nourrice came, or sent a message, telling how he was. She would arrive by night, with the Indians.

"If Madame could see the baby now!" she'd cry. "Madonna, how he's grown! He takes my sister and me, the both of us, to nurse him now. The spit of his father, I should say"—if Monsieur de Bonaventure happened to be there.

Then he would look at her or take her hand; and they would smile together tenderly, each of them thinking:

"I have ruined him."

"I have ruined her."

It was sad in that little house, waiting for the snows to melt and the first ship to arrive from France, bearing, they knew, the answer to the letters sent by the St. Vincents and Monsieur de Goutins in the fall. The Governor had warned them of the letters, gone to join the others, in the dossier. Therefore, the two clung closely, loving each other more than before—more deeply and more fundamentally. It was as though they had grown up over-night, coming into their long-deferred maturity.

As long as the Governor ruled the settlement and Raoul's Indians patrolled it for him, there was no physical danger to be feared for her; but when the ships came, they might contain orders from a higher authority than the Governor. They would certainly make him responsible for what had happened. Poor de Brouillan, Madame de Freneuse thought. Having wanted her, he would be censured because another man had given her a child. It was sweet to have Pierre's child. She thought of all those other children she had borne. Except for one who had died—may the Virgin rest his soul—they had not counted. They had been little animals, running to and fro. One was kind to them, but one did not care or associate them with oneself. Strange that the only two who called forth all her maternity were Gervais, dead, and this unwanted baby. Poor Antoine! She touched his father's hand, tentatively. De Bonaventure responded with a movement of his shoulder against hers. His shoulder was comforting. It gave the illusion of security in the hostile world.

De Bonaventure constantly told her that when her health returned, if she did not want to stay in the settlement, they would go away. She smiled at that, knowing that it might be impossible. De Bonaventure, a responsible officer in the King's service, could not just go away. What would happen to his wife and children in France? Could she see them disgraced and beggared, perhaps even worse? Assuredly not. His children! Looking perhaps, exactly like Antoine. She patted his hand.

"Do you love me, Pierre?"

"More than my life," he said, his eyes full of tears.

She brushed them away as they kissed.

"The sun on the snow is blinding," he said huskily.

CHAPTER LXV

THE vessels from France came in early that year. It was May when they were sighted sailing up the Basin, two of them, the *Soleil d'Afrique* leading. De Bonaventure, standing on the palisades, turned pale as he saw her.

"My ship!" he murmured. "That it should be my ship!"

"Heart up!" de Brouillan counseled. "There's many a loophole twixt procès and rope. We'll wiggle out yet. I wager de Goutins is rubbing his hands. That ever I should be censured over the increase of population in my command! There's a bounty on babies. By rights I should pin a decoration on your virility."

De Bonaventure smiled a little wanly.

"I hope she doesn't see them yet," he thought, "not till I get home!"

But Madame de Freneuse was standing at the window with Denise.

"That's the *Soleil d'Afrique*," she said, "his ship! Oh, Denise, if you had seen him as I have, in command, at sea! He's out of place here on the land, though they do say he's the most competent King's Lieutenant this place ever had! But his heart's at sea."

"Is it?" Denise said. "I should say, from what I've observed, his heart's with you."

"A man's heart can be in two places at once, Denise, and only then is it undivided."

"I want all of Raoul's heart," Denise said suddenly, thinking aloud. But Madame de Freneuse, luckily, did not heed.

"My Captain," she was murmuring. "My Captain. Pierre."

Suddenly she was afraid of what news he might bring. It was so near now. It was today.

But Pierre, when he came, was absurdly gay.

"The Governor's had a sheaf of dispatches about us," he said. "They all contradict each other. The worst of them only asks if the story is true! That gives us plenty of time. De Brouillan says we must lie."

"Lie?"

"Certainly! Throw sand in their eyes just as long as we can. He is drafting out a letter to send, for me to sign, at this minute. He sent a bundle of letters down to de Goutins, too. I'll wager the damned shark is sick! Beloved—don't you see?—it means a blessed respite, perhaps even we may go scot-free!"

"But, Pierre, lie? You mean lie about Antoine?"

"Certainly! They'll find out in the end; but that will give us time, and by then the Ministry may change. They may get tired of probing into such a personal matter happening out here. De Brouillan says take a high tone with them; that's what they are asking for, what they want to satisfy themselves that they've done enough. After all, it's only a lot of gossipy old women's words and a notary's against the Governor's and mine."

"I see."

She had never seen him so excited, or so pleased, as when he handed her a little packet.

"This came on the *Soleil d'Afrique*."

She opened it wonderingly. It was a christening mug, in hand-wrought carven silver with a motto and a crest. The motto was "Fideliter," the crest de Bonaventure's with a bar sinister, and underneath it "Antoine."

"It's not for you," de Bonaventure said; "it's for him, later."

She turned it over and over in her hands, looking at it through a blur of tears.

"I never gave the others anything," he said, taking it from her gently to set it down. "But he's our own."

She thanked him with a smile and a long kiss. Satisfied, he said:

"Now I must go. I left the Governor struggling with his dispatches. He has a visitor, too: Monsieur de Subercase, the Governor of La Plaisance. They have a lot to talk over and not very much time, since the *Soleil d'Afrique* departs tomorrow."

"I shall be sorry to see her sail; she's such a beautiful vessel. You should be aboard her, Pierre."

"I have other decks to walk," he replied, "and other storms to weather, and so that I come to harbor in your heart I am content."

Denise listening from the embrasure thought this the prettiest speech she had ever heard, and pictured Raoul saying it. He must be down at the port, watching the unloading, talking to the men fresh from France with news. Everyone was there, everyone except her aunt, Monsieur de Bonaventure, the Governor, and Monsieur de Goutins, who had been first on board, had borne away his mail, and was sitting now, in the gloom of his back room, where angrily he took up his pen and began to write anew. He would not be put off by courteous words. He would show the authorities that he was not a negligible person to be trifled with. He would humble the de Freneuse hussy yet.

CHAPTER LXVI

THE answer to Monsieur de Goutins' second missive arrived in the fall of 1704 and was peremptory enough to satisfy even him. It ordered the exile of Madame de Freneuse to her husband's seigneury, or to Kebec, and the immediate return of de Brouillan to be tried for maladministration of the colony, he having acted, the paper set forth, with a mixture of harshness and laxity that was not fitting for the duties of his station. It ordered him to appoint as administrator in his absence the officer most capable of filling his place and the most competent to carry out defensive measures against the English, who were rumored preparing a vast attack.

"Just as though we did not know it," de Brouillan grumbled, "but must hear it, certes, from *them*!"

There were no instructions to, or about, de Bonaventure except that he and Madame de Freneuse must separate. The Governor laughed.

"My orders are plain enough," he said. "I am to appoint the best person for the command and, therefore, I have no choice. I appoint you!"

De Bonaventure started back.

"Not me," he begged. "I must go with her to Kebec."

The Governor shook his head.

"How far do you suppose you would get? The Bishop of Kebec has his orders, too. He will incarcerate her in some convent, and send you back or, if you refuse, have you executed for treason. You know that as well as I do."

De Bonaventure started to make a gesture.

"No! Leave it to me," de Brouillan continued. "I am still Governor here. She is not going to Kebec."

"But, sir, you cannot disregard a direct order from the Minister! De Goutins, de St. Vincent, the rest—they will report you. They are waiting now to see what you will do."

"Soit! Of course, I cannot disregard a direct order from the King's Ministers. Why should I dream of such a thing? The order says to her husband's lands. Her husband is dead, and his seigneury laid waste. To send her there would be to murder her, which is in itself a criminal offense. To send her to Kebec, on the other hand, demands an escort through the woods, a vessel of some kind to take her along the coast, expense and responsibility. I cannot be sure she will not escape. Therefore, since I am responsible for her, as the order says, answering to the Minister for any further complaints and for your good conduct, too . . . They like your work, and they know your worth, mon vieux; they do not suggest that we dispense with you—ah, no!—only with her. . . . Since I am responsible, I say, I choose to exile her to a place where I can keep an eye on her and have her within reach. I shall send her up the river—twenty miles or so. Say to the house of the habitant who has her child. How will that do?"

De Bonaventure seized him by the hands.

"Then I shall be able to see her. She'll be safe!"

"She'll be safe, but you will not be able to see her. I am sorry, man, but you must give this thing time to die away of itself. You must wait a while. When my case is over, yes; or when the malice of these brutes has expended itself, then yes again. Meanwhile caution! Meanwhile injured innocence, meanwhile surprise! You know what you must do, if you wish to save her, not to mention what you must do for me. I shall be in France and in their hands. You must conciliate the people here, press on the defense, show yourself the soldier and administrator that you are. You must keep the Indians contented, through your nephew. I have already stressed the relationship to the Minister. You must put aside your dreams of personal happiness for a little while, and so must she. It may not be so hard if she is with her child and kindly treated. If you do well, I shall be able to say to them . . . You see? I shall be able to tell them that you deserve a little latitude. It is our hope."

De Bonaventure bowed.

"Governor, you are good to me—to us. I will write to the Minister. You shall see what I say."

·[274]·

Accordingly he composed a draft that night. The Minister had sent him a letter full of dignified remonstrance, like a curé wagging his finger at a little boy. De Bonaventure stuck his tongue in his cheek and began:

"Monseigneur,[8]

"I have received the letter that it pleased you to write to me on the eighteenth of July, and I cannot enough express my surprise to you and also my grief at seeing how my enemies' calumnies have triumphed over me. I never would have believed that they could turn against me, to my disadvantage, a conduct always conformed to the needs of religion and also to the desires of His Majesty, as that which I have always maintained up to this day; since, innocent as my conduct has been however, it has had the misfortune to displease His Majesty and your Eminence, I shall be very careful not to continue it, although charity alone prompted it.

"If there were anything which I might desire on this point, it would be, Monseigneur, that you should have enough kindness toward me to bring the facts to light. I would even implore your Eminence to give me this satisfaction if I did not fear to importune you after the protection which you have extended me in this affair, without which I should certainly implore you to send a commission of inquiry here at my expense.

"Monsieur de Brouillan will report to you what he has done with regard to Madame de Freneuse, and my own behavior in this matter. What have I done, Monseigneur, to the clergy and the justices that can deserve a reproof? Was I in command here? Has not Monsieur de Brouillan always been at hand to oppose my violations? Have I had anything to do with either of these parties to bring upon me such a sorrow? No, your Eminence must be persuaded to the contrary if you will give your attention to the matters reported to you."

De Brouillan added this:[9]

"Monsieur de Bonaventure is so mortified by the accusations made against him that he thinks himself obliged to ask permission to return to France, to justify himself, unless His Majesty judges his services more necessary here. In that case, he begs permission for his wife and family to join him, and also would point out that his salary is not sufficient to support him here."

De Bonaventure looked blank when he read this.

"Do not worry," the Governor said. "They will not raise your salary nor send your family out. But it looks well."

·[275]·

CHAPTER LXVII

BEFORE Monsieur de Brouillan sailed on the *Soleil d' Afrique*, Monsieur de Bonaventure and Monsieur de Perrichet conducted Madame de Freneuse to her new quarters, twenty-three miles up the Dauphin River, in a little hamlet called Beaulieu. They reached it by boat and deposited her there with Denise, Dahinda, and two Indians to act as messengers and go-betweens. Then they returned to speed the departing Governor. Raoul took to the forests, with his braves, to see about the Indian affairs he had left too long, while de Bonaventure settled grimly to the task of administering the settlement so that the King's ministers might be pleased with him and repeal the edict against his woman.

Madame de Freneuse, installed in the bedroom of the peasant family, who now lived—all of them—in the kitchen, dug herself in for the long winter and tried to fight her despair. They were kindly people, these habitants; she had Denise and the baby, who was lively enough to keep anyone busy as he trotted in and out on his unsteady legs. When he fell, he frowned so like de Bonaventure that her heart turned over; but she did not need the baby to remind her of Pierre. She thought of him all the time. She shut her eyes and pictured them together in her little house. At first she could not believe he would not come to her, but as the days and weeks went by and the Indian runners brought her only messages or a letter, hastily scratched, she ceased to hope. Evidently she was exiled, she told Denise, from more than the settlement.

"I am banished from his heart."

"Nonsense!" said Denise, oversharply for her years. "He is eating his heart out, but he cannot come. If he did, the trouble would begin again."

"The old Pierre would not have minded a little trouble," Madame de Freneuse muttered rebelliously, pressing the top of Antoine's head to her knees. The child looked up at her. He grinned toothlessly and gnawed at her knee.

"Behold," she said, "even he would bite. Men are alike."

Denise burst out laughing.

"Now, my aunt, you are more childish than Antoine! Monsieur de Bonaventure wishes to see you restored to your house and all to go on as before. In order to do this he must stay at his post and satisfy the King's Ministers in France; he must also wait till the grumbling of the settlers has died down."

"They should all be boiled and given to the savages to eat," Madame de Freneuse muttered. "Father Francis as the entrée."

"He would be tough."

"De Goutins would be all strings!"

"Madame de St. Vincent would be a heap of grease."

"Poor savages."

They laughed, but Madame de Freneuse's mood remained black and melancholy. It was almost as much for her as for herself that Dahinda was glad to see Raoul appear one morning, unexpectedly. He came in, tall and brown, dressed in his Indian leggings, with red cheeks and snapping black eyes that laughed in his usually serious face. He kissed Denise absent-mindedly on the cheek and then, seeing her blush, stopped, a little confused.

"You have grown such a lot," he said. "I forgot, Denise."

She tried to laugh at him; but her lip trembled, and he saw that she was troubled. A sudden realization swept over him, and he looked again. She was standing by the door lintel, with her head resting against it, her copper-colored hair flowing on her shoulders, and her wide blue eyes cast down. Raoul took her by the chin and raised her face so that he could see into her eyes. What he saw there apparently both pleased and satisfied him, for he gave an exultant laugh. Then tenderly he kissed her on the lips.

She was fiery red now, and she wrenched herself away from him.

"Don't go," he said. "I mean no harm. I have only been blind too long. I have only passed by the doorway to my home. I have not known where my true happiness lay."

But she was not reassured. She dreaded being trifled with by him. He watched the trouble in her face and caught her by the hand.

"Will you marry me?"

"Am I to be fourth squaw?"

·[277]·

Raoul went red in turn and snatched his hand away.

"No," he said after a moment. "There is much that I want to talk · with your aunt about, and now with you. I am leaving the savages to return to France."

"Leaving? But, Raoul, the war against the English . . ."

He shrugged. "I can't help that. Hamogom will carry on. Besides, I cannot go yet. I mean eventually. When I have money enough. You know, of course, that de Brouillan, my uncle, and I have been mining for copper and gold and trading for pelts? We will be quite rich by and by, Denise, and then we will leave this country and go home."

"Home, Raoul?"

"Home to me is Provence. Home to my—wife, as well."

She blushed again, but her eyes grew bright.

"And the squaws," she whispered, "will we have to take them, too?"

"Never a one!" he cried, exultant, for he saw that she was jealous. After so many years of indulgent indifference from Madame de Freneuse, it was pleasant to come first with anyone, especially with a beauty like Denise. The sun came out for him, and he felt young, and proud of being young, for the first time. He threw out his chest.

It was in this attitude of pouter-pigeon and blushing hen-bird that Madame de Freneuse found them.

CHAPTER LXVIII

O N A day in June, when the fruit trees blossomed, even in
Beaulieu, and the whole world seemed to mate, Madame
de Freneuse, restlessly wandering with Denise, distraite at
having heard no news from her fiancé for the space of a whole fortnight, came to a clearing on the edge of the tiny settlement where
they could see the river rolling beneath them, swollen, to the Basin.
Madame de Freneuse followed the course of it in her mind.

"Just think, Denise," she cried, "it flows past the house and to the
fort where he is working. I wish I were the river, free to go where
I would go!"

Denise was not listening. Her mind was with Raoul in the woods
among his squaws. She had just got to the point where he had
yielded to her entreaties and had the third and last squaw turned
out when her eye was caught by something on the river. She jerked
her aunt by the arm.

"Look!" she said. "There's a boat! Oh, ma tante! It looks like the
one we came in; and there are people in it, not Indians. See!"

Madame de Freneuse looked, and saw, and turned very pale.

"It is he," she whispered, as though such a secret must not be
heard. "Oh, Denise, it is he!"

She sat quite still as though she were stunned, and then suddenly,
breathlessly, took to her heels and ran all the way back to the
habitant's house. She rushed through the kitchen where the old
woman was sitting, knitting on a comforter, and spread-eagled
Antoine out of her way. He fell among the cinders of the hearth
and started whimpering.

"Pick him up," she shouted to a staring little girl, thumb in her mouth, who was watching her. "Pick him up and dust him! His father's coming here!"

Later de Bonaventure, with a lady and a gentleman each side of him, arrived at the habitant's house. Much had happened in the interim. The kitchen had been swept and the door of the unused little front room flung open wide. Madame de Freneuse was seated there in a very becoming gown, her hair newly coiled, sewing on a piece of tapestry. Denise sat with her, half smiling.

"You are like a young girl," she whispered, "ma tante, who is in love."

"No young girl knows how to be in love," Madame de Freneuse answered. "That is something left for one's middle age."

Denise pouted. She loved her aunt, and she had always viewed her love affair with de Bonaventure indulgently and, even when she was younger, considered it romantic; but now it did seem quite absurd, now when she knew what it was to love! One must have a handsome lover, young—above all, young—before one knew what loving meant. To give up one's place in the settlement, one's home, and everything, to bear an unwanted child . . . Denise shuddered. All that was not love, but craving for excitement probably. Her aunt was strange, she mused—twice married, and now this! No wonder the nuns shook their heads and sighed. Perhaps, after all, they could envisage the outcome, seeing further ahead than Madame de Freneuse. It was sad to think of the outcome. For the hundredth time since Raoul had told her and vowed her to secrecy, Denise wondered what her aunt would say if she knew! Perhaps that was what Monsieur de Bonaventure was coming for— to break it to her that his wife was there, and two of his other children, living in the fort with him, welcomed everywhere.

"La tante Jeanne," Raoul had said ruefully, "is impossible! She and the de St. Vincent woman are as thick as thieves. It is awful for my uncle. He looks like a walking ghost. He is afraid someone will tell *her*."

He had nodded his head to the room where Madame de Freneuse had retired to leave them alone for a little.

"Doesn't he want her to know? But, Raoul, she'll find out!"

"That's what he dreads, and you must help him, Denise; you must keep her from knowing, from hearing chance gossip, if you can. No sooner had we returned to the settlement, it seemed, than the *Profond* sailed in with her aboard! I wish you could have seen my uncle's face! That dumpy little woman walked off the boat

·[280]·

as though she owned the place, and she has behaved so ever since. My uncle feels that perhaps if he stays quiet and accepts the situation, on the face of it at least, the Ministry will revoke *her* banishment. He'd do anything for that."

Denise was thinking of all this, and wondering if the moment had come for her aunt to know and what would happen afterward when de Bonaventure and the de Falaises, who were with him, walked in. There were unheeded curtsies from Denise and the de Falaises, but Madame de Freneuse was in de Bonaventure's arms. Her face over his shoulder—eyes shut, mouth smiling in ecstasy— looked quite unreal; and when she released him at length, and began to stammer apologies to the de Falaises and to bid them belated welcome, her eyes held such a light that Denise could not look at them.

"Don't let that light go out," she prayed incoherently to all the saints that she could bring to mind.

But chiefly it lay in Monsieur de Bonaventure's power to keep it there. If he must tell her, let it not be too much of a blow to her pride, to her jealousy, to her love!

The de Falaises said to Denise:

"We do not know this part of the river, Mademoiselle."

"Does it extend very far, the settled cultivated land, Mademoiselle?"

She took the hint.

"If you would like to walk a little way," she said, "we can see the edge of the settlement. It is pretty there; the deer come down to drink sometimes."

The other two did not see them go. De Bonaventure took her in his arms again and kissed her hungrily.

"I'm working hard," he said, "harder than you know, to have you released and returned to your house."

"Our house," she said, "ours, Pierre! You are living there still, aren't you?"

"No," he said. "I have to be at the fort. It's easier."

"Oh? But you go there, Pierre?"

"Often," he assured her. "It is just the same, just the same pretty place."

"Ours!"

"Yes—ours. Let me look at you!"

"Do you see all the gray hairs?" And then: "Oh, Pierre!"

"I know, I know," he said, folding her close. "Oh, my dear love, what misery!"

She was satisfied. She lay in his arms, reassured, at peace, and comforted.

When the de Falaises came back, and it was time for them to return, they found Madame de Freneuse watching de Bonaventure playing with his son.

"What an idyl!" exclaimed Madame de Falaise, who was romantic.

"What a catastrophe!" said Monsieur de Falaise.

Denise said nothing. She could see that the light was still there; her aunt did not know.

CHAPTER LXIX

MONSEIGNEUR:[10]
"Permit me to complain again of the accusations made against Madame de Freneuse and myself. I had the honor to ask you, last year, to order that work be started upon my case. This has never been refused to anyone. It is a matter of indifference to me by whom the case is drawn up. I do not ask for clemency if I am guilty; but also, Monseigneur, if I am innocent, grant me, if it please you, that the author of such a calumny be punished.

"I implore you to consider whether it be just that this lady should be banished like a miserable criminal if she is innocent, who has neither goods nor establishment elsewhere than at Port Royal. It is impossible for her to live at the St. Jean River, since that settlement is entirely abandoned. She has the children of the Sieur des Chauffours, her brother-in-law, to look after, he being a prisoner in Boston. She is bringing them up as though they were hers. Although she has little money, she does not cease to provide for all her family by her careful management.

"If, Monseigneur, you absolutely will not have her alleged crimes brought to light, nor allow this lady to live upon her own property so long as I am at Port Royal, then have the goodness, Monseigneur, to withdraw me rather than her and return me to my former employment in the Navy. It is more just for me to leave the country than for her to do so, since it is I who am the cause of her misfortune."

De Bonaventure signed and sealed this dispatch with a gloomy frown. Then he drew another piece of parchment toward him and began to write more rapidly.

"My beloved:

"It was like sight to a long blind man to see your face again. You have no conception how one may suffer here, deprived of your presence, seeing you everywhere—upon the street, in the house, and in the room where I write, which is the Governor's ordinance room. Sentries are standing to attention, watching me engaged upon my important affairs on behalf of the government! If they only knew that I am writing to you! It is a relief after the affairs of the settlement, which are very bad, very bad indeed.

"We are in for another famine, I fear, and certainly an attack by the English and the Bostonians. Everywhere the scouts report massing of the troops and collection of vessels fitted out against us. And what do we do? Nothing! With Acadia to win or lose, we sit here, and the Government meddles with our private lives—with you and with me; with Allain, who has displeased Madame de Bellisle; and with poor de Brouillan, who writes that his case is not yet called, and Dieu sait when it will be. With all this detailed interest in us, when I write (as I write, by every mail-bearing vessel that leaves, for men, for money, for supplies) the Government is deaf; it is even, miracle of miracles, dumb! It has nothing to say to me in guidance upon such matters as the defense of the settlement, but plenty to say upon my private life! Ciel!

"These thoughts are treasonous to have, no doubt, but they occur to a thinking man. And I fear that they will occur only too forcibly to those in authority when we lose the settlement. Yes, beloved, it is most certainly a question of that. Nicholson, who commands the English forces, is an able soldier and a ruthless adventurer. He is of a different stamp from the pinch-penny courtiers at home! He has with him a queer card, Sir Samuel Vetch—like retch, is it not? And certainly we should all be doing it were he to come here, as he boasts, as Governor. This is how it stands.

"And in the middle of all this, when the harvest is failing this year and the pirates report plague among the Indians, Raoul falls in love; and this has rendered him, apparently completely useless! He no longer cares to control his men; he no longer looks upon himself as Indian. (Look upon yourself how you like, I told him, but do your work.) Ah, no, he is full of some crazy idea of marriage with your niece! Decidedly the women of your family are troublemakers to the authorities! I only hope he has one-tenth the happiness that I have had with one of them! Have had? Have, I mean, for happiness is in the future, too.

"One of two things will happen: my importunities and de

Brouillan's verve will bring about a recall of the edict, a vindication for the Governor and you; or else we will be plunged in war and lose the settlement to the English, and you and I will hardly care what they think at home. We will take to the woods and live on roots, like Raoul, or we will go to Boston and be prisoners. I hear they feed them very well. Seriously, unless someone can waken His Majesty's Government and extort some supplies from them, some help, some encouragement, we shall all be learning how to curtsy to Queen Anne, and you will wear English fashions. I hear they are very frumpy in comparison with ours, but you would look well in anything.

"My pen is blunt, and my arm tired. I would give much to rest my head where it rested when I saw you, light of my life! But there, one must have something to look forward to, Father Francis said in his sermon yesterday something to make a man support the troubles of this life. He meant some harping heaven; but I nodded agreement to him, thinking, my love, of you. The little Antoine is a fine little man, and sturdy. He is privileged in his mother.

"Salute him for me, and that young baggage of a niece who has created havoc in the well-laid plans of the Administrator (who will yet be the death of many, scalped because of her renegade Raoul), and he signs himself, this poor Administrator of everything but his own affairs,

"Your affectionate, and loving, and devoted, Pierre."

He finished and was laying down his pen when the door opened and Madame de Bonaventure came in.

Fresh from his visions of Madame de Freneuse, Monsieur de Bonaventure looked at his wife with dismay and distaste. She was a stout, bustling, dowdy little woman with a formidable goodness of character. He stood up, politely, to bow to her. At the same time he summoned the young Latouche with a crook of his finger.

"Take this to the Indian you will find outside," he said.

Latouche grinned and disappeared.

"Well, my dear?"

Madame de Bonaventure sat down heavily.

"I find," she said, "that the savages in the convent have no summer shoes. They are actually running barefoot!"

"Well," said de Bonaventure, "they and their ancestors have done so for generations, and may do so again."

"But think of the immorality! Some of them are quite grown girls!"

De Bonaventure thought of it, threw back his head, and laughed heartily. Madame de Bonaventure waited until he had finished.

"Pierre, you must write for shoes," she said. "You are the Administrator here; it must never be said that you encouraged immorality."

"Oh, never," he agreed.

CHAPTER LXX

FROM rumors, dispatches, visits from Raoul, Madame de Freneuse gathered the desperate state of the colony. Her heart was hot with anger against the home authorities and with concern for de Bonaventure. How could he hold out against the English when they attacked unless there were more supplies, more men, and, above all, more money? Money was needed to pay the corsairs and to bribe the pirates. Money was needed to keep the Indians loyal. Money was needed to pay the peasants for their labor; they could be forced to give it for nothing, but then they neglected the fields and the crops. Money was needed, above all, to purchase supplies.

She pondered the situation and came to a decision. Instead of languishing here within a tantalizing distance of the settlement, shunned like a leper—the only gift in her power to bestow upon Pierre, her absence—she would pick up her skirts and go to France. She would see de Brouillan there and aid him with his case. She would see the authorities; tell them firsthand what was happening to the settlement, the danger they ran of losing Port Royal to the English, of losing all Acadia. She would ask for nothing for herself unless she saw the moment favorable, when she would beg to be allowed to return and take up her duties in the siege that was surely coming. That was all.

The idea smiled at her. She told Denise and said that she would take her, too.

"We will get Raoul to come, instead of digging in his copper mine, neglecting his savages and you!"

Denise tried to dissuade her, but Madame de Freneuse was fired with enthusiasm. To get away from here, to be active once more!

To meet with men and women of the greater world, to sharpen her wit upon them in a salon once again! These were the reasons she gave Denise, over and above the settlement's desperate need of somebody to champion them, to attack the Court, to explain. But there was another reason which weighed further with her and was at the bottom of the whole idea—she would have to sail from Port Royal; it was her nearest port. She would have to spend at least a night there, possibly some days. She would see Pierre! De Goutins and the others might object; but as long as she was sailing for France, they had no word to say of blame against him or her.

She dispatched one of the Indians to find out what vessel would be leaving, and when. Then she set about her preparations. They were simple, consisting chiefly of instructions to the habitant and his wife about Antoine's welfare. The child was active and intelligent for his age. He came running to her whenever he could, bringing this and that to show to her, and always stood at her knee looking up at her with eyes so like Pierre's that she was startled. He was better here than anywhere else. If there were a siege or the English attacked, they would hardly be likely to burn or pillage so small a place as Beaulieu. The habitants had seen three attacks and always came through quite unscathed. They satisfied Madame that they would take to the woods with the baby and hide till it was over. Meanwhile they grew enough food, and there were the hogs; they would not starve. They were too far away from the fort and the sea to be in any danger.

Madame de Freneuse asked the two Indians attendant upon her —they were usually asleep in the sun, or absent on mysterious trips to the woods—to fetch a canoe and be ready to paddle her downstream to the fort.

"Send word to Ruwerera," she said, "that I need him at once. Bid him come to Port Royal, to the fort, before two nights are gone. Tell him I take the big boat, and he is to come with me; tell him *she* goes, too."

The Indians nodded; one of them disappeared. He would give the word to his waiting comrades, who would run with it on tireless feet to the copper mine where Ruwerera worked.

Madame de Freneuse, in a fever of excitement now that she did not have to face another long, agonizing winter—shut in, shut away, shut off in Beaulieu—bustled and scolded and ran about, catching up her flowing dresses, tripping Antoine up twenty times a day, until the morning dawned when she could take her place in the canoe.

Denise was upset because they had heard no word from Raoul. She wanted to wait, but Madame de Freneuse refused.

"You can, if you like," she said, "but I am going. The *Faulcon d'Or* is sailing tomorrow at noon. I propose to catch it. Raoul will probably be waiting at the fort, you foolish child. Come at least as far as that and see."

But Denise was nervous and afraid. She did not know what she should do. Madame de Freneuse did not know that de Bonaventure's wife was with him. Should she break it to her or leave her to find out? If she told her, would she not say: "What! You've known it all this time!"—and feel much worse than if she discovered it for herself?

If only Raoul had come, Denise would have made him tell it. But Raoul was mysteriously absent.

Madame de Freneuse, trailing her fingers in the water as they left the shore and struck out to midstream, was singing to herself. She raised one hand and waved it toward the bank, where the habitant and his family were standing, one of them holding up Antoine. Though she loved the child, she could not stop looking happy. Happiness welled up inside her as she thought that she would see Pierre soon, surprise him, spend the night. She kissed her fingers to the shore, settled herself, and closed her eyes.

It was afternoon. She had timed the arrival carefully. It would be about dusk. She would land at the wharf near the fort and proceed at once to the northern gate. Latouche would be on guard there probably. No matter what sentry it was, she would give the countersign and be let in. Perhaps no one would observe her from the settlement. If they did, and followed or made inquiry, then she would make it known that she was sailing the next day for France and needs must see the Administrator. . . . Pierre! Pierre!

She hummed beneath her breath. Denise looked at her anxiously. The rhythmic stroke of the savages brought them swiftly forward. They would be there soon. Denise tried to turn her mind from the approaching catastrophe. She thought about the voyage to France. She had never crossed the seas. She would see the Court, the King and the Queen, and the fashionable ladies. Best of all, she would see Raoul's own home. They would be married. She would not return. She shut her eyes and fell into sleep.

When the canoe grated against the sand as they beached, she

woke, bewildered. Madame de Freneuse sprang out, slipped as she came to shore, and almost fell. She gathered herself up and hastened, nearly running, to the postern gate. Looking up at the sentry, silhouetted against the sky, she flung the password at him. It was Latouche! She was through in a moment, running toward the Governor's quarters. She burst through a door, and another, running with swift instinct to the ordinance room.

There Pierre was, writing at a table. He did not turn his head as she came in. She stole nearer, cautiously. His blood leaped up, and he turned round.

"Louise!"

His arms went round her with a sound like a sob or a grunt. He strained them closer. Then he remembered, putting her away from him.

"How did you get here? Why did you come?"

"I had to! I had to! Oh, Pierre, I had to! But it is all right"—as he looked wildly round—"no one will censure you. I am sailing to-morrow on the *Faulcon d'Or*. This is an official visit, Monsieur l'Administrateur!"

She laughed and took his arms and put them about her again, pressing her lips to his.

They stood a long moment thus. Then she felt weak and wanted to sit down. It was after he had taken her to a seat and was standing in front of her, a good three feet away, that the door opened a second time and Madame de Bonaventure bustled in.

"Mercy on us, Pierre," she said, "here's the table set the longest while! My husband"—now she wheeled on Madame de Freneuse—"is tiresomely droll. He did not tell me we had the pleasure of a visitor. Present me, Pierre. I vow it is a pleasure, Madame, to meet new faces here." She sank in a curtsy even before her husband could mutter:

"Madame de Freneuse."

He looked at Louise imploringly, but she gave no sign that she saw. Instead, she sank in a long, official, deep-set curtsy, rising slowly out of it to stand upright and pale.

"Madame," she said, with only the slightest catch in her voice, "Monsieur de Bonaventure is, indeed, very droll."

"De Freneuse?" inquired the dumpy little woman with an important frown. "A relation of the little youth here, studying for the priesthood?"

"His mother."

·[290]·

"And the cadets?"

"My other sons."

"Enchanted, Madame, that you will sup with us."

"I do not want to put you to that trouble. I sail in the morning, and I needed papers from the Administrateur. I came at once because there was so little time."

"Of course, of course. You are staying here?"

"In the country, at the moment."

Evidently Madame de Bonaventure had been spared the scandal. That was unlike the gossips of the place. Could it be that this woman's worthiness and the real goodness of heart beneath her volubility had touched them into sparing her the truth? No help from Pierre. He stood there dumb, looking at her—she knew it, though she did not catch his eye—with all his soul in his eyes. He knew it hurt. But she would keep her hurt till the evening was over and she could examine it by herself.

Together, according each other a hundred delicate little attentions, the two women preceded him to the large Salle d'Armes. There Madame de Bonaventure presented her to the officers, assembled awaiting them. Madame de Freneuse raised her eyes and looked at each in turn. It was enough. Every man among them took his cue. One by one they came to kiss her hand, while Madame de Bonaventure explained to them who she was and Monsieur de Bonaventure stood there gray to the ears. In the middle of the introductions Denise came in with Raoul, who stopped short and gave a little crow of dismay until he, too, caught Madame de Freneuse's warning eye.

So, with Madame de Bonaventure at the head and Monsieur de Bonaventure at the foot, Madame de Freneuse took her place at the table where she had presided—ah, how many evenings! Monsieur de Bonaventure, desperately, raised his glass to her. She looked across her own and smiled. The smile was mechanical. Her eyes were blurred with tears.

CHAPTER LXXI

THE *Faulcon d'Or* was a week at sea before Madame de Freneuse found courage to leave her cabin. In spite of entreaties from Denise and embarrassed pleas from Raoul, she declined to move from the place where Pierre had placed her. Here, on this little roughly made cabin bunk, they had said their farewells. What farewells! It was almost worth going away from him, it was even almost worth leaving him with That Woman, to have such a farewell. She wanted to retain it in her memory. She had no curiosity about the last sight of land, the first whale, the distant flutter of white on a passing vessel; she wanted to lie here with her memories. It was different for Denise—her first trip to France, and Raoul with her. What a setting for young love! She smiled, thinking of Raoul's embarrassment.

"He does not like to feel that he has ever loved me," she thought, "and yet he cannot bear to be disloyal. He doesn't know where he is. Questioned, he would say that he was not in love with Denise, just marrying her. But one look at his face when she is there tells the whole story. Ah, if only Pierre and I could have married at their age! What a difference!"

She sighed. It was hard to think of Pierre's wife—sent out by the Minister, Pierre said. But perhaps he had wanted her to come? No, she must put that thought aside or she would grow bitter. After all, as Pierre had pointed out, he had to put up with Mathieu de Freneuse and, before that, Charles Tibaut. She had forgotten that. She had forgotten everything except the sweetness of being with him, the overwhelming urge they had to be together. Exile changed nothing. When de Brouillan returned, triumphant, one must hope. When the fight against the English was over—also triumphant, one hoped, although it would be a miracle unless the home authorities did something to help their colonists—then would come readjustment. The poor little dumpy woman would be sent home with her brats, and she, Louise, would be with Pierre instead. That's all she asked—to live with him.

"But that is everything."

The door of her cabin opened; Raoul poked his head in.

"Come up on deck with me," he said. "There's a most glorious sunshine on the sea, and dolphins."

She shook her head.

"I saw dolphins before you were born."

"Don't be superior. These may be a new kind. Besides, there's a vessel sighted."

"What else would there be on the sea?"

"It is coming toward us, belike from France."

"Well, well!"

"You'll grow pale in here, moping, always moping. My uncle would not like it. His last words to me were: 'Take care of her!' Come on, walk with me."

"Where's Denise?"

"She is trying to fish with a piece of rope. The Captain's with her."

"I thought there was some reason for this throwback!"

He went crimson to the ears, and she put out her hand.

"Sorry, Raoul."

He took her hand to his lips and looked at her.

"Then you will come?" he said, and won the day. She flung a heavy cloak about her shoulders, tied a kerchief to her head, and followed him up the rope ladder to the hatch and through it to the midships deck.

The sea was, in truth, blue and beautiful; the air, keen and cold. It was autumn, and there was a winter nip in the wind. The sails of the *Faulcon d'Or* spread in the sun glinted and gleamed like the plumage of some silver bird. They strained forward, and the ship plunged after them striving to keep up with her own wings. Madame de Freneuse drew a long breath. She had ever loved the sea. She thought of it as Pierre's. It was a fitting background to his life. But it was also great in itself and friendly, even when it was rough; even when it reached up and took you, it was kind. There was nothing small about the sea.

·[293]·

Raoul stood beside her, rolling his sea legs. Together they held to a spar and looked forward.

"Where's the vessel sighted?" Madame de Freneuse shouted, her words whipped away by the wind.

"For'ard to port!"

She looked where he pointed and fancied she saw a gleam of white.

"English?"

He shook his head.

"Too soon to know."

"If there's a fight . . ." she began, but the rest of the sentence was drowned. "Look, Raoul, look!" A sperm whale blew not five yards away. Some of the water spattered the deck.

"Big fellow, that," said Raoul sagely. It was the first time he had seen such a thing, and secretly he felt anxious. Would it upset the boat? His eye sought for Denise. If there were an accident, his place was beside her, the future mother of his children.

"And not so future either," a small voice pointed out. Raoul grinned, sperm whale and seas forgotten.

Madame de Freneuse left his side, wandering forward. She greeted a couple of taciturn sailors and plagued the lookout by asking for his glass.

Then, feeling suddenly desolate, she turned to go back to her cabin—at least one could lie down there, dream and cry and dream.

A shout went up from the d'artimon. The lookout cupped his hands and hailed.

"Aieeeeee, it's the *Profond*!"

"Nonsense," said Madame de Freneuse crossly to herself, startled by the cry. She had nearly slipped, and now she looked upward balefully. "You cannot possibly tell at that distance whether it's a ship at all, let alone the name of it!"

But it was the *Profond*. An hour later, when Madame de Freneuse was clutching the pillow in the second part of her program and tears were easing her, the watchers on the *Faulcon d'Or* could see her colors clearly through the glass.

"She's half-mast!" the Captain said. "Run up a signal. Who is dead; Can it be the King, do you suppose?" Denise and Raoul stood hand in hand while the vessels neared each other. Eventually, after a long cold wait, the *Profond* passed within hail.

"The Governor. It's the Governor. They've got his corpse on

board. It's Monsieur de Brouillan, dead at sea. He died two days ago."

The news spread round the ship. Raoul went to find Madame de Freneuse.

"Cry one more tear," he said as he opened the door and saw her weeping. "This time for a friend."

She looked up, startled.

"Monsieur de Brouillan has passed us, lying in state on the *Profond*. They bury him tomorrow, off La Plaisance."

"De Brouillan!" she said. "I wonder whether he won his case?"

"He comes up for judgment now before another tribunal," said Raoul, with the sententiousness of the happy young.

Madame de Freneuse crossed herself. She flung the cloak on for the second time and went on deck. For a long time she stood, silent, looking aft across the rapidly darkening waters. The sun was going down.

"He was a brave man," said Raoul, by her side.

She smiled. She was not thinking of the Governor as others thought of him. She saw again a day in June when he came from the forest, opened the Salle d'Armes door, and saw her there. Strange, eager boy, beneath his Governorship. Strange hour! It would stay with her always. Peace and rest to him. Her lips moved, and she prayed.

CHAPTER LXXII

"FROM Marseilles to Draguignan is a weary way," thought Madame de Freneuse. She rode a stocky little horse, Provençal breed, with an uncomfortable cross-stick saddle. It was better than a mule or a donkey, but that was all. Raoul rode beside her, with Denise a-croup behind him. He was a different Raoul, young and excited and boyish and shy all at once. He pointed out old landmarks all the way: there was the de Callians' mill, and the farthest part of their land; there was the convent to which one of his sisters was sent. Denise, admiring, turned her head this way and that, drinking in the sunshine, the orange trees, the gay flowers, the old stone buildings, the fountains in the villages, the little donkeys, caked with sweat, trotting sagely up the hills, and always Raoul's face against this new background.

Madame de Freneuse thought wearily: "What am I here for? This does not advance me with the supplies, the Court, the needs . . . But I suppose it is wise, for Denise. She will marry, from Raoul's home, and live here with him. This is where he belongs. And yet I have seen him capering and yelling in the forests! Strange! I am glad he is not in love with me, glad and yet a little lonely. It is like missing a favorite dog. Denise will marry; and I will send her sister to her and her cousins, too. She will be good to them. It is a very good thing to be the Comtesse de Perrichet, no doubt. I wonder how much of a place he has? I must make them like me, for Denise's sake. How strange it will be for them to see him return, so many years away! What would I feel if it were mine? Antoine or . . . Gervais? Or Jean-Marie," she added hastily, "or the others. Good sons, all."

She sighed a little, shifting her weight. "I am too old for all this

·[296]·

exertion," she thought crossly, and fell to thinking how differently she would ride if Pierre were at the end of it, waiting for her or, better still, riding beside her. Here she would meet his relations, by marriage, and have to speak of him. Quelle corvée! What a nuisance! It was bad enough to have left him behind with That Woman, but to talk of him to her relations would be terrible.

"Look!" said Raoul. "We are beginning to climb the hill toward home! Now we can see the town, the church, the château. See!"

Denise looked. People were moving about the square and round the château gates.

"Whose place is that?"

"The de Callians'." He spoke self-consciously. The vision of Vanina, as he had last seen her, rose before his mind. He laughed at it. Since then he had loved one woman and married—four, if you counted squaws! He laughed again.

A woman dressed in black came out of the church. She made toward the château, passing the little cavalcade with unseeing eyes. Raoul did not recognize her. Some old servant perhaps, slipped into vespers to pay a visit to the Blessed Sacrament. She was shape-less and shrouded in respectability. He idly pitied her. What did such a stuffy old matron know of anything? Thus he passed his first love, all unwittingly. Madame de Callian turned in the gates of her château, pulling the black shawl closer. One grew colder earlier these days.

Raoul and his cavalcade rode on. They turned a corner. "And there," he said, "is home!"

The animals clattered across the courtyard. No one was in sight. Raoul lifted up his voice and shouted:

"Ohé! Here!"

A gnarled old man came forward to take the horses. Raoul slid to the ground.

"Henri, is it not?" he inquired. The man touched his hair.

"Don't you recognize me, man? I'm Monsieur Raoul! Where are my father and mother? Are they—are they well?"

"Heaven bless us!" The man crossed himself. "Monsieur Raoul! Té, you have grown a sight! And alive, and safe, from those strange savage lands! Monsieur le Comte is well," he went on hurriedly, sensing Raoul's impatience, "except for the ache in his bones. And Madame, too. She has grown quite deaf. But she'll hear *you*, no doubt. Will these be friends?"

"More than a friend, you old dog, you." Raoul gave him a push. "This is my bride-to-be."

Denise blushed fiery red. The old man chuckled.

"Santé, santé à tous," he said, leading the horses away, looking back now and then.

Raoul started up the steps. The door flew open, and an elderly, plump woman flew out.

"My son!" she cried, laughing and crying in the same breath. "My son!"

She turned after that and tried to curtsy, but she was too excited in the middle of it to follow it through. She flung her arms about Raoul again, nodding and smiling over her shoulder at the others, as much as to say:

"Time presently, for you. This is my son!"

At length she disengaged herself and held him at arms' length.

"Mother, this is my betrothed."

The woman and the girl looked hard at each other. What they saw, they liked. Each was all smiles, and there was a good feeling in the air.

"This is Madame de Freneuse, her aunt."

Again the scrutiny, again the mutual liking.

"You will come in," Madame de Perrichet said. "Of course, you will stay with us—a long, long time. There is so much to hear, so much to say! I could have died when I heard his voice and looked out of the window. At first I did not know him; but now, see! He has not changed so much after all."

"Where are the others, Mother?"

"Your sister is married, your brothers—one of them is gone from here, and the other two are dead. We have had sad times, son, since you were here; there was a plague, you know, but such a plague. I did not write about it for fear you should be sad."

A buxom, smiling woman came toward them.

"Tiens," said Madame de Perrichet, smiling and nudging her son, "an old friend of yours!"

Raoul looked bewildered. He did not know the woman at all.

"Marie, here's our wanderer home at last! You recognize Monsieur Raoul!"

Marie flung her arms up and called on heaven; then she ducked in an excited bob and danced about him, exclaiming, "Boudie! Sacré Nom," and other expressions of intense surprise. Raoul politely bowed. He did not know her at all.

·[298]·

"Monsieur remembers *me*," she said at length, seeing that he didn't, "la petite Marie?"

It all came back to him then, and he blushed and started back.

"Marie is our best dairyman's wife," his mother told him placidly. "Marie, you must pay your respects to Monsieur's betrothed."

Marie and Denise greeted each other, without expression. Denise was shy, and Marie uninterested.

Madame de Freneuse, working a toe into the ground, thought: "Can I endure it till the wedding? Must, I suppose!"

She followed the chatting group into the house.

CHAPTER LXXIII

RAOUL was married before Madame de Freneuse left for
Paris. Denise made a pretty bride. The wedding took
place in the church at Draguignan; and the bridal procession walked beneath the huge old yellow trees of the square, with
ribbons and laces fluttering in the breeze that swept the valley.
Denise leaned on the parapet and looked out over Provence. She
saw mile upon mile of small cultivated fields, and little walled
towns of stone houses with gaily painted shutters and roofs. It
looked so joyous after the grim and desolate wastes of forests and
water she had known all her life in Canada that she felt a lifting of
the heart. Though the old world had troubles, plague, high taxes,
wars, it was a friendlier place. She had come home.

Madame de Freneuse kissed her, blessed her, and gave her the
small dowry she had saved for her niece. Denise clung to her at
parting, and Raoul walked with her to the coach. The de Perrichets were sending her in state back to Marseilles. From there she
would take the courier to Paris. Raoul handed her in, bowing over
her hands. She leaned forward and kissed him upon the cheek. It
was the first unsolicited kiss she had given him. It made her feel
very old. But he took her by the cheeks and kissed her lips.

"Remember," he said, "to call upon us for anything you need."

Then he stammered and stood on one foot. The de Perrichet
servants, in their sober livery, took their places on the coach, and
the driver in his plumed hat cracked the whip. There was a crack-
ling of wheels on gravel and the sound of straining feet. Madame
de Freneuse placed her face at the aperture, smiling at both of
them.

"Good-by," she said. And to herself: "I have lost a lover, to find a friend." She waved again as the coach swung to turn the corner, then gave herself up to her thoughts.

The mission ahead of her would be very arduous. She had counted on being able to see de Brouillan, finding out from him where the land lay. They would discuss the situation together; he would advise her what to do. Now he was tossing in his shroud a thousand leagues away; and she was alone among scheming, clever, unscrupulous men, to find her path without him.

She spent no time in Marseilles. The courier was leaving immediately; she left on it. They bowled along dusty highways, between orange and olive trees, through little walled Provençal towns, till they reached Avignon. Here Madame de Freneuse spent the night, heard mass, and changed her clothes. They plodded on. She grew so tired at length of the journey, that she did not notice anything, leaning back with her head against a cushion. Her fellow passengers, two gentlemen, paid no attention to her after the usual perfunctory gallantries, and she was able to think until she was too tired even for that.

The courier traveled day and night for the latter part of the voyage, with brief halts to change the horses and for the travelers to get hot food. They dashed through the forest of Fontainebleau, with the guards sitting, gun and pistol cocked, on the lookout for highwaymen. They reached the outskirts of Paris at eventide on the last day. They entered along the quais and drove toward the Ile de la Cité. There, at an inn opposite the Cathedral of Notre Dame, they halted for the last time. Hostlers ran to take the horses; fat chambermaids ran to assist the passengers; a group of loiterers became animated, talked with the postboys, and ran to dissipate the latest news from the South. A lean cat rubbed itself against Madame de Freneuse's skirts as she stood unnoticed in the throng. The bustle and the excitement tired her. She did not like the look of the inn, but she knew no other place to go until the morrow. The de Perrichets had given her letters to relatives of theirs; she had other letters from de Bonaventure to his friends; but it was late, and she was tired. She followed the chambermaid, who finally took notice of her, into the inn and engaged a room.

It was a little room under the eaves. The price of it astonished her. One could buy a team of oxen for the same amount, and cattle were the most expensive things, in the New France. At this rate she must work fast to succeed. She marshaled her plans in her head once more, going over them point by point.

The great bells of Notre Dame tolled the quarter hours and rang the hours with mellow boomings. They kept Madame de Freneuse awake. Toward dawn she rose and pushed her lattice open to look out. The moon's rays still shone on the great rose windows, and the dawn's light began to mellow the stone. Notre Dame towered above her, so beautiful that she caught her breath. There was nothing in the new world to rival the glories of the old. But opposite the Cathedral rose the cruel walls of the prison and the courthouse, the torture chambers and the dungeons, where men, miserable relics of humanity, sweated out their dark days in blood and fear, in misery and cowardice, in cringing and betrayal, or in useless martyrdom. She wondered how the Cathedral and the prison could so front each other and not raise questions in men's minds. For a moment, as she shuddered, the tortures of the savages beneath wide skies seemed cleaner, less degrading, than the King's paid executioners. She shut her window hastily and climbed back onto her narrow, high, quilted bed, homesick for the house at Port Royal, sustained only by the thought that before she could go there, freely, she must attack the authorities, convert them to her view. Unless the King's Ministers sent help, there would be no settlement to go to. It would fall.

CHAPTER LXXIV

MONSIEUR DE POURTCHARTRAIN, His Majesty's Minister for the Navy, the Colonies, and the Dependencies, sat in his suite of State in the Louvre Palais, surrounded by secretaries and flunkies in the King's livery. He was a tall, fleshy-looking man, with an expression of having lived upon his face, disguised beneath a hasty veneer of sanctimoniousness, acquired with difficulty lately. Since Madame de Maintenon reigned over the King, many of his Ministers and courtiers, who had been with him before her, wore the same expression, while it was illuminating to see ladies of the Court beneath their penitent black veils, disguising eyes and lips meant for laughter—and used for license in the pre-Maintenon era—beneath a sudden pious austerity.

Monsieur de Pourtchartrain had the harassed air of one striving to do too many things at one time and fearful of not doing them to the satisfaction of his royal master's mistress, another expression which he shared with those about him. When one of the flunkies brought a card to him, he frowned at it impatiently.

"Madame de Freneuse, Monseigneur, introduced to Monseigneur's attention by Admiral de Bœuvelin."

"De Bœuvelin? What does that old stick dig himself out for nowadays? Thought he had retired long ago to the grave. Hmmm, Freneuse . . . Freneuse? What does that remind me of? Something to do with New France. Acadia. I have it! Jean, get out the Acadian File, Port Royal; look me up Freneuse. Give me the dossier here, when you have it. Tell the Admiral to wait, with my compliments," he said to the flunkey with the card. "Tel! him I am

·[303]·

at present in audience, but will see him afterward. De Bœuvelin? Isn't he that de Bonaventure's cousin? Yes, of course, of course!" He smacked his lips and rubbed his hands together. "I shall like to take a look at Madame de Freneuse. She appears to have set the whole place by the ears. Must be a pretty woman. Take a look, Jean, and see!"

The secretary bowed, and glided on his black-encased legs toward the antechamber where the Admiral and his protégée were waiting.

"Monseigneur is chagrined to keep you waiting," he said, taking stock rapidly. ("Not pretty," he thought, "not young, not the usual strumpet—something more than that, striking, unusual, vivid. Mon Dieu, yes, this is a woman for a man to lose his head about. I understand Monsieur de Bonaventure now; Monsieur de Brouillan, too.") Aloud he made his excuses, called a flunkey to fetch wine, and left.

"Well?" said de Pourtchartrain looking up. "Shall I see her?"

"Yes, Monseigneur. She is not what one would expect."

"She may not be; her petition is. I'll wager she comes to be justified, to return to Port Royal, to begin all over again. Hein? What use was it to send out the fellow's wife and crowd of brats if there is to be another scandal there! She has misjudged her time, Jean; she is not à la page. She forgets we have gone pious now in a big manner! Oh, là, là." He rolled his eyes and crossed himself. "That ever a man should sleep with a woman out of wedlock, fie! But if all the world had been of the de Maintenon's way of thinking, many of us would not be here, eh, Jean, my son?"

The secretary looked about him furtively. "Not so loud Monseigneur," he begged. "Her spies are everywhere!"

The Minister pouted, but he was silent.

"Well," he said, "I have only the problem of how to embark our troops for Spain without any ships and without any money, how to build seven new frigates without any funds, how to mount guns on seventeen of the old type without any money, how to administer the dependencies without any money, and how to retain my place without any money. With nothing but that for my morning's work, I may as well see this woman."

"Without any money," the secretary put in. "She did not sweeten the palms of the flunkeys. It is a wonder she arrived as far as Monseigneur's door."

·[304]·

"That's the old Admiral. One of the old-school boys, all ramrods and equity. Dieu, what a morning, Jean! Show them in."

He was standing when they entered—a fine figure of a man, if a little too fat and white of complexion. He bowed and extended his ringed hand.

"Admiral! It is a joyful occasion which brings you to the Court! You have neglected us shamefully. Madame!"

He bowed again, and Madame de Freneuse curtsied. Her dark brown dress was copied on that of Madame de Maintenon's. Her plain black veil was severely draped; but the face which looked out from under it, straight into his eyes, was not the mock sanctimonious one he was prepared for in a woman of her reputation. Jean was right, the woman was unusual; there was a certain freshness about her—piquante, that was the word. Hmmm . . . Perhaps it came from living overseas, in the wild colony he had administered for twenty years without really caring to know anything about. Perhaps.

"Madame," he said again, "what is your will of me?"

"Monseigneur," she answered, "I have taken this long voyage from Port Royal here to see you, and to acquaint you at first hand with the situation in the settlement, knowing that if you heard it you would act."

The Minister smiled. She would ask for a repeal of her sentence of exile, which he had in the dossier before him. He would grant it—at a price. That would be one intrigue that promised safety from Madame de Maintenon and her spies; for the woman would sail right afterward (he would see to that) and she would not talk (he would see to *that*)!"

But her next words took him by surprise.

"Monseigneur, there are only a hundred and sixty officers and men in the garrison. The English are amassing men, ships, and ammunition against us. They have, our scouts report, at least two thousand seasoned troops now."

(" 'Our,' and 'we'! Tiens, tiens! The lady identifies herself pretty completely with the Administrateur.")

"Even so, we might make a stand. But ammunition is lacking; money is lacking."

"Ah, always money!" said the Minister.

"Unfortunately, money is a necessity in the defense of colonies, Monseigneur. The crops have failed; plague has set in among the Indians and along the coast. There is a shortage of everything, in

·[305]·

fact, that could make a spirited defense possible, or, indeed, any defense at all!"

"It would be sad, Madame, if such a mercenary spirit as you describe existed in His Majesty's colonies! I understand that the needs of the settlers are simple, in keeping with the life they lead. Why do they not work a little harder and wring from that rich soil the food they need?"

"Monseigneur, already winter is setting in. Your Excellency can have no idea of the cold of the winter, when all the earth is buried six feet deep in snow and a man has a hard enough time to keep alive at all without thinking of anything else."

"The cold must also affect the English, Madame, and keep them occupied."

"Then comes the melting of the snows. The rivers run; the sun shines; the quick, rich earth lies waiting; and the habitant creeps out of his hole to set about wrestling with nature for the brief time allotted him."

"You speak like a poet, Madame, I vow you do."

"Monseigneur, before we can sow a crop next year, the English will attack and we shall starve. Unless we can receive supplies, food, ammunition, men, and money speedily, the fort will fall to the English, and Acadia may be lost to France.

"Madame, that is a loss we shall all feel and deplore. But you will permit me to be frank with you. I think it best, and kindest. Since you have the fate of the colony so much at heart, you cannot be unaware of the fact that Port Royal and, indeed, Acadia have cost His Majesty's Government more than the most prosperous settlement could ever hope to repay. Money has poured into Port Royal as into a sink, and so far we have had not the smallest return."

"The fur trade alone ——"

"Ah, yes, the fur trade. Even the few livres that might bring back to His Majesty's coffers have been grudged him. The colonists cheat and lie and sell the furs elsewhere. They steal and smuggle them; they do not feel that all they do belongs by rights to His Majesty's Government, who sent them ships and financed their expeditions in the first place, who pays their Governor and his staff their salaries. Oh, no! Nothing but complaints pour in from the colony, complaints and demands for more money and more money. The settlement at Port Royal, Madame, has forgotten that His Majesty has other cares and concerns than the doings of a small handful of malcontents half the world away! We are at war, Madame. The Spanish succession, vitally affecting His Majesty's interest, has perforce drawn us into war with England and her allies. We need every man, every gold piece here at home! Do the colonists at this time send us their help, their support, their furs, their tobacco, their maize, and their money? No. They do not even send their sympathy, their loyalty, their expressions of devotion to His Majesty's cause. No, they send you, Madame to beg for more, at a time when we are hard put to it for ourselves! They send you to ask for money, food, ammunition, men; they send you with a story of plague and famine! Look about you, Madame; here in France you will find plague and what amounts to famine! Go back and tell those who sent you that we ask them for maize, for help, for money, or we may lose France, and see what they say!"

"Monseigneur, nobody has sent me here. I come as a private individual."

"Then it is to private individuals that you must address yourself! There are still enough soft hearts and long purses in France to be robbed."

"Robbed, Monseigneur!"

"Madame, your colonists have a great country, full of resources; they have friendly Indians, ready to exploit these resources for them; they have copper and gold mines; they have pelts; they have the rich, productive earth; they have a fort and guns; and if they had any manhood, Madame, that should suffice!"

"I would you could see the conditions there, Monseigneur."

"I would you could see them here, Madame! Perhaps, if you stay long enough, you may. It would give Madame de Pourtchartrain and myself great pleasure to entertain you while you are here."

"You are too good, Monseigneur; but I am a quiet person, and I would fear to incommode Madame de Pourtchartrain with my presence. I am well disposed of with Admiral de Bœuvelin."

"You could not be better." He bowed. "But I hope you will allow us the pleasure of hearing many curious and interesting details of the habits and customs in Acadia? Will you sup with us tomorrow?"

Madame de Freneuse sank in a curtsy. She hesitated a moment, looking for courage to the Admiral, then she stammered:

"Monseigneur, there is a small personal matter I would bring to your attention."

"Let me see if I can spare you the trouble, Madame. You have, doubtless through no fault of your own or of Monsieur de Bonaventure, incurred the dislike of the ecclesiastical and legal authorities of the colony. You are at present, if I mistake not, under an edict of exile?"

Madame de Freneuse nodded. Her eyes pleaded with him. He shook his head.

"I trust you do not think of me as an enemy, Madame," he said. "Yet, if I were to permit your return to such a dangerous place as you have convinced me Port Royal is, I should be acting hostilely toward you. I cannot grant your request." He waved his hand. "Jean, see that Madame is informed where to come for the supper and is well attended thither. You will join us, Admiral, will you not?"

"You see," said the old man, when they were safely out of earshot and the avalanche of curtsying and bowing was over, "it is as I told you; he will do nothing. From his point of view he has reason. He is not a free agent, and the King will spend no more money on his colonies. He told you to turn to private personages, and that was more than I expected. He might have ruled out any mention of Acadia. You had better follow his advice, and also go to the supper. It is wise. I will come with you, though I swore I would never set a foot there. We will see what we can do together. You might appeal privately to Madame de Maintenon. She is sometimes generous in a good cause."

CHAPTER LXXV

I T WAS some weeks before Madame de Freneuse could obtain
her audience with Madame de Maintenon. The weeks passed
quietly in the Admiral's household, which consisted of himself and a widowed sister, her son and two daughters. They lived
quietly in a beautiful old family house in the Rue de Bellechasse.
It had a garden, with lime and lilac trees. Madame de Freneuse,
passing under the grim and noncommittal portal with its grille of
iron gates and heavy oak door studded with nails, always felt that
it was like passing into another world to find oneself in this garden. She did not go out much, spending her time sewing tapestry
with the Admiral's sister or reading aloud to the two daughters,
one of whom was blind. She took part in the modest dinners that
were given to retired officers of the Navy and their families; she
listened to the news that was given forth; and when she was called,
she gave the news of the settlement as it had been when she left,
described the rigors of the Acadian winter and the difficulties of
the coming siege. She grew heated about the shame and disgrace
of losing the colony permanently to England. The old seamen
shook their heads.

"But yes," they said, "it is a disgrace and a shame; unfortunately,
it is also a saving. The King has holes in his coffers now, and a
miserly woman to make him heed the leaks. Too much has been
spent on Port Royal already. He will not spend more."

Nevertheless, they came to her sometimes, privately, with a few
louis d'or for her growing fund.

She made a list of supplies, medical herbs and foodstuffs, grain,
rice, corn, oil, wine, cloth. Ammunition was beyond any means

she had; but she hoped to obtain a sum from Madame de Maintenon to cover that, or an order on the King's armories.

She dressed herself with care, when at length the day arrived,
in a black dress, with the black veil, and a silver crucifix about her
neck. She looked like a nun and could not help smiling to think
what reputation the pious robes covered and also what manner of
woman she was going to see—a strumpet, but a royal one; and now,
of course, a wife. Why, she wondered, did Madame de Maintenon
derive such comfort from being a morganatic, unacknowledged
wife? "Religion," Madame de Freneuse said to herself, "I suppose." She remembered how the Admiral's sister had told her that
Madame de Maintenon made the King fast in Lent.

"Fast?" she had inquired. "Do not many people—in fact, all of
us—fast to some extent in Lent?"

"I mean," said Madame de Vaillant, blushing, "fast from other
things."

"From the use of her body, do you mean?" said Madame de
Freneuse, amused and astonished.

"Hush, Madame!" She looked about her, to see whether her
daughters heard. "I do mean . . . That is, Madame de Maintenon
denies the King her wifely duties during the entire season of
Lent."

"Hmm," said Madame de Freneuse. "What does His Majesty
do? I suppose Lent is the season most of the royal bastards are
conceived."

"Madame! I beg of you! High treason! If we were overheard!"

"Who could overhear us behind these walls?"

"But I vow you amuse me vastly," Madame de Vaillant said,
when she had recovered herself. "I've heard"—she sank her voice
to a whisper—"she recommended the King to take purges when he
felt the desire rising!"

"Seigneur Dieu! I am glad I am not a king!"

She thought of this conversation as she found herself, with the
Admiral escorting her, driving under the archway to the Louvres.
Just as they approached the western gates, a cry went up; their
driver pulled his horses up on their haunches and backed them out
of the way. A carriage bowled by, with footmen in the royal
livery attending it. A sallow, livid face appeared at the window,
draped in black.

"That is Madame de Maintenon," said the Admiral, "driving
with the King." He uncovered his head and bent his knee.

They followed, discreetly, taking care not to arrive until the occupants of the carriage had disappeared. Then Madame de Freneuse showed her audience card and was escorted to a waiting room. The Admiral went with her. The room was full of people. Madame de Freneuse counted seventeen priests, fourteen women who looked like Mother Superiors, one girl in fustian gray, a bishop or a cardinal, and a man with a long white beard.

She took careful stock of the faces. They all had the same expression, a prevailing fanaticism, whatever their age or degree. The Admiral kept an austere silence. He was the only man not clothed in black in the room. His wig, tied with a bunch of ribbons, in the old school, gave him almost a rakish look among these crop-haired people. Poor dear Admiral, if he looked out of place, how would Pierre seem here?

They sat for three hours before Madame de Maintenon granted them audience. Following a lackey, they penetrated into a large gloomy room, so cold and damp that Madame de Freneuse shivered. The windows were shut and sealed; the air was stuffy, but not warm. Madame de Maintenon sat upright before a needlework frame, where she was embroidering an altar cloth. A number of ladies round her were engaged in the same kind of work, sitting in silence on uncomfortable chairs.

Madame de Freneuse curtsied and came forward. Madame de Maintenon looked up. Little beady eyes in the yellow face bored into her.

"Be seated, Madame," said the prim lips. Madame de Freneuse demurely complied.

The work went on in silence, while the Admiral, ill at ease among so many women, sat against the wall. He had been accorded a cool nod, a gesture of dismissal, and a stare. He sat there rebelliously, remembering the gracious welcome of other royal personages—in particular the lovely, young, enchanting Duchess of Burgundy. "Where," he quoted to himself, "are the snows of yesteryear?" This was cold enough to be snow, in all conscience, without the beauty of whiteness.

Madame de Maintenon spoke presently.

"I have heard that you are a woman from New France?"

"Yes, Madame."

"You were born there?"

"Yes, Madame."

"You have lived there always?"

·[311]·

"Yes, Madame, except for brief visits, such as this, to France."

"Your father was a Conseiller du Roi, was he not?"

"Yes, Madame."

"And your late husband—heaven rest his soul"—all the ladies crossed themselves except Madame de Freneuse, left at the post; she hastily remedied this and bowed her head—"was one of our well-thought-of settlers, owning the seigneury of Freneuse?"

"I see that you know everything, Madame."

"We are well informed, and interested in the matters pertaining even to the outer world."

There seemed no answer to this. The next question came abruptly.

"Do you read?"

"Why, yes, Madame."

"Write?"

"Yes."

"Script or print?"

"Both, Madame."

"Where did you learn to read and write?"

"In the convent at Kebec."

"Ah!" The yellow face nodded, satisfied. "It is as I said to the dear Cardinal—the nuns uphold our civilization to the four ends of the earth. Were there any savages in your convent?"

"Many, Madame; we had a number of little Indian girls."

"No boys?"

"No, the convent did not take the Indian boys. They stayed with their families in the woods. When they came to visit their sisters, there was such a difference! The little Indian girls, clean and smiling, dressed in little robes the nuns made for them and their hair neatly braided. The little boys, dirty and unkempt, scowling at them angrily. The little girls sometimes would not speak to their brothers; none of them wanted to leave the convent or to marry, for after marriage, of course, the picture changed. The man, then, had the good clothes; the squaw was a dirty beast of burden."

Madame de Maintenon leaned back for a moment and closed her eyes.

"I have been praying for my sisters, the Indian women," she announced after the interval. All the ladies murmured "Amen" except Madame de Freneuse, caught napping once more. The audience was almost drawing to a close, and she had not begun her appeal. She gathered herself together.

When she had told of the dangers, the hardships, the plague, and the need the settlement was in of strong support from France in order to survive, Madame de Maintenon said:

"I am persuaded that the good work done by the nuns among the savage children needs support. Every soul baptized, every squaw converted, is another soul saved to eternal graces and glory of the Church, our Universal Mother. You have interested me very much, Madame. I shall contribute gladly to your fund; but the money that I send, or my friends send, is to be spent uniquely upon the propagation of the faith among the savages, the decent clothing of the women and girls. My secretary will give you my donation. I shall expect a strict accounting from the Mother Superior of the convent. Madame, I give you good day."

She rose and sketched a curtsy. Madame de Freneuse bent deep in another. The Admiral, who had not been addressed and had not spoken a word, led her away. In another room they found the secretary. He presented them with ten louis and a tract for the savages, written by Madame de Maintenon's own hand. He obtained a receipt and a written pledge that the money should go to the convent and the converted savages, to be used in the best interests of decency and religion.

"You see?" said the Admiral, when they were out of earshot and Madame de Freneuse dared release the furious breath she was holding. "That is how it goes here now!"

CHAPTER LXXVI

TOWARD the summer of 1706 Madame de Freneuse had collected from her friends and her acquaintances, from kindly disposed societies, and from the de Perrichets enough supplies and stores for the settlement to form a cargo. She had not been able to collect ammunition or arms or to secure any official help whatever. The authorities were not interested. They grew less and less interested. The colonies, so far as King and Court and King's Ministers went, might just as well be left to any fate that came along. They were expensive and a nuisance, and there were more important things to think about—the War of the Spanish Succession, for instance, and the new tax on bread, which was causing one of those popular uprisings so tiresome for the people that took part in them.

Madame de Freneuse decided that she would sail with what she had. Repeated attempts to have her exile lifted and her home restored met with blank refusal. She knew, for the Admiral had seen the procés itself, that Monsieur de Brouillan had been acquitted and that, when he had sailed on the *Profond* and died at sea, he sailed as Governor of Port Royal once again, vindicated, free. But so far as Monsieur de Bonaventure's affair with herself went, that was another story. She was afraid to agitate too much for what she wanted, in case her determination might draw down a worse fate. The more she saw of the workings of the Court and the King's Ministers, the less reliance she placed on their honesty or justice. She was hungry for the freer air of the New France.

Even Paris stifled her, its narrow, ill-lit streets and stinking houses. Refuse washed down the center of the pavements; beggars with sores clamored round her when she walked or drove; people with pinched white faces crawled about the alleyways; and over everything there was a feeling of restriction, of cruelty, of stagnation. She had looked forward to a winter in Paris, in the larger life—why, everyone she knew in the New France longed to be able to come "home" as they still called it, even when their families had been in New France for three generations. Now she was home; she was able to enjoy the company of distinguished men and women; she went to the play at the Court and saw the King; she talked with men whose names were spoken with fervor and faith in Acadia; and she was disgusted with it all. She longed for the clean seas, the fair land, the spacious skies, the freedom, of the New France. What if there were savages, and hardship and disease, and famine? These things were in Paris; they were everywhere—worse, in the Old World, because disguised and distorted.

The only interview she enjoyed during her stay in France, one which lingered in her mind and was retold by her repeatedly, was when the Admiral took her to the house of an old lady whom he had admired and loved all his life, the famous, or infamous, Ninon de l'Enclos. Madame de l'Enclos, about whom there were so many stories, was ninety, yet retained all her faculties. She was to die very soon; but on the sunny afternoon when they met, in the autumn, not long after Madame de Freneuse had come away from her interview with Madame de Maintenon, she was having one of her "good days" and was exceptionally good company.

She sat in the bed that had seen so many fantastic episodes, wearing a fichu of lace on her head; her face was painted and rouged, her hair dressed à la fontanges, and, unlike Madame de Maintenon, she wore a negligée of the brightest blue imaginable. It made her own blue eyes stand out in the worn face. She received her visitors eagerly, and with a charming courtesy that won Madame de Freneuse's heart. She had only to say that she retained the most tender memories of Monsieur de Bonaventure's father, one of her lovers in his early youth, to complete the attraction. Madame de l'Enclos, still vividly interested in everything—in the colonists; in their hardships; in their amorous intrigues, which reminded her of forgotten affairs their fathers had; in all that she could glean of news from the life around her—professed herself glad to help the settlement.

"Ammunition is nothing that an old woman can do much about," she said reflectively; "the only powder I know goes with patches. But money is something I do know about. I have enough and to spare for all my needs. I should hate to see Port Royal go to the English. I dislike the English. They wear their dresses badly, and their teeth are long from tearing at the raw food they eat over there. I had only one English lover, and he snored. So I will help. There are my jewels, some of which must go to my relatives, some of which you shall sell and exchange for what you need. I do not need accountings. I do not fear robbery.

"If you had wanted money for yourself, my dear, you would have turned pious and stayed at Court, or be in a little house at Neuilly visited by Monsieur de Pourtchartrain. He has no imagination in the houses that he gives his mistresses, just like his father before him. I could tell a de Pourtchartrain love nest half a mile away. Don't tell me he did not ask you to sup with him? He did? Well, my dear, as I said before, your honesty is obvious. De Pourtchartrain has more money than he knows what to do with, made out of the colonies. Of course. What else are the colonies for? When there comes a hard year, as you say there is now, or it looks as though there might be a little fighting, then the colonies are good to be abandoned until they right themselves and are paying once again. Thus it goes. You do not need to tell me. I have been in this world a very long time and seen something of men, especially Ministers. Oh, my dear, Ministers!

"Take the ruby necklace. Beautiful, is it not? Red like the blood it will go to spill. And the pearls. And I think I could find you a few louis d'or, say fifty? You are kind; you are gracious with your thanks! It has been a pleasure to see you. I like to see people; oh, how I like it! When you are old and helpless as I am, then you will like to see people, too. But few are as vivid as you are! Tell me, in confidence—no, do not tell me anything. Take the jewels and the money. Tell *him* that I have the greatest affectionate remembrance of his father; don't forget to tell him that."

Madame de Freneuse pressed the old fingers gratefully. She would have something to tell Raoul as well as Pierre—that Ninon de l'Enclos retained her charm to her ninetieth year, and her memory of friends.

CHAPTER LXXVII

MADAME DE L'ENCLOS' jewels and her louis d'or chartered a ship for Madame de Freneuse. It was a little packet, the *Midi*, with a crew of seventeen men and no passengers. It bucketed across the ocean, taking five weeks before land was sighted. Madame de Freneuse made friends with the wild-looking Captain and the rough crew. Her one fear was that they might run afoul of an English frigate and the precious stores be confiscated.

The *Midi* rode low in the water, carrying seventeen bales of warm cloth, a hundred barrels of salt pork, fifty casks of red Bordeaux wine, several tonneaus of oil, twenty hogs, seven oxen, twelve brace of poultry, and five female hares already in a promising family way.

"Regular Noah's ark," Raoul commented, seeing them weigh anchor at Marseilles.

She bore, besides, some sacks of bullion and a scant store of private ammunition purchased from a friend of Raoul's who was in with some obliging highwaymen. Madame de Freneuse thought she had done well with the means at her disposal.

"It would be just my luck," she said, "to lose it all to the English."

But the only sails they sighted were the French fishing fleet in the North Sea and an unidentified vessel off Greenland, which the Captain suspected to be a pirate.

"He won't overhaul *us*," he said. "He's after bigger fish. Throw out the lines, boys, and we'll be trawling, should he come up to ask."

So they ambled along, like a belated fishing smack, for any eyes to see. Under cover of night the pirate vessel disappeared; the sun came up and showed a deserted sea. Madame de Freneuse sighed with relief.

"If there is much of a famine," she said to the Captain that day, "and there was when I left, over a year ago, we may be in danger from desperate settlements, at the mouth of the river, or from the corsairs. If they think we've got supplies, they may attempt to stop us."

"I carry my two guns," the Captain said. "They're a bit unhandy to use, but they'll serve. Never you fear; we'll run you to port. It's a rare woman would risk her neck to save her fellow colonists. I've sailed to Canada a mort of times, but never to Acadian parts. Have always given them the wide berth and passed north to the St. Laurent. It will be quite an experience to drop anchor at Port Royal for a change.

"And maybe," he added, to his beard, "I'll stay there! I'm sick of the King and the Court. It's too hard for a man to make a living out of the sea these days. What with press gangs and taxes for the war, and English ships sinking us or searching us and pressing more, and French frigates firing across us on dark nights, and the pirates atop of all. It's a good time to turn landlubber. I've an idea I'd like to sell the *Midi* and go ashore."

"It's a bad time you've chosen, Captain, to join the colonists. The King is leaving them to the English and the Iroquois. It will be no fault of his if Acadia is lost to him."

"You've got a good Governor, I've heard, in Monsieur de Subercase. My brother served with him, in La Plaisance. He's a terror, plucked to the last ounce of him. He'll put up a fight for Acadia, never fear."

"We had a good Governor in Monsieur de Brouillan and a good Administrator in Monsieur de Bonaventure."

"I've heard of *him*. Sailed the *Soleil d'Afrique*, fastest ship on the seas."

"Yes"—her heart beat, and the blood came to her cheeks—"he did."

"Ah," said the Captain, spitting expertly overside, "a man I would be proud to serve from all I hear."

"Run me and the stores safe to port, and so you shall," she promised. "How many more weeks will it be?"

"Nay, not weeks now—days," he answered, without humor.

And suddenly she was impatient for the end of the endless sea.

They were lucky to have fine weather all the way across, mostly a following wind. It was when they reached the Baye Françoise and the mouth of the Basin that their troubles began.

Two ships, anchored in the Baye close to the Basin, guarding the entry to the gap, challenged the *Midi*, firing across her bows.

"Englishmen," said the Captain angrily, "although they fly no flag. If we don't make the tide, we'll have to wait six hours till she comes again. Don't believe they can follow if we make it now; they draw more than we do, by a long reckoning. Still and all, the water there looks dangerous to me."

"It's the rip tide," said Madame de Freneuse. "I've fished there with Monsieur de Bonaventure. If you keep in to the shore, Captain, you can pass. But the English ships are there, where you should go."

He considered this.

"Run up the surrender," he said to the mate. Madame de Freneuse protested, white with fury. "No!"

"Let be," said the Captain, with a twinkle.

The English ships signaled: "Stand to."

"No boats, will come alongside," answered the *Midi*'s flags.

The Captain took the helm himself and maneuvered the *Midi* slowly forward to meet the foremost frigate. Then, when he was so close that they could see the red-coated soldiers aboard and the curious sailors leaning on the sides, and too close for the guns to come into play, he twisted the *Midi* under the Englishman's bows and slipped toward the shore.

An angry yell went up; but still the *Midi* was too near for the guns to get into play, and out of reach for the grapnels. The Captain caught the in-shore breeze, and the *Midi* drew away. Madame de Freneuse let out her breath, as now the shots began dropping round them and they had to meet the angry seas, twisting the little vessel into danger on that most dangerous coast. The Englishmen did not attempt to give chase and ceased, presently, to fire, evidently thinking their ammunition would be wasted. The *Midi*, shaking herself rode on.

Now Madame de Freneuse could see Isle au Chèvre, and beyond it the first rough houses of the settlement. They lay scattered along the banks of the Basin, until the fort itself came into view. She craned her neck and took the Captain's glass to get the first sight of her house. It was still standing.

The settlers had seen the sails and were hailing the packet with signal fires along the shores. A gun fired from the fort. The *Midi* fired in salute, the first time that her guns had been used and clearly a nervous business. The report almost blew the little boat out of the water, and the Captain sponged his forehead.

Thus, to the lowing of the oxen and the squealing of the pigs, the cheering of the men and the medley of sounds from the shore, the *Midi* dropped her anchor near the quay to the fort. A boat set out to meet her. De Goutins was on board. His jaw dropped when he saw Madame de Freneuse.

"This time I bring my welcome with me," she said, with a sweep of the hand, indicating the cargo piled below hatch and on the deck. "Shall I take it up river to the Indians, or shall I land it here? It is all paid for, Monsieur de Goutins, out of my own means."

She looked past him to two officers of the fort, who were greeting her in pantomime.

"Does the garrison need hogs, oxen, food, cloth?"

The young men groaned.

"Not a bale goes ashore unless the notary here signs me a paper, Captain, that I shall not be molested nor forced into exile again."

"I cannot go against the authorities," Monsieur de Goutins said, moistening his lips.

"Naturally not, Monsieur," Madame de Freneuse agreed, "but you need not stir them up by letters and dispatches. I have seen the Minister's dossier and I know my enemies."

The people on shore began waving and shouting anew.

"Vive the *Midi*! Death to the English! Give us food! What is the news? Holà, ahoy!"

"Well," said Madame de Freneuse, "do I get my paper? Would you like to see some of the supplies?"

The notary groaned. He was painfully thin, she noticed, and very white of face.

"Has it been a hard year?" she inquired sympathetically.

It had apparently. Monsieur de Goutins proved only too glad to sign her paper—written in terms that would compromise him if he complained of her to the authorities—in exchange for a hog and one of the hares, a bale of cloth for his own use, and a sack of grain.

He signed the Captain's papers, and they all went ashore.

CHAPTER LXXVIII

D AWN rose over the north-shore hills, and the first rays of the sun slanted upon the palisades and the sober roofing of the fort, where the fleur de lis was flying, tattered in the autumn breeze. Jean Latouche, on sentry-go, coughed upon his rounds and tried to keep himself warm by stamping his feet. It was late summer yet, but the cold mist of the morning chilled his bones. He was very thin. So were all the garrison; and the settlers, too. A year of famine, two of war, and no help from France—that was the painful record under the new Governor.

In 1707 the English had appeared, sixteen hundred strong, against the garrison's one hundred and sixty men. They were beaten off. In August of the same year they appeared again under Colonel March, known and feared throughout Acadia for his inhuman cruelty. They were beaten off again. Monsieur de Subercase wrote to France asking for munitions, for provisions, for soldiers, strong in the hope that such a courageous and magnificent defense, against such overwhelming odds, would draw some response. But the authorities left him to rot. And rot the whole colony would unless help came. Jean Latouche coughed again. He looked hungrily at the river. Perhaps he could get a fish when he came off his guard. Meanwhile he should be keeping his eyes for other matters than fish. He stared wearily across the marsh.

The flutter of a skirt caught his eye and provoked a moment's curiosity. There were few women left in the settlement. All those who could leave had gone to France or to Canada—all the officers' wives, Madame de Bonaventure, the notary's wife, Madame de St. Vincent; oh, all of them! Only Madame de Freneuse remained. He grinned. There was a woman! She stayed in the fort, among

·[323]·

the officers. She cheered them through the long winters. She cooked strange foods; she rallied the Indians, poor devils riddled with plague, to hunt and fish for the settlement and paid them out of her own stores of beads and feathers she had brought from France. She went fishing with Monsieur de Bonaventure and brought back pollack and cod. Right under the Englishmen's noses, she ventured; she did not have any fear. And she was kind to everyone, nothing stuck up about *her*! He fingered the comforter she had knitted him two winters ago for the New Year's eve. It was Madame de Freneuse walking out there, across the marsh! Dieu sait what she'd been up to—something dangerous, no doubt.

"That's a woman for you!" he said out loud.

As though she heard him speak, Madame de Freneuse looked up, toward the fort, and quickened her pace. She brought exciting news with her, gathered from an Indian along the river bank. He was wounded and, after the custom of his tribe, left there to die or to recover by himself. Madame de Freneuse, on the lookout for moving game, had taken a pistol and slipped out of the fort. She had come upon him at the water's edge and almost fired, thinking he was a deer come down to drink. She bandaged him and gave him a drink of wine from the flask she carried. In return, he gave her news. She would see the Governor as soon as he awoke.

Monsieur de Subercase was her idea of a man. She liked him best of all the Governors that had come and gone—except Pierre, who had only been Administrator and was different anyhow. There was no man like Pierre. It was terrible to see him now, so thin, so wretchedly ill, but no more than the others. They had been through hell.

Monsieur de Subercase ruled with firmness, justice, and authority. He was popular with the Indians, because he was always fair with them, and worshiped by his men for his bravery and simplicity. He had taken Madame de Freneuse's part when the old trouble started up and a letter came from France demanding her exile again. She traced the trouble to its source. The supplies she had brought were exhausted, and Monsieur de Goutins had bestirred himself once more with Father Francis. Monsieur de Subercase took a firm stand. He wrote that the malice of Monsieur de Bonaventure's enemies was unbelievable and that the story against him had been "pushed as far as hell could desire," also that it was desolating, coming from a quarter where only Christian charity should be expected—the Church.

"If they would only take one-tenth the notice of my demands for men, supplies, and munitions as they do for the scandal mongerers' petty stories," he said, "we would be in better case."

He declined to do anything further. De Bonaventure was his right-hand man; he liked Madame de Freneuse.

"They would send away the only woman of any use," he complained. "The others have run of their own accord. I declare the place would be as melancholy as a pesthouse if Madame de Freneuse were to leave us, too."

So Madame de Freneuse came and went, attended by Dahinda and one or two of Raoul's men. She hunted; she fished; she trapped; and she cooked for the Governor and the officers of the garrison, with help. She kept house for de Bonaventure, wounded since the last engagement with the English, weakened and ill. She cheered them with music, with laughter, and with whatever other means came to her hand. She was the mascot of the garrison.

She was also the outpost for news, having friends among the Indians, the habitants, the trappers, and the Coureurs de Bois. The Captain of the *Midi*, turned corsair, was one of her staunchest friends. He brought her cuts in all his raids upon Boston and New York or any of the vessels that he captured and sank.

Now there was this news. It was not good. It was ominous, indeed, but the Governor must hear it immediately.

Nicholson's army of colonials, Bostonians, and Iroquois, thirty-four hundred strong, were embarking in a fleet sent out from England and would be on their way against the settlement with the first fair winds.

Against this force, when it came, de Subercase could muster only one hundred and sixty soldiers, three quarters of whom were undisciplined young men shipped out from Paris, Marseilles, and other big towns in France which did not desire them longer on the streets. All his forces were, moreover, weakened by three years of hardship and semistarvation and by the lack of everything they needed for defense.

It looked black, indeed, Madame de Freneuse thought, an impulse of pity stirring in her for the Governor. He had worked so hard; he had tried so often to rouse the apathy of the home authorities. He might, even now, have made another stand like the two he had commanded in 1707; but this year even the corsairs

·[325]·

who had helped him then, were lacking, driven out of Acadia by the fear of plague. It was rife among the Malisites and the Micmacs, on the outskirts of the settlement, as well. And the crops had failed.

"The bon Dieu seems against us," she mused. "What a black year! Ah, well, let the English come. At least we are together, Pierre and I."

Her heart sank as she reflected that Pierre might join his ship. The *Soleil d'Afrique*, disabled by an engagement with the English fleet, was laid up in the Basin, refitting. Pierre went down once a day and was rowed out to her.

"Put the *Soleil d'Afrique* across the Gap," he said, "and she would hold a fleet off."

Now the fleet was coming. Madame de Freneuse paled. She was so happy, even among the hardships, even eating dog and crows and endless eels, even without fuel, even without cloth—so happy because his wife had returned to France and she was with him again. He had grown older. Under the wig there were streaks of white hair. She had grown older, too. But they had grown together. Their love was like an autumn evening, mellow and harmonious, with crisp sparkling frost and larger stars to come. Madame de Freneuse asked nothing more of life than to continue living with her love. But this was threatened now, as it had been threatened twice before. Pierre was a brave man. He would do what he thought right. If only she could be with him to the end! If they might die together by the same cannon shot! But these were weakening thoughts, and she would need her strength. She turned in the fort gates, clutching her cloak around her and waving to the sentry, who grinned and kissed his hand.

CHAPTER LXXIX

THE Captain of the *Midi* finished his portion of eels and
sagamite at the Governor's table, wiped his hands and his
beard, leaned forward, and thoughtfully smoothed the fine
linen cloth upon which the meager meal had been served.

His lookout had sighted the English ships, already out of Boston harbor. The *Midi* had run before them, slipping through the
Gap, to bring a warning.

"The largest fleet I have ever seen," said the Captain, "all new-
seeming ships, and mounted—from what we could make out,
through the glasses, before we ran—with the new guns the Indians
told us about last year, and the scouts described."

"Hmm," said the Governor.

"We'll hold them up at the Gap, never fear," said the Captain,
looking toward de Bonaventure. "With the *Soleil d'Afrique* and
the *Midi* anchored across, and all guns trained on the mouth, we
should keep them in the Baye for a while, at any rate."

Madame de Freneuse shot a glance at Pierre. He was dressed in
his old naval uniform, frayed and mended, with the gold braid
thinned out to go further. She had worked and worked at that
uniform these last troubled days. He met her glance, smiling
wistfully.

"We had best be getting on our way," the Captain of the *Midi*
said. "They were hard enough on our heels to be here on the next
tide, I think."

De Bonaventure said nothing; but he rose, saluted the Governor,
turned on his heel, and gave his arm to Madame de Freneuse.

"I will be with you, Captain, immediately," he said over his
shoulder.

They walked out onto the fort grounds, toward the chapel. Monsieur de Subercase watched them go, with a sigh. He was thinking of his wife and children in France and, not without bitterness, of Monsieur de Pourtchartrain and the other Ministers, who could have saved the settlement, had they wanted to. His eyes followed the curve of Madame de Freneuse's shoulders, pitifully thin as they escaped her dress, and Monsieur de Bonaventure's stiff, erect carriage limping beside her.

"A gallant pair," he said to the Captain of the *Midi*.

They stepped onto the grass and paused beneath the bright afternoon sky.

"Beloved," said de Bonaventure gently, "do not be anxious. I have been in action often before."

"But you are a sick man, Pierre, weakened by privation. It is different now. And"—she faltered—"they have so many ships!"

He pressed her arm in silence. They stood looking toward the gap, which they could not see from the fort, reflecting on the strange traffic it had seen sailing through its narrow opening.

"Will you stand where I can see you, on the palisade," he whispered, "waving me? Then I shall go forward with courage. You could fire any man, and . . . and I have loved you, Louise; you have fired me!"

"Have loved, Pierre?"

"I love you, dearest." He kissed her long upon the lips. "I shall always love you. I shall wait, Louise. Do you understand? I shall always wait—out there."

"I understand. But I do not think it is for this time, Pierre. I do not feel it, here."

She touched her heart lightly and smiled at him. Her lips trembled, and her eyes filled suddenly with tears.

"We have had what we wanted," he said; "we have had more than most. We have lived, and suffered, and loved. We have not been alone. We are not alone now, even when I sail out there and you are here. I carry you with me, dearest, in my heart."

"Brave words"—she faltered. "Kiss me again, beloved; kiss me hard!"

He took her by the shoulders and pressed his lips to hers. The kiss was without passion, with an infinite tenderness.

"I must go," he said huskily. "God keep you, my Louise, the dearest, best, bravest woman . . ."

·[328]·

"Hush," she said, clasping his hand in hers and passing it across his lips. "God will keep me, dear; may He keep you."

They looked at each other in silence, de Bonaventure pale and drawn with the pain and sickness of his wound, she pale and drawn with fatigue, hunger, and her fears for him. They looked like two phantoms in the rich sunlight, eying each other with a desperate yearning.

"Now go!" she said, pushing him on the shoulder.

He straightened himself and went. She watched him cross the fort grounds, without looking back, and pass beneath the western gate. Then she crossed herself and prayed. When she opened her eyes, the Governor was beside her.

"Shall we watch them weigh anchor?" he said, taking her by the arm. She smiled at him, speechless. They climbed the palisade together and stood beside the sentry, looking out.

"But you have preparations to make," she said at length, when she had recovered her self-control.

The Governor shook his head.

"There is nothing to do," he said. "When we see them in the Basin, then we man our posts. After that, nothing but a miracle can save us. We must fight, though; for if we surrender without resistance, the peace terms they will make will be so horrible that not a man, woman, or child in the settlement will go unscathed. We must do what we can. With the Indians to help, we should be able to conserve our own men for a time at least."

"You!" he called to the sentry. "Send word to the people of the settlement that they are to leave their houses and to drive their stock into the fort grounds. They are to come themselves, within the hour, here. Tell them that we face an attack by the English, that we hope to beat it off, that they are to come upon pain of death to their posts within the fort."

The sentry saluted and withdrew.

"Ah!" breathed Madame de Freneuse. She saw the *Soleil d'Afrique*, all sails set, go slowly forward up the wide basin to the entrance of the Baye. She moved gracefully, the sun shining on her full white sails; a southerly breeze bore her smoothly onward, against a background of dark forests on the northern shore. She dipped her colors in salute to the fleur de lis on the fort. Madame de Freneuse took the fichu from her dress and waved it with both hands above her head. Monsieur de Subercase bared his head.

They stood together, watching her grow smaller till at length she passed behind Isle au Chèvre—out of sight.

An hour later the sound of guns came clearly on the breeze. Before nightfall the English ships were anchored, opposite the fort, in long neat rows.

CHAPTER LXXX

ALL morning, after the settlement woke to find the English fleet anchored before Port Royal, Monsieur de Subercase was besieged by frightened men, pitiful wraiths with bones sticking through their skin, beseeching him to surrender. Madame de Freneuse was with him when Monsieur de Goutins appeared, clamoring one of the loudest, even having spirit enough to threaten the Governor.

"I will see that this is reported," he raved.

The Governor listened with a patient shrug and, when the notary paused for breath, replied:

"Monsieur, the authorities to which you would report me have left you as they have left me—to rot here, to die. Perhaps if you had not complained so constantly the King's Ministers might have listened to me, instead, might even have supplied us with some of the things we need. No matter. We will defend this fort as long as it is possible to do so."

"But . . ."

"I know what you would say. I agree with you. It is quite true that we cannot hold out, that miracles do not happen for a third time, that we have nothing with which to withstand the English but a hundred and sixty men—boys, mostly, famished and ill. The *Soleil d'Afrique* and the ketch with her have been defeated, possibly sunk."

Madame de Freneuse gripped her hands together convulsively.

"But we have no choice. We must fight. You, Monsieur de Goutins, have stirred up trouble constantly during my Governorship. If you have any manhood in you, stir up trouble for the

English, now, instead. I am not asking you, or any of you, more than I ask of myself and of my garrison."

He turned to the door. Through its opening they could see rows of gaunt soldiers in the courtyard, struggling to parade as though no sagging knees or empty stomachs made them faint. Their officers, boys with puckered faces, hollow-eyed, stood in the sunshine shouting orders. Madame de Freneuse looked with unseeing eyes at her son, a lieutenant, strapping his sword belt tighter as he flourished his lace gloves. She caught Monsieur de Goutins' eye. It fell before her own steady gaze. The notary mumbled something, fumbled at his buckles, and was gone, followed by the group that had come with him.

Monsieur de Subercase laughed ruefully.

"Curs!" he said.

She nodded.

The Governor sighed.

"Well," he said, "have you and Dahinda found a new way of cooking sagamite?"

She did not answer. He looked at her and looked away, again quickly.

"The men on morning relief caught seven crows," he said. "Have they been given in?"

A sound behind him interrupted her distracted answer. A Micmac glided in. He held out a paper. Monsieur de Subercase took it, glanced at it, exclaimed under his breath, and looked at Madame de Freneuse. She read his expression.

"News!" she said, catching her breath. "At last! The *Soleil d'Afrique*! Is it definite?"

The Indian broke into Micmac before Monsieur de Subercase could stop him. Madame de Freneuse listened, her expression changing as he spoke. Despair, bewilderment, relief, and horror passed across her face.

"Poor little boy!"

The Governor waved the messenger aside and took her by the waist, supporting her.

"Poor Paul-Marie," she said at length, wiping her eyes into which a sudden rush of tears had come—tears of relief for Pierre, of sorrow for her son. "He was always a gentle boy." She signed herself. "He studied for the priesthood because he was unfitted to become a soldier. Now . . ."

·[332]·

"He died for France, like a missionary martyr," said Monsieur de Subercase firmly. "Etienne!"

An aide de camp came running, saluting smartly, with only a slight stagger as he came to a halt.

"There is a last bottle of brandy in the cupboard beneath the secret stairs," Monsieur de Subercase said. "Get it."

He assisted Madame de Freneuse to a chair. When the brandy came, he poured her a liberal measure. She began to drink, unthinkingly, but suddenly remembered and put it aside.

"For the wounded," she said. "And you. I do not need it."

"Tell Monsieur de Freneuse to come here," the Governor ordered. Madame de Freneuse sighed. When the tall young man, pale with privation and fatigue, was facing her, she said:

"Your brother, Paul-Marie, has been taken by the Iroquois and killed. He was in his seminary clothes. They took him for a priest. He—he died well."

The Governor departed, leaving them together. The young officer paled and looked at his mother dumbly.

"I must go," he said after a moment. "The English are disembarking. We can see them from the palisade. Men, men, men! Guns, ammunition, food! They are well off, those God-damns. I'm sorry, Mother; I'm sorry about Paul-Marie. But he is well out of it now."

He hesitated. "Bless me."

She blessed him hastily, and signed him to go. Then she sat still while the noise increased outside.

"I wish," she said after a moment, "that we had been better friends, Paul-Marie."

Her mind went back to the scene where he spat at her. She passed her hand across her lips. She felt remorseful that the death did not affect her as Gervais' had done, as Antoine's would have. Antoine, sleek and fat, was safe in Canada—with cousins in Kebec. They had sent him there as soon as she returned from France, and money with him to last for several years. The cousins were kind, and she had word of him. He at least was out of this. Kebec would not be taken; it was prepared and strong. Antoine would play there happily, unaware that his mother was in a siege, that his father . . . his father . . . she choked back a sob. Then she wiped her eyes, summoned Dahinda, and began to supervise quarters for the wounded. Dahinda was cooking the seven crows over one long spit.

·[333]·

"There will be many wounded, Dahinda, and much work. They are all sick now with famine and disease. This is not war; this is murder. But the Governor says we must fight."

Dahinda nodded.

They went about their work to the accompaniment of bugle calls, scurrying feet, the sound of the fort guns firing at intervals, and other less reassuring sounds. The English ships were pouring shot into the fort. Soon there would be attacking parties assailing the tired men who manned the walls. Madame de Freneuse, thinking of the famished boys mustering for battle, cursed wars and battle. There seemed no end to the cruelties of life. She thought of de Bonaventure on the *Soleil d'Afrique*; she thought of nothing else. Day and night, through the long sleepless hours, feeding men in batches from meager soups and stews, fetching water in careful measurement, there was only Pierre—and Pierre's fate—lying upon her heart.

She was sorry for Paul-Marie; but he was out of it, finished with suffering, among the blessed dead, perhaps in Paradise, certainly in Purgatory, wearing his martyr's crown. Absurd to think of it, Paul-Marie, her solemn little son! She crossed herself again. Her thoughts returned to Pierre. Anguish assailed her. She forced her mind to concentrate on the work at hand. Wounded men were carried in. Dahinda held a candle while she examined them. Pitiful skin and bone; one was surprised to see red blood flow from such skeletons. She bent over a sentry's leg, drawing shot from his wound, while Dahinda held him. Then she returned again to her thoughts of the *Soleil d'Afrique*.

CHAPTER LXXXI

O N THE eighth morning of the siege there were fourteen
rounds of ammunition, no food, four casks of fresh water,
and fifty-four wounded in the fort; but the English had
no means of ascertaining the misery of the besieged. They had been
repulsed six times from the palisades. So far they had respected the
settlement; the houses were not set on fire, nor the fields laid waste.
All the attack was directed against the fort. Canon shot from the
sloops and frigates in the Basin pounded against the fortifications;
arrows from the Iroquois, many of which were poisoned, fell in
fountains on the defenders as they massed to make a stand; storm-
ing parties scrambled up the palisades, to be beaten back by hand-
to-hand fighting with the weary, hollow-eyed French soldiers
serving a twelve-hour watch. Madame de Freneuse, her heart
turned to stone, moved among the wounded, doing what she could
to ease their pain, doling out water in her thimble to moisten fevered
lips, all the time thinking:

"Pierre! Pierre! Pierre!"

There was no news of him. The *Soleil d'Afrique* was sunk or
captured; the *Midi*, too. She must wait, effacing herself before the
stark heroism of these wounded men. She must smile to cheer their
pain. Monsieur de Subercase, all eyes, like a walking ghost, decided the moment had come to play his last card. He sent a messenger with a white flag to ask if he might parley with the Commander of the English forces.

The answer returned: "Yes." An escort was sent for him. He
swallowed the last dregs of brandy he had kept for the end, brushed
his best suit, and donned his tallest wig. Then he set forth, alone,
for the English camp.

"Monsieur," he said, in tolerable English, to the burly Nicholson, as they faced each other, "I have come myself to parley with you because I know you to be a fair and honorable man. This is the truth. I can hold out for several weeks, perhaps months; but capture of the fort is certain in the end. I would avoid too great a loss of life and mitigate the hardship of my people. If I offer you surrender now, will you conclude a peace with me on honorable terms?"

The English Commander, after the taste of two former campaigns against Monsieur de Subercase, was inclined to believe his word. He knew that every attack of his men had been beaten back. He admired the Frenchman for his courage, knowing, as both of them did, the inevitable outcome for the French. He also wanted to spare his men. He could see no flaw in such a proposal. He inquired:

"Upon what terms would you surrender, Governor?"

"I shall require the safe-conduct of my garrison to France."

The Englishman bowed.

"The most scrupulous respect for the inhabitants who remain beneath your rule."

The Englishman nodded.

"The surrender shall comprise the fort of Port Royal and one league around the fort," he said, "the settlers therein to take an oath of allegiance to our Gracious Queen Anne, or else to depart within two years."

Monsieur de Subercase bowed his head. There was nothing else he could do.

"Monsieur," he said at length, while the terms of the agreement were being written, "there is one other condition I would ask, throwing myself upon your generosity. We have fought you honorably and well these last three years . . ."

Nicholson said: "Yes."

"Permit us, then, to retire with the honors of war. We would march out of the fort, flags flying, drums beating, arms at the salute. Then you can do with us what you will, provided you return my men to France."

Nicholson retired to confer with his officers, leaving Monsieur de Subercase leaning against the oak chest where the fourth officer was putting the terms of the treaty into script. His knees were shaking, and his hands trembled from fatigue and humiliation. He tried to stand without moving, steady and straight.

"After all," he reflected, "the dishonor is not mine, but theirs at home who have betrayed me. But it is mine to take," he added wryly, as the English officers returned.

"Provided," said the English Commander, "you agree to lay down your arms within twenty-four hours, during which time hostilities shall cease, you may withdraw from the garrison with military honors. Your men shall embark without delay, for France, on board as many ships as shall be necessary. You may keep your sword. You have fought well, Monsieur de Subercase."

The French Commander bowed. His eyes suddenly full of mistiness, and his mouth of a bitter taste. This was the end of his Governorship, the end of the fort at Port Royal, the end of years of endeavor, uselessly thrown away for want of a little help.

"We have made miracles succeed each other for years," he thought; "there comes a time when a shoulder to the wheel is necessary after all."

He took the papers handed to him, read them through carefully, and signed them in the presence of the English officers, with a firm flourish beneath his name. Then he stepped back a pace and proffered his sword. Nicholson touched it on the hilt and pushed it back to him. The other officers stood at the salute as Monsieur de Subercase saluted them. Then he wheeled, looked about him for the escort, and marched off. He had been gone three hours and pulled the bluff of his life. There would be no more wounded, no more famine-stricken soldiers, no more misery. They would march out as if they went to parade . . . as if they went to parade! His eye traveled to the fleur de lis, and the sharpest pain he had ever felt went through his heart.

Madame de Freneuse was waiting near the gate. He went straight to her.

"It is done," he said. "I have surrendered."

She took him in her arms.

"You have done more than any man could do. Be comforted, Governor."

He bowed his head for an instant against her shoulder, then he threw it back and said:

"We have been accorded all the honors of war. The terms are generous beyond measure. We have fooled the English after all."

He beckoned behind him. An orderly staggered forward, attempting to run.

"Summon the buglers," Monsieur de Subercase said. "Tell them

·[337]·

to blow the retreat. We have surrendered. There will be no more fighting. Dress parade tomorrow, full-dress uniforms. Tell the standard bearers to pay particular attention to their uniforms. Pipe clay and polish, men, for the honor of France!"

He turned away. Madame de Freneuse followed him.

"Governor," she said, "did you hear news of the *Soleil d'Afrique*?"

"No," he said sadly. "I . . . dared not ask!"

CHAPTER LXXXII

O N OCTOBER 13, 1710, the garrison of Fort Port Royal marched out, for the last time, beneath the stone archway of the western gate. Monsieur de Subercase stood by the English Commander to receive the last salute.

First came the wounded, carried in stretchers by the settlers, then the garrison itself. Monsieur de Subercase stiffened to attention as he perceived the first of its uniforms coming beneath the archway.

A young ensign led, Monsieur de Villieu's son; after him came the standard bearers, among them the young de Freneuse and his cousin; then the body of the men, ninety-seven in all.

They marched gaily, in a valiant effort to keep up the quick-step to the tune of the Chasseurs du Roi played on the fife. Pipe clay and paint had done its work. Some of them had sat up half the night, working on their tattered uniforms. They sloped arms, saluted the Governor and the English Commander, and marched away toward the river, where they would entrain. De Subercase relaxed. It was over now. He had not disgraced his men.

"Where are the rest?" said Nicholson, after they had waited a little while.

"There are no more."

"No more! But that was scarce a hundred men."

"Truly, Monsieur. Scarce a hundred men."

"And you kept us at bay eight days. I honor you, Monsieur de Subercase, I honor you!"

De Subercase bowed.

"One ship will suffice to carry the garrison to France," Nicholson said. "I had ordered six. Lieutenant Markison, report to Cap-

·[339]·

tain Trent; tell him to detail only the *Resolute* to return the French soldiers to France."

The young officer saluted, and followed the marching French. Monsieur de Subercase looked up at the fleur de lis, still flying from the fort.

"I have to thank you for your courtesy," he said. " I will rejoin my men. But I have a question. Did you, when you entered the Basin, engage with two of our ships at the Gap?"

Nicholson nodded.

"We sank them," he said; "I'm sorry. The survivors have been sent to Boston. They will be exchanged for prisoners from France."

De Subercase received the news in silence. Then he asked:

"Did you take Monsieur de Bonaventure, who commanded the *Soleil d'Afrique*?"

Nicholson swept his officers with mute inquiry. One of them volunteered:

"I think so, sir. He was wounded. He was put on board the *Victory*."

As Monsieur de Subercase watched the fort with unseeing eyes, the fleur de lis came down and the English flag went slowly up instead. An English officer came up, saluted, and said:

"We can find no provisions, sir, to send with the French garrison to France."

"No provisions?" He shot a glance at de Subercase, who smiled.

"They gave out completely two days ago," he said.

Nicholson bit his lip. He did not like to be bluffed; but he had signed the treaty, and his respect for his opponent increased.

"Give orders for some of our provisions to be sent with them," he said.

Another officer appeared, looking puzzled.

"There is no ammunition," he said, "except in one of the powder magazines, where we found a few rounds."

Nicholson threw back his head and laughed. "I suppose that had given out, too."

"Correct, sir," de Subercase said. "We had thirteen rounds this morning. As it was the thirteenth of October, we considered it suitable to fire them in a last salute. Perhaps you heard us, at dawn? There are a few odd rounds left, gathered from here and there. You surely did not suppose," he added, "that Frenchmen would

·[340]·

surrender while they had food and shot? That was not to know us very well."

He saluted, turned on his heel, and went to the shore. Nicholson stood looking after him, envy and irritation on his face.

"Tell those people they may not go in and out of the fort until they have signed the oath of allegiance to the Queen," he said. Madame de Freneuse, walking out of the fort with a little group of forlorn habitants, halted as the officer approached them.

"They ask to go to their houses," he reported. "Is that all right, sir?"

"For the present." Nicholson waved them away.

"Well," he said to the group about him, "we have won the fort. We hold Port Royal. It will never be given back. We had better rename the place."

"After the Queen," someone suggested.

"What could be more appropriate? Let us call it Annapolis, Annapolis Royal, from henceforth."

Madame de Freneuse ran after Monsieur de Subercase.

He stopped and took her by the hands.

"He is wounded," he said. "They put him on the *Victory* for Boston. He will be sent to France."

"Alive!" she cried. "Alive! God be praised! I can bear anything if he is alive. Good-by, Monsieur le Gouverneur, good-by!"

She sank in a curtsy to him, while he bowed and made a leg. English soldiers, watching, nudged each other.

"Fancy!" said one of them. "I ain't seen her curtsy to Nicholson yet."

"Nor likely to. Them Frenchies are proud as proud. Diddled us proper, they have. Shouldn't wonder if they didn't want their old fort no more."

Two Iroquois, searching for arrows, passed by.

"Them fellows gives me the creeps," the English soldier said.

"Don't you forget they're our brothers now. They did most of the fighting," the other one said.

"Yes, and they'll be quartered on the habitants, most like. Shouldn't fancy it myself."

"You should stay at home if you're so squeamish, instead of enlisting for overseas."

"Watch me stay, if I had the chance!"

They wandered off to see the Frenchies embark. Madame de Freneuse was watching them, too, from the window of her house.

·[341]·

There came a sudden loud knock on the door. She went to open it.

An English soldier was standing there with five Iroquois.

"These are quartered here," he said. "You're to look after them."

"Han!" grunted the Indians, shouldering her aside. She watched wide-eyed as they installed themselves in the living room.

"Dahinda," she called, "come here. Ask these what they desire."

Dahinda came out shrinking. Like all the Micmacs and the Malisites, she went in terror of the Iroquois; but she asked the question bravely. One of them laughed and spat. The others squatted on their feet and began to pull at their beads. The youngest brave answered:

"We are to live here, squaw. The English say it. We are the white men's brothers. You and the French squaw are to cook for us."

Dahinda translated. Madame de Freneuse shivered with distaste. She would go to the English Governor and get them removed. It was probably a mistake. It was likely they had not known her house inhabited. She would endure it for a day or so till the English had digested their victory. She went into the bedroom and locked the door. She had seen too much of the tortured Malisites and the Micmacs not to hate the Iroquois. Besides, there was Gervais! Perhaps these very brutes—she must not think of that. She pulled out her rosary.

"Ave Maria," she said, "I thank you for preserving Pierre's life. Holy Mary, Mother of God, protect him now and ever. Amen."

The Iroquois were howling now, in one of their bestial chants. She put her fingers in her ears to shut out the noise of it. Then she lay down upon her bed, exhausted. She was frightened and half-starved, alone beneath a hostile government.

CHAPTER LXXXIII

SAMUEL VETCH, who now became Governor of Acadia, had not been present at the taking of the fort and was not a party to the terms of surrender. In his opinion the French had been dealt with far too leniently; and he proceeded to put things right by a series of stiff ordonnances, with fines and stripes as penalty for breaking them. He quartered the Mohawks and the other Iroquois braves permanently upon Madame de Freneuse and others, taking a delight in singling out the houses of the nobility for the purpose. He forced the habitants, weakened by siege and famine, to repair the fort, to erect winter quarters for some of the troops not accommodated in the garrison, without compensation for the time they spent or payment for the materials which they were to provide. He instituted curfew and forbade the habitants to carry firearms, although he knew they must depend upon what they could shoot and stow away through the winter for their food. He executed several men and one woman for being found with pistols; and he shut Father Francis in a dungeon for refusing to sign the oath of allegiance to Queen Anne, couched in such terms that it was impossible for the priest to do so and be true to his vows. He interfered with the convent in every way that he could think of, forbidding the ringing of the sanctus bell, the shutting of the gates at any time, and the wearing of the religious habit outside of the convent grounds.

When Madame de Freneuse interviewed the Governor and begged for the removal of the Iroquois from her house, pointing out that there were two vacant houses a stone's throw down the street, Vetch replied that an Iroquois was worth two Frenchmen any day and she should be glad to be in the house with them; that if they complained to him about her treatment of them or the food she gave them should not be sufficient, he would have her publicly whipped. She did not doubt that he would keep his word, for she saw every day his soldiers at the whipping post chastising some poor creature. In order to satisfy the Iroquois, she and Dahinda were constantly put to it to find food. It became a dog's life.

Some of the more courageous of the people left within the two-mile area surrendered to the English gathered together and wrote to Monsieur de Vaudreuil, the Governor of Canada, to see if he could intercede for them. The letter was sent by Indian runners to Kébec. It went like this:

"As your goodness extends over all those who, being subjects of His Majesty, have recourse to you to relieve them in their misery, we pray you will vouchsafe us your assistance to withdraw ourselves from this unhappy country. M. de Clignancourt will tell you better than we can do by a letter the harsh manner in which Governor Vetch treats us, keeping us like negroes and wishing to persuade us that we are under great obligations to him for not treating us much worse, being able, he says, to do so, without room to complain of it. We have given to M. de Clignancourt copies of three ordinaries which Monsieur Vetch has issued. We pray you, sir, to have regard to our misery and honor us with your letter for our consolation, expecting that you may furnish us with the necessary assistance for our retiring from this unhappy country." (12)

Madame de Freneuse watched her house become filthy, the house where she had known so much happiness. The Iroquois relieved their natural needs against the walls, cooked fires in the middle of the brick floors, and spat tobacco juice on the furniture. Madame de Freneuse lived for the most part shut in her room, endeavoring not to hear the savages grunting, spitting, and yowling in the next room. Filthiest and most cruel of all the Indian tribes, the Mohawks and the other Iroquois were allies of the English and had been used by them in many encounters. Madame de Freneuse had never seen them except as prisoners or howling outside the walls of a besieged palisade. The more she saw of them at close quarters, the more she loathed them. They stank of unwashed bodies and raw flesh. They wore bundles of drying scalps at their belts. Their faces were bestial and stupid. Worst of all, they began to cast lustful glances at her.

But it was not until Dahinda had been dragged before the Governor by one of the Iroquois for refusing to sleep with him, and had been sentenced to a flogging, that Madame de Freneuse was shocked out of her stupor to a struggle for escape. She ran to the Governor, pleading for her servant.

"She has married a man of her own people, sir; she cannot be treated thus."

"Can she not?" said Vetch.

The soldiers took hold of Dahinda, screwing her poor frightened brown face into the expressionless mask of her people in pain, and tied her to the whipping post. They stripped her, taking their time about it, while Madame de Freneuse pushed her way nearer and took her by the hands. The first brutal lash descended; Dahinda quivered; Madame de Freneuse knelt beside her and kissed the straining hands.

"Dahinda," she moaned, "I love you, and you suffer this for me. Forgive me that I brought you here. Oh, Dieu!" she exclaimed, as the lashes continued and Dahinda's blood began to run in long streams down her heaving sides.

"I will give you money if you will lay them on more lightly," she whispered to one of the soldiers. He shook his head.

"Can't do it, ma'am," he replied briefly. "Don't you take on," he added, seeing the desperate agony on Madame de Freneuse's face, "it's only an Indian. They don't feel pain like you and I. She'll be up and around in no time, most likely. But you best see that she does what's wanted of her; and you had best do so, too. Get back now, out of the way."

Madame de Freneuse went back to her station, crouching beside the suffering creature. At each blow she thought she could not endure the pain of seeing another. When at length they stopped and Dahinda, unconscious, was untied roughly to slump upon the ground, Madame de Freneuse gathered her up as well as she could and dragged her to the convent. She did not dare take her home for fear of the Iroquois quartered there. The convent was nearer.

When she arrived, exhausted beneath her burden, staggering through the gate, a nun ran out to help her, regardless of the edict against wearing robes on the street. Together they pulled Dahinda in. Madame de Freneuse explained, in gasps, what had happened. The nun shook her head in pity. She went to fetch oil and bandages.

"It is the holy oil," she said when she returned, "but we will use it to anoint her wounds."

Madame de Freneuse asked for the Mother Superior.

"She is ill," the nun replied. "These are dreadful times. We have only one consolation, that the children entrusted to our care are safe in Kébec—your own among them, Madame."

Madame de Freneuse started. She had forgotten for the moment that she had nieces in the convent and that the nuns had disapproved of her. An awkward silence followed. Dahinda groaned and moved her head.

"She will be feverish," the nun said. "Poor thing."

She glided away to fetch what soothing drink she could find, and Madame de Freneuse stayed with the sufferer. She stayed there for three days and three nights, during which Dahinda remained in a delirium. On the fourth day she died.

They buried her in the convent cemetery. Madame de Freneuse said:

"The money with which I might repay you is hidden in my house. I dare not go there for fear of the Iroquois quartered upon me, who did this to her. I am going away from this desolate place; and as soon as I can do so, I will send you what I can."

"Do not trouble yourself, Madame," said one of the older nuns. "We are not allowed to take money for acts of charity. If there is anything we can do to help you on your way, we are at your disposal. It might be wise for you to leave here soon. Periodically the soldiers search the convent. If they found you here, they would bring you before the Governor for neglecting the savages quartered on you, like poor Monsieur de Flang. Did you hear about his execution? Dreadful times! Sad barbarity. But we are in the Lord's hands; better days will come."

She smiled. Madame de Freneuse smiled back. They were both brave women, and each could appreciate courage when she saw it.

CHAPTER LXXXIV

I T WAS late November, but the snows had not yet fallen; Indian summer lingered long that year. Madame de Freneuse, in what warm clothes the nuns could provide, with Dahinda's leather leggings and jacket over them and her own black hair in plaits, her face stained brown, left the convent by night for the woods behind the fort. It was her intention to find the Micmacs and to pass from encampment to encampment round the whole long peninsula till she could come to her husband's seigneury on the River St. Jean. There she would be among her own friendly tribe of Malisites. They would hide her among them. Possibly she could find, among the debris of the burned house, its store of money and valuables that had been hidden away. The Malisites had plague; the journey to the St. Jean was many hundred miles; she was alone and a woman, but she set out unafraid. The English under Vetch were worse than anything else she had encountered. One expected savagery of savages, but not the sort of thing she had seen done here. It was not like their usual gallantry.

Fighting was still going on in Acadia. The French were endeavoring to retain their hold on the colony. Perhaps the time would come when the English would be driven out of the fort. She might take part in it. She might raise a band of Malisites from the River St. Jean and the hinterland and lead them against the fort. At any rate, to go there was all that was left to her.

She stole apprehensively from the convent grounds, crossed the marsh by the path she knew and had often followed, climbed the hill behind it, and was lost in the forest gloom. She camped the first night beneath a tree, not daring to make a fire, keeping herself awake—on guard against wild beasts. There were lynx in the woods, and bear; even wolves, though it was early for them. She kept herself awake by counting the number of Micmac words she could remember and what they signified.

Early the next morning she fell in with a Micmac encampment. She made them understand that she was Ruwerera's friend, that she brought news of him from across the big waters, where he was living now, and that he wished her to be taken to the Malisites at St. Jean.

The Micmac braves believed her, assigned her a tepee, and sent her with a small escort upon her way. They used canoe and dog team indiscriminately. The weather turned, and the snow fell fast; they wrapped her in bearskin and buffalo. They took her silently and swiftly through the woods, all for the memory of Ruwerera.

It was strange to journey through the forests alone with Micmac Indians, not going this time to an assignation with a treaty to be signed, but alone, a fugitive, returning to a desolate and ruined seigneury, with even more desolate thoughts, for she could get no word of de Bonaventure. Monsieur de Subercase had promised to write on the first occasion. His letter would come to the settlement; she would be gone. It would be a long time before Madame de Freneuse heard. Pierre might be dying or dead. She herself might succumb to the rigors of the winter. With these grim thoughts she traveled on, taking no count of the days and nights, crouching indifferently by this or that smoky fire, fed on scraps of sagamite and dog meat and other things she did not like to examine too closely.

Ruwerera's name was passport everywhere. The Indians believed, she discovered, that since his departure many miseries had come upon them—wars, plague, dissension among themselves, famine, discouragement. If Ruwerera would return, all might go well. Some of them went so far as to make a legend of him. He was not Ruwerera, they insisted, but Glooscap in a disguise. Glooscap, or Kuluskape, as Madame de Freneuse had heard of him, was the red man's Savior. He lived at Blomidon, and he had promised that any of his children who made the pilgrimage to him would get what he desired. There were many songs of Kuluskape. Dahinda sang them all, and Madame de Freneuse heard them again round evening fires. There was one she always liked. She sang it to the medicine men, on her journey, as she had learned it from Dahinda.

Kuluskape gave the names
To everything on earth;
He first made man and woman
Bestowing on them life;
He also made the winds
To make the waters move.
He was merciful at heart,
Knew all that was passing
In the hearts of his Indian children,
Observing and pitying them,
Came to them all at once;
For he ever came as the wind
And no man e'er wist how.[11]

"Yes, yes," said the medicine men eagerly, when they heard it, "even so will Ruwerera come again to us, the white squaw is wise."

They passed her from tribe to tribe through the winter snows, lending her dog teams and men to drive them, until at length she reached familiar land.

There, uncoiling in a vast silver ribbon, lay the St. Jean River, with snow upon its banks. Another day's journey, and she reached Freneuse.

There was nothing there but the ruined stones, the site of the mill, the broken chapel, the overgrown fields; but Madame de Freneuse dismissed her escort and set about preparing to live there on her seigneury. At least it was French.

She found one room with a roof and stuffed buffalo hide in the windows and door. Then she made the Indians gather firewood and leave her a stock of provisions before they returned to their camps. She sat, the first night, chin in hand, before a fire that burned on her own hearth, while the snow fell outside and there was silence everywhere about her.

CHAPTER LXXXV

FOR a year Madame de Freneuse lived among the Micmacs near her husband's lands. They took her in, built her a hut, cooked for her, and kept her informed of what went on in the outside world. In return she nursed their sick, helped their women to bear children, sang to them, and told them stories of the great lands over the sea. The Indians never tired of these stories and would clamor for her to sing cradle songs of Provence, or hymns, to them. Madame de Freneuse complied. She was sick at heart, lonely beyond telling, and discouraged as the days rolled on.

She wrote letters to everyone she could think of—to Raoul in France; to Monsieur de Vaudreuil in Kebec; to Monsieur de Subercase, care of the Ministry in Paris; to Monsieur de Goutins, even—asking for news of Monsieur de Bonaventure, telling them where she was hiding and the poverty she suffered living like a squaw. She got replies from Monsieur de Vaudreuil, who informed her that her sons were safe in France, her nieces in Kebec, Antoine with them, but did not mention de Bonaventure. The Indians, knowing that she was unhappy, were sorry for her. They looked upon her as a medicine woman. They were proud of her presence among them and willingly sent their young men east and west to pick up news for her. But the news was for the most part bad.

The French, it appeared, were driven farther from Port Royal. The English were securely entrenched there. It looked as though it would be hard to drive them out. Madame de Freneuse pitied the inhabitants still beneath the enemy rule.

Crouching over her fire on wintry days, with the smoke in her eyes, she would wonder whether it were possible that she had ever entered a lighted room in silken dress; and when she picked at her

·[350]·

sagamite with a wooden spoon, she wondered whether she had ever eaten at long tables, covered with silver, among men and women of her kind. She was lucky, she told herself, to be taken in by the Indians, housed, and fed. But sometimes, as she thought of the long years ahead, she was desperately frightened. Then processions of the faces she had known would come to her by night and stand at her rough couch. They would say nothing but look long at her, surprised. Always the last to come was Pierre. Sometimes she stretched out her arms to him, and woke to find them spread apart. She concealed her depression as well as she could from the Indians, knowing them to be lighthearted children with little sympathy for things they did not understand.

She taught them to be clean at their cooking, to make the best of the material at hand. When the spring came, she set them to sowing in the still-fertile fields about Freneuse. When they raised a good crop of maize and another of beans, she showed them how to make bread and cakes with the flour, ground in a mortar she found at the house.

She played with the children, teaching them to count and to say their prayers; she joined in all the tribal festivities, dancing or singing, as the occasion required, at spring and autumn festivals; she helped the squaws prepare regalia for the lodge and heated stones for initiation ceremonies; but all of her outer life was purely mechanic. She lived an inner brooding desolation hidden beneath activity.

Once she went to the chapel, as near Christmas day as she could reckon, and knelt where the altar had been, to pray. She fancied Father Francis' face if he could see her kneeling there and, with a sudden rush of pity, prayed for him among the rest. That night the Virgin came among the procession of faces, to look down on her, with Antoine in her arms.

Summer succeeded spring; autumn succeeded summer; winter was upon her again. The Indians were rubbing themselves with bear oil. She must do so, too, if she were to survive; but she put off the day until her fingers grew too stiff to hold the paddle. One of the few things in the new conditions of her life to bring her real relief and pleasure was canoeing. The Indians taught her all they knew, and allowed her the use of one of the canoes as often and as much as she liked. She would go out upon the river and stay there day after day, watching the moose swim to shore, scrambling up with a clutter and a shake, or the delicate deer come down to drink. She grew acquainted with the wild life of the forest in a new way. Now it would be time to put up the canoe and dig herself in for the long icy winter. And so it would go on, year in, year out, until she died. When this thought came, she spoke to the nearest Indian about anything that came into her mind.

It was a day in January that the Malisite messenger came. He had been running through the woods for a week when he fell in with a party of English soldiers, who wounded him. He crawled away from them, continuing upon his journey, through the snow, desperately hoping to reach his destination and deliver his message before he died. It was a point of honor among the Micmacs and the Malisites, when entrusted with a message, to get it there; otherwise their spirits would not rest in the hunting grounds, and they would not be able to take their place round the totem of their fathers before the Great Spirit.

This youth crawled out of the forest on his hands and knees toward the encampment, gasped a word or two, and died at the feet of the squaw who reached him first.

Madame de Freneuse came out of her hut, glad of a diversion. The squaw turned to her.

"He said: 'The Great Bear, Baye Françoise, at the Gap, a cove to the right,'" she explained.

Madame de Freneuse screamed and shook the messenger.

"Monsieur de Bonaventure? The Great Bear? Is this true talk? Oh, at last! At last!"

"No good," said the squaw stolidly; "the messenger is dead."

"But he said the message," she said wildly. "Was that all he said? The Great Bear! I know the place. I will set out at once. Run, Wosedek; find out which of the young men will come with me in the canoe."

"Across the great water, now, in wintertime?" They shook their heads. "No one will go with you. No one. It is mad."

"Then I will go alone!" said Madame de Freneuse.

She set about her preparations feverishly, hysterically relieved that the time of dull inactivity and hopeless misery was over; the time for action, with hope and joy at the end of it, begun. To cross the Baye Françoise alone in a canoe in wintertime would be madness, perhaps impossible; but, equally, to stay a moment longer, separated from Pierre, who was waiting there, would be worse madness still.

She rubbed herself with the hated oil and dressed herself in

·[352]·

the only European clothes she still possessed, a dress that had been hanging in the ruins of Freneuse. Over this she drew on all the thick clothing she could lay hands on, everything that the squaws would lend. After a hasty consultation two braves decided that they would go as far as the waters of the Baye with her, and launch her on her journey. They were generous to give her the canoe.

As they set off, Tegoa, a little boy whom she had petted sometimes, shrilled out:

"I'll come with you. Take me for ballast if I may not paddle."

The boy had no parents to forbid. So he joined the canoe, crouched by the two braves, and the mad venture started.

CHAPTER LXXXVI

WHEN they came to the waters of the Baye Françoise, at the mouth of the river, and saw the great gray sea heaving in the moonlight, Madame de Freneuse drew a long deep breath. After so many weary months shut in among the trees of the forest, with no spacious places even in one's soul, this breath of the infinite, the spacious lordly sea, was like a draught of wine to a thirsty man—comforting, and soothing, setting tortured nerves at peace.

Madame de Freneuse smiled. Pierre's element, the sea, and he was waiting on the other side of it!

They camped that night on the shore. The sound of the waves breaking among the stones was music to her; the wild chant of her own heart joined in. She tried to sleep, knowing the strain ahead; but there was no sleep for her—only joy, the fierce delight of action to come, and the hope . . . the hope!

"I shall be in his arms again! I shall be in his arms again!"

The sea might be kind, or cruel; it was never dull or mean. (And at the end of it, Pierre!) The hours crawled till she could make a start. Dawn came at last; the Indians stirred and grunted. One of them looked from the breaking waves to her.

"You still want to go?"

She nodded. Then she said:

"My thanks for your help."

She stooped to the little boy.

"Tegoa, the sea is big and hungry. It may be that the waves will swallow us. Will you stay with these wise braves?"

The boy looked at the sea and drew in his breath.

"I will go with you," he said; "I am not afraid. Give me the paddle. When we arrive, you will take me with Great Bear, the Untamed One, to the lands across the sea."

The tallest of the braves stooped to the canoe and launched it between two waves. Then he held out his arms for Madame de Freneuse. Wading out with her, he put her in the stern, while his companion held the canoe for the boy on his shoulders to slide into place. They gave it a final push and waded to shore, where they stood silently dripping, watching the outgoing tide whirl the canoe to sea.

Madame de Freneuse, dipping ineffectually into the sliding hills of water, thought for one wild moment: "I am beaten before I start."

But the sight of the boy's little black head lifted proudly against the wind rallied her courage. She set to work in earnest, paddling strongly as each wave lifted the canoe up, up, and dropped it down again, into the hollows. Tegoa paddled steadily, crouched over the bow as though he were shooting rapids, looking out for rocks.

"I did not know there was so much water in the world," he shouted back to her.

The tide was doing most of the work, and there was little wind. Unless a storm came up, or the seas roughened, the feat might be possible after all. Only now did she realize that she had never quite believed in her own strength. She looked up at the sky. The sun was rising, and the freezing cold would bite less chill with every crawling hour. The canoe rode the huge crests buoyantly as though it had sea wings, shipping a little water with each wave, but only a little.

"Tegoa, bail," she said; "there's a dipper beneath your knees." The boy felt carefully where he was kneeling, stooped, and, cleverly balancing his weight, bailed out the water. Then he took up his paddle again.

Sea gulls swooped about them screaming and squawking; the wind moaned a little past their ears. Slowly—imperceptibly, almost —they were drawing out from land toward the opposite shore. They could not see it from where they sat; they would not see it for hours yet; but it was there—blue hills, like those they had left, with patches of white for snow.

Madame de Freneuse knew by the sun that she was headed in the right direction; but she also knew that she could not change the course, for the canoe must meet the waves head on. She would fetch up somewhere near the Gap and creep along the shore. She reckoned:

"At this rate it may be low tide when we arrive. I hope it is. But not going out. To get that far will be good enough, beyond all record."

She threw back her head, exultantly filling her nostrils with the sharp salt of the sea; wintry-gray and black, it slid past her, cold, deep. Its coldness seemed to her the integrity of a friend; its depth, that same friend's silence. She had no fear of the sea. She rested her aching arms for a moment.

"Change sides, Tegoa."

The boy obeyed.

Slowly fatigue set in. She began to count each stroke, and each stroke grew harder. Although it was bitter cold, she sweated freely; then the sweat froze in particles of ice about her forehead. Her clothing steamed and was damp. Her muscles ached. The wind rose a little, and the slight opposition irritated her. Always the straining slide, the paddle poised, the dip, the swerve, the descent, the climb. She began to feel slightly sick. Tegoa vomited. For a moment she thought that she would vomit, too, but there was not time for that; she controlled herself.

"One, two, three; strain, lift, dip, guide; hold one's breath at the descent; don't look back as the canoe stands on its tail and it seems it must fall over!"

Her mind repeated these admonitions to her faculties over and over. Everything was becoming dulled. She dared not stop for a second or she would never get the cramped muscles to move again. Every nerve in her screamed for rest.

"Pierre!" she said to herself. "Oh, Pierre!"

Even that did not help by the time five hours had passed, with five more to go. Tegoa, hunched over the bow, appeared like a wooden figurehead. Madame de Freneuse crouched behind him, wild-eyed and white, with ever-working mouth. She lost all count of time, of existence even; and still she paddled on through the wild seas.

A packet, on her way out through the Gap, caught sight of them moving over the swollen waters, and all her crew came to the rail.

"Just look at that! Two savages in a canoe! Crossing the Baye!"

"They must be running from famine, sir, or plague. I've heard there's both on the other side."

Madame de Freneuse did not see the packet; she saw nothing but her paddle and the waves. The sky darkened above her, and the stars came out. The moon rose slowly, like a witch ball of silver ice. Madame de Freneuse paddled on.

Black in the moonlight rose the coast—so black, so near, that she was startled into consciousness. They had arrived! There, there, to the right, was the little cove. An hour or two away; but she could make it, before dawn perhaps.

"Tegoa," she croaked. "We have almost won."

The small head stirred, slowly, dully, and the boy looked round. Seeing her, he smiled faintly in the moonlight, coming back to himself—though all the time he had never ceased paddling, paddling steadily into the crests.

The hardest part was ahead. They faced the turn of the tide. Now the strength of a strong man was needed to succeed. They would be swept away. But when dawn broke and the sun began to rise, they saw that they were nearly at the cove. Madame de Freneuse bit her lips till the blood ran down her throat, refreshing her with its warmth, and strained anew, calling on all the saints to hear her, lend her strength. A wave lifted the canoe, tossed it about this way and that, and flung it sideways toward the beach. Another took it from there and turned it upside down. Madame de Freneuse gasped as the icy waves closed over her and hurled her toward the rocks. She clawed her way to safety, scrambled out, and struggled through the spray. A fire was burning, and a man stood there. He turned as she came near.

CHAPTER LXXXVII

RAOUL DE PERRICHET started forward. He seized the dripping figure stumbling toward him and drew her close to the fire. Then he began to tear the clothes from her, snatching up blankets and his own coat to cover her. A movement near the shore attracted his attention, and a small shape rolled on the beach. At first he thought it was a dog; but as he ran near to help, he saw it was an Indian child, unconscious from the cold. He picked Tegoa up and took him to the fire.

"Raoul!" gasped Madame de Freneuse, as he returned and she recognized him. "Where is Pierre?"

He took her in his arms.

"He is dead," he told her quietly, and held her close while her scream tore the mists.

"He sent you this," he added, reaching for a package in his doublet.

She held out a groping hand, undid the package, stared at it dully.

There was a letter, wrapped about the little silver crucifix she had given him years ago—her crucifix de première communion. The letter said:

"Beloved, when you receive this you will know that I have left you for a little while and am waiting for you on the other side of death. I have loved you more than even you have known. God be good to you, Louise."

She turned the cross about in her hand, this way and that.

Raoul said:

"He died at sea. He was on his way here, with me, to find you and to bring you to France. Neither of us could rest while you were here. He has left you money. Will you come home, Louise?"

She did not answer, lifting her head and staring out to sea.

"Come home," he said; "live with us. My uncle would have wished it. Denise and I wish it, too."

She pressed his hand and shook her head. The dripping ringlets fell across his face and stung him with their cold. He held her closer and began to rub her hands in his.

"You are frozen! The boat will come for us soon; you will find warmth aboard the packet. Every day they have landed me here to wait for news from the Indians. I sent out over a hundred runners. I would have gone myself, but I didn't know where to look. I have been crazy waiting here. But Ruwerera is still a strong name to the Malisites. They tried again, and one of them has found you!"

He broke off, seeing that she did not listen to him but was looking, always looking, at the sea. There was a hungry, desperate look upon her face.

Sun broke through the mist and shone upon the cove.

"You will be warmer soon," he said, not knowing what to say yet feeling a rush of tenderness toward her. "We shall be so happy to have you with us in Provence."

"I shall stay here," she said, speaking at last with an effort to control her voice.

The life had gone out of it. Raoul started, so unlike her voice it sounded, dead and flat, against his ear. Then she pushed him aside and walked a few steps toward the sea. He followed apprehensively. She raised her arms in a gesture of abandonment and longing, a gesture so revealing that for an instant's space he shut his eyes. Then she spoke, and now her voice recaptured its old fire.

"Farewell," she said, "Pierre, my lover; Pierre, my friend. Farewell."

She bowed her head. The sun shone on the waves, and for a momentary lull the water appeared to subside and flow more evenly.

"See!" she cried, whirling on Raoul suddenly. "See, how quietly he lies! Yes, *quietly my Captain waits*, and I will come to him!"

Raoul stepped quickly forward and took her by the arm.

"You do not think of—*that!*" he said, shuddering toward the sea.

She shook her head. Her voice broke in sobbing, and she leaned against his shoulder. He stood, holding her there, his eyes wet with tears. Through the mists in them he saw the little figure by the fire rise and stagger over to them. It pulled her by the blanket.

"Is this the Untamed Bear?"

"No, Tegoa," she said, putting her hand upon his head. "But you will go with him across the Great Waters all the same."

"We will sail home," Raoul said. "Louise, you will be among friends."

She disengaged herself and looked into his eyes.

"No. It is kind of you. I must stay here."

"Louise . . ."

"I must stay here. There is work for me to do. The English must be driven out of Acadia. We must push them into the sea. Then he will not have died in vain, Raoul."

"What can you do," he pleaded, "alone against the English? Oh, come home with me!"

She put the hair back out of her eyes and smiled. He read the answer in her eyes. While they stood there staring, they heard the sound behind them of a boat beached on the pebbles. Tegoa capered toward it, shouting in the sunshine. Madame de Freneuse slowly shook her head.

He stretched his hands to her; she took them, putting them gently aside. In silence he held out a heavy bag of gold. She took it, turned it over, and raised her head.

"This will help us to retake New France."

Then as he looked at her, mutely imploring, she said:

"I am not alone. I have his son. You must remember that when you think of me. Farewell, Raoul."

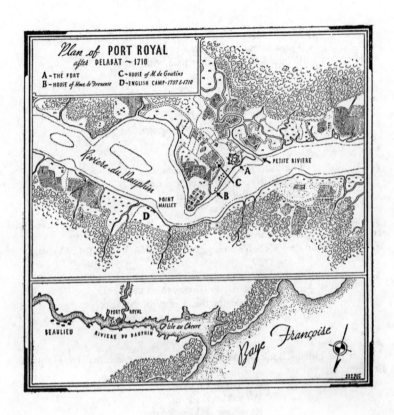

Plan of **PORT ROYAL**
after DELABAT ~ 1710

A ~ THE FORT   C ~ HOUSE of M. de Goutins
B ~ HOUSE of Mme. de Frenerie   D ~ ENGLISH CAMP · 1707 & 1710

Rivière du Dauphin

PETITE RIVIERE

A
C
B

POINT MAILLET

D

BEAULIEU   PORT ROYAL   RIVIERE DU DAUPHIN   Isle au Chevre

Baye Françoise

APPENDIX

Translations of French Songs in the Text

*Extracts from Correspondence in the Public Archives of Halifax,
N. S., and Originals of the Letters Incorporated in the Text*

I.   Sweet gallants of France,
       Going to war,
       I pray you, an' it please you,
       To salute my love.

They vanish, things of my existence,
Those eyes, those lovely eyes,
Whose splendor makes pale with envy
Even those of the skies.
Gods, friends of innocence.

What have I done to deserve
The annoys into which this absence
Will precipitate me?

2.　　　　The third day, Phyllis, unwise,
Would have given sheep and dogs
For a kiss, which the rascal
Gave to Lisette free!

3. Extract from a letter written by Monsieur de Villebon and preserved in the New Brunswick Archives.

4. Extract from de Villebon's writings, in ACADIA by Dr. J. C. Webster.

5.　　　　Cloris, whom in my heart I have so long served,
And whom my passion shows to all the world,
Will you not change the destiny of my life,
And give mellow days to my last winters?

6.

From the Indians Book by Mrs. Nathalie Curtis—published by Harper & Brothers.

Ah, tsiksu rutatiku
We raki retkaha ra.
Kaw-kaw, rakuwak-tahu,
Kaw-kaw, rakuwak-tahu.
Operit we ra ti kuhruri,
Operit ti ra-hu.

Letter from Monsieur de la Touche to the Ministry in France.
"Le lieutenant du roi ne cause pas moins de scandale ayant chez lui une femme veuve dont trois enfants passent pour soldats dans les compagnies."
Translation: "The King's Lieutenant is causing no less of a scandal, having in his house a widow, who has three children enlisted in the Companies."
7. Monsieur de Goutins, the judge of Port Royal, writes to the Ministry in France:
"Il y a ici une affaire qui cause un grand désordre, et fait gémir les pères et mères de familles par le mauvais exemple que cela donne à leurs enfants—c'est l'accouchement de la veuve de Freneuse, des œuvres du Sr. de Bonaventure, arrivé le 7 septembre dernier entre six et sept heures du soir, sans secours d'aucune femme, sans apprets ni dispositions pour recevoir l'enfant,

étant toute seule avec M. de Bonaventure, la servante étant dans une chambre à côté de celle où cette femme accoucha.

"Je passe les circonstances qui se débitent ici publiquement des mauvais desseins de la mère, pour dire que M. de Bonaventure partit dans le moment pour se rendre au fort, qu'on le vit tout affairé, ayant de la peine à mettre son épée et s'en fut chez la dite dame ou il donna de l'eau à l'enfant, qu'on envoy a chercher la demoiselle Burat et sa servante et le même soir sur les dix heures, un soldat gardien du port avec la femme du Nantais, habitants, le portèrent à quatre lieues chez un autre habitant pour le faire nourir.

"Si cela était arrivé à d'autres, j'aurais agi dans l'ordre, mais ne le pouvant ici, je fus trouver le lendemain M. de Brouillan. Je lui dis ce qui se débitait publiquement le danger ou était l'enfant pour le faire baptiser, et après avoir raillé, il dit qu'il l'avait ondoyé, et qu'on ne devait pas se mettre en peine.

"Cette affaire étant publique, M. de Bonaventure sachant qu'on en parlait, fit savoir que s'il apprenait que quelqu'un fut aussi hardi d'en parler, il le ferait mourir sous le baton.

"Le Docteur Poutz, notre chirurgien, s'étant trouvé en compagnie ou on en parlait, ce qui ayant été rapporté, M. de Bonaventure l'envoya chercher, après le jour couché lui disant: 'C'est donc vous B. de coquin qui avez parlé de Madame de Freneuse?' Et voulant se justifier, Monsieur de Bonaventure lui avait donné plusieurs coups de baton et l'avait fait conduire dans le cachot. On avait pressenti le Sr. de Poutz mais n'ayant pas répondu à ce qu'on voulait de lui, il tomba deshors en disgrace, lui ayant fait essuyer tous les chagrins possibles, même de grandes pertes en batissant sa maison qu'il a fait comme d'autres à ses dépenses, laquelle a servi d'hôpital sans rétribution."

Letter from de Brouillan to the Ministry in France.

"Cette officier (de Bonaventure) est très mortifié des accusations faites contre lui. Il affirme que c'est un très bon sujet, qu'il ne lui connait aucun défaut et que c'est le seul en qui il puisse prendre confiance lorsqu'il s'agit de quelque chose tant soit peu considérable, mais les reproches qu'on lui a fait l'ont si touché qu'il supplie de lui permettre d'aller servir en France et si sa Majesté veut qu'il reste à l'Acadie, il supplie d'accorder passage à sa femme sur le premier bateau qui partira de France."

Translation: "This officer (de Bonaventure) is very mortified by the accusations made against him. He (de Brouillan) affirms that he is a very good subject, that he knows no fault in him, and that he is the only one in whom he can have confidence when there is any affair of the least importance afoot, but the reproaches that have been made to him have so upset him that he begs leave to return to France and serve there, and if his Majesty wishes him to remain in Acadia, then he begs permission for his wife to take passage on the first boat that leaves France."

Notes in margin of letters in the Minister's office in France:

Toujours de l'argent! (Always money!)

Laver la tête à tous les deux (de Brouillan and de Goutin) et qu'ils ne recommencent plus! (Give both of them a good talking to, and let them not begin again.)

Letter from Monseigneur l'Évèque de Québec (the Lord Bishop of Quebec), 30th November 1703.

"Il propose d'éloigner deux femmes de l'Acadie qui y causent beaucoup de scandale. La femme est la dame de Freneuse, que tout le monde sait avoir un mauvais commerce avec le sieur de Bonaventure. Il seraient nécessaire d'ordonner à M. de Brouillan de l'obliger de retourner au Canada avec ses enfants ou dans ses terres qui sont au près de la Rivière St. Jean."

Translation: "He proposes sending two women away from Acadia, who are causing a big scandal there. (Note in the margin: Send de Bonaventure to Canada.) The woman is Madame de Freneuse, whom all the world knows to have had nefarious dealings with the sieur de Bonaventure. It would be necessary to order Monsieur de Brouillan to force her to return to Canada with her children, or to her property near the St. John River."

8. De Bonaventure writes:

Monseigneur,

J'ai reçu la lettre qu'il vous a plu m'écrire le 18 juillet et je ne puis assez vous témoigner quelle a été ma surprise et ma douleur en voyant l'avantage que la calomnie de mes ennemis remporte sur moi. Je n'aurais jamais pu croire qu'elle eut pu tourner à mon désavantage une conduite aussi conforme à la religion et aux intentions de sa Majesté que celle que j'ai tenue jusqu'à présent; puisque toute innocente qu'elle est, elle a eu le malheur de déplaire à sa Majesté et à votre grandeur je me donnerai bien de garde de la continuer, quoique la charité seule y eut eu part. Si j'avais à désiré quelque chose sur ce sujet, ce serait, Monseigneur, que vous eussiez assez de bonté pour moi pour éclaircir le fait. Je sollicitrais même votre grandeur de me donner cette satisfaction, si je ne craignais de l'importuner après la grace qu'elle m'a faite de me proteger dans cette occasion, sans quoi je supplierais d'envoyer un commission à mes dépens pour en informer. M. de Brouillan vous rendra compte de ce qu'il a fait à l'égard de Mme de Freneuse et de la conduite que j'ai tenu à cet égard. Qu'ai-je fait, Monseigneur, aux eclésiastiques et aux officiers de justice qui puisse mériter une réprimande? Ai-je commandé en ce pays? M. de Brouillan n'a-t-il pas toujours été présent pour s'opposer à mes violences? Ai-je eu rien à démèler avec les uns et les autres pour m'attirer un tel chagrin? Non, votre Grandeur doit être persuadée si elle veut bien faire un peu d'attention à ce qui lui est revenu.

9. Le sieur de Bonaventure a été si mortifié des accusations qu'on a fait contre lui qu'il croit être obligé pour sa justification de demander à repasser en France (note: wait) à moins que sa Majesté ne le juge nécessaire à son service dans le pays, en ce cas il supplie de donner passage à sa femme et à sa famille pour l'aller trouver (note: approved) et d'avoir égard que ses appointements ne peuvent le faire subsister. (Note: No.)

10. De Bonaventure writes:

Permettez-moi de me plaindre encore une fois au sujet des accusations que l'on a faites contre la Dame de Freneuse et moi. J'ai eu l'honneur de vous demander l'année dernière d'envoyer l'ordre pour travailler à mon procès. Cela n'a jamais été refusé à personne; il m'est indifférent par qui le procès soit instruit. Je ne demande point de grace si je suis coupable, maise aussi Monseigneur si je suis innocent, accordez-moi s'il vous plait, que l'accusateur d'une pareil calomnie soit puni. Je vous supplie de considérer s'il est juste que cette dame soit bannie comme une misérable criminelle si elle est innocente, qui n'a ni bien ni établissement qu'au Port Royale. Il est impossible qu'elle puisse vivre à la Rivière St. Jean, puisqu'elle est tout à fait abandonnée. Elle a les enfants du Sr. Des Chauffours, son beau-frère qui est prisonnier à Boston. Elle les élève comme les siens. Quoique elle ait peu de bien, elle ne laisse pas que de faire subsister toute sa famille par son grand ménagement. Si absolument, Monseigneur, vous ne voulez point que l'on éclaircisse ses prétendues crimes, ni que cette dame demeure dans son bien tant que je serai au Port Royale, ayez la bonté, Monseigneur, de m'en retirer plutôt qu'elle, et de me remettre dans mon emploi de la marine. Il est plus juste que je sorte du pays qu'elle, puisque c'est moi qui lui cause son malheur.

De Goutins writes:

La dame de Freneuse ne s'étant pu rendre aux Mines par la maladie qui lui survint en y allant, ne pouvant aller à la Rivière St. Jean qui est abandonné, passe en France, et laisse ici sa famille. Elle est restée depuis près d'un an en haut de cette rivière chez un habitant. M. de Bonaventure monta au mois de juin dernier avec M. de Falaise et sa femme, ou était la dite dame de Freneuse, mais lorsqu'on lui fit connaître que cela faisait du bruit, il n'y a plus été depuis.

4th Dec. 1705.

Translation: Madame de Freneuse not having been able to go to Minas, on account of her illness, and not being able to go to St. John, which is abandoned, returns to France, leaving her family here. She has been in a habitant's house, above the river for nearly a year. M. de Bonaventure went up there last June with M. de Falaise and his wife where Madame de Freneuse was, but as soon as it was made known to him that it was causing talk, he has not been there since.

11. From "Kuluskap the Master and Other Algonkian Poems," translated by Charles Godfrey Leland and John Dynely Prince, by permission of the publishers, Funk & Wagnalls.

12. Translation of a letter in the Archives at Halifax.